FORGED IN SHADOW

FORGED IN SHADOW

Book One of
THE WAR OF THE
NINE FAERIE
REALMS

MEGAN HASKELL

ISBN 13: 978-1-950307-04-3 (Paperback)
ISBN 13: 978-1-950307-03-6 (eBook)

Sword Concept Art: Emanuele Galletto
Cover Art: Sam Kim
Cover Design: Shawn King
Editor: Kimberly Peticolas

Trabuco Ridge Press | 22365 El Toro Rd #129, Lake Forest, CA 92630

Dedicated to the man who has encouraged my every word. I couldn't have a better partner in life.

PROLOGUE

Othin, King of the Upper Realm, master of spirit, and ruler of the glittering throng, stood before the most powerful leaders of the realms of the fae. Summer, Winter, Autumn, and Spring—even the dark elves of the Shadow Realm gathered for the centennial summit. The table was round, but he had long since claimed its head.

Now, he would claim his crown. After more than two thousand years leading the most prosperous and powerful of the new elf lands, he deserved it. He met the gaze of each seated leader as he opened the summit agenda.

"—where once our fathers fled their ancestral lands and the wars that divided us, now is the time to reunite for the benefit of all fae—"

Rindae, King of the Shadow Realm, lord of the dark elves, slammed his hand on the table and stood from his seat.

"This is a mockery of our ancestors' sacrifices in leaving their home realm," he said. "I will no longer participate in what has become a misguided ploy to control us all."

"You haven't heard our proposal yet. You must sit." Othin's

fingers, hidden in the folds of his formal robe, curled into a claw. He pulled on the energy of his people to expand his own aura and encourage the shadow king's compliance.

The dark elf king took a step in the right direction, but his heir rose and placed a hand on his arm. King Rindae shook his head. "The Shadow Realm will take no part in this."

With a synchronized bow, the pair left the room.

Othin could do nothing but watch them flee with clenched teeth and a carefully composed expression as his power and position were undermined, the position he had been building ever since he first stepped onto the fertile soil of the Upper Realm.

The shadow king would pay for his impudence. Othin was the greatest spiritmaster to have ever lived and Rindae would come to know it. They all would.

The kings and queens around the table whispered and grumbled, their voices rising in the echoing chamber of his great hall, as Othin stood motionless, his thoughts fixed on what was to come.

It was time to craft Thúlentur, a sword enchanted to amplify the spirit magic in his blood. With it, he would drop entire cities to their knees. None would dare rise up and rebel, not if they wanted to survive.

If he couldn't take the high seat with diplomacy, he would take it with force.

CHAPTER 1

Hammer struck iron. Again. And again. The rhythmic clang lulled Curuthannor into a dream-like trance. His human assistant held the ingot of red-hot steel on the anvil with a set of tongs nearly half as long as he was tall, while Curuthannor pounded the metal into shape. Sweat dripped from his brow to sizzle on the anvil. Finally, he stepped back and nodded to the holder who placed the ingot back in the forge. The second piece was golden hot and ready to remove.

Curuthannor wiped his face with a rough towel and stretched his shoulders. At his nod, the assistant removed the bar and Curuthannor pounded again.

Blades were his life, but this . . . this was monotonous at best. This was Curuthannor's least favorite part of the entire process of crafting a weapon.

His gaze wandered around his father's smithy. His middle brother sat at the grinding wheel, sharpening and shaping the edge on a decorative dagger for a lesser noble of the high elves, while his elder brother was instructing one of the newer humans in the preparation of the ceramic crucible that would be used to smelt the raw iron into steel worthy of only the greatest warriors.

Curuthannor's hammer slipped, striking the holder's tongs. The human shouted in surprise as the metal fell into the dirt. Luckily, he pulled his foot out of the way before the heavy lump smashed and burned his toes.

Godsdamnit, Curuthannor swore in his head, though he kept his mouth shut. His mother was strict about invoking the gods without reason—and a curse was always without reason in her opinion.

Eyes wide, the assistant grasped the dropped steel with the tongs and placed it back on the anvil.

"Apologies, Curuthannor," he whispered.

"It was not your fault," Curuthannor replied, bringing the hammer down in hopes no one noticed the mistake. His hope was in vain.

"No, it was my son's fault," Hatholdammon, Master Smith of Rómesse Gulch and Curuthannor's father, replied. His voice was low and gruff and filled with disapproval. "The forge is no place for distraction or wandering thoughts."

Curuthannor could do nothing but stand and take the criticism, chin up, eyes gazing straight ahead. It was what he had been trained to do under the strict tutelage of the master smith.

Hatholdammon shoved a recently crafted longsword into Curuthannor's hands. "Take this, tell me if it's good enough for the lesser of the king's guard. Hadhion finished it this morning."

Curuthannor frowned, disappointment and humiliation raging through his blood. Though well into his third century, Hadhion was new, and the only high elf apprentice who was not also Hatholdammon's son. He had chosen to pursue the life of a blade-smith after realizing he was more interested in the tools of his father's game-hunting business than he was in the act of hunting and butchering the meat. He'd taken to the forge with purpose and zeal, and Curuthannor was well aware that soon he would be displaced if he didn't focus on his own work with more care.

"Yes, Father." Curuthannor hefted the blade in his hand. There was a slight issue with the balance, a little too heavy toward the tip for Curuthannor's liking, but he would have to practice with the sword for awhile to be sure.

"Take your time. There is no immediate rush. When you're done, bring Hadhion and report your findings to me."

"Yes, Father." Curuthannor bowed and excused himself to the practice field behind the small estate that was their home. Dismissed from his work, Curuthannor's shoulders sagged. It was becoming increasingly common that he was sent out of the forge to test the great works of his father and brothers . . . and now Hadhion. If he didn't find his place soon, he might find himself permanently on the outside, a fate he refused to consider.

With a deep breath, Curuthannor settled himself in the training yard. He set his feet and held the sword in a low opening stance, as his father had taught him. He swung the sword in a slow arc overhead, then sliced across the body of an imaginary foe. Lifting the sword once more, he circled it in the other direction and down to the opposite side.

Definitely heavy in the tip, but perhaps correctible. The wire-wrapped hilt dug into the palm of his hand. That was a larger issue in the moment, but easily fixed with a bit of leather. He lunged forward, and back, stabbing the sword into the gut of the invisible soldier who would strike him dead if given the opportunity.

Hatholdammon believed that every great smith should be able to wield the weapons he created. He should understand their strengths and weaknesses in order to improve on their design, and he should intimately know every blade in order to match the right weapon with the right warrior. All three of his sons had been taught to wield a weapon practically from the moment they could walk, but only Curuthannor had reveled in the daily physical practice. Where his brothers moaned and complained, he had jumped at every opportunity to enter the training yard.

Curuthannor turned and parried a new imaginary enemy. Slice

up and across. Spin. Lunge. Block. The moves flowed into a seam-less mock battle, the rhythm dragging Curuthannor away from conscious thought into pure movement. Sweat trickled down his spine as he gave himself over to the rhythm. His breath surged in and out of his lungs, nourishing the strength in his limbs. He never felt so alive as when he practiced with the sword.

It wasn't until a horn sounded in the distance that Curuthannor emerged from the pattern. The ram's horn blew for one reason, and one reason only: High King Othin had crossed the portal from Caralávar, the capital city, into the village of Rómesse Gulch. And since Hatholdammon was the only master craftsman residing in the village, there was only one place the king could be visiting.

Curuthannor hurried to place the new sword in the testing rack and sprinted toward the smithy. The whole family would need to be present for a proper showing of respect and solicitude, and the estate was only a few leagues from the portal. The king would arrive in mere moments.

The family and all the servants had already gathered at the end of the arbor-covered brick path that led from the street to their home and the smithy beyond. Curuthannor dashed into place at the end of the row, his breath heaving in ragged gasps.

"Where is your shirt?" Curuthannor's mother, Tunniel, hissed as he tried to catch his breath.

Curuthannor looked down at himself in embarrassed shock. He had completely forgotten he'd taken it off while testing the sword. "I was out in the training field," Curuthannor replied with a grimace. "Should I run and find one?"

"No time for that," Tunniel growled. She tossed him a small soft towel she'd tucked into the deep pockets of her stylish but func-tional dress. "At least wipe your face and dry off the sweat."

His brothers snickered. The smithy was much closer to the road, and they'd been blessed with a few extra moments to wash up in the house before the king's arrival. Plus, their day's work had involved sitting and polishing and instructing, not hammering and sparring and sprinting. Why was it Curuthannor was always the one out of line? Curuthannor hurried to wipe off as best he could.

After a quick examination, Tunniel nodded her assent before turning back to face the road. Hooves clacked on the flagstone road as the first of the king's guard appeared over the small rise that led into the village center. Curuthannor wadded the towel into a tight ball and stood at attention with his hands behind his back. The rest of the family and their servants did the same, the three human assistants standing with their heads bowed behind the family and Hadhion.

"Remember, bow deeply and hold the pose until the king tells you to rise," Tunniel whispered. "Keep your eyes downcast unless the king is addressing you directly. Say nothing unless asked a question."

King Othin glowed with brilliant light as he approached on the back of a pure white horse. Four mounted guards escorted him down the road, two in front and two behind. The soldiers wore the armor of the golden army and the helm of the king's personal guard, men who had been trained since the day of their maturity to protect and serve His Majesty. They were the elite warriors of the realm, but Curuthannor had only ever seen them at a distance. They were far more impressive up close.

The king himself wore a shirt of golden chain, but no other physical armor. Curuthannor supposed he felt safe in his own realm, protected as he was by his men. However, as he neared, Curuthannor could feel the power emanating from the king's aura. Magic buzzed along Curuthannor's skin, and intentional or not, Curuthannor felt the threat of His Majesty's presence. He prayed for his heart to calm as he prepared to face His Majesty, King Othin.

The horses stopped before the family, the guards circling around to flank their king. Curuthannor kept his gaze trained on the animals' polished hooves.

As the highest ranking member of the family, having once been a lady at court, Tunniel was the first to speak. "Welcome, my King." She curtseyed, keeping her eyes downcast.

"Your Majesty," Hatholdammon bowed low from the waist. "We are honored to have you visit our humble village."

Curuthannor and his brothers followed with deep bows of their own, and the servants each dropped to one knee.

King Othin stared down at them from the back of his horse, but made no move to dismount. It was a bit unsettling, but Tunniel had trained them well. No one moved or shifted under the king's scrutiny, even though he didn't invite them to stand.

"Why does an apprentice stand before us unclothed?"

"Apologies, Your Majesty," Tunniel replied. "We were not informed you would be visiting today. We were unprepared. My son was in the distant yard testing one of the new blades."

King Othin shifted in his seat. "Are you certain this is the smith in question? Perhaps we have arrived at the wrong establishment."

"No, Your Majesty," one of the guards replied.

"Surely Hatholdammon, Master Smith of Rómesse Gulch, Enchanter of the First Order, and last living apprentice of Luhtaro himself would be better prepared and more presentable," King Othin insisted.

Curuthannor's cheeks heated, but he remained bent over at the waist and said nothing. He would do nothing else to disgrace his family before the king.

"I am Hatholdammon," Curuthannor's father replied. "Forgive our rude appearance, but we are a working smithy. The heat of the forge is unforgiving."

"Indeed."

Curuthannor could practically feel the displeasure and disbelief emanating from that single word.

"Well, if you truly are Hatholdammon, then you are the smith we seek. We require a master-level work—a longsword that can be wielded against our enemies in defense of our great realm. The sword must amplify our ability to drain the energy of armies and store that energy until we require it. It must be unstoppable by any other magic. Can you do this?"

Still bent at the waist, Hatholdammon hesitated to respond.

"Well?" King Othin asked, impatiently.

"Your Majesty, a sword of that nature requires rare materials not available in the Upper Realm. I would need a flawless diamond as large as an orange, at least four bars of the purest silver to contain the enchantment, and iron from the lava flows of Nalakadr to craft the steel. The expense will be significant."

"The cost is immaterial. Can you do it?"

Hatholdammon hesitated once more. "Your Majesty, it is possible, but it could take years to craft. There is only one day in the year that the enchantment can be performed: the summer solstice. The ceremony must be executed with exacting precision. Even a minor error may turn the gods away from the metal. Moreover, as with any blade, there is a high probability of error resulting in the failure of the sword's construction. If anything goes wrong, we would have to wait another full year before the enchantment could be attempted again."

"Then you had best make the first attempt perfect. We will expect delivery of our sword on the second day of summer." King Othin nodded toward his lead guard, who tossed a large bag of gold at Hatholdammon's feet. "There should be enough there to buy your materials. Twice that will be paid for the sword on delivery."

Curuthannor stiffened. The bag must hold at least a thousand gold coins. This commission was enough that they could buy the whole village if they wanted to. Maybe even the Crimson Mountain mines. He and his brothers could each have their own estate.

"Yes, Your Majesty," Hatholdammon replied. "I will have it ready for you."

"Good. And while you are working on our great sword, your apprentices may practice their craft on arms and armor for our army. The arms master will send you a requisition of the required items along with additional payment."

Hatholdammon's voice sounded strangled as he choked out a response. "We work at your pleasure, Your Majesty."

"Remember that." The king turned his horse and began the stately ride back to the portal and his palace. "Oh, and one more thing—buy your son a shirt. One should never appear before us in such a state of disrepair."

Curuthannor squeezed his eyes shut and swallowed the last bitter drops of his pride. This might officially become the worst day of his three-hundred and forty-seven years. If he could hide under a bridge or bury himself under a rock, he just might make the attempt. Instead, he was forced to wait motionless until the last of the guard rode out of sight.

The family straightened with gasps and shocked expressions. Curuthannor waited for the imminent censure, but none came. Instead, Hatholdammon hefted the leather bag with two hands.

"Gods above, thank you," Tunniel whispered, her gaze never leaving the purse.

"Do not get ahead of yourself, my dear. I was not exaggerating the materials' cost. It will take at least this much just to gather everything we need." His gaze raked across the assembled family. "I must work on the design immediately. We haven't much time."

"It is only the beginning of fall, my love," Tunniel replied. "We have many months before the deadline. Surely we can celebrate?"

Hatholdammon shook his head. "There is travel and time differentials. There isn't a moment to lose. Nambamahtar and Minyondor, you will take over the forge and handle any new requisitions. Hadhion will follow your lead. Curuthannor, you will gather our materials. Go first to the dwarves. They will drive a hard bargain, but they will deal honestly. Bring back the largest flawless diamond you can find and four bars of the purest silver. Unfortunately, you will have to acquire the iron from the new goblin master."

"What happened to Master Krin?" Curuthannor had been making most of the supply trips to the Shadow Realm over the last few decades, and had developed a bit of a rapport with the goblin. He hated to start again with a new partner and lose what little goodwill he'd earned.

Hatholdammon shrugged. "According to the smith's guild, he disappeared several months ago. No one has heard from him. But his undersecretary, Ger, stepped into his place and has apparently been challenging to deal with. You mustn't let him get the better of you."

"Understood. I won't let you down." Curuthannor would use this opportunity to prove his value to his father and his family. He would make a great deal and bring home only the highest quality supplies at the best possible prices. The king's sword would be immaculate, Hatholdammon's legacy secured, and Curuthannor's future bright.

"Good. Then pack now. You leave tomorrow."

The family broke apart, each returning to his work while Curuthannor strode toward the house to prepare. Tunniel joined him, wrapping an arm around his waist and ignoring the lingering sweat that glistened on his skin.

"Do not fret over the king's words. You couldn't have prepared," she said.

Curuthannor's cheeks reddened once more. "I failed the family," Curuthannor replied, keeping his voice low. Though determined to make it right, he still felt the weight of this day's failures.

"Nonsense. If it hadn't been you, he would have found something else to displease him. He needs your father and that makes him angry. He does not like to be beholden to anyone for anything, nor does he like to show weakness. He must always feel more powerful than those around him."

Curuthannor frowned, not quite believing her attempts to comfort him.

"But Curuthannor?" she asked.

"Yes, Mother."

"Don't forget your shirt." She gave him a squeeze and a smile, and a gentle nudge toward the house. "I'll bake some travel cakes to take with you, too."

CHAPTER 2

Blush pink silk fell to the floor in a wrinkled heap.

"Too pale," Princess Faeliel complained. "The ladies here wear colors so bright they would make your eyes bleed in our court. I must have something that both stands out and fits in. Do you understand what I mean?"

Lhéwen nodded, though she had no idea what the woman wanted. Stand out *and* fit in. Bright colors that hearkened back to the preferred pastels of the Upper Realm. Right.

She sifted through a closet that was as large as a bedroom in a modest elvish hall. They'd packed in a hurry, Princess Faeliel insisting that time was of the essence. Lhéwen had filled four trunks with her ladyship's best dresses for the journey. For the princess, that was traveling light, especially since she had chosen to limit her entourage to just her personal bodyguard, a half-dozen loyal guards, and one handmaiden.

Lhéwen smiled, imagining the jealous expressions on the other ladies' faces when they'd found out Princess Faeliel had selected her for the position. They would have been outraged, particularly the lesser nobles who expected to be given every advantage despite their reticence to serve. Lhéwen was one of the best seamstresses in the palace, and had spent most of her life in Princess Faeliel's company while her mother had been a handmaiden to the late queen. She knew her place and had earned her position, along with the princess's trust.

Lhéwen's hand brushed across a sparkling gold gown with long translucent bell sleeves, a scandalously open back, and a flared skirt that ended in a fluttering train. Golden leaves wrapped the bodice from the right shoulder across the waist, highlighting the curve of the waist and arch of the low back. She pursed her lips with a knowing smile.

"Perhaps this one will suit better," Lhéwen murmured, avoiding eye contact as she lifted the gown from its hanger and held it before the princess.

Faeliel gasped. "Perfect," she breathed.

Lhéwen smiled. She had designed this particular gown herself, to the consternation of the head seamstress. It was far too glamorous for the elder woman's conservative sensibility. Lhéwen had known Princess Faeliel would love it. Lhéwen inwardly preened as she carefully laid the shimmering silk out on the bed.

Her Royal Highness had already bathed and brushed her hair to a glowing fall of summer sunlight. They would want to accentuate the low back of the dress, and the pale skin beneath—so different from the inky black of the dark elves.

"My lady, may I suggest a braided knot at the nape of your neck, positioned slightly off to one side? I believe it will heighten the effect of the gown."

Princess Faeliel's lips pressed together in an amused smile. "I trust your judgment, especially since I do believe I see your hand in the design."

"Indeed, Your Highness. I am particularly pleased that you approve."

"Your taste is impeccable for every occasion." The princess sat at the small vanity, the backless stool giving Lhéwen free movement to rein in the waist-length locks of the princess's hair. "It is why I insisted you come along."

Lhéwen allowed herself a small smile at the compliment, then proceeded to prepare the princess for her appearance in the throne room.

"What do you know of King Rindae?" Lhéwen asked. It was perhaps a bit impertinent, but the princess had never refused idle conversation. They'd been together so long now, they were practically sisters in all but rank and title.

"He is my father's rival and a dark elf. What else do I need to know?"

"You've met him before, haven't you? What kind of king is he? Compassionate and kind? Proud and vindictive?" Lhéwen paused, letting her lips slide up into a knowing smile. "Handsome?"

Faeliel gently slapped Lhéwen's hand where it rested on her shoulder. "Enough of that. Rindae's insistence on independence has been a stain on my father's reputation. I am simply here to help the Shadow Realm see the value in an alliance."

"Of course, my lady," Lhéwen grinned, meeting Faeliel's eyes in the mirror. "As you say."

"I do say. Besides, he's a dark elf and I am of the glittering throng. A fling would be too conspicuous."

"Unlike your romances in the high court?" Lhéwen teased. The princess was notorious for her highly unsuitable and very public relationships with the handsomest of the high court nobles. All to make her father take notice. Which he did, to the detriment of the men involved. It had become a joke amongst the serving staff that to appear in public with the princess was to risk life and limb, but the man who finally tamed her would reap the greatest reward.

Princess Faeliel sputtered a breath, then caught the twinkle in Lhéwen's eye. "Someday my king will have to realize that though I am his daughter, I am also a woman. He cannot keep me as a jewel, locked behind mirrored glass, only to bring me out to decorate his throne and tempt his ancient cronies when the mood strikes. He cannot control me forever."

"Hmm." It was all Lhéwen could say without risking censure. The fact of the matter was, King Othin desired power above all else, and control of everyone. It was why they were here. He could not fathom a realm that refused to bow to his will and superiority.

"It is well that he allowed you to take on the role as delegate. Perhaps he is beginning to understand you're more than an ornament for the great hall."

Princess Faeliel wouldn't meet her gaze in the mirror. "Perhaps."

Lhéwen placed a final pin in the princess's hair, then examined her handiwork. The loose, yet controlled arrangement was beautiful and perfect for the gown, but there was still something missing. She tapped a finger against her lips. The dress needed no adornment, and the hair was a perfect complement. The soft golden slippers were appropriate footwear, though they wouldn't be seen.

"My lady, with your permission, I would like to create a small enchantment for your person. Something to draw the admiration of all who see you."

"You do not believe this dress will suffice?" Faeliel asked in disbelief.

"The dress will do wonders, but I would like to ensure your success. King Rindae has resisted all prior delegations and is politically astute enough to avoid causing offense in the process. I believe I can use my modest skills to draw him to your favor."

Faeliel gazed at Lhéwen with shrewd eyes. "What do you have in mind, exactly?"

Lhéwen grinned. Like all high elves, she had an affinity for spirit magic, the ability to control mood, emotion, and energy. However, where most high elves were able to affect people directly, Lhéwen had been blessed with the rare talent to imbue *matter* with altered effects.

Lhéwen removed a twisted wire ear cuff from Faeliel's jewelry box. The gleaming silver was a perfect conductor for the affinity spell she had in mind, and the vaguely floral vine would complement her dress, seeming to extend the embroidery up from the right shoulder to the tip of her ear.

"This will be subtle. It will have to be."

Though Lhéwen had little skill with the manipulation of magic herself, she could copy the pattern of another spirit and impress it on the metal to create greater effects. She opened her mind's eye to the magical spectrum and examined the princess's aura. Faeliel had an innate charisma, a passive magic that drew the eye and made others wish to please her. Lhéwen ran a finger along the wire, strengthening the princess's natural abilities like an extra dash of fragrance behind the ear.

"What is it?" Faeliel asked, still admiring herself in the mirror.

"Just a simple charisma enhancement. It will encourage others to align themselves with your point of view. Your words will be more persuasive, your expressions drawing empathy from the audience."

"In other words, I will be a master diplomat without effort."

Lhéwen smiled, finishing the spell. "Perhaps not a master, but well on your way. And none will be the wiser." The shadow king and his court couldn't know they were being manipulated, even in such a small way.

With gentle fingers, Lhéwen clasped the ear cuff on her ladyship's ear lobe, arranging the loops and whorls to highlight and extend the princess's tall pointed ears. It looked spectacular as the only jewelry on display.

"There. I believe you are ready."

The princess stood from her seat at the vanity and strode to the full-length mirror in the corner. Shifting a little from side to side, she practiced several variations of poses and expressions. Confidence and carefree sexuality oozed from every pore. Not a man in that room would be able to tear his eyes away.

CHAPTER 3

Afew moments of quiet were all Curuthannor desired. A drink and a meal and this day could end. Luckily, the Crossroads Inn was known for having the best of both, and though the sun had set bells ago, it was still early enough in the evening to avoid most of the crowd.

Most, but not all.

A cloud of rancid blue-green smoke drifted across the outdoor bar, the tell-tale scent clinging to everything in its path. Curuthannor coughed and shot a pointed glare at the group of leipreachán men three seats away. He wasn't sure they could even see him through the fog, but their rough giggling and the stench of something that wasn't tobacco had the other patrons clearing a wide space around them. Only Curuthannor remained, and only because he preferred an isolated seat at the bar to the communal tables nearer the entertainer's stage. If they would just get the hint and move toward one of the private gazebos on the hill, he could dine in peace.

"Won't do ye any good," a rumbling voice growled. "Ye know

they're incorrigible. They're more likely to come over here and blow that smoke in your face than leave."

"I will take that under advisement," Curuthannor replied with a tired chuckle.

Tryg was a troll, young and small by trollish standards. Standing merely elf height, he hadn't yet gained the equal width and stocky stature of his older brethren. In fact, he didn't much act like a troll at all, choosing instead to work as a bartender and body-guard for the inn's proprietor, Tharbatiron. Tryg had a talent for it—he never forgot a face, name, or favorite food and drink.

"So what can I get ye this evening?" Tryg asked while wiping the counter clean with a damp rag. Another non-trollish behavior.

"My usual, if you would. And something to eat, as well."

"Black mead, on its way. And I'll bring ye a bowl of the dumpling broth, if ye like."

"That will do fine."

While Tryg moved away to fill the order and greet other customers, Curuthannor leaned forward against the silky smooth polished stone in front of him. He crossed his arms and rested his forehead in one hand. His father had told the truth. The new goblin master was impossible to deal with.

Damn goblins. Master Ger demanded three times the price for the same iron Curuthannor had bought less than a year ago. The fat little man had rubbed his belly and sneered, completely unwilling to negotiate, but Curuthannor was certain the local gremlins weren't paying the same. No, Master Ger thought he saw an easy payout in Curuthannor, and would probably claim half the money for himself. Based on the way his ladies draped themselves around his office, they agreed.

At least the previous master had been civil and dealt more or less in good faith. Krin had enjoyed a good negotiation and a fair bit of conversation over a cold ale as well. Too bad he'd died. Suspiciously. With Master Ger as the only witness. That much Curuthannor had learned from the gossip in the goblin mound.

What Ger didn't realize was that Curuthannor's funds were limited. King Othin had been generous with the materials costs, but Curuthannor had already spent a small fortune on the diamond and silver, which should have been the most expensive materials to acquire. The black hills iron was high quality, but it wasn't worth its weight in gold.

Regardless, Curuthannor would have to go back to the mines tomorrow. He couldn't return home empty handed, not with the king's blade in question and the humiliation of that day still top of mind. He'd only returned home long enough to store the diamond and silver in the family's safe before crossing the portal into the Shadow Realm. Unfortunately, with the time differentials what they were, more than a month had already passed in the Upper Realm. Time was not on Curuthannor's side.

Curuthannor sighed and lifted his head. He couldn't let himself sulk, nor could he do anything to fix the situation until he returned to the goblin mines. Better to focus on the moment and take refuge in the fact that he wasn't slaving behind a hot forge at home under the ever critical gaze of his father. Instead, he was sitting in his favorite seat in his favorite drinking hall in all of the nine realms.

The open air pub was the centerpiece of the Crossroads Inn. Strategically located at the base of a natural amphitheater, it was the perfect place to see and be seen, or hide in the shadows and obscurity of a crowd. The bar itself was created from natural stacked stones and topped with a slab of obsidian that gently glowed in the gleam of soft wisplights. No matter where you stood in the inn, you could see the flickering torches that encircled the patio, arena, and its hub of activity. And from the bar, you could gaze out at the crowd perched on an eclectic mix of tables and chairs, everything from rough wooden logs to ornately carved high-backed chairs to blankets laid out on the distant hills.

Tonight's growing crowd was as eclectic as the furniture. Two trolls, each at least three times the size of Tryg, hunched over an entire spit-roasted boar, tearing great hunks of meat from the animal with greasy fingers. Four dark elf ladies sat ensconced within a small gazebo festooned with dancing fireflies, their white hair and bright clothing seeming to sparkle in the dim light while their deep black skin blended with the background night. An eight-man squad of high elf guards in polished gold armor laughed and drank ale at a long table carved from a single piece of wood. A few sellswords—obvious in their dark attire and numerous weapons—were scattered around the outskirts of the bar area, waiting for their patron or a new commission. And, of course, there were the leipreacháni, giggling at the bar with their long pipes.

Curuthannor grimaced and waved a hand in front of his face to clear away the smoke that burned his eyes and coated the back of his throat. He turned his gaze to the sky, finding a pocket of fresh air.

The sun had set bells before, the moon rising large and bright over the city of Nalakadr. Days were short here—even the longest lasted only a few bells—which meant most business was conducted by the light of the lesser orb. This was the capital city of the dark elves in the Shadow Realm, their center of commerce and economy. The city had grown even in the short time that Curuthannor had been visiting its environs, but it had yet to rival the great cities of the upperworlds.

Curuthannor missed the glittering halls and gleaming rooftops of his home world. It was a nice change to visit a realm that only rarely saw the sun, but he'd already been here too long. He had to negotiate a good deal, and soon.

A thunk from behind him had Curuthannor turning around. Tryg pushed the black mead and a steaming bowl toward him.

"So, what has ye staying with us this time? More of that iron for your father?" At Curuthannor's nod, Tryg continued. "Business must be good then."

"Indeed."

"Have anything ta do with the soldiers here in town?" Tryg pointed his chin toward the rowdy knot of high elf soldiers.

Curuthannor glanced at the men in question. They'd grown more raucous in the half bell Curuthannor had been sitting at the bar, and might as well have been in a spotlight on stage for all the notice they drew. Even the brightly colored attire of the Shadow Realm citizens did little to distract the eye from the gleaming metal and glistening white skin at the center of the gathering.

"There are rumors that the summit was not the resounding success King Othin had hoped for," Curuthannor replied noncommittally. His gaze caught on a knot of dark elf warriors entering the amphitheater space. With deep black skin, black leather and plate armor, and gleaming white hair tied back into slick buns and tight braids, they were an intimidating group even without their blades in hand. Yet as they wound their way through the tables, toward the golden warriors, Curuthannor's stomach soured.

"Ye mean the shadow king refused ta bend the knee, and Othin isn't happy 'bout it."

Curuthannor deliberately turned his back on the impending mess and lifted his mug in salute. "Your words, not mine. I'm not privy to discussions of that sort."

Nor were the actions of the soldiers any of his concern.

A shout echoed from across the clearing, and a glass shattered.

Curuthannor couldn't help himself. He swiveled toward the noise.

"Apologize for your impudence," the high elf guard at the front of the squad demanded.

The prickle of magic lifted the hair on Curuthannor's arms. It was his one magical skill, the ability to sense magical energies when they were in use. And in this, the high elf guards were manipulating the dark elves into a fight.

Gods damn it all, Curuthannor thought. Couldn't he eat his meal in peace? He set down his spoon, while his eyes scanned the courtyard. The soldiers could handle themselves in a fight, of that he was certain, but as representatives of the Upper Realm they were making a spectacle of themselves.

The shadow guard opposite sneered. "My impudence? Do you know who I am?"

"Dark elf filth. That is all I need know."

The dark elf in question burst forward, his fist snapping toward the high elf's nose with a roar of indignation. The high elf dodged while his arm pulled back for a strike of his own. In less than a heartbeat, the rest of the soldiers joined the fight, rallying around their leaders.

Bystanders scrambled out of the way, chairs and tables toppling in their haste to escape the melee. A few of the mercenaries jumped up, placing themselves between the fracas and the ladies in the gazebo, but they made no other move to engage with the warriors.

Tryg put the mug down with a thump and a scowl. "There they go. Knew it was gonna happen eventually."

With one meaty hand, he lifted a club the size of Curuthannor's leg from a stand beneath the back counter and thumped his way around the bar toward the escalating fight. He might not be as large as his brethren, but he was still far stronger than the elves. He could also take at least three times the damage without even breathing hard.

Curuthannor resolved himself to stay out of the fight. He would let the trolls deal with the troublemakers. It wasn't any of his concern. He was simply a guest of this establishment, here on business, nothing more. He already had enough to deal with in Master Ger, he shouldn't add to his troubles.

He took a sip of the warm broth in his bowl and popped a perfectly wrapped dumpling into his mouth, savoring the burst of game fowl and spring onion. The shouts and sounds of shattering wood continued on behind him.

He glanced over his shoulder. Tryg slammed into the soldiers like a battering ram, but they kept coming back. The trolls from the hillside had come down, but instead of helping their younger cousin, they taunted the fighters, alternately cheering and insulting their skill. Furniture was flying, along with the blood.

Curuthannor sighed. The Crossroads had been like a second home to him. He could hardly stand by and watch the place crash down around him. Not if he could do something to help. It didn't look like anyone else was going to step in.

Pressing his eyelids closed, he blew out a breath and drew his sword. Leaving his soup to cool and the mead to warm, he wove a path toward the fight.

"Enough," he shouted, to no avail. Not a single head turned toward him. He wasn't sure what he expected them to do—he had no authority here—but it had seemed worth a try before he added to the bloodshed.

A dagger thrust toward his middle. Curuthannor parried, then used the pommel of his sword to crush the dark elf's nose. The man fell back, his hands rising to his face. Curuthannor kicked him in the stomach, knocking him to the ground where he rolled under a table and out of the way. If Curuthannor could avoid killing anyone, that would probably be for the best.

Unlike the warriors on both sides of the battle, Curuthannor was not wearing heavy armor. He preferred the speed of hardened leather to the stopping power of metal plate. He'd honed his reflexes in the weapons arena at every opportunity, but still he had to be cautious and quick, precise and unpredictable.

Another dark elf barreled toward him with a wicked glint in his eye and two mid-length curved blades in his hands. He swung the blades in a rapid figure-eight motion that set Curuthannor back on his heels. A blade sliced across his arm, drawing blood. Curuthannor hissed, but set aside the pain. Two more steps backward and then he found the rhythm of his opponent's movement, but the swirling blades were a near-perfect guard.

Curuthannor's leg brushed up against an empty chair. His father liked to say, 'When finesse doesn't work, try brute force.' Curuthannor swung the polished wood at the man's head. The dark elf ducked, losing his rhythm. Curuthannor connected a fist to his temple. The man slumped to the ground. Hopefully he still breathed.

Finding himself near the leaders who had started this fight, Curuthannor saw his opportunity. The two fighters were too focused on their personal battle to notice the other men and women around them. Curuthannor kicked out with a swift heel strike to the gap behind the high elf's knee. The man's leg buckled. The dark elf made for a killing blow with his sword, the point aimed at the high elf's throat. Curuthannor blocked with his own weapon, preventing the golden warrior's death while at the same time keeping him on the ground.

The dark elf turned his attention to Curuthannor, his sword at the ready.

"Stop this madness," Curuthannor shouted.

A body slammed to the ground, as if to emphasize the point. Tryg thunked his club into the downed man's chest, breathing hard as he leaned on his weapon like a cane. The rest of the fighters were either unconscious in the dirt, or groaning from injuries. One of the dark elves lay unmoving.

"Who are you to command us?" the dark elf asked, his eyes tight with battle lust.

"I am no one. Simply a merchant passing through. But I seem to have more sense than the rest of you."

"How dare you—" the dark elf's words cut off with a gasping cough and he lifted up onto the tips of his toes as if trying to release the pressure from an invisible hangman's noose.

"Cendir, that is quite enough," a voice called from the wide gates leading into the inn. A man strode forward, his steps purposeful. Behind him ranged a group of at least a dozen men and women clad all in black, their expressions hard.

The dark elf—Cendir—suddenly dropped. He leaned over, hands on knees, as he gasped for breath. "Your Highness," he panted, the words raw and pained. He remained bent over, but repositioned himself into something that looked more like a bow.

The expression in his eyes, however, was furious and anything but respectful.

Curuthannor and every other patron of the inn bowed to the new arrival. Even the men on the ground did their best to raise themselves to a knee, clutching bleeding wounds and broken bones.

So this was Prince Aradae. It must be. Curuthannor had never met the man, never even seen him before, but he was the second son of the king and general of the dark elf army.

"You put us all at risk with this little diversion," Aradae continued. "Our guests are not to be molested."

"It was not my fault, sire. The high elves started the conflict."

"Perhaps. Regardless, you are all called to account for this . . ." the prince hesitated for a beat, his lips curling in distaste, ". . . scuffle."

"Yes, sire," Cendir replied, but his lips were pursed as if he'd eaten something sour.

Curuthannor sheathed his sword without lifting his head. Now that the fight was settled, he was looking forward to returning to his soup and his mead. Perhaps they hadn't become too cold and warm, respectively.

As the soldiers picked themselves up and dusted themselves off in preparation to leave for the palace, Curuthannor moved out of the way toward his seat.

"Soldier, where do you think you're going?" Prince Aradae asked.

Curuthannor dared a glance up, finding the prince's gaze trained on his face.

"I am no soldier, Your Highness," Curuthannor murmured. "Merely a guest who couldn't stand to see the entire inn destroyed by these men."

Prince Aradae lifted a single eyebrow. "So you put your own body on the line to save some furniture? That hardly seems likely."

Curuthannor shrugged. "Likely or not, it is the truth, sire."

"Well, soldier or not, you will still be joining us. Your testimony will be required."

Curuthannor gazed longingly at his meal, but he blew out a resigned breath.

All he'd wanted was a little peace and quiet, an end to this endless day. But even if this wasn't his realm or his liege, he was a foreigner at the mercy of their laws, and he was duty bound to comply.

"As you wish."

CHAPTER 4

A knock at the door. Lhéwen froze, still holding a hairpin in her hand. It was time. It would be the princess who negotiated with the shadow king, and yet Lhéwen's nerves fluttered in her stomach as if her own future depended on the outcome of this meeting.

Princess Faeliel rose from her seat in front of the mirror and brushed her hands down the golden length of her skirt to smooth it into place. She nodded toward her bodyguard, giving her assent to open the door. Belegeth lifted her battle axe and complied.

A tall, dark-skinned male wearing a carefully pressed black and gray wool suit with asymmetrical lines, long tails, and silver trim stood at the entry, his hands clasped behind his back. "Your Highness's presence is requested in the throne room," the courier intoned without preamble. "Please follow me."

"Of course," Faeliel replied, dazzling the young man with a smile. He blinked wide eyes, as if stunned.

Lhéwen smirked to herself. She'd known it was a good dress.

After a few more heartbeats of awkward paralysis, Lhéwen cleared her throat. Someone needed to break into the poor boy's thrall. With an embarrassed half-smile, the dark elf bowed and backed away from the door, motioning with one hand toward the right.

Belegeth was first to step out into the passage, axe and shield held at the ready. Though Lhéwen had seen her smile once or twice when not on duty, the woman was intensely focused when at work. Her fierce expression held no hint of emotion, though the lines of her face were relaxed and alert. She wore a golden cuirass that must chafe despite the soft wool beneath, but not a shred of discomfort showed, no matter how long she was forced to stand at attention nor how quickly she needed to move.

Lhéwen couldn't help but admire the woman's strength. It wasn't a fashion she wanted to emulate, however it was nice to see a woman who could not only stand up to a man, but physically defeat most any who made the mistake of attempting an attack. Standing in the hall, her head turning from side to side and senses obviously attuned to danger, Lhéwen doubted any would take that chance.

Unfortunately, the woman might be their only protection in the current moment.

"Your Highness, the other guards seem to have disappeared," Belegeth said.

Faeliel waved a hand in dismissal. "Nonsense. I gave them the evening to carouse. No one will dare bother us here, in the shadow king's castle, with you at my side."

The princess grinned at Belegeth who frowned in return. Lhéwen's lips pulled down in agreement with the guard, but what was she to do? She was only a lady-in-waiting, a glorified tailor. She had no right to admonish a royal decision. All the same, what would happen if the shadow king decided to play them all for fools? They were in his territory, visiting his realm under his forbearance, at a time when tensions between the kings were at their peak.

Then again, what would a few more guards have done to stop a king set on treachery in his own castle? He was honor bound to protect them, and they had to trust that he would do so.

Still, Lhéwen tried to keep her eyes open to any danger. She didn't have Belegeth's training, but at least she might provide a moment of warning if the worst were to happen. If only she could see what was to come.

Unfortunately, the black castle seemed designed to thwart a visitor's sense of direction. With few straight lines and fewer stairs, she felt like she was walking through the innards of a giant beast, rather than along the prestigious paths of the dark elves. Spiraling ramps led to the upper levels, while peaked archways led deeper into the dark recesses of the keep. Dim wisplights provided the only illumination, forcing Lhéwen to squint her eyes in an effort to see into the shadows.

Meanwhile the courier never hesitated, leading them with the soft susurration of leather on smooth stone. Finally, they approached broad double doors, behind which the muffled sound of voices could be heard.

Princess Faeliel paused a single step behind the courier, motioning for Belegeth to take position on her right. She once more smoothed a hand over the skirt of her gown, and lifted her chin. It was the pose of a woman in command of her audience.

Lhéwen fell into position behind her mistress, hands clasped at her waist. The princess would pose and preen, drawing the eye. It was Lhéwen's duty to keep watch and remain invisible. She'd learned long ago that the less attention she garnered the better for her likelihood of survival, whatever may come.

The courier nodded to the guards on either side. "Princess Faeliel of the high court of the Upper Realm, here to see the king."

With an answering nod, the guards pulled open the doors. A cacophony of sound erupted from behind the heavy wood. Lhéwen shrank away from the near physical bombardment of sound. Men and women shouted in virulent anger. Whatever they argued about

—and Lhéwen couldn't understand their words, only the emotion behind them—it divided the room.

No one noticed the princess at the doors. Princess Faeliel's jaw clenched. If there was one thing she hated more than her domineering father, it was being ignored. Lhéwen had been forced to listen to countless complaints of the slights against Faeliel's honor when some lord or lady failed to make the proper obeisance instantly upon her entry into a room. Luckily for everyone involved, the Shadow Realm had an announcer at the door.

The courier scurried to the herald, cupping his hands around the man's ear and leaning in. Without betraying a shred of surprise or a hint of unease, the man lifted a staff taller than his person, and slammed it onto the ground.

The room fell silent. Every dark elf head turned toward the new arrivals at the door. The vast majority snarled with unhidden fury or disgust.

"Her Royal Highness, Princess Faeliel, daughter of Othin, Crown Princess of the high court of the Upper Realm." The herald's words boomed and echoed across the throne room, easily four equestrian arenas long.

As if on silent command, the brightly dressed crowd of black-skinned, white-haired elves stepped back and cleared a path from the door to the king's seat on a raised dais at the end of the room. Black to match the rest of the castle, the throne was carved from some kind of dark wood and made to look as if dragons rested beneath the king's hands. A silver seal of the royal crest, a dragon wrapped around an orb, graced the top center of the tall peaked back.

The man who sat on the throne was equally imposing, his black and silver formal robes draping the wood and puddling around his feet. He sat in the chair with his back as straight as a spear, his expression unfathomable. His first son and heir stood at his right shoulder; the man was a younger replica of his father, down to the black robes and long braided hair.

Lhéwen's shoulders tightened, the relentless dark invading her mind in a way the golden shine of the high court never did. Even with the brightly colored fabrics worn by the rest of the court, there was too much black, too much shadow.

Princess Faeliel, however, didn't seem affected. She posed for several heartbeats, letting her audience view and admire her presence. After a careful few heartbeats, the princess strode forward, swaying her hips ever so slightly as she proceeded down the hall. A low murmur of whispers and hisses rolled through the room as she walked, but the princess never hesitated. Lhéwen followed three steps behind, carefully keeping her expression passive and eyes focused on the train of her ladyship's golden skirt.

Faeliel had practiced this walk and confident facial expression in the mirror more times than Lhéwen could count, and with each iteration she modified and perfected her performance. Some might call it narcissistic, but Lhéwen thought it was more about survival. She had taken to the practice as well, though her expressions and poses were geared toward invisibility and subservience rather than fearless pride. No one need know her true emotions, whatever they might be.

Ten steps from the dais, the princess paused, posed once more, and dropped into a respectful curtsy, low enough to give honor, but not so low as to imply obeisance. Lhéwen, however, dropped lower, her rank giving her no option but to present the greatest possible deference.

"Your visit is quite unexpected, my lady," King Rindae intoned after Faeliel returned to a standing position. Lhéwen followed suit with relief, keeping her eyes downcast. "The palace is in an uproar, the staff all aflutter. I trust your accommodations are to your liking."

"I do apologize for any inconvenience my arrival may have caused," Faeliel replied with a bow. "You may assure your staff the suite is perfectly suitable to my needs, and those of my ladies."

Lhéwen glanced at Belegeth to catch her reaction to being called a lady. One so fierce could hardly be described in the same breath as a lady of the high court. Belegeth made no sign she even heard the princess's words. Her right hand rested on the haft of her axe where it hung from her belt, while the left remained ready with the shield.

"I am glad to hear it."

Princess Faeliel was quick to continue. "But after your rather abrupt departure from the centennial summit, my father was concerned that something had been said or done to cause you offense. We deemed it prudent that I follow quickly to reassure Your Highness that though the summit is over, we hope to resume negotiations and reach a mutually beneficial agreement for the sake of all of the fae realms."

Lhéwen risked a glance up at the royal dais and its occupants. While the shadow king's jaw twitched ever so slightly, his expression remained placid as a lake on a hot summer's day.

"I'm afraid such delicate negotiations will have to wait as there is a more immediate matter that must be addressed regarding the members of your guard."

"Oh?" the princess replied, her lips pursing into a subtle pout. "And what could my guards possibly have done?"

"There has been an altercation at a local establishment."

The princess lifted a perfectly manicured hand to her lips. "Oh dear, I hope no one was injured."

"I'm afraid there was indeed some damage. Luckily, the commander of my guard was nearby, and able to apprehend all parties concerned. Now that you are present, I will question your men."

"That was very considerate of you to wait. I will, of course, defer to your judgment."

Lhéwen had been in the princess's inner circle for long enough that she thought she heard a hint of displeasure in her tone, though she doubted anyone else noticed.

With a graceful curl of his hand, the king motioned for the prisoners to be brought in. The commander entered first, leading the way for the rest of the guard and the prisoners. A fierce-looking dark elf, he bore a striking resemblance to the king and his heir, with the same silvery pale eyes and penetrating gaze. Could he be another member of the royal family?

The shadow guard prisoners were next in line, their leader a dark elf with a sneer that belied his defiance. All wore the characteristic black armor of their office but they could be differentiated from their captors by their lack of weapons and the numerous bleeding lacerations and bruises forming on their faces and exposed skin—not that there was much of the latter.

Behind them came the princess's guards, who still wore the golden livery of the Upper Realm. Like the shadow guard prisoners, their weapons had been removed and many were wounded.

The last man to file into the throne room was a younger-looking high elf Lhéwen didn't recognize. He kept himself apart from the guard, and wore only dark brown travel leathers and a resigned expression. Like the other prisoners, his weapons had been removed, but it didn't fit that he was involved in this mess.

"Commander Aradae, report," the king said.

The commander of the shadow guard stepped forward, a single eyebrow raised while his lips pulled up into a half smile.

"There was pub brawl at the Crossroads Inn. These men were found fighting in the courtyard, destroying private property, and causing a general disturbance of the peace. Weapons were drawn on both sides."

"And how did the altercation begin?"

"I have not had an opportunity to interrogate the prisoners," Commander Aradae replied. "I felt it prudent to allow you to question them."

"Wonderful. I do enjoy a good story." The king turned toward the shadow guard prisoners first. "Cendir, you are a trusted soldier and leader amongst my guard. How did this happen?"

The sneering dark elf at the front of the queue lost some of his defiance as his back straightened at the praise. "Your Majesty, the high elves knocked into us, spilling our drinks, then demanding recompense as if they were the aggrieved party. When we refused to apologize, they attacked."

"An insult!" A male voice called from the crowd. Others joined in. "Let them hang!"

Lhéwen kept her face carefully bland. It wasn't uncommon for King Othin to harshly punish even slight offenses, so it could only be worse here, where the violence occurred every day on the street.

"Silence!" King Rindae shouted. The crowd grumbled, but kept their voices down. Lhéwen was surprised when he didn't do more.

"That cannot be true," Faeliel interjected. "My men do not start fights without cause."

"Perhaps they had a reason," the king replied. His gaze paused on Faeliel, a subtle charge passing between the royals.

Faeliel's lip turned up a fraction. She held the king's gaze while she turned her head toward the imprisoned members of her guard.

"Is this your recollection of events?" she asked the high elf captain, still holding the king's gaze.

"No, Your Highness," he replied. "The dark elves intentionally crashed into our table. An ale poured over my head in the process."

"And that justified an explosion into violence?" King Rindae asked, keeping his tone level despite the obvious answer.

"My men can hardly be expected to allow a slight against their honor. They were due an apology," Princess Faeliel replied before her captain could say more.

"Your Majesty, they lie. That's not how it happened," Cendir said, his tone urgent.

"Perhaps our third party will have a better perspective."

The high elf at the back of the crowd of warriors looked up, his brow furrowing as if startled. The blue of his eyes reminded Lhéwen of the flowering vines that grew in her mother's garden, while the strength in his jaw gave him a sense of purpose.

"Apologies, Your Majesty, but I did not see the start of the fight. I only helped to end it."

"You are not a part of the high elf guard?"

"No, Your Majesty. I am simply a merchant passing through."

Lhéwen cocked her head to the side, examining the man more carefully. Indeed, he looked the part of a merchant, his functional travel leathers scarred from use but obviously oiled and well cared for. His hair, worn long and braided in the common style of the high court, hung around his shoulders. But something about his posture and the fit of his gear made her doubt that merchant was his only title. He carried strength within his lean muscles, as if coiled and ready for use.

"Passing through for what purpose?" Rindae asked.

"For business, sire." The merchant wrinkled his brow, as if the answer was obvious.

Rindae lifted his gaze to the ceiling for one brief moment of exasperation. Clearly he had no problem showing his emotions. "Yes, but *what* business?"

"I am Curuthannor, son and apprentice of Hatholdammon, guildmaster of the smithy in Rómesse Gulch. I am here to acquire iron from your master of mining."

"Iron? Doesn't the Upper Realm have its own mines?"

"Yes, sire, but my father prefers the strength and flexibility of the metal from the black hills lava flows."

"Interesting." Rindae turned his enigmatic gaze toward the princess once more, giving her a knowing smile and a subtle wink. "It seems we have something that the Upper Realm wants."

The princess's lips turned up at the corners in an amused smile. She licked her lips, putting the charm on in full force. "I do believe that is the point of this visit, is it not? I'm certain *I* want more from the Shadow Realm."

CHAPTER 5

Curuthannor coughed, covering his mouth with his hand. The princess was laying the charisma on thick, and every male head was turned in her direction. He refused to be one of them.

Princess Faeliel was a performer. Though he'd never been to court, even Curuthannor had heard the stories. Everyone in the Upper Realm knew she was a vain coquette, not that they would ever say it to her face.

She was also vindictive, narcissistic, and self-serving, or so he'd been told, and seeing her here made him nervous.

"Tell me, Curuthannor, why it is that you felt it appropriate to fight your own kinsmen?" Faeliel asked.

Curuthannor swallowed hard. He wouldn't consider these high elves his kinsmen—only his brothers and parents could claim that right—but he supposed realmsmen was too much of a mouthful.

He glanced at the high elf prisoners standing near, but not too near him. By common unspoken agreement, they and he had made the clear distinction. He was not part of their group. Nor did he want to be. The guard, though filled with skilled fighters, was also filled with men who had little respect for the common elves of the realm. They seemed to feel it was their right to lord over the untitled craftsmen who provided their armor and weapons. Curuthannor had seen it time and again in his father's smithy. The men coming in with their sneers and their demands, with no regard for the time and attention to detail required for each new project.

The men today, in their gleaming gold metal, glared at him from paces away. Their opinion didn't concern him. Their vengeance, and that of their princess, might.

"I did not intend to fight them, but felt it was imperative that they refrain from embarrassing our realm."

"He drew his sword," one of the high elf soldiers protested. Curuthannor thought it might be the man he had pinned at the end, though he couldn't be sure.

"Their behavior reflected poorly on the ideals and values of the Upper Realm. We are not a race prone to violence and destruction," Curuthannor replied.

The princess glanced beneath her lashes at the shadow king once more. Curuthannor took a deep relieved breath as her attention was drawn away from him.

"This is true. There were no deaths, were there?" she asked.

"No," King Rindae replied, voice low. "No deaths."

"If my men had truly wanted to cause 'violence and destruction' as our dear merchant phrased it, they would have simply drained your guard of their energy. The captain alone has the power to end a life with his magic."

Rindae's expression turned fiercely speculative. "So you would argue they showed restraint? Perhaps that they needn't be punished for their actions?"

Faeliel lifted her hands in a graceful placating gesture. "I only mean to say that the incident could have been far worse. Thanks to the quick thinking of our merchant, and to the *restraint*—as you so pleasantly put it—of my men, no permanent damage was done. I will make reparations to the inn, but I cannot be deprived of my guard. I suggest that we put this matter aside and discuss more relevant topics to my stay here in your court. "

"They must be taught a lesson!" a voice called out.

"Already she seeks to usurp your rule," another shouted.

The king glanced up with a lifted eyebrow, but didn't respond. Instead, he turned a speculative gaze on the princess. "Perhaps you would prefer to discuss our current trade agreements? Or should I say, the new export tariffs your king has imposed on all Upper Realm agricultural goods. I suppose his intent was not to raise our food costs and deprive our people of the basics for life? Perhaps his treasury is running dry?"

Princess Faeliel tilted her head in a coy nod. "The cost of living is going up everywhere."

No longer in the spotlight, Curuthannor felt his attention begin to drift from the royals' careful wordplay to the Shadow Realm throne room. Though he'd never officially trained as a soldier, his father was a skilled swordsman and paranoid by nature. His admonitions about being caught unprepared had taken root in Curuthannor's daily habits. One day, he would put those lessons to good use. In the meantime, it was smart to practice in unfamiliar territory.

Black marble—or perhaps it was the same obsidian as the walls—covered the floor, a slick surface that could be challenging in a fight without enough grip to secure one's footing. Matching black columns held up the distant ceiling, which could provide a bit of cover if necessary in a skirmish. The main public door was at the farthest end of the hall away from the king. It was probably the worst exit from this room, at least in a panicked crowd. The doors behind the king's throne were likely a better choice, but would also be protected by the king's guards.

He scanned the room, looking for the hidden men who would be ready to protect their king. The obvious soldiers, including both princes, stood behind the throne and off to either side. But they weren't the king's true protection. There had to be hidden assassins and warriors in the crowd.

Curuthannor examined the faces of the individuals closest to Princess Faeliel. Two alert men in traditional silk robes stood behind the princess and her ladies, but their stances were too straight and balanced to be mere nobles. Their gazes flicked around the room, mostly avoiding the royals, their expressions focused and hard. They weren't here for the business or the entertainment. Curuthannor wondered if the princess and her small entourage had identified the danger.

His gaze turned to her party. The lady warrior kept behind the princess. Her hand was loosely clasped on the haft of her large battle axe and her shield rested in a relaxed but prepared position on her hip. Standing taller than most high elf males, the woman was thick with muscle and could hardly be called a lady. No, she was clearly the princess's personal bodyguard.

The other woman was harder to read. She was pretty enough in the way of the glittering women of the high elves—certainly more attractive than the guard at her side. Tall, but not too tall, golden blond hair that gleamed but failed to outshine the princess's perfect tresses. She wore a well-designed but neutral dress and no jewelry or other ornamentation. In fact, she seemed designed not to stand out. She kept her head tilted down and her expression bland as plain rice, but every so often her gaze would flicker up from beneath long black lashes and a twinkle of repressed emotion would shine through.

The woman lifted her head, catching Curuthannor's gaze for one brief instant. Curuthannor's breath caught in his throat. And then her eyes turned to the king and the moment passed.

King Rindae stood from his throne, drawing Curuthannor's attention back to the conversation going on between the royals. "Very well, we will take this discussion into more private quarters."

"And what of my guards?" Princess Faeliel asked.

King Rindae looked over his shoulder at Prince Aradae, the

commander of the shadow guard. "Take them to the guest barracks and confine them to quarters. They will be allowed to guard the princess outside of the palace walls, if necessary, but their weapons will not be returned until they are needed. Beyond that, you may punish your own men as you wish."

The guards grumbled and growled. "Your Highness, this is not right. We are here to protect you, not waste our time in quarters."

The princess snapped her gaze to the commander of the guard. "You should have thought of that before," she hissed. "The king is being lenient. I would not protest, if I were you, or things will go much worse."

Ah, there she is, Curuthannor thought. The princess's true personality was showing. But she was quick to conceal it once more.

"Apologies, King Rindae," she said with a modest curtsy. "My guards will comply."

There was no mention of Curuthannor. Had he been forgotten, or lumped in with the princess's guard? Would he be allowed to return to the inn? He didn't want to draw attention to himself if he didn't have to, but he did need his sword and knives returned.

The handmaiden glanced his direction. Her eyes flicked from his face to the royal dais and back, as if trying to tell him something. Should he speak up?

The woman blew out a breath and stepped forward with her hands clasped before her in a deferential bow. She leaned in to whisper in Princess Faeliel's ear.

"Of course," the princess replied to the handmaiden before speaking up to King Rindae. "And what of the merchant? He is a high elf, but he is not of our party. May I suggest he be released?"

The king shrugged, indifferent. "The story remains consistent across all parties. He had no part in the disagreement, except to try to stop it. Return his weapons. He is free to go back to his business, but should weapons be drawn again, I suggest he allow the shadow guard to do their duty."

"Thank you, Your Majesty," Curuthannor murmured with a low bow, hoping to hide the heat that rose to his cheeks at the reprimand.

While Prince Aradae returned the weapons, King Rindae held out an arm for the princess, which she gracefully stepped forward to accept. Once again, her charisma surged forth, drawing the male gaze. The crowd in the hall murmured like swarming wasps as the royal couple exited toward the doors at the back of the hall.

Curuthannor hoped it would be the last he would see or be seen by those two. The faster he purchased the iron he needed and returned home the better.

CHAPTER 6

Catching the subtle finger wave his father cast at him, Aradae and his elder brother, Daeturion, trailed behind the princess as they left the public throne room. Careful not to step on or trip over the train that shushed along the ground, Aradae's eyes were still drawn to the long expanse of gleaming white skin that lay bare for inspection to all eyes.

She was beautiful, of that there was no doubt, but she was also a temptation that was too risky to contemplate, even for his father, though he would never dare give the king advice.

"Your Highness, please sit down," the king said, addressing the princess. "My staff will be here presently with refreshments." Rindae swept a hand toward the cushioned chairs near the desk in his private chambers.

The princess murmured her thanks, but sauntered over to the chaise lounge near the window instead. With a practiced hand, she drew the train out from beneath her and leaned against the curled riser, her chin resting on her knuckles. An enigmatic smile touched her lips, as if challenging the king to move her.

With a tip of his head and a gleam in his eye, Rindae acknowledged the subtle power play but said nothing about her choice. That in and of itself was telling. The king was intrigued.

"I must speak with my sons for one moment, and then I'll return to our discussions." The king ushered Aradae and Daeturion back out into the hallway before shutting the door behind them.

Aradae would have been shocked at leaving a powerful noble from another realm in the king's private study, except he knew this was all a facade. There was nothing confidential or private in that room. The king's true study was attached to his private quarters and remained locked except when in use by the king himself.

"Daeturion, I want you to mobilize your spies. The observers must follow and track that merchant," the king ordered Aradae's brother, his voice turning to business. "If what he says is true, then our iron may be the true reason King Othin wants to control our realm. It may be our only active pawn in this game."

"I have already activated the network. He won't go anywhere without our knowledge."

"And if he returns to the guild?" Aradae asked. The merchant may have seemed rustic, but Aradae had seen him fight. He was quick and determined. He wouldn't willingly leave the realm without completing his mission. Aradae was sure of it.

Rindae glanced in Aradae's direction, but ignored the question as if it hadn't even been asked, instead continuing to give Daeturion his orders.

"We finally have a bit of leverage, which we can use to our advantage. Send a message to Master Ger. We will no longer support the armies of our enemies. Iron exports are banned."

"Yes, Father," Daeturion replied.

Aradae scowled, but said no more. It wasn't worth it. His job was not to question his father's edicts, no matter how much they might antagonize a powerful enemy. His only job was to enforce those laws.

"Make sure Master Ger understands that if he attempts to

subvert the law, he will find himself in the same position as his predecessor, along with anyone he sells to."

"As you command."

"And Aradae?"

Aradae lifted his head, wiping any and all expression from his face. "Yes, Father?"

"Don't let a merchant best you or your men, ever again."

Without further comment, the king returned to the room and shut the door.

Aradae curled a lip. *Godsdamn Cendir.* It was bad enough that the king ignored him, far worse that he think him incompetent and his army undisciplined.

"When are you going to learn?" Daeturion hissed as the brothers returned to the throne room. They would have to find a courier quickly, before the merchant had a chance to return to the miner's guild hall. "You must keep better control of your underlings."

Aradae's shoulders tightened as he instinctively defended himself from his brother's rebuke. "How was I to know the high elf guards would be at the Crossroads? Or that Cendir would take his off-duty time there today?"

"Cendir and his thugs love that pub. They're there nearly every evening."

"It's so easy for you, isn't it? You know everything that everyone is doing."

Daeturion's Observers were the Shadow Realm spies and information gatherers, and Daeturion was their central hub. No one did anything without his knowledge, and he was adept at manipulating their behavior, even without the high elves' spirit magic.

Aradae loathed politics. At times he wished he could remain obscure, a simple soldier in the king's guard, rather than their commander.

"Knowing what they *are* doing and predicting what they *will* do are two entirely separate skills. It's the latter you need to improve on. Think three steps ahead of your enemy and prevent the nega-tive outcome."

Daeturion turned away, as dismissive of Aradae as their father.

"You there. Boy," Daeturion called to a courier at the scribe's station outside of the main throne room doors. "I have a message."

"Yes, Your Highness," the boy squeaked.

Normally, Aradae wouldn't trust a throne room courier, as they tended to be less experienced and more likely to slip information to the wrong parties, but speed would have to prevail over caution if they were to prevent any iron from leaving the realm. This partic-ular courier was blood sidhe, which meant faster than elf. It was a worthwhile risk.

Daeturion must have agreed, because he bent to scribble out a note. That done, he folded the paper into the complicated square that would close all edges, while the boy heated wax for the seal. The boy poured the wax over the seam and Daeturion pressed his signet ring into the rapidly cooling black goo.

"Take this to Master Ger," Daeturion ordered. "Tell him I'll be by to discuss terms before first light."

"Yes, Your Highness." Apparently it was all the courier knew how to say. A good sign.

As the courier scurried away, Daeturion turned back to face Aradae with a frown. "Get yourself cleaned up. We'll be watching the merchant and I'll let you know if you or your warriors are needed."

A pounding on the door of his private quarters jolted Aradae awake. In an instant he was on his feet, short sword and dagger in his hands.

"Aradae!" His brother's voice called through the thick dark wood. "Open up!"

Aradae sheathed his sword and dagger and pulled on his

trousers. If Daeturion was here this early, something must have happened. He opened the door.

"What is it?"

Daeturion stepped into the room, looking as fresh and cleanly pressed as if he were about to enter the throne room. Aradae admired his brother's constant poise, and yet he couldn't bring himself to make the same effort. Those robes were a pain if you moved at anything other than a sedate walk.

"Get your leathers on." Daeturion said, tone urgent. "The merchant is on the move, headed to the miner's guild. Master Ger acknowledged the king's edict, but he won't hesitate to 'lose' a few bars if he thinks he can get away with it."

"Damn greedy goblins."

"Be glad for it, brother. If he hadn't tried to triple the price on the high elf, the merchant would have already left with his supplies. We would have missed this opportunity for leverage."

"And someone would have ended up dead at the Crossroads, as well."

"Aye. We owe the merchant a debt. One that can be repaid by letting him keep his life."

"Our king ordered his removal if he became a problem. I assumed that meant death." Aradae pulled his tunic over his head, wondering at his brother's minor rebellion.

Daeturion lifted a single quizzical brow. "Were you looking forward to killing an innocent over a bit of metal?"

Aradae shrugged. It wouldn't be the first time he'd killed for no better reason than his father ordered it. After all, that was his job. "I follow my orders."

"Well, even if you are truly that indifferent, think through the ramifications. If the merchant fails to return home, his king will never hear that the iron trade has been stopped. Better Othin hear it from one of his own citizens than lash out at one of our couriers. Plus, if we can avoid being the first to shed blood, we can avoid the stain of starting the war. That alone may save us if the upperworlds refuse to back a power-hungry high king."

"I think Father's edict is tantamount to a declaration of war. He's spitting in Othin's face."

"Tantamount, perhaps, but not declaration in truth. There is still room to negotiate. With the princess in residence, I have hope that amicable terms can be reached."

"Always the diplomat."

"I'd rather not have all five upperworlds slavering for blood. It's bad enough that our king has antagonized Othin and the high elves, but if the fire sidhe and wood elves join him, our days of independence will be numbered."

"You doubt our guard?" Aradae asked. He'd spent the last three centuries building up the army and its warriors. It stung that his brother would question his effectiveness.

"You have a few hundred soldiers? Maybe a thousand? Do you really think that's enough to defend our city, let alone our entire realm? Besides, Othin has no right to claim authority over our lands and our resources, but we still need each other. They have the agricultural bounty. We have the mineral wealth."

"Then you would bend the knee? You would swear allegiance?"

"Of course not," Daeturion scoffed. "Why do you think Father walked out of the summit? I *Saw* Othin's plot to claim the high crown through the memories of his assistant. I will do what I can to secure our future, and I will make sure our king does the same."

Aradae cinched the last buckle on his black leather bracers, and patted his weapons. The time for talk was over. "If we're not going to kill him, what's the plan?"

Aradae exited his rooms with Daeturion at his side, the brothers picking up the pace down the corridor.

"Master Ger has closed off the above-ground entrance to the guild hall. Take the subterranean route. Go alone. Scare him off," Daeturion said.

"Simple."

"Exactly."

"And if he won't go?"

"He seemed a reasonable man. Make him understand there is no other option. He will leave."

"You're sure?"

"I'm not gifted with foresight, so no, I'm not sure. But I'm confident in your powers of persuasion. Besides, my observers will report if he does anything unexpected on his way out of our fair city."

CHAPTER 7

Curuthannor rubbed the sleep from his eyes. Even after two cups of hot dark tea, and a warm sausage and biscuit breakfast, he couldn't seem to return to the realm of the living. It didn't help that even at fifth bell, the sun had failed to rise above the mountain peaks. It wasn't called the Shadow Realm for its abundant daylight.

Yet that wasn't the only reason his body dragged with fatigue. Sleep had come fitfully during the night, his thoughts turning over the altercation in the bar, followed by the events in the throne room, and the woman's twinkling eyes. He couldn't shake her image from his mind. So much had happened in such a short amount of time.

He blew out a breath and stretched his shoulders, refocusing his energies. He couldn't allow himself to become distracted. He had business to attend, and would need every bit of clever wit he could muster to deal with Master Ger.

The mining guild headquarters were located on the outskirts of the city, near the northern gate in the foothills of the black mountains. Glancing at the skyline, the dark peaks seemed to push down into the bustling capital, the slow lava flows running down their sides like glowing red tears. But it was all an optical illusion thanks to the oppressive darkness. The active volcanoes were hundreds of leagues away, though their lava still flowed beneath the streets of the city. In fact, it was the local goblins who had mastered the redirection of the flow and learned to parse out the minerals. Which was, of course, why it was the purest and strongest form of iron. And only available here.

Curuthannor scowled. It was that monopoly that gave Ger the audacity to demand triple the gold for the iron. But even if the black hills iron was the best, it wasn't worth *that* price. Curuthannor would find a way to bring the cost in line with reality and maximize his family's profit. He had to.

Dodging one of the steaming lava vents that lined the thorough-fare, Curuthannor thought through his options. A bribe was out of the question; past experience had shown that one bribe led to another and another, until they were paying more to keep people complacent than they were for the iron itself. Besides, that was likely exactly why Master Ger was demanding triple the price in the first place. He would keep much of the excess for himself.

Was there another way to gain favor? Perhaps if he mentioned the commission from King Othin, and the likelihood of increased business as a result, the twisted creature would look to the long-term revenue instead of the short-term profit.

Given the death of the last mining master, Curuthannor doubted Ger cared much for long-term planning. He would be taking as much advantage of his position as he could muster before some other enterprising goblin stretched him out on a rack until he burst at the seams.

The buildings that lined the street began to grow squat and wide, like the pedestrians that trundled the alleys and walkways. This was goblin territory. Only a few members of their prolific race chose to move above ground and into the city, but those that did made their homes as close to the old northern gate as possible.

Finally, the gate itself appeared; a high stone arch made of shining black volcanic rock that marked the edge of the city. Beneath the peak he could see the domed earthen structure on the hill that was the entrance to the mining master's estate. No guards watched the doors. There was no visible sign of habitation at all. But Curuthannor knew outward appearances could be deceiving. There were tens of thousands of goblins living beneath that calm surface in tunnels that had been carved out by hand and by molten rock.

A massive stone slab covered the rough entrance to the building. A tormented goblin's face had been carved into the rock, the visage screaming with its tongue extended. Though Curuthannor had seen the image on previous visits, the door had always been open and he could just walk in. That wasn't an option this time.

Curuthannor banged a fist against the rock. The stone didn't make a sound. All he achieved was a bruise on the side of his fist. While rubbing the pain from his hand, he tried pushing on it with his shoulder, just to see if it would shift. It didn't move a finger's-width.

Gently knocking a row across the stone slab, Curuthannor listened for some kind of variation in the sound, any indication that there was a way to alert the residents inside that someone waited on their doorstep. He didn't hear a thing.

With a frown, Curuthannor walked around the exterior of the building. The low building had a living roof, covered with shrubs and grasses. Really, it was less of an edifice and more of a mound in the dirt, a hatchway to the deeper interior. There were no windows, only the single rough entry.

No wonder it didn't need any guards.

Curuthannor returned to the front entrance, studying the hatchway once more. He'd never needed to inform them of his presence on his previous visits, he had simply walked inside and been greeted by some peon of the guild master. What was he supposed to do now?

"You could just ask," a sniveling voice said from above and to the right.

Curuthannor's head jerked upright. His gaze darted around the doorway until at last he spotted a creature sitting on a ledge, leaning over with his hands on his knees. Dull brown wide-set eyes stared down at him from between broad ears and two nubby horns. A twitching pink nose sniffed in disdain.

"Ask?" Curuthannor asked, dumbly.

"You know, use your words to request information, or in this case, access to the guild headquarters."

"Who are you?"

"Who are you? Tell me your name and I'll see if the master wants to speak with you."

"The master?"

"You ask a lot of questions. Not so smart questions, if you ask me, but what do I know. I'm basically a doorbell."

Curuthannor swallowed and gathered his wits. This creature could get him inside. He didn't really need to know anything else about the minuscule goat-rat-man.

"I am Curuthannor, son of Hatholdammon, the greatest smith in Rómesse Gulch. I'm here to see Master Ger."

"More information than I need, but I'll pass it along."

With a pop of displaced air, the creature disappeared.

Curuthannor leaned his back to the stone door and removed one of his mother's travel cakes from his bag. Chewing on the salty-sweet concoction reminded him of home. He could almost smell the warm bread and roasting meat that she was probably working on right now. She would be humming a lilting tune as she kneaded the dough, or slapping his father's hand away as he attempted to steal an early bite of the roast. Or maybe it was time for the midday meal, and the whole family would be gathered around the table for a smorgasbord of cold cuts and yesterday's leftovers.

Curuthannor took another bite from the cake and felt his mother's love wrap his aura and feed his energy, even as the sweet bread filled his stomach. No matter how delicious Tryg's menu, nothing would ever compare to his own mother's cooking.

Just then, the little imp returned, a wrinkle in his brow. "Go away."

Curuthannor snorted at the complete lack of political grace. "I cannot simply go away. I need to see Master Ger."

"Master Ger doesn't want to see you, unless you can pay what he asks. He's busy."

"Tell him I have a commission from King Othin himself. I cannot pay what he asks now, but if I mention Master Ger in my report, I'm sure the high king will look favorably on future business with the guild."

"He already said no, but if you give me a taste of that cake, I'll run the message," the imp said with a lick of his lips.

Curuthannor frowned but tore a small chunk from the travel cake, handing it up to the imp on the shelf who promptly shoved it in his mouth with the grace of a ravenous bear. After sticking his fingers in his mouth to clean off the last of the honey, he grinned and popped away once more.

He was gone longer this time, long enough that Curuthannor worried he wouldn't return. He leaned his back against the door, resigned to wait until someone opened it, even if it meant he slept right there in the dirt.

Finally, a clatter sounded above his head.

"The commander is on his way," the imp said without preamble. "Master Ger says you can talk to him."

Great. The last thing Curuthannor wanted to do was talk to Prince Aradae, the man who had forced him to stand before the court like a common criminal. It was the thanks he got for trying to stop an intra-realm incident.

Still, he couldn't go home empty-handed. They needed the iron. His father would settle for no less, not for the high king. Curuthannor couldn't return a failure. Not again. Not in this.

Sensing the imp about to pop away once more, Curuthannor jumped and snatched him off the ledge. In a panic, the imp translocated, bringing Curuthannor with him into the guild hall.

Curuthannor let go before the imp could send him back outside. He looked around, finding himself in a room he'd never visited before. Thick fur rugs covered the floor and walls, making the elf feel as if he'd arrived inside a warren of brerhoppers that had exceeded the advisable population limits.

A throat cleared behind him. Curuthannor spun to the sound, a hand on the hilt of his sword.

"I told you to go away," Master Ger said, his voice a raucous crow of sound. "Ye're not wanted here."

The man lay on a wide pillow, his hairy chest bare. Luckily, his body was covered from the waist down in the same rugs as lined the room. Given the thickset and mostly naked goblin ladies on either side of him, Curuthannor would hate to see the rest of him. The ladies didn't bother to cover up, simply stared at him with glassy eyes and empty grins.

Master Ger's four eyes blinked in random order, watching Curuthannor expectantly.

"You would turn down a prospective client with so little civility? That hardly seems like a good sales practice. This could be a highly profitable deal for you."

Movement at the edge of his vision caught Curuthannor's attention. A hanging fur was pushed aside.

"Then ye've found the funds to pay the price, after all?"

Curuthannor shook his head. "No, I cannot afford a triple increase. But I can offer more business. Once the king sees my father's blade, he will want more. I guarantee it. And my father will require the black hills iron for his work."

"It matters not. Yer business is no good," Master Ger declared.

"Says who?"

"Me."

Curuthannor pivoted to the left as the rug fell back into place behind Prince Aradae. Curuthannor dropped into a low bow that would have made his mother proud, even as he suppressed the anger that wanted to bubble to the surface. It wouldn't do any good to start a fight. Not here. He didn't even know the way out of this room, though obviously the exits were covered by the furs on the walls.

"Took ye long enough," Master Ger snapped. "He's been bugging me for bells."

Hardly, Curuthannor thought. He kept his head low and gaze on the floor. The prince hadn't invited him to stand, yet.

"At ease," the prince intoned. "There's no need for formality. Not here."

The goblin master chuckled as if the prince's words were some great joke. Curuthannor didn't understand the punchline.

"Then may I ask why I am not permitted to purchase the iron I need for my business?"

"Certainly. I'll even answer. We need it. Master Ger's entire inventory has been spoken for."

Curuthannor glanced at the goblin from the corner of his eye. The four-eyed man gaped at the prince, puffy lips spread wide in shock. It seemed this was news to the mining master, as well as to Curuthannor.

"I am here to bargain in good faith. There must be some arrangement that can be made."

"I'm afraid not," Aradae replied. "Every bar is claimed for Shadow Realm use, and Shadow Realm alone."

"For what purpose?" Curuthannor demanded. Without knowing exactly how much iron was pulled from the lava flows each day, he couldn't be certain, but there had to be enough stock-piled for an army's worth of weapons.

"That is one question I cannot answer. However, rest assured Master Smith, your business dealings will not be lacking."

"I am no master, but I will pass along your . . ." Curuthannor paused, searching for the politically astute word to use in this situation ". . . edict to my father. He will be most disappointed."

"I'm sure that can be remedied in some other way," Aradae replied without emotion. Curuthannor was fairly certain the man didn't care one way or another what the outcome of this conversation was. "For now, I suggest you return to your rooms at the inn and pack your things for the journey home."

CHAPTER 8

King Othin clenched his jaw as he paced a circle around the gilded desk in his office, unable to sit still. The steady rhythm of his slippered heels striking cold marble focused his thoughts.

His high elf advisors—the landed lords who had supported his early ascent to the Upper Realm throne so long ago—were weak and lacked vision, but they had bought him some time. The export tariff on all goods sold to unallied realms would erode the dark elf supply lines. It wasn't nearly enough, of course, but it was a start. Already, it had borne some small sour fruit.

The Winter Realm had signed the alliance. So had Spring. Like the Shadow Realm, they were dependent on the agricultural bounty from Othin's lands. They'd practically begged for the more favorable trade terms.

The high elf lords believed the shadow king would soon follow suit. Othin knew better. But then, he was also a king.

And he would be High King. No filthy little soul-stealer would deny him.

Othin growled as he pivoted to circle the opposite direction. The summit was supposed to have been his greatest political victory, the moment in which the realms joined for a united future under his benevolent leadership. Instead, only the weakest of the realms had joined him. Rindae's stunt had not only broken the union of the nine, it had shaken the faith of the strongest warriors outside of his own golden army.

The Summer Realm soldiers—the Tirnor—might decide the outcome of the coming war. They were warriors fueled by fire. They were powerful, but not yet numerous enough to defy the strength of the Upper Realm. At least, not by themselves. If they aligned with another realm . . .

He could *not* allow them to ally with the dark elves. He would show them why he was their king, give them a taste of what would happen if they refused to sign. He needed them to fight for the *right* side, the side of light. For a people that worshiped the sun god, that side should be clear.

If not . . . well, he would make sure they understood their true position.

In the meantime, he would bring the high elf advisors, his so-called small council, tighter into his influence. They must feel the insult to their realm as he did, must understand the threat Rindae represented to their own interests. To achieve that, he must first inflate their egos and their belief in their own importance. His advisors must be honored as the wisest of men, so that when they called for war, they believed it was their own idea.

Tonight's feast—the celebration of the new inter-realm alliances —would be the first opportunity to lay the foundation for their future voluntary subjugation.

He needed his best assets in play.

Othin yanked on the bell-pull at his desk, ringing for his assistant outside. Within moments, the door opened. A bony arm gesticulated as the obsequious weasel of a man made his formal obeisance on entering the room.

"Yes, my king?" Rolimdornoron's nasally voice grated on

Othin's nerves, but the man was efficient in his duties, and entirely loyal.

"Send for our daughter."

Othin hadn't spoken with Princess Faeliel since before the kings and their courts had arrived for the summit weeks ago. He had seen her fluttering around the edges of the gathering like a moth drawn to the flame of power, but she had not been invited to sit. She was still too brash and impetuous, a liability in a tense situation.

But at a party, she was the perfect addition to the decor. He needed her at his side for the dinner feast, if only to distract and tempt the unencumbered lords who were vying for greater position. And perhaps she could seed some fear into the daughters and wives, put a little pressure on their fathers and husbands. She had a knack for influencing others in her direction, when she wanted to.

"Apologies, my king. I thought you knew. Princess Faeliel left the palace and has not yet returned."

Othin's eyes narrowed as his anger flared. "Where has she gone?"

If she wasn't present at the feast, things would not look well. The lords would question her absence, the lusty, grasping fools, and they would know his house wasn't in order.

"I do not know, Your Majesty. She disappeared in the night." The man bowed lower, until his nose practically touched his knees. "There is a rumor that she was intrigued by King Rindae and his entourage. Perhaps . . ."

King Othin stood from his chair, drawing his shoulders back. His jaw clenched and twitched in consternation. "You are dismissed."

"Yes, Your Majesty. As you wish." Rolimdornoron scuttled backward out of the room, somehow managing to remain in his bow at the same time.

Othin began once more to pace around the room. The last thing he needed was another crack in his authority. She could not have timed this latest rebellion with worse consequences.

Except . . .

His steps paused, his thoughts narrowing in on a plan that might give them all exactly what they wanted. His greatest weakness, his heir, could perhaps be turned to his advantage.

CHAPTER 9

Rothruinil was ready. She waited in the shadows of the front hall, watching the edge of the jungle where King Othin would emerge. Word had been sent ahead that he was on his way. A fire sidhe escort had been assigned to lead the king from the portal, across the network of bridges and waterways, to the jungle covered palace island at the center of the Summer Realm capital. His journey would take a bell, maybe a little more, but he had to be close by now.

The barong roared a warning. The red-faced sentient winged lions swooped overhead, their silhouettes dark against the clear blue sky. Rothruinil grinned to see them soar.

Rumor had it that after the failure of the nine realms summit, the Upper Realm king was desperate to forge the alliances that would unify the five upper worlds. He already had three oaths, but they were weak and their populations small. The fire sidhe were the last. But what could he offer them that they didn't already have? He demanded allegiance in exchange for protection and trade. The Summer Realm didn't need protection, and their lands were as fertile as the Upper Realm.

Rothruinil chuckled quietly to herself. She wished she had been invited into the throne room for the meeting. She would have loved to witness King Othin's frustration and consternation at being refused. But the Tirnor had elected her as their chief for the traditional welcoming greeting. It was an honor she didn't take lightly. Even as the daughter of the Summer King and Queen, she wasn't given special privileges. She had earned her place in their ranks.

She grinned again, and bounced lightly on the balls of her feet, anticipating the show that was to come. On instinct and reflex borne of thousands of hours of training, she twirled the thick, carved-wood tavahatal mallets that had become an extension of her own arms. They had been her weapons of choice for over a century, a traditional weapon of the fire sidhe. Specially treated to contain and control the fire within her blood, they would never fail to burn and yet would also never blacken.

Four other Tirnor warriors had been chosen for the greeting ceremony. Two carried tall staffs and the others carried arm's-length clubs, all treated with the same enchantments. The fire dance for the Upper Realm King would be unforgettable.

At last, King Othin emerged from the thick jungle foliage that had been burned back from the stone palace walls. Riding a bright white horse and wearing formal white robes shot through with golden thread, he practically glowed with radiant power. Rothruinil's nerves suddenly spiked and her stomach clenched.

This was the king of the high elves, the ruler of the Upper Realm, one of the most powerful men alive and an original settler of the nine faerie realms. As powerful as the Summer King and Queen were, they couldn't boast his age and experience. The weight of his strength was carried in the hard lines of his eyes and the haughty, disdainful expression on his face.

It was the latter observation that set Rothruinil's resolve. This king might be powerful, but he was not *her* king. He would come to understand the strength of the fire sidhe.

The escort led the king and his four golden-armored guards to the steps of the palace gate.

"You may dismount here. The horses will be taken to the arena, fed and watered," the younger warrior informed the king.

The king gave a nod, and he and his guards dismounted as two stable hands emerged from the edge of the jungle to take their reins. Two of his guards led the king up the three steps to the top landing of the palace.

"Welcome," the younger fire sidhe said as he stepped out of the way with a slight bow and a wave of his hand.

It was time.

Keeping her body hidden within the shadows of the unlit hall, Rothruinil willed fire to blaze forth from the tavahatals. The magically enhanced wood burst to life in a blaze of orange and yellow flame. She let out a ululating war cry and began the fire dance.

Rothruinil became the flame. She spun in a vortex of fire, her tavahatals on their leather wrist straps spinning around her. The golden-armored warriors quickly stepped in to surround and protect their king. Rothruinil lunged toward the nearest golden warrior, but kept out of reach of the longsword that was suddenly in his hand. She spun away with a grin. *Success.*

The goal was not to start a fight, but rather to intimidate and gain a reaction. She danced backward, giving the king and his soldiers room to step deeper into the hall. Lunge, spin, jump, and twirl. Rothruinil screamed her defiance. These were welcome guests, but they would know the power of the flame.

With a final twisting jump, Rothruinil froze, landing with her left leg bent, right leg extended to the side, right hand touching the floor, left hand high in the air, pointing the tavahatal to the sky. She gave three short bursts of wordless sound, the signal for the others to begin.

The club-wielders jumped down from the ledges above and on either side of the king and his men. The spear wielders appeared out of the darkness behind her. Like her tavahatals, their weapons blazed with fire, and their war cries echoed through the chamber. This room was kept dark and windowless for a reason: the dancers were the only source of light. One had to face the flame and earn the right to move from shadow into the sun god's dominion.

One of the club-wielders thrust his weapon into the face of the golden guard. The guard slapped the weapon away with the flat of his sword. A spear-wielder lunged forward, the point of his weapon stopping within a hairs-breadth of another guard's belly.

"Enough!" the king roared. He clenched his hand in the spear-wielder's direction. The Tirnor warrior, one of the best in the Summer Realm, fell to one knee, then to the floor. Rothruinil rushed to his side, extinguishing her tavahatals as she cradled his head in her lap. The warrior, a man named Valyaro with whom Rothruinil had trained with for the last two decades, gasped for air. His eyes bulged from his head, the whites showing all the way around his iris. No words were spoken, and yet Rothruinil could feel his desperate plea for help.

"Stop it!" she shouted at King Othin.

The king stared down at her with indifference.

Valyaro continued to struggle to breathe. The skin of his face grew wrinkled and ashen, his appearance aging thousands of years in mere moments. The energy for which he took his name leached out of him.

Fire burned within Rothruinil's soul. Impotent rage welled up inside her as she watched her friend waste away in the prime of his life. The tattoos that told his life story would never be finished.

King Othin's gaze examined Rothruinil. She returned the stare with naked aggression.

"This barbaric ritual is a waste of our time. Take us to the fire king. Now." King Othin demanded.

"Return his life to him, and perhaps the sun god will show you mercy," Rothruinil replied. Heat radiated from her skin in visible waves, her blood temperature rising with the magic inside. She lowered Valyaro's head gently to the ground. Her tavahatals once more burst into flame as she channeled her rage into the carvings in the wood and stood before the high elf king.

Rapid footsteps approached from the direction of the throne room. Rothruinil didn't take her eyes off the threat before her. He had disrupted the welcome ceremony, had mocked their tradition and turned it from heart-pounding joy into despair. He didn't deserve the sun god's blessing, and he didn't deserve their respect.

"Your Majesty," Queen Norgeledil extended the peace blossom on both hands with a modest bow.

Rothruinil gaped. The man didn't deserve the peace blossom, couldn't be allowed in the throne room.

"Queen Norgeledil," King Othin glanced at the offering with a disdainful sniff, but did not take it from her hands.

"Mother!" Rothruinil hissed, offended on behalf of every fire sidhe in their realm. The king couldn't be trusted. "He's taken Valyaro's life! You cannot be serious, accepting him into the hall."

Queen Norgeledil shot her daughter what may have been the most remonstrative glare she'd ever received in her life. Rothruinil clapped her mouth shut, but fumed beneath the surface.

Valyaro had been her friend. He deserved better than this.

"She is your daughter?" King Othin's lip lifted in a disdainful sneer. "She would perhaps do well with a remedial diplomacy lesson. Her tongue is sharp and her wits are slower than I would expect for a royal heir."

"Succession's chosen by the clans, Your Majesty."

"All the more reason to teach her better manners in the presence of her betters."

"Please accept this sign of our good intentions and welcome in our hall," Rothruinil's mother insisted, still holding the peace blossom.

"Very well," the king lifted the bloom from her outstretched hands with two pinched fingers. "Now take us to Thanûr. We have business to discuss."

"Please, follow me. You are welcome."

King Othin sniffed, but he and his guards followed Norgeledil toward the light at the end of the dark hallway.

Rothruinil fell to her knees at Valyaro's side. No breath of life stirred in his body. The king had drained his spirit entirely. She pressed her face to her friend's chest and prayed the sun god bless his soul on its journey to the summerlands.

"Find peace in the warmth of the sun," she murmured.

With a sense of dread, Rothruinil watched King Othin and his guards disappear into the throne room with her mother.

CHAPTER 10

After three bells of careful teasing and suggestive double entendres, the princess was exhausted. The good news was that King Rindae seemed to be interested, his gaze frequently traveling the length of the dress Lhéwen had created. And she could feel the charisma ear charm pulling at his emotions as well. With a little careful maneuvering, Faeliel might just succeed where all others had failed.

As it turned out, Lhéwen had been more than a convenient pawn. She was also an obvious asset to keep in her arsenal.

The guards on the other hand couldn't keep their testosterone from ruining everything.

"What were you thinking?" Faeliel demanded, turning on the captain of the guard as soon as the door to her suite was shut behind them. Lhéwen had been dismissed to her own quarters and Belegeth stood outside the door.

"Apologies, my lady," Arhesto replied with a defiant gaze. "But this is not a failure." He stood straight, eyes forward, with his hands clasped behind his back.

"You were supposed to gather information, not participate in a pub brawl. You nearly ruined everything."

"Again, my apologies, but I strongly disagree. We tested their strength, but no lives were lost. And you were right about the Crossroads Inn," Arhesto replied. "The amphitheater was filled with warriors. Some were clearly shadow guard, others looked like mercenaries hoping to be hired."

"Is King Rindae preparing for war?" It would make sense, given his disrespect and continued defiance of King Othin, but if there were proof and she could bring it home, her father would be most pleased. He would finally be able to call his lords to arms.

That is, *if* she decided to return. That seemed less likely after this afternoon's efforts.

"I cannot say with any certainty, but there must be rumors of imminent battle. The sellswords wouldn't be here otherwise."

"Are the soldiers well-trained? How challenging would it be for the Upper Realm to defeat them?"

This was the real question. To break free of her father's control, she needed to find someone with the strength to support her. Someone with a capable army. Only then would she be able to oppose him.

Still, she had to move carefully and keep her options open. If Rindae's forces weren't prepared, she would need a way to justify this venture and bring home the victory for her father.

"They were skilled, yes. The squad leader, the one called Cendir, would have skewered me if it weren't for the merchant. He was entirely shielded against a spirit drain and he moved as if he could predict every outcome. But Prince Aradae is the true power. He was able to control us all from across the room. It felt like my very soul was being manipulated like a puppet on strings, and my body just followed along."

"That makes sense, considering the power that lies in this land." If the son was that powerful, his father—one of the last remaining fae to cross the portals from the Origin—must be far stronger.

Faeliel paced across the room, throwing open the heavy curtains to gaze out the window. The rooms looked out over the bailey but were high enough that she could see the moat and the city beyond. Shadows of all sizes scurried around, lit only by the faint wisps and lamps that floated over the causeways or hung from the sides of buildings. What did the people do? And more importantly, how could she capitalize on it?

Footsteps approached, and the captain's broad hand came to rest on her shoulder. He was too familiar with her, too sure of himself.

"Do not worry, Your Highness. I will protect you."

Faeliel mentally laughed. Her captain was good with a sword, and she hadn't been lying when she told the shadow court he could have drained his enemies in the pub—at least the ones not shielded —but he wasn't as strong as she.

Faeliel shook her head. "How is it that a *merchant* and a *bartender* were enough to stop an entire squad of my best guards?" It seemed absurd, but that alone should prove his limitations in this realm. He was out of his depth. But she wasn't.

"You said no deaths." His body moved a fraction closer. "Unshackle me if you want satisfaction."

Faeliel suppressed a shudder at the obvious and inept double entendre, but hardened her voice while she moved out from beneath the unwanted touch. "The goal was to observe and uncover the strength of the Shadow Realm, not decimate my own guard. You are lucky King Rindae is reasonable. You risked too much."

"I am no spy. Subtlety is not my strength."

"No, I suppose not. Perhaps I chose the wrong tool for the job."

The captain bristled. "I am no tool."

"Of course you are," Faeliel snapped. "We all are, to one extent or another. The sooner you realize that, the happier you will be. For now, you are dismissed. I must retire to bed. I am afraid this will be a much longer visit than anticipated."

Longer than her entourage anticipated, anyway. Her own goals were much more ambitious.

Arhesto's jaw clenched and he leaned forward as if to move closer. The look in his eyes spelled trouble. Warrior men were all the same—they couldn't bear to be seen as weak in any way. She could feel his bruised ego rippling through his aura, and the internal compulsion to overpower her.

It wasn't going to happen.

Faeliel lifted a hand with a graceful flick of her wrist, palm facing the warrior. He dropped to his knees so fast the bone cracked. His head drooped and arms trembled to hold himself up from lying prone on the ground.

He would learn this lesson and learn it well. She would not play the damsel in distress any longer. She was taking control of her future.

"Do not presume to believe you can intimidate me. I am heir to the high court. You will do as I say, not the other way around. Do you understand?" She kept her voice saccharine, the volume calm and level.

"Yes, Your Highness," the captain whispered. It was all the energy she'd left him.

Pushing a bit more of his spirit back into his body, Faeliel gave him the strength to stand. "Always remember your place. It is a lesson I learned young, and one you would do well to learn quickly."

"Yes, Your Highness." His voice was stronger this time, and his eyes flashed with suppressed anger, but he dipped his head in acquiescence.

She would need to find a new captain. That is, *if* she returned to the high court.

"Very well. Return to the barracks with your men, and do not leave until I call for you. Do not give the king cause to reprimand you again."

"Yes, Your Highness."

Maybe he had learned his lesson after all. She waved him away with a flick of her fingers.

"Please call for Lhéwen on your way out. She is resting in her room."

As soon as the door shut, Faeliel retired to the bedroom and fell back on the bed, the deep feathers cushioning her fall with a puff of dusty air. *Who cleaned these rooms?* she wondered absently, as her thoughts rambled away from the current predicament. She closed her eyes.

The memory of her father's last words to her floated through her brain. *Your thoughts are not necessary. Your words are not necessary. You are an asset to my court only so long as you are seen and not heard.*

It was what her mother, the queen, had done for so many hundreds of years. She was the bauble at Othin's side, the proof of his virility. Beautiful and empty. That's what he expected of his daughter.

No longer. She'd tried again and again to prove her worth, to demonstrate her value. He refused to see it. She refused to wilt beneath his disfavor.

This was it. The final confrontation. One of two things would happen at the end of this adventure: she would return to the Upper Realm a heroine for bringing the Shadow Realm beneath the banner of the Upper Realm and earn a place on King Othin's council, or she would become a queen in her own right. There could be no middle ground.

The bedroom door opened, drawing Faeliel's thoughts back to the present. Lhéwen's footsteps were nearly silent on the thick rug, but Faeliel could See the woman's sunny aura approaching, even with her eyes closed.

"I am awake," Faeliel said.

The mattress shifted and sank as Lhéwen sat down and immediately began massaging Faeliel's temples. She was loyal to her duty, as all good servants should be. If only Arhesto had realized it sooner. But Faeliel could still feel the tension in the air, the unspoken words that wanted to burst from Lhéwen's lips.

Faeliel blew out a breath. "Speak," she ordered. "You have something on your mind."

"I would never presume to second guess your plans." Lhéwen's fingers were strong, yet gentle, the pace steady. "But are you sure it's a good idea to tempt King Rindae? Your father will not be pleased with the relationship."

Faeliel almost snorted. 'Not pleased' was the nicest way of describing her father's foul temper she'd ever heard. King Othin had sent previous 'unsuitable' lovers to The Pit just for having had the audacity to be seen in public with her, for fear they might taint her reputation.

"Perhaps not, but if I can use Rindae's admiration to convince him to bend the knee, my father will not complain," Faeliel replied. "The ends will justify the means."

Faeliel smiled to herself, her thoughts returning to the steely gray gaze that sizzled along her nerve endings. There was much contained power behind those eyes. He might even be able to stand toe to toe with her father. Which was precisely why Othin wanted Rindae to come to heel. Until he could be brought into allegiance, he would remain a threat to Othin's power.

"I should take word to the high court, provide an update on the situation here and explain your plans. I am certain it will go a long way toward alleviating the king's wrath when he discovers your tactics," Lhéwen continued.

Sweet, simple Lhéwen. She believed this was a sanctioned journey, a mission assigned by the high king himself. Why would she believe otherwise? Faeliel had been careful to ensure that the plans were kept secret until the last possible moment, and had personally executed the logistical details. No one in the Upper Realm, save the group she'd brought with her, had been involved. And she'd made sure they had no remaining ties to the high court. There were no families left behind, no communication to leak to her father until she was ready to reveal her success, whatever form that took.

Faeliel sat up from the bed and shook her head, feigning worry. She looked directly at Lhéwen, ensuring the woman understood her sincere intention. "You might be right, but I cannot risk you. If he takes his anger out on your person . . ." Faeliel paused a beat, as if horrified at the thought, then quickly shook her head. "No, I need you here. Besides, the dark elves would be suspicious if you suddenly left my service to return home without me."

"If King Othin's spies report a liaison between you and the shadow king, the king's wrath will be swift and severe." Lhéwen argued. "Isn't it better he hear the truth in your own words, rather than presumptions? I would simply deliver a message, written in your hand. I would not be at risk."

That wasn't entirely true. King Othin had been known to take his anger out on the messenger, but it was rare. Lhéwen likely hadn't ever witnessed such an event.

However, Lhéwen had a point about high court spies in the Shadow Realm. She hadn't really considered the information gatherers a threat, but if they were here, and if they revealed her actions before she had snared a place at the shadow king's side, all would be lost. Rindae would simply hand her back over to her father rather than put his realm at risk. She needed more time. A vague explanation of an intent to return with information sealed with her sigil might delay any action on King Othin's part. At least, it might confuse him enough to slow him down.

"No, I still need you. We cannot raise suspicion. We need someone trustworthy, who is not part of our entourage—that would be too conspicuous. Someone who can travel the portals without suspicion, but who will do his duty without a separate agenda."

Faeliel had just the individual in mind, but it would be best if it were Lhéwen's idea. Then if things went wrong, all the blame could be placed at her handmaiden's feet, instead of her own.

"Perhaps the merchant would do it," Lhéwen said. "The one who broke up the pub fight between the soldiers. He seems strong and capable, and also loyal to the realm. I am certain he would be willing."

Faeliel pursed her lips, as if unsure, though her heart lifted with glee. Once again dear Lhéwen had fallen into the plot, but she would need additional security. "We do not know him. He could be one of father's spies. It feels risky."

"Perhaps I could enchant the message so that anyone who opened it—other than the king himself, of course—would be instantly drained of their energy and put into a deep sleep. I would need your help for the enervation, but it would ensure that if he did break his oath, he would be easily apprehended. And since you would gain his energy, we would know immediately what had happened and be able to find him."

"Would that work through the portals? At such great distances? It seems unreliable."

"Time and space wouldn't matter because you wouldn't be maintaining the connection. It would be a stable, independent charm. I'm certain it would work."

"In that case, I think we should do it." She would add a little extra power to the drain as well, to make sure that if the merchant *did* open the message, he wouldn't just sleep, he would never awaken. However, there was no need to tell her sensitive hand-maiden as much. The woman clearly had a soft spot for the man, since she had spoken up to make sure he was released from the throne room.

"Only, he is not a spy, not trained in the ways of the court. His lack of credentials might be a liability. He might not be able to reach the king." Lhéwen bit her lip with obvious uncertainty.

"We will send him through the west gate. With my seal in hand, the guards will not hesitate to fulfill my orders."

Over the years, the west gate guards had become allies and accessories to her adventures. They'd also become accustomed to the bribes and favors that went along with each exploit. They would not stand in his way.

It was a solid plan.

"The merchant is probably staying at that inn where the fight happened. When you take him the scroll, you can also make my apologies to the proprietor and negotiate payment for damages."

"As you wish, Your Highness."

"Then tell me, what did you think of Rindae?" Faeliel couldn't help but ask. If this sprouting idea was to bear fruit, its inner strength would have to be tested.

CHAPTER 11

Lhéwen wrapped a brightly colored scarf over her head and around her neck to hide as much of her skin and hair as possible. She knew it was a useless gesture, but it was better than standing out like a lit beacon in the dark of the Shadow Realm.

"Belegeth, you are to go with Lhéwen. Help her find out where that merchant is staying and track him down," Faeliel commanded into the hallway.

Lhéwen peeked around her ladyship's shoulder to find the large woman standing at attention to the right of the door.

"Who will guard your rooms?" Belegeth questioned. "With your personal guard confined to quarters, you would be left unprotected."

"I swear on my mother's grave, I won't leave these rooms. A guard will not be necessary."

"A guard is always necessary, Your Highness," the bodyguard insisted. "The palace may seem safe, but tensions are high. Even if the king himself intends no harm, there are others who may have access to these halls, others who would hurt King Othin through you."

"You make it sound as if my father actually cares."

"Belegeth is right," Lhéwen interjected, keeping her voice soft and subservient despite the contradiction in her words. "You must be kept safe. I will be fine on my own." In truth, Belegeth was an intimidating presence, and Lhéwen was sure she would be less noticeable without the other woman at her side.

"And who is princess here?" Faeliel snapped.

Lhéwen flinched away, quickly turning her gaze to the floor. Princess Faeliel was a fair mistress, but at times her father's rage bubbled up from within. At those times, it was best to return to invisibility and avoid stirring the wrath.

With visible effort, Faeliel calmed her breathing. "Belegeth will go with you, Lhéwen. She will ensure that you are not molested along the way, and that you are successful in your duty. All of the ladies of this court have bodyguards and protectors, and so shall you."

"Yes, Your Highness," Lhéwen replied, still keeping her head down. It was kind of the princess to consider her a lady. Truly.

"Good. Return here when you have accomplished your goal." The princess shut the door to her suite, closing the women into the darkened hall. Only a single wall sconce lit the passageway. Lhéwen was beginning to get used to maneuvering in shadows and darkness, but it still unsettled her nerves. She would be glad to get outside; even though it was dark, the open expanse and moon shining above would surely alleviate some of her discomfort.

"Do you know where we should begin?" Belegeth asked as they made their way through the gently curving hallways toward the front gate.

"The fight was at the Crossroads Inn. It is likely he keeps a room there." Lhéwen replied. "If not, the proprietor or barkeep might know where to look next. We must meet with them as well to discuss payment for damages."

The question was, would the barkeep be willing to give them information? Certainly, she and Belegeth had a valid reason to go to the merchant. Lhéwen had watched the princess write the letter, and had sealed the wax herself, tying Faeliel's magic—the draining of the spirit—into the pressing of the seal. The trap had been set. Lhéwen prayed to all the gods that Curuthannor wouldn't attempt to open it. Faeliel had been a bit more enthusiastic about this particular enchantment than usual. It wouldn't just drain the victim to insensibility, she feared it would end in death.

She didn't want that for Curuthannor, but it was too late to alter course now. She could only trust in the honor and loyalty she sensed in him that day. She believed he would not only accept the task, but would succeed. And for that reason she hadn't objected to the princess's modification of the enchantment. When the king opened the message, the trap would dissipate and none would be harmed.

Gods, let it be so.

As they made their way out onto the main street, Lhéwen couldn't help but watch for signs of pursuit. They weren't trying to be sneaky, not really, but it would still be preferred if they weren't observed. But whether it was the presence of Belegeth or simple indifference, it didn't seem anyone was inclined to follow or stop them. There were a few raised eyebrows, perhaps, but nothing more.

At least, Lhéwen didn't notice anything, and Belegeth seemed unworried. Lhéwen took that as a good sign.

"So what do you think of the Shadow Realm?" Lhéwen asked. "Is it what you expected?"

It was Lhéwen's first trip beyond the borders of the Upper Realm, but she wasn't sure if that was also true for Belegeth, who was at least three centuries her elder.

The woman didn't turn her head, didn't even let her gaze drop to Lhéwen's shorter height. Constantly scanning the crowd, her response was tightly controlled.

"The city has expanded some since I was last here," she replied. "But the people are the same, the noise is the same." She sniffed. "The smells might be worse, however."

Lhéwen grinned. Perhaps the woman had a sense of humor after all. Lhéwen's foot splashed in some kind of gray muck that had pooled between cobbles. The scent of ammonia and cooking grease wafted toward her nose. Maybe Belegeth wasn't joking after all.

"Careful where you step. The feral ashcats are notorious for marking their territory, and their scent is near impossible to get off."

"I will keep that in mind," Lhéwen grumbled. She hoped that puddle was something else. "When were you here? Before, I mean."

"Approximately one hundred fifty years ago."

Apparently that was all the response she would get. Direct answers to direct questions. She wouldn't let that deter her.

"Why? And with whom?"

"I was included on the first delegation as a squire to one of the older warriors. We protected the ambassador then, as I protect the princess now. It is my duty."

Lhéwen nodded. She could understand duty. Her mother had been a handmaiden to the queen before marrying her father. As Lhéwen was a handmaiden now. Duty was often passed from parent to child, along family lines, whether they liked it or not.

Winding their way around a cart filled with dark-skinned fruit, Lhéwen stifled a yelp as a female troll glared at her. The low brow, large nose, and single chipped tusk left Lhéwen at a loss for words. Lank, greasy hair hung down the woman's shoulders, which were covered by some kind of thick woolen wrap that looked far too hot to wear in the humidity of the Nalakadr city streets.

Apparently she stared too long.

"What do you want?" the woman demanded.

"Nothing," Lhéwen hastily replied.

Belegeth's hand gently pushed Lhéwen out of the way, guiding her toward a section of the road with faster moving traffic.

The troll grunted, watching the pair with narrowed eyes as they hurried away.

"Do not antagonize the trolls."

"I did not mean to," Lhéwen replied. "She startled me."

"Then do not be startled. It is easy to cause offense in this realm, warranted or not."

"So I have come to realize." Lhéwen mentally shook off the encounter, and focused more carefully on her surroundings.

The streets were crowded as fae of all races hurried to close their businesses before the sun rose above the horizon. At this time of year, daylight would only last two bells, or so she'd been told, but most of the residents preferred the dark.

The farther they traveled from the castle, the more narrow and congested the streets became. Shoulders brushed past, knocking Lhéwen from side to side. Talking became near impossible. The rattle of wagons, clatter of hooves on cobblestones, and banter from shopkeepers drowned everything else out. Eventually, Belegeth had to use her shield to protect them both from being knocked to the ground.

Finally, they arrived at the inn. Belegeth pushed open the heavy wood gates with her shoulder and they stepped inside.

Lhéwen wasn't sure what she had expected, but it wasn't this. A wide open hillside plain stretched out before them, seemingly endless despite the high stone wall at their back. Lhéwen glanced over her shoulder, just to be sure they hadn't walked through a portal, but no, it was a simple wood gate. She turned back to the vista before her.

A gravel path lined with torches wound its way down and between the hills. Every few dozen spaces a new path would branch off to one side or the other, leading—Lhéwen guessed—to the various rentable living quarters and meeting spaces. Groups of fae gathered here and there on hillsides, mostly dark elves as far as

Lhéwen could see, but a leipreachán family was also having a picnic on a blanket, and a goblin was hustling to clean up what had obviously been a rather rowdy party, with mugs and debris scattered over and around a small gazebo.

Lhéwen looked up at the sky, which was gradually lightening from the orange and pink of sunrise to a solid indigo blue. Unfortunately, the sun rose behind them and they had missed most of the transition, but at least the crowds had already gone home.

"I suppose most of the fae here are relatively nocturnal. Perhaps they have gone to bed. But the dark elves still function on a normal business schedule," she mused to herself.

She didn't expect a response from Belegeth, and she didn't get one. Instead, she pushed her sleeves up and held her arms out from her sides to absorb and enjoy every possible moment in the sun.

They continued down into the valley, where a natural amphitheater carved out the central area. A small stage had been set up to one side, a convivial group of musicians playing a lively tune, though no one was there to dance.

"Do you think they are rehearsing?"

"How should I know?" Belegeth replied. She sounded bored.

Ignoring Belegeth's disinterest, Lhéwen's gaze scanned the seating area. Dozens of empty tables, large and small, scattered around the space. It was an eclectic mix of fine furniture and rough-hewn wood scarred with cuts and stains. Only one patron sat in the bar area, a dark elf woman with the longest braid Lhéwen had ever seen. She had looped it over the back of her chair and then coiled the remainder in her lap, where she sat playing with the ends in time with the music. She smiled when Lhéwen caught her gaze, but returned to watching the band.

Curuthannor was not present.

Hoping to find a bartender or staff person still on duty, Lhéwen wound her way through the tables to the expansive bar at the center of the gathering space. On the other side, the outer wall of a small building had been covered with shelves and drinkware ready to be used by the inn's guests. A door to the interior of the building stood open.

"Can I help ye with somethin'?" a thick baritone voice called from inside.

Lhéwen peeked around the doorframe, squinting her eyes into the gloom, then jumped back when she saw the massive troll peering back at her. The man had to be at least two heads taller than Belegeth and at least three times as wide.

Belegeth surreptitiously stepped up and to the side, placing herself in position to defend Lhéwen if necessary. Though, truth be told, Lhéwen got the feeling this particular troll was unlikely to become a threat.

"Two things, actually. I would like to speak with the proprietor, and I am looking for a high elf named Curuthannor. Do you by chance know if he's staying here?"

The troll stepped out of the room holding a thick-bristled curry comb. Tufts of white fur dotted his rough-spun tunic. A long-haired goat trailed out after him, bleating its displeasure.

"Hold on there now, Bessy. We've customers to attend. Ye know the rules," the troll murmured.

Lhéwen stifled a grin.

"Who's askin'?" the troll asked.

"My name is Lhéwen, and I am handmaiden to Her Highness, Princess Faeliel. I am here to pay for the damages our guard caused on this establishment, and I must find Curuthannor on behalf of her ladyship."

The troll gave her an appraising stare. Lhéwen lifted her chin. She spoke the truth, she had nothing to hide.

"I see," he finally replied. "Well, Tharbatiron is the proprietor, but he's in a meeting right now. I'm sure he'll be out after awhile. And Curuthannor has been here, but he's not here now."

"Do you know when he will return?"

"Nay, he's out on business."

Lhéwen turned to her companion. "I suppose we will have to

wait then, we cannot return to Faeliel until we have spoken with him."

Belegeth dipped her chin.

"Woudja like somethin' ta eat?" the troll asked. "I'm Tryg, by the by."

"Perhaps a light snack," Lhéwen's stomach twinged. She hadn't eaten anything since the early morning meal with the princess.

"And ta drink? I've a fine light cider that might appeal."

"That sounds wonderful," Lhéwen replied.

"Water for me, if you please," Belegeth added. "I cannot inhibit my reaction times."

"'Course," Tryg replied. "Understood. We've quite a few warriors through these halls. Pull up a table wherever you like. I'll be right out with the food and drink."

Lhéwen dipped her head in gracious thanks, but Tryg had already turned back to shoo his goat into the shed. She hoped the food wasn't stored near the goat's pen. Somehow that seemed . . . distasteful.

"How about we sit at the bar instead of a table," Lhéwen asked Belegeth. "Would that be acceptable?"

Belegeth nodded. "This is a good vantage point."

"Wonderful." Lhéwen wanted to roll her eyes at the woman's intense focus, but repressed the urge. Belegeth was only doing her job. Instead, Lhéwen swept her skirts out of her way and sat on the high bar stool, running one hand along the smooth obsidian. It felt slick, as if it had been treated with some kind of lacquer or varnish, but the irregular patterned waves in the surface suggested that little else had been done to process the material.

That seemed to be the theme of this realm. They used materials in their natural state, or as close as possible, rather than forcing form on the substance. Twisting branches, rough stone, braided vines . . . it was as if because there was so little native flora, they wanted to preserve what they had while making it functional.

Lhéwen could appreciate that. In fact, it gave her some good ideas for dress designs that could incorporate more 'flawed' fabrics to great effect. She wished she'd brought her design book.

Tryg reappeared with a platter of mixed cheeses, cut fruit, and salted meats in one hand, and thin flat bread with a selection of different sauces and dips in the other.

"Now, since I haven't seen ye here before, and ye're high elves, I imagine ye haven't had much cause to try our Shadow Realm fare. So I figured I'd give ye a sampling of my personal favorites."

"This looks wonderful," Lhéwen replied, sincerely meaning it. "I look forward to trying everything."

Tryg grinned, clearly pleased and proud to be of service. "Ye can mix and match. Just spread some sauce on the pulka—the bread right there—choose yer meat, and cheese, and ye're off. Watch out for the green one though. If ye don't like spicy, that one might not be right for ye."

"I'll keep that in mind. Perhaps Belegeth will enjoy that one."

"I prefer simple foods," the woman was quick to answer, her gaze never straying from the empty amphitheater.

"There's no need to be so vigilant. Not at this hour," Tryg said. "The regular customers won't start to arrive until full dark in another couple'a bells, and the guests will come in sometime after that, after business is done for the day."

"Are all your guests merchants?" Lhéwen asked, scooping a bite of a yellow sauce onto the bread and mixing it with a thin slice of gently spiced meat. She liked that one.

"'Course not," Tryg replied. "We get all types. Even tourists and occasionally high placed ladies," he glanced at Lhéwen from the corner of his eye as he absentmindedly dried an already dry glass.

"I am no lady, if that is what you are wondering," Lhéwen replied.

Tryg gave a deep belly laugh. "Ye caught me. But ye look the part, all the same. Certainly worth the question."

"I am only a servant, nothing more," Lhéwen reassured the troll.

"No?" a sonorous voice asked. A dark elf strode toward them from a separate building. His robe was the same dark shimmering black of his skin, while his starlight white hair flowed down his back, giving him the appearance of an apparition in the already fading light of the Shadow Realm day.

"I'm Tharbatiron, the owner and operator of the Crossroads Inn. Welcome."

Lhéwen stood from her stool and gave the dark elf a low bow. Belegeth followed suit, though she immediately returned to her vigilant stance, keeping her gaze turned outward toward the main seating areas and showing no threat to the man. He might not be a royal, but he was certainly distinguished. Possibly a first generation displaced from the origin. As a simple messenger and lady-in-waiting, Lhéwen remained in the obsequious bow.

"My name is Lhéwen, handmaiden to Princess Faeliel of the high court of the Upper Realm. I have come to apologize for the destruction caused by Princess Faeliel's guard, and to discuss reparations."

"Reparations?" Tharbatiron brushed his robe out of the way as he took a seat at the bar next to her. Lhéwen didn't rise. "I see. And what does your princess offer?"

"She will gladly pay for the repairs on any and all structures and furnishings damaged in the altercation. If there are other less quantifiable damages that must be compensated, please just let her know what those might be."

"What about my reputation, and that of my inn? We can't have our customers thinking they might be accosted at every visit."

Still holding her low bow, Lhéwen used her hair to hide her own expression while looking up through the long tresses to assess his. A small smile curled the corner of his lips and a flicker of his left eyebrow suggested more humor than ill-will. He popped a small bite of one of the hard cheeses into his mouth and chewed as he awaited her response.

"As I understand it, there are a considerable number of fights in this establishment. I have been told it is part of the attraction in a place where so many races meet and mingle."

Tharbatiron's smirk grew wider. "You've done some small amount of research, perhaps. Then why offer reparations?"

"It is not our custom to endorse violence."

"Ah. Right. Well, then, I suppose damages plus a small disturbance fee would be welcomed. I will write up a bill you can take to your princess. Now, come sit and eat before Tryg's favorites go to waste."

Lhéwen rose from her bow and returned to her chair, all while keeping one eye on the dark elf next to her.

Lhéwen continued eating the platter of delicacies while Tharbatiron discussed the day's business with Tryg. Apparently he carried quite a bit of responsibility in the bar. He was not as dimwitted as she would have expected, and despite his girth—which was still lean compared to the other trolls she had already seen in the city—he was rather agile around all the glass.

It was already near full dark by the time Lhéwen finished her meal. Lights from under ledges and around the bar blossomed to life all at once, eliciting a gasp.

Tharbatiron chuckled, sending Tryg off to greet a few new arrivals. There still weren't many customers, but certainly more than had been seated when Lhéwen arrived.

"So tell me, can I help you with any other business before you return to your princess?"

"I cannot return yet. I must speak with Curuthannor, the merchant who was also involved in the altercation yesterday."

"What for?"

"Her ladyship has a simple request for him, if he will accept it."

"Ah. Well, I suppose now would be the time to ask him." Tharbatiron surreptitiously pointed a finger toward the entrance path. A man strode down the hill with ragged steps and a fierce gaze. As the only other high elf in the entire inn, Lhéwen would have been hard pressed to miss him, but even had this been an establishment in the Upper Realm, she wouldn't have been able to avoid noticing his presence. Which was funny, because there was nothing overt that would make others notice him. No, it was his intense internal focus and the lack of obvious peacocking that drew Lhéwen's attention.

He still wore the same scarred but well-oiled brown leathers as in the throne room. Whatever business meeting he may have had, he hadn't bothered to change into something more formal. His hair, worn long and braided back at the sides in the fashion of the Upper Realm, was golden straw in color, lustrous, but not glimmering, well-cared for, but not fussed over. His eyes were the brilliant blue of a cloudless day in the mountains.

His boots were utilitarian and functional, designed for long treks and tough terrain, not the smooth marble of court. Come to think of it, Lhéwen couldn't remember ever having seen the man before, which meant that he was probably a rural craftsman, rather than a city merchant. That would explain a lot.

"Curuthannor!" Tharbatiron waved at the man, drawing his gaze and turning his feet toward their spot at the bar. "You have an admirer."

Lhéwen felt her cheeks heat as she stood once more from her stool. She dropped a half-bow in his direction by way of greeting, not yet trusting her voice. She hadn't meant to stare, but she *had* been admiring Curuthannor from afar. She only wished her notice hadn't been . . . well, noticed, she supposed.

CHAPTER 12

Curuthannor could feel his teeth grinding together, but he couldn't stop himself from the frustrated march through the city and into the Crossroads Inn. He had been dismissed like a low-level servant. Told to go home like a misbehaving child.

The truth was that he didn't matter to the dark elves. His business didn't matter.

Still, what was he going to tell his father? They were depending on that iron for the king's blade. Hatholdammon would never be content with the Upper Realm iron. Maybe Curuthannor could propose going to the dwarves, but as far as he knew, Hatholdammon had never forged dwarven iron. It would be risky to work with a product for the first time on such a high-value commission.

Lost in his thoughts, Curuthannor wasn't paying close attention to his surroundings. Tharbatiron's voice caught him by surprise.

"Curuthannor!" Tharbatiron waved at him from the bar. "You have an admirer."

Curuthannor's gaze locked onto the woman next to the dark elf.

The princess's handmaiden stood from her chair, presenting him with a very proper court bow. The bodyguard at her side faced him, but remained standing. She crossed her arms over her chest, keeping them far from the haft of her axe in a clear sign of non-confrontation. Either she didn't view him as a threat, or she had been expecting this encounter. Were they here for him?

"Greetings," Lhéwen murmured, rising from her bow as Curuthannor approached the final few steps. "I apologize for intruding on your evening, but I would like to speak with you in private, if you have time available."

"You are Princess Faeliel's handmaiden, correct?" Curuthannor asked. What a stupid thing to ask. Of course she was. It wasn't as if he could forget.

"Yes, my lord. My name is Lhéwen."

A beautiful name, he thought. Unfortunately, what he said was, "I am no lord."

Gods above, could he not say something civil to the woman? At least he could pretend to have manners.

"Then the two of ye'll get along just fine," Tryg interrupted with a grin. The troll was eyeing them with mischievous interest, as was Tharbatiron.

What could the troll possibly mean by that? Bristling, Curuthannor would have jumped to the lady's defense but for the genuinely amused smile that lifted her expression. He must have missed something.

"Tryg is correct, I am not a lady of the high court."

"No? I thought all servants to the royal house were nobles in their own right." And now he went and questioned her lineage. What was wrong with him? His mother would have been shocked and dismayed.

"I am one of few, it's true, but my mother was handmaiden to the queen prior to her late majesty's rise to the throne, and was brought along to serve in the castle. I was granted the same boon upon my apprenticeship, and given over to serve Princess Faeliel."

"You were grandfathered in, so to speak," Tharbatiron grinned.

Curuthannor felt like a spectacle for the dark elf and the troll. Only the bodyguard didn't seem to be paying much attention to their conversation, her gaze still scanning the nonexistent crowd for threats. Curuthannor envied her stoic silence.

"I suppose. But it has given me the opportunity to study with some of the best seamstresses in the realm. I am her ladyship's primary dresser."

"Ah." Curuthannor's mind flashed to an image of Lhéwen getting dressed and his cheeks reddened. He cleared his throat. It wasn't that he hadn't had intimate relations before, but no woman had ever made him feel so discombobulated as Lhéwen.

"What does her ladyship's primary dresser want with a simple merchant?" he asked.

There. Back to the facts. Emphasize his low status and her importance to the princess. Perhaps not the smoothest transition, but at least it would move the conversation along.

"I'd prefer to speak in private, if that would be acceptable? Perhaps Master Tharbatiron would be so kind as to lend us a meeting room?"

"I know just the place. Tryg, please show our guests to my private garden."

Tryg grunted his agreement, and extricated himself from behind the bar.

"Follow me. Ye'll have some privacy."

Curuthannor trailed behind Tryg, Lhéwen, and the lady's bodyguard. Despite Lhéwen's assurances that she was not noble, he could think of her as nothing less than a lady of the high court. She was graceful and demure, with an understated beauty that captivated his attention.

What was he doing? He had no business even being in the same room with the woman. Gods. She had daily contact with royalty, probably shared the princess's confidences, and kept her secrets.

She would have been at least secondarily involved with every one of the princess's exploits in the high court.

He was outclassed. What could they possibly want with him? He needed to get back to the forge, find a way to make this iron situation right again. As much as he hated the work, he couldn't leave his family to suffer because of his failure. Whatever the princess wanted, she would need to find someone else to assist her.

"Here ye are." Tryg gestured the last few feet down the gravel-paved path. A small building covered in white-leafed vines squatted off to the left, a table and chairs nestled under an arbor outside. To the right, a curated garden was laid out in neat boxes and rows, the plants carefully tended on trellises or pruned into manicured shapes. Curuthannor wasn't much of one for plants, but he could appreciate the order and structure required for such an undertaking, especially here in the Shadow Realm where every ray of light was precious to growing things.

In the center of the garden, a gazebo made of stone with a high peaked roof was lit by floating blue wisplights. A wrought iron table and four chairs sat in the center of the space. The illumination was dim, but would be enough to see a companion without stumbling.

"No one'll disturb ye here. It's Tharbatiron's private garden." Tryg turned back toward the central amphitheater and bar. "I must be getting back to work. Give a shout if ye need anything." The troll stomped away without looking back.

"Shall we?" Lhéwen asked, gesturing toward the gazebo. "It looks lovely, and it will be obvious if anyone comes near enough to overhear our conversation."

"That would be quite the insult to the hospitality of the Cross-roads Inn, if someone were to invade the owner's private quarters without permission."

"Indeed." Lhéwen smiled.

Curuthannor's heart stuttered a beat.

Making their way into the garden, the woman bent to smell a

white flower with a yellow center, the petals unfolding in a complicated symmetrical design. "Amazing that these can grow here," she commented.

"Amazing that anything can live here at all," Curuthannor replied. The Shadow Realm was hot and humid, practically devoid of sunlight, and unforgiving. That elves had chosen to settle in such a place baffled him. He had heard stories of the thinness of the veil between this realm and the afterlife, giving the dark elves greater strength in their magical abilities, but the greatest feat he'd seen so far was Prince Aradae's puppet master trick. Really, it seemed the dark elves thrived on violence and aggression.

Of course, they had more opportunity to practice, given the general lawlessness of their society.

Lhéwen took a seat under the gazebo and Curuthannor sat opposite. The bodyguard, meanwhile, paced the edge of the garden with her axe in hand.

"I suppose you're wondering why I requested a private audience," the woman began, drawing Curuthannor back from his thoughts. Her eyes sparkled with reflected blue light, and perhaps a small amount of amusement.

Curuthannor pursed his lips. He didn't care to be the butt of someone else's joke. Or any joke, for that matter. "Yes. I have no dealings with the royals. I could hardly be of interest to anyone from the high court."

"Perhaps not," the woman replied. "But you're one of only a handful of high elves in this land of darkness, and the only one that can be spared to return to the high court. Your princess needs your service."

Curuthannor's jaw clenched momentarily. He didn't like being ordered around, even less so by a royal that he didn't know . . . or respect. Whatever she wanted, he guessed it would mean trouble.

"In what capacity?"

"It's a simple task, really, and shouldn't take you far out of your way. We need you to take a message to His Majesty, King Othin. He will be waiting for word from Her Highness, but we cannot trust the Shadow Realm messengers—I mean couriers—in this task."

"Why me?"

"As I mentioned, you are the only high elf we can trust to be loyal and fulfill his duties with honor. You rose to the occasion, stopping the guard from making fools of themselves—"

"I was hardly successful at that. I just kept them from completely destroying my favorite accommodations."

"Perhaps, but you didn't even have to do that much. With the guards confined to the guest barracks after the events of last night, we can't give them a message to take home. And Belegeth and I—" Lhéwen nodded toward her bodyguard, "—must remain with her ladyship. You are conveniently situated to leave without notice, and without attracting attention."

"I wish that were the case, but I'm afraid my business dealings here have soured and I am under similar scrutiny. Prince Aradae himself instructed me to leave immediately."

"That's wonderful."

"I beg your pardon?" He didn't see any benefit to an early departure with failure hovering overhead.

"Apologies," Lhéwen demurred, her gaze dropping to the hands clasped lightly in her lap. She was hiding behind that cloak of neutrality she liked to wear. "I didn't mean to offend. But the timing is ideal. Her Highness's message must be taken to the king immediately."

Curuthannor swallowed. Wonderful. Not only would he have to admit his failure to his father, but he would have to take the words to the king directly.

"May I ask why you're being told to leave?" Lhéwen asked.

Curuthannor's cheeks flushed. "It will become public knowledge soon enough. I've been barred from purchasing the iron I need from the goblin master of mining. Prince Aradae himself informed me that every bar in the guild is spoken for. They will allow no further sales."

Lhéwen cocked her head to the side, her gaze focused on a distant unseen point. "Why would they do that? It will only increase tensions with the Upper Realm."

"I don't know, but they will not sell even a single bar."

"You cannot tell this to King Othin. Not yet. I will inform Her Highness. Let Princess Faeliel bring home the iron for her father, and yours."

"You are certain of her success?"

Lhéwen nodded eagerly. "This could be the opportunity she's been looking for. In the meantime, take this message to the king and return with his response." She pressed a rolled and sealed scroll into his hands. "I'll meet you here in three Shadow Realm days time."

"What am I supposed to do for nine days in the Upper Realm? I can't return to my family's hall, or they'll ask about the iron."

"Take a holiday. Tour the city. I don't know. But give us some time to work on the problem. You won't regret it. I swear it."

CHAPTER 13

A soft knock at the door. Daeturion looked up from the stack of off-world reports on his desk.

"Come in," he called.

Ethires stepped into the room, her long braid draped around her shoulders like a scarf. He couldn't understand why she insisted on growing her hair so long. It was impossible to care for.

"Apologies for the interruption, Your Highness, but you asked for immediate updates on the movements of the merchant and any of the princess's entourage."

"What can you tell me?"

"The merchant returned to the Crossroads a quarter bell past. He looked frustrated and angry. Tharbatiron called him over to the bar, where he met with the princess's handmaiden. The bodyguard was there also. The merchant, handmaiden, and bodyguard followed Tryg back to Tharbatiron's private garden. I was unable to follow."

"Do you know what they were discussing?"

"The handmaiden spoke with Tharbatiron about repaying the

damages incurred at the inn, then said she needed to speak with Curuthannor regarding a request from the princess."

"Interesting. Are they information gathering?"

"Unknown, but I think unlikely, at least on the part of the merchant. As far as I could tell, he was not expecting the meeting. He seemed surprised and awkwardly uncomfortable during the small bit of conversation I was able to overhear before they left."

"And what of the handmaiden?"

"Unknown, sire. I saw no message, no other form of communication, but without being able to observe their conversation I cannot say what the princess's request might have been."

"I feel we're being played, somehow. The timing is all too convenient."

"You think the bar fight was staged?"

"I think we don't know the princess's true purpose here. She is clearly intent on seducing our king, but the question is why. Is she doing it at the behest of King Othin? It seems unlikely given the rumors I've heard of his protective nature, but at the same time it seems doubtful he would have allowed her to come here at all if he didn't think she would be able to influence our realm."

"King Rindae won't be fooled, will he?"

Prince Daeturion lifted one eyebrow and shot her a chastising look. She was a common elf with no business questioning the king's choices.

"Apologies, sire. I step out of place."

"Our king acts in the best interest of our realm, always. Never dare question him again."

Ethires dipped her head. "Apologies."

"For now, continue tracking the handmaiden. If we can uncover their purpose, we can better advise our king."

Ethires pursed her lips to one side. "I'm afraid that might be a problem. The handmaiden saw me at the Crossroads. I was listening to the musicians warm-up before the evening entertainment. I can continue to observe the inn, but it will be difficult to follow her movements outside its walls."

"Understood. In that case, keep on the merchant, make sure he leaves this realm. I'll assign one of the palace observers to continue the watch on the handmaiden and the princess."

After Ethires's departure, Daeturion leaned back in his chair and pressed his fingers together beneath his chin. There was a game afoot, and the princess was a worthy opponent. So long as her interests were not antithetical to the interests of the Shadow Realm, they could remain amicable. But, if she attempted to bring the Shadow Realm under high court rule, by force or by manipulation, Daeturion would do everything in his power to prevent it. The Shadow Realm would not surrender to the high elves.

CHAPTER 14

Rothruinil rose a bell before dawn and dressed in white linen. It had been six days since Valyaro's death. Six days since King Othin had barged into their world and ended the warrior's life. As was tradition, the seventh day would be his final day in the sun.

The drapings of death shrouded Rothruinil's figure and dimmed her sight, but for once she was grateful. The veil would hide the silent tears that threatened to fall at any moment. Glancing at herself once more in the mirror, she was grateful that no one would see her face.

Taking a bracing breath, she left the palace and made her way to the temple of the sun god where Valyaro had lain for the last six days. It was there that the body had been oiled and blessed and wrapped in fine linens. And it was there that she met Valyaro's wife and son, and another Tirnor warrior to carry his body to the pyre. Together, the four of them would bear the body in silence.

Rothruinil took her place at Valyaro's feet while the others stood at his head and shoulders. They lifted the pallet from the low altar in the chamber of dusk where the honored dead waited for their final rites. It was time.

Valyaro's wife led the way, her place at his head unquestioned. Rothruinil admired the woman's strength. There was no hint of the inner turmoil she must be experiencing, no shaking of her shoulders to indicate sobs. The woman might not have been of the Tirnor, but she was a warrior in her own way, stronger in spirit than in body.

As they walked through the still-dark city, friends and neighbors, all who wished to honor Valyaro, fell in line behind the pallet. In the dim light, the city itself appeared to be in mourning, its colors muted. The mourners all wore white and pale gray, the color of the ash that would float to the sky. The only sound that could be heard was the steady fall of bare feet on tile and stone, and the gentle beating of the waves against the walls and bridges of their island homes.

By the time they reached the mainland, it seemed like every resident had emerged to honor the dead. Though the fire sidhe were a war-like people, there hadn't been a death due to intentional violence since the clans had united under Rothruinil's grandmother's rule. They trained and they sparred, and certainly there were occasional accidents that resulted in death, but never intentional.

Until now. Until the high elf king decided he needed their banner for his collection.

Rothruinil swallowed down the bile that wanted to rise to the back of her throat. The king and queen hadn't thrown him out of their palace. In Rothruinil's opinion, that had been a terrible mistake. She couldn't bear the thought of owing allegiance to such a man, but she also hadn't been a part of the royal meetings.

For four of the last six days, King Othin remained in residence, though he spoke with none but her parents. At last he had left, but without the fanfare of his arrival. He rode out with his guard before dawn, with the same haughty scowl on his face. He neither appeared victorious, nor defeated, though she could hope she sensed frustration in the set of his shoulders.

When questioned, King Thanûr had refused to share what had been discussed. He told her to focus on Valyaro's funeral, that the rest would come in time. She wasn't certain whether she should have hope that they had rejected King Othin's proposals, or whether she should despair that they were now allied with the volatile king.

But her father was correct. Now was not the time to dwell on the injustices of the realms. Now was the time to honor the dead. Later, she could seek justice.

The pyre could be seen rising above the jungle foliage, the wooden struts having been built especially for this day. It stood at least three stories tall, high enough that no shadow would fall across Valyaro's face.

Carefully, the pallbearers began the final climb up the stairs that would lead them to Valyaro's last resting place. Rothruinil was forced to lift the pallet to her shoulders to keep his feet level with his head. Her arms and legs trembled with the effort by the time they reached the top.

At last they placed Valyaro on his death bed. The four pall bearers would remain standing on their own separate platforms on the four sides of the compass, far enough from the body to keep from getting burned themselves, but close enough to witness the return to ash that was the destiny of every fire sidhe.

As dawn broke over the edge of the forest, the pyre glowed with dawn's light. Rebirth and renewal, dawn was the face of redemption, the face of forgiveness, and the face of new beginnings. On this last day of Valyaro's mortal body, dawn's light would bless his journey into the afterlife.

Below them, a single clear note of song lifted into the air. The wailing woman sang of a life well-lived, of a wife and a son well-loved, and of a warrior who would not be forgotten. A tear streaked down Rothruinil's hidden face at the bittersweet beauty of the singer's words.

Food was carried up to the pallbearers at mid-morning, a simple meal of fried flatbread and cold water. Rothruinil choked down a few bites but couldn't find the appetite to eat more. Her thoughts kept drifting back to the events of the welcoming ceremony, the fierce joy at being selected to lead the dance, the satisfaction of seeing the high elf guard draw his weapon. Had they not known it was all for show? It was a demonstration of power, an intimidation tactic, but they should have been aware of the ceremony. Surely, King Othin knew. After all, he'd called it a barbaric tradition. But who was the true barbarian?

The sun slowly made its way overhead. They would light the pyre at exactly noon, the midday sun revealing the truth—Valyaro would not rise again. Conflict and revelation, these were the faces of the midday sun. The path had been laid, and now it would be traveled.

The war drums beat the final rhythm for the warrior on his way. Only moments left, a few long heartbeats. Rothruinil could feel the vibration in the soles of her feet, the sound building as another drum entered the call, and another.

As one, everything stopped. Silence fell. Even the call of the birds in the distant trees ceased.

The four pallbearers lifted their right hands to the sky. Rothruinil sent up a silent prayer for Valyaro's everlasting soul. He would be honored, and he would be missed. May he find peace in the summerlands.

The pallbearers lowered their arms, pointing their hands at the pyre. Rothruinil willed a spark to light within the wood. As the flame took hold, she fed it more and more energy, forcing the red to turn orange, then the orange to turn blue. The flames ate through the fuel, catching every last twig in its endless appetite, until finally the flame touched the oil-soaked linens wrapping Valyaro's body. A ball of fire erupted from the corpse.

A heartbreaking scream pulled from the depths of mourning shocked Rothruinil from the hypnotizing flame. Valyaro's wife took three long steps and launched herself from the pallbearer's platform onto the pyre. Screams tore from her throat as her body caught flame alongside her husband.

"Mother!" their son shouted. He fell to his knees, both hands outstretched to the flame for an instant before he covered his face with his hands. His body shook with sobs, but he didn't attempt to follow.

Tears flowed freely down Rothruinil's face now, soaking the white linen veil where it touched her cheeks and making it cling to her skin. They must have been lifemated. She hadn't known. Lifemates rarely outlived each other by more than a few days or weeks. Sometimes even less. Only the strongest of reasons could keep a bonded survivor in the mortal coil.

Lifemate bonds were honored and sacred, but they could also be a liability. Rothruinil couldn't imagine being so deeply connected to someone that you would rather die than continue to live after their death. It was one of the reasons she had never sought to entangle herself in romantic relationships. Well, that and she hadn't found anyone she deemed worthy of more than a friendly shared release.

As Valyaro's wife fell silent, and the flames consumed the last of their fuel, Rothruinil wiped the tears from her cheeks. The sun neared the horizon and called in dusk, the face of death and decay, the time to give over the ashes of the deceased to the sun god's care. Her vigil was almost over. Valyaro and his wife would find their final resting place together in the summerlands.

Rothruinil worried that it was the living who would suffer the consequences of his death.

CHAPTER 15

Portals made Curuthannor itch. The trips were becoming more common, but even still, he didn't enjoy being in the presence of such a mix of magics. Their combined energies were too chaotic and confusing; his own abilities couldn't sort them into their proper places.

Unfortunately, he couldn't do anything about it. They were a necessary appliance to travel between realms. Without them, the elves would still be stuck in the over-populated dysfunctional Origin. Or so they'd been taught as children. Even his parents no longer knew the truth.

Regardless, the original elves had created the portals using every magical discipline, opened the way to the nine, and then shut the way behind them. There was no going back. And there was no other way to travel through the veil, from one realm to the next.

Curuthannor blew out a breath. There were only three people left in front of him in the queue. Hopefully they would be fast. He was impatient to get rid of the scroll.

His gaze dropped to examine the seal once more. There was some kind of magic inlaid into the golden wax. He couldn't tell its function, but he could sense that it was there. Spirit magic. Energy magic. He simultaneously wanted to touch the seal and throw it as far away from him as he could. He would resist both options.

The paper at least was mundane in nature. It rustled slightly as his hand moved, but otherwise seemed to be plain cream-colored parchment with a clean edge. High quality paper, tightly rolled, but that was to be expected from the hand of the princess. She would only use the best in anything she did.

Like the best seamstress. Lhéwen wouldn't be here if she weren't the best at what she did. Companionship and fashion, he imagined both were critical to Her Highness. He wondered how attached the women truly were. The princess had the reputation for being a taskmaster, manipulative and quick to anger. Lhéwen didn't fit that mold at all, but perhaps she was a calming influence, someone who could talk the princess down out of her moods.

The bigger question was what influence the princess had on the seamstress. Would Lhéwen ever question her mistress, or would she simply follow orders?

The woman in front of him drew her final rune on the stone and stepped through the gate. At last.

Curuthannor approached the rune stone. Lhéwen had given him the code to travel through the public portal directly from Nalakadr to Caralávar, the capital city of the Upper Realm and the seat of the high court of faerie. He would emerge from the central portal, and then find his way to the West gate of the castle, where the guards were friendly to the princess's eccentricities.

Like receiving a common messenger with a private scroll for the king. Or sneaking out at night to visit a paramour, as she'd been known to do. Or so went the rumors.

Curuthannor placed his finger on the flat stone slab to the right of the arch, beginning the drawing of the first rune. When the symbol was complete, the stone archway began to hum. After the second, a crackle of lightning split across the empty gap. The third increased the tension and the fourth made the hair on the back of his arms stand straight up.

He swallowed. There were more people waiting behind him, but he needed half a moment to force the magic to do his bidding. Manipulating energy had never been his forte. Sensing it, funneling it, sure, but he struggled to bend it to his will.

He'd always been a disappointment to his father for his lack of magical skill. Martial skill was another story, but that could be learned and practiced over time. Magic, to some degree, was innate to the bearer. It could be uncovered over time, and its use perfected, but its raw essence was decided at birth.

Curuthannor forced his finger to draw the fifth rune, the symbols glowing softly with blue light. Just one more and the portal would open. Then a brief moment of disorientation as he stepped through and he'd be home. Rather, he'd be in his home realm. He didn't particularly care for the city, would have much preferred to return to his family's hall in Rómesse Gulch.

He blew out a breath on a frown. At least there would be light in Caralávar. He was tired of straining his eyes in the oppressive dark.

With a pop of displaced air and sizzle of electricity, the portal opened. The view cleared from the shadows to a brilliant day in Caralávar. Curuthannor almost covered his eyes from the glaring light, but a high elf shouldn't be afraid of, or sensitive to, the light in his home realm. It was what he had just been grateful for, after all.

"Are you going through? There are others behind you," a female dark elf with a long white braid asked from immediately behind Curuthannor. She shaded her eyes against the light pouring through the veil.

Curuthannor didn't bother to respond. He grit his teeth and stepped into the archway. The portal squeezed the breath out of his lungs before pulling him cell by cell through the artificial gate and into the reality of the Upper Realm. The sensation always left him feeling as if he'd been turned inside out, as if he'd been wrung out like a wet towel and his guts now rested on the floor. Luckily, that wasn't how it actually happened, though he'd heard a few horror stories about the creation of the first portals several thousand years ago.

Doing his utmost to keep his spine straight, he stepped forward onto the polished marble of the central terminal. The portal closed behind him with a snap and immediately reopened for a new traveler. Curuthannor quickly side-stepped out of the way.

Tears sprang to his eyes as he gazed out at the terraced city, not because he was emotionally overwrought, but because the light reflecting off every mirrored, polished, and gilded surface pained his eyes. The high court and its occupants were known as the glittering throng for a reason. Though the intensity of the light was the same in Rómesse Gulch, the simple buildings couldn't have been more opposite. Where Caralávar was filigreed and formal, Rómesse Gulch was all straight lines and practical materials.

He missed home more than he'd like to admit. He missed his mother's fresh bread slathered with homemade brickleberry preserves. He missed his brother Minya's teasing and Namba's quiet presence. He even missed his father's gruff critique of his work. At home he knew where he came from, even if he struggled to find his place.

He couldn't fail them. He had a job to do, one that could help his family acquire the iron they needed to complete the king's commission. Without it, they would be ruined.

Course set, Curuthannor blinked away the wet and found the path that would take him to the castle on the hill.

Caralávar was built on a series of terraces that wrapped around more than a dozen rocky hillsides. The location had been chosen so it wouldn't interfere with the fertile valley lands that supported the nobles in their city manses. However, over the course of millennia and multiple generations, the city had needed to spread. Protecting the valleys had been deemed of utmost importance after the destruction of the Origin, so rather than venturing down into the grasslands, the city had bounced from one hilltop to another, and wide bridges connected each of the new districts.

The central terminal was located on the most heavily populated and easily accessed of these hillsides, but King Othin's castle maintained its own private mountaintop location. In order to get to the West gate, Curuthannor would have to circle around the perimeter of the city, traveling through three other hilltop districts.

He glanced at the sky. The sun was at its zenith, which meant he had plenty of time to arrive before nightfall.

Crossing over the first of the three bridges into the basta district, Curuthannor was overwhelmed by the smell of baking bread and sweet preserves. The ovens were working at full capacity to feed the sedate throngs of pedestrians who wandered from shop to shop during the midday bell. Servants scouted for new delicacies their lords and ladies could try, while the nobility lunched at delicate tables, their food equally small and fraught with pretension. There was no rustic fare to be had here, no rough-chopped vegetables or thick cuts of meat to be enjoyed with gusto after a long day of labor. These men and women didn't understand the meaning of the phrase.

Curuthannor shifted those thoughts out of his mind. He wasn't a noble, and had no desire to become one. Give him a sharp metal stick and he'd be content. Especially if he could convince a golden-haired maiden to stand beside him.

Leaving the Basta District with its bread and pastries behind, Curuthannor continued onto the hill of the Santírima. Unlike the other districts, this hilltop had been dedicated to the enjoyment of the natural—if manicured—flora and fauna of the realm. Flightless birds walked across smooth stone pavers, their long shimmering tails dragging along behind them. Artistic seating areas for the leisurely enjoyment of the district were arranged on balconies or under gazebos. Much like Tharbatiron's private garden, come to think of it. Curuthannor briefly wondered if Tharbatiron had gotten the idea from the Upper Realm, or if it had been his idea first.

A flock of fist-sized birds with bright yellow beaks scattered up into the temperate afternoon air. That was another nice thing about being back in his home territory; the humidity was actually bearable. He didn't immediately find himself with sweat running down his spine.

Curuthannor glanced at the skyline, gauging his distance to the palace. The castle rose high into the air, golden rooftops gleaming. It was good he'd chosen this route. Now that he was closer, he could see the guards posted on the southern entrance. Their staffs were crossed, and the portcullis was down, blocking all entry. He hoped Lhéwen was right, and the western guards would be amenable to helping him.

He hurried out of the Santírima gardens and into his favorite district: the Maciltam hill with its armorers and swordsmiths. He glanced once more at the sun. Barely into afternoon, he could relax his pace somewhat and peruse the tables that would be lining every major thoroughfare.

"You won't go wrong purchasing a new blade from me," a man said, drawing Curuthannor's gaze to the blades laid out on a soft velvet cloth.

Curuthannor shook his head and moved on. The man's wares were subpar at best, purely decorative. Thin rapiers with golden wire-wrapped hilts already showed a slight bend in their length, and Curuthannor could see from a distance that the bejeweled daggers had a dull edge. They might make the untrained nobles feel safer in their homes, but they wouldn't be of any use in a real fight like the one at the Crossroads. These daggers would break before piercing even a hairsbreadth into hardened leather, let alone plate armor.

Winding his way through the streets, Curuthannor found himself rarely impressed by the craftsmanship on display. It was no wonder King Othin had commissioned a blade from his father. The metal on offer here couldn't compare.

A table in a corner—the elderly proprietor quiet and unconcerned with the passing shoppers—caught Curuthannor's eye.

"You look like man who knows his metal," the man called when Curuthannor paused, his voice rough with age. He was easily two, maybe even three generations Curuthannor's elder. He seemed far too old to hold a hammer or brace against an anvil, yet the quality of his blades was far superior to anything else Curuthannor had yet seen in the market. What's more, there were some new shapes he'd never encountered before.

Curuthannor picked up a pair of hands-length knives with an odd, bulbous curved tip. The man said nothing as Curuthannor examined the blades, letting the work do the talking for him.

"What are these called," Curuthannor finally asked.

"Khukuri knives," the man replied, his voice like the whisper of wind through the leaves of the aspen trees. "Stab, slice, or chop, they are a versatile style for practical tasks."

Curuthannor frowned. "They're kitchen tools?" That didn't seem right, not for these blades.

The old man laughed, the chuckle resolving into a fit of coughing.

"Not exactly, though I'm sure you could put them to good use there. They are the everyman's weapon and a tool for the road. They will allow you to chop your way through the densest forest and then skin the hide off your hunter's kill. They are not for everyone though. They serve a purpose."

"Weapons?"

"Could be. They're light and fast, but don't give the reach of a sword. If you're looking for a fight, I've a broadsword that might be to your liking."

"No, these will be fine. I will take the pair."

"And you've the coin to pay?"

"Aye." His father wouldn't be keen on the expense, but he'd call it research. They were a beautiful shape and well-made, but Curuthannor knew his father's make would still be superior. He and his brothers would have a fine time perfecting the blades for use in close combat. And Curuthannor would enjoy the challenge of a new fighting style and weapon.

"Two gold, then."

Curuthannor's eyes widened. "They are of fine quality, but the steel is . . . " Curuthannor turned the blade over in the light, ". . . Krevish? Good, not great. And the shape is not perfectly symmetrical for the pair. The weight is off a mite toward the handle . . ." Curuthannor paused again eyeing the blade directly and the shopkeeper in his peripheral. "I'll give you three-fourths gold and not a sliver more."

"Like I thought, you do know your metal. One gold. They're sturdy and well designed. A new design. Which I imagine you're thinking about modifying for your own use."

Curuthannor's eyebrows lifted and the man raised his hands in a settle down motion.

"I don't mind, not in the least. This pair has been overlooked already for far too long. If they can find a home and be a prototype for others, I'll be satisfied. With one gold in my pocket, of course."

Curuthannor grinned. He liked the man's style. "Deal. One gold, for the blades and the knife pattern to go along with it."

His father wouldn't mind the gold at all if he also got the pattern.

The bent little man beamed. "Done."

Curuthannor handed over the gold and the shopkeeper sheathed the blades in simple leather, then wrapped them again in oilskin.

"Take good care of the girls and they'll take good care of you and yours."

Curuthannor dipped his head in a small bow, tucked the knives into his traveling pack and whistled a merry tune. Things were looking up.

CHAPTER 16

Purchase made, Curuthannor approached the barbican with a spring in his step, expecting the guards to take the scroll and be done with it. The king wouldn't deign to meet with a simple smith's son. Even the princess had only sent her handmaiden to deal with him. A trusted, valuable handmaiden, but a servant nonetheless.

He didn't mind. In fact he preferred it. He could do without the pomp and circumstance and court politics that went along with it. It was his father and elder brother who dealt with the high-end customers. Curuthannor preferred the good working men and women who provided their supplies.

The castle perched high on its own hill, four bridges marking the four entrances on the four cardinal points of the compass. The tall, gilded edifice caught the first and last light of day, reflecting its glory onto its surroundings and proclaiming its dominion. To the north, the mammoth herds marched across the tundra. To the south, plentiful fields of maize and grain were harvested while vineyards produced the finest elvish wines. The east brought in the forest lumber and wild game. And the west was the mountainous home of the mines and quarries, and all their related goods.

The west was home. It seemed fitting that it would also be the gate ordered by Lhéwen for this particular delivery.

"Halt and state your business," a bored voice called out from ten paces away.

The portcullis was down. Curuthannor didn't know if that was normal or not, but he didn't much care. He lifted his hands, the still-sealed scroll on display in his right fist.

"I am Curuthannor, son of Hatholdammon, Master Smith of Rómesse Gulch," Curuthannor replied out of habit more than any sense that his heritage would garner him any kind of acclaim. "I have a message from Princess Faeliel for His Majesty, King Othin."

"How did you come to have this message?" a more suspicious voice asked. Apparently, calling out the princess had piqued their interest.

"I was in the Shadow Realm on business for my father. I came into contact with her ladyship's handmaiden, Lhéwen."

"Lhéwen?" The guard sounded surprised, and perhaps even more interested. For some reason that irked Curuthannor.

"Indeed. She is traveling with her ladyship. They asked me to carry this to His Majesty for them, as they are unable to leave the current negotiations in the Shadow Realm."

"Step forward. Show me the scroll," the guard said. His voice was harder than it had any right to be under the circumstances.

Curuthannor offered no threat, but kept his gaze focused on the man's chest as he scanned his surroundings with his peripheral vision. The barbicans at each gate had been trapped and spelled to repel or destroy intruders with ill-intent. He wasn't one of those, of course, but it was still sound advice to pay attention to the defenses in place.

Two guards in heavy gold plate impressed with the King's sigil —a crown centered on a sunburst—stood just inside the closed portcullis. They carried long steel pikes that could reach between the bars to impale an intruder. The creak of a board overhead indicated there were soldiers above. A shifting shadow behind the arrow slits suggested crossbows or arrows were also pointed in his direction.

Plastering a false smile across his cheeks, Curuthannor hoped the men didn't notice his nerves. He had no intention of harm, but one wrong move could spell disaster.

"Open it," the guard on the left—the suspicious one—commanded.

"I cannot," Curuthannor replied. "It was given to me in trust for the king. The contents are not my business to know."

"And how do we know that your words are true?"

"Examine the seal. It is the princess's signet." He had looked at it enough already to know it couldn't be any other. And Lhéwen wouldn't have steered him wrong.

He held the scroll out in front of him, the seal bared to the gate. The bored guard on the right came closer to the iron to peer at the design. "It appears authentic," he said.

"Then you open it," the other guard said.

"I would not tamper with that seal," Curuthannor interrupted. There was magic tied up in the wax. He knew it. He just didn't know what it did.

"Why not?" the suspicious guard demanded.

"It is the king's business. Not ours." The magic could be nothing. Or it could be something. Maybe it just prevented anyone but the king breaking the wax. If that was the case, there was no cause for alarm. If it wasn't? Curuthannor had no idea what to tell the guards.

The bored guard rolled his eyes. "You are obviously not a frequent visitor of the high court. Everyone knows everything on this hill."

Curuthannor doubted that was true.

The guard sliced through the wax with his belt dagger. His eyes rolled back into his head. He fell to the ground, the thunk of meat hitting stone.

The other guard lunged forward, tension pulling the skin of his face taut as he raced to help his companion.

"Alimno!"

As if on cue, the guard on the ground shuddered. Screams tore through his throat, the sound a continuous wail that pierced the eardrums and sent Curuthannor's hands to cover his ears. The guard curled into the fetal position. His fingers scrabbled at the golden chest plate that covered his torso. The visible skin of his face and hands shriveled into old age, the formerly healthy golden hue turning gray as if dusted with ash. The screams petered out as the last of the man's breath left his body. He lay still.

The whistle of wind through the cracks in the stone could be heard in the shocked silence that followed the guard's demise. The remaining sentry lifted his gaze to Curuthannor's face. His eyes were wide with shock and accusation, his mouth hung open in dismay. Curuthannor could almost feel the targets painted on his body where the bolts and arrows from their hidden comrades would hit.

He fell to his knees, lifting his hands high into the air in surrender and dropping his chin to his chest.

"It was not my doing! I was not told of the message's trap." He couldn't say he had no idea of the spell—he'd known of the magic —but he could say honestly that no one had told him about it.

Lhéwen hadn't told him about it. She had to have known, but she hadn't said a word.

If he had tried to open the scroll, he would have suffered the man's fate.

He shuddered at the close call, praising all the gods for their small gifts of honesty, loyalty, and magical sense.

Metal grated against stone. "You will come with us."

CHAPTER 17

Faeliel leaned forward conspiratorially, brushing a hand across King Rindae's forearm. "The Shadow Realm will become a preferred trade partner. In fact, the king has agreed he will never impose tariffs or fees on allied realms. They will be free to purchase or trade for any Upper Realm products or services at the going market rate. Plus, your citizens will be allowed free access to the Upper Realm portals."

This was all true, assuming King Othin would apply the same agreements he'd made with the Autumn Realm and Winter Realm to the Shadow Realm. The written attestations she had intercepted had been clear. Every allied realm was a 'preferred trade partner' in his mind. Of course, he hadn't made that same offer to the Shadow Realm, King Rindae had left too soon for that, but she had to keep up the charade of trade negotiations until she was sure she could trust the shadow king with her life . . . and her freedom.

"We already have free access to the portals, that's not a great benefit . . . unless your king has plans to start a conflict. We won't go lightly into isolation."

"Of course not. I meant no threat." Faeliel carefully dipped her chin and tilted her head to the side in a somewhat submissive and conciliatory gesture, glancing up at Rindae from under her lashes. "My father has been clear about my role in his court. I am only allowed to share his words, not my own."

That should plant the seed. Place the offense at Othin's feet while reminding Rindae of her political relationship, and also imply her own dissatisfaction with her role. This was a game she knew how to play. She only feared she played it too well at home.

Rindae lifted an eyebrow. "You are so controlled by your king?"

"Would you send a woman to treat with a foreign monarch without first coaching her in her duties?"

"I suppose it would depend on the woman, and her diplomatic skill."

Faeliel allowed a pleased smile to warm her expression. She felt for the energy in the room, her magical senses opening wide to test the emotional output.

Lhéwen was bored, that was no surprise, nor was Belegeth's vigilance in the hall. They didn't interest her. The king's attraction, however, was far more enticing. His aura pulsed against her senses with deep-seated want.

Just then, a stubby-tailed cat with tufted ears wandered into the room. Faeliel had felt her presence as a vibrating warmth on the magical plane, the creature a living embodiment of the Shadow Realm. She rubbed her long body across the king's leg, then jumped into his lap. She rested her chin on his left arm while he absently petted her thick fur. The creature eyed Faeliel from between slitted eyes.

"What a lovely animal," Faeliel murmured, leaning forward once more to bridge the short distance between herself and Rindae. Her arm rose in a sinuous wave. "May I pet her?"

The king dipped his chin toward his pet. "You will have to ask Mithmuig. She has quite the mind of her own."

The cat eyed the princess another half beat, then meowed her apparent approval.

Faeliel slid her fingers through the cat's fur, her gaze all for the king. He was a handsome specimen of male physical strength. The only drawback might be the gray irises that almost disappeared into the white of his eyes, but the intensity of his stare sent shivers to all the right places. She dropped her gaze to his full lips, wondering what it might be like to kiss them.

"So soft," she said, drawing her attention back to the cat. "What is she?"

"An ashcat. She was a stray runt begging for scraps at the castle kitchens when I found her. I rescued her before the larger beasts could eat her."

"That was generous of you," the princess replied. Truly, it was. She could admire compassion in a man, so long as it didn't interfere with his effectiveness to rule.

The cat began to purr, its voice a rhythmic murmur. With her magical senses wide open, the cat's approval of her petting and her words was evident.

A new force of energy slammed into Faeliel's body. Her shields were down. She couldn't control the flow.

"Oh!" the princess sat back, her hand lifting to her throat. Her heart rate sped as her eyes grew wide. Energy poured into her like a flash flood through dry desert canyons. She rode the wave as it crested through her body, filling her cells with the excess spirit of another sentient being.

The message's seal had been broken. Someone was dying for his treason.

The princess's eyes closed and her head tilted back against the plush couch cushion behind her. She licked her lips and swallowed. Every sense was heightened. She stroked a fingertip across the smooth, well-oiled leather beneath her hands. The smells of ancient books and dark peppermint combined in a masculine warmth. She wanted to take a bite of . . . something.

Her gaze connected with Rindae's amused and intrigued smile.

"Mmm," the princess's purr was almost as loud as the cat's. She was high on the energy of another. She would need to expend some of it or risk losing control.

"Are you feeling quite well?" Rindae asked, his gaze emotionally stroking Faeliel in all the right places. She could hardly respond.

"My lady, I believe it is time for you to retire to your rooms," Lhéwen interrupted.

She was a wonderful seamstress and a good companion, but she didn't understand the risk of interrupting this moment. Faeliel had never taken an entire life before, not of a sentient creature at any rate. The power was . . . exquisite. It needed to be shared or she felt like she might explode.

"Nonsense," she murmured. Her vision was clear even if her judgment was less so. "There are still . . ." she paused, her breath hitching as Rindae gently moved the cat from his lap to the floor, ". . . negotiations to be undertaken."

"My lady, I don't think that is wise at this juncture. Belegeth and I will escort you back to your quarters."

"Lhéwen, I know you mean well, but your services are no longer required." Faeliel's eyes were locked onto the small cleft in the shadow king's chin. He was strong. Powerful. He would help her funnel this excess into more . . . exciting avenues.

"You may go." The deep timbre of the king's voice took command.

Lhéwen rose with a bow and backed out of the room.

Yes, this was a man she could tangle with without fear or hesitation. Faeliel would have this king.

CHAPTER 18

Lhéwen closed the door silently behind her, the murmurs and gentle laughter no longer audible after the latch clicked shut. For a brief moment, Lhéwen wondered if the king had spelled his door to occlude all sound, and if so, who had done the work. Sound was perhaps the most difficult energy to manipulate as it was disconnected from its source.

"Where is the princess?" Belegeth asked, her gaze ever alert.

The words snapped Lhéwen back to attention in the present. "With the king. They . . ." *how to put this delicately,* ". . . may be awhile."

It was hardly a sufficient explanation, but it would have to do.

"Stay here," Lhéwen continued. "Don't let anyone enter these chambers, even the king's servants. She can't be discovered alone with him. We can't protect her from herself, but we can protect her from the scorn of others, and the wrath of her father."

"I hardly think that's true, either, but I'll do my best. What will you do?"

"I'm not sure, yet." The scroll had been opened, the seal broken.

120

It was the only explanation for the princess's behavior. "I must find another way to get a message to the Upper Realm."

"Go. I will protect Her Highness."

Lhéwen left the castle with her thoughts in a tangle.

Curuthannor had opened the scroll. Gods protect him. Lhéwen had never seen the princess so overwhelmed with energy. She'd lost her senses in the thrall of power. Lhéwen knew Faeliel had made the seal enchantment stronger than they'd discussed, but this . . . it could only mean she'd absorbed a full life. She had killed someone. She had killed Curuthannor.

And Lhéwen had been her weapon.

Gods above, what had she done? She imagined his blue eyes faded and gray, his skin drawn and ashen in death. It normally took millennia for an elf to age and fade away. This would have been mere heartbeats. Excruciating. And now his body might be decaying in a nameless alley or windowless room, lying undiscovered and dishonored. It could be days, weeks even, before anyone found him.

She should be the one to find him. To make sure the message didn't get into the wrong hands. But where would he have gone? Would he still be at the Crossroads?

Lhéwen turned a corner and slammed into the solid chest of a dark elf man. Only his hand on her arm kept her from falling to the ground.

"Apologies, my lord," Lhéwen said defaulting to the neutral honorific. "I was not paying close enough attention to where I was going."

She looked up to meet the amused gaze of Prince Daeturion, heir to the shadow throne. Behind him stood a young male blood sidhe in page's livery, holding a thin board with parchment and a quill attached to the top.

"You look quite distracted," Daeturion mused drawing her attention away from the scribe.

Lhéwen bent into a deep curtsy. "Apologies," she repeated.

"No harm was done, though I'm glad you didn't fall. Where are you headed in such haste?"

"I have some business to attend, that is all," Lhéwen replied, keeping her response as vague as possible without being rude.

"Anything I can assist with?"

Daeturion's voice was soothing to her frazzled nerves. It made her want to trust him, to divulge the truth, but she knew better than to reveal what had happened. The prince would get the wrong idea. Or maybe the right one, which would be just as bad. Even if the royals of this realm knew in theory that the princess would be communicating with her home realm, they would still want to know the contents of those messages. It was only practical.

It was imperative they not find proof of the princess's true designs.

"No, Your Highness. I am confident I will be able to perform my duties."

Daeturion tipped his head in a modest bow. "As you wish. I will let you pass." His lips twisted up in an ironic grin as he rose to his full height.

Lhéwen dropped into another low curtsy, then hurried on her way down the hall and out into the streets of Nalakadr.

Her thoughts immediately returned to Curuthannor and the predicament she was in. She had trusted him, believed in his honor and loyalty. She had been the one to convince the princess to use him as a messenger. It looked like the princess's choice to strengthen the charm had been the right decision.

"Stupid girl. Your heart overturned your head." She'd only known the man a few bells. She'd watched him in the throne room and decided he was trustworthy based on almost no evidence. She couldn't even be entirely sure that he was a merchant. She'd never seen him in court, didn't know his family or his references. How could she have been so blinded by his good looks and honest appearance? They were high elves, manipulators of energy, including the emotions. She should have known better.

Gravel crunched beneath her feet. She pushed her way through the dancers in the Crossroads' central amphitheater, not even hearing the music coming from the stage. The patrons sitting at the bar must have taken heed of her fierce expression; three of them moved from their stools, giving her the right of way to sit in their seats.

Tryg approached with a full mug of cider, his expression grim. "Ye look like ye could use one of these right about now."

"What do you know of Curuthannor's business dealings?" Lhéwen asked abruptly.

"Nae, I cannot betray the confidence of our patrons. Ye know that would be bad for business."

"Bartenders deal in information as much as food and drink. Tell me, please. Is he a good man? Loyal? Or did I mislay my trust?"

"What're ye talking about? Curuthannor is one of the most honorable men I've had the pleasure of serving in this place. Yer trust is not misplaced in that one. Not a chance."

Lhéwen blew out a relieved breath, but it still didn't explain Faeliel's sudden energy. The simplest explanation was usually the truth.

"He broke the seal." Lhéwen dropped her face into her hands. Even knowing there was no other logical explanation for Faeliel's behavior, she couldn't believe he would have so completely turned on his own realm.

He had broken up the fight in this very bar in an attempt to protect the reputation of the High Guard.

Or so he said.

"He did what, now?" Tryg asked. His ever present rag swirled in circles on the bar top, cleaning away invisible food and grease.

Lhéwen shook her head. She'd misplaced her trust once already. She couldn't do it again. Even if Tryg were the most honorable troll in the history of elven-troll relations, there were others nearby who might overhear.

"Well, whatever you think he's done, I'll vouch he didn't do it.

He's a good man, is Curuthannor. He'll kill a man in a fair fight, but he'd never stab him in the back."

"I hope you're right."

"I am. I swear it."

"Is he still here?"

"Nae, he left this morning. Said he was headin' home."

If he'd left this morning, then at least he hadn't opened the message here. There might still be hope that the contents hadn't been spread amongst those who would use it for ill.

Lhéwen tilted the mug of cider to her lips. There was only one solution. She would have to return to the high court to find out what happened for herself. If the message hadn't reached the king, she could deliver it in person. And she would find out why Curuthannor had lost his life to the trap she'd placed in his hand.

The cider turned sour in her mouth. If Curuthannor was dead, it was her fault. Faeliel may have been in command and reaped the benefits, but it was Lhéwen who reaped the blame.

CHAPTER 19

Daeturion wiped his hand on the silk of his robe, wiping away the remnants of the vision. Hindsight always felt like a personal invasion. As a child, he had felt cursed. He couldn't touch a soul without knowing their darkest, most terrifying secrets. There had been a time when he was forced to wear gloves or go mad from the visions.

In time, he had learned to control the ability, to wield it as a surgeon's knife. Centuries of training had honed his ability to parse the details of the past and See only what he wanted to see.

Like what the handmaiden was running from.

Faeliel had successfully seduced his father, which was neither surprising nor necessarily unwelcome. An alliance between the realms, one of parity and familial ties, would be good for the high elves and dark elves alike. Marriage had been a political strategy for eons.

He had Seen Faeliel's actions through the handmaiden's eyes, knew exactly what the princess had done, and how his father had responded. The women's reaction should have been pride at their success. Instead, the handmaiden had been shocked and dismayed by the princess's sudden seduction. It scared her. What Daeturion didn't know was why. It related to something deeper in her memory, but she had pulled her arm away before he could delve into the past to find it.

Daeturion turned to Tecindo. "Activate the web. We must know where she goes and who she sees."

The young scribe immediately and without question sprinted up the hall toward the courier station. The blood sidhe were the fastest of the greater fae. Tecindo and his brethren would spread the orders to every observer in Nalakadr before the handmaiden could walk a block through the city.

Daeturion would find out where the handmaiden was going, and why she ran from her own success.

CHAPTER 20

The portcullis groaned as the chains pulled tight, lifting the heavy defensive gate from its mooring. The suspicious guard's armored footsteps strode forward. Though his heart rate sped and his hands grew clammy with sweat, Curuthannor kept his head down. He wanted to run, or better yet fight, but he couldn't afford to offend or antagonize the man who might have his life at the end of his pike. If he did anything dramatic, he would be proving his own guilt.

A metal blade lifted his chin. "Hands behind your back. You will come with us."

"I am innocent, I swear it. I have been tricked. This is not my doing," Curuthannor pleaded with the men. "Please, just let me speak to someone. I will explain as much as I can."

"I want no explanations from you. My brother lies dead by your hand."

A constricting band of emotion wrapped itself around his chest. Gods above, he couldn't have worse luck. He couldn't even imagine what it would feel like to watch his own brother die in front of him, especially not in such a horrific manner. He would be devastated. Furious. And ready to kill the man who had dared harm his family.

Curuthannor's muscles shook, but he put his hands behind his back for the chains. This wasn't his fault, and he would prove it, but he wouldn't ignore another's pain.

"I am sorry for your brother."

The guard's armored foot smashed into Curuthannor's side. Tears sprang to his eyes, but he held them back while curled into a fetal position, clutching his ribs.

"Never mention my brother again, traitor."

Curuthannor couldn't respond as the pain froze all thought. It was all he could do to keep himself from whimpering. He didn't deserve the punishment, and yet if it weren't for him, the man's brother would still be alive.

Two soldiers ran out from the gatehouse, a length of stiff rope dangling from their hands. His arms were yanked behind his back. A boot pressed his face into the stone while the rough bindings were tied tight around his wrists. A fast but thorough search removed his weapons, including the two new knives in their oilskin wrapping.

"On your feet."

Curuthannor rolled to the side, gritting against the screaming pain. He lifted a foot, pressing down into the ground with as much grace and balance as he could muster.

Gods, he wished he'd asked more about the scroll and its message. The princess couldn't have intended to assassinate her own father, could she? That seemed unlikely, but then again, they'd always had a contentious relationship.

Had Lhéwen known? She must have. Perhaps? If the princess was truly trying to murder the king, would she have told her hand-maiden? But the spell was unique, not something just any spirit master could accomplish. It took a special set of abilities to imbue an object with enough power to drain a grown man to the point of death. The princess was an enervator like her father, but as far as he knew, she wasn't an enchantress. Was Lhéwen?

Striding through the gatehouse, Curuthannor kept his chin up. He wouldn't cower before whomever would judge his actions and his future. He had done no wrong, only performed his duty as a loyal citizen of the Upper Realm to the best of his ability.

They would have to recognize that. They had to.

Curuthannor stared at the dead man lying on the stone. He couldn't have been much older than Curuthannor, yet now he appeared to have died amongst the elders. Enervators could be harsh in the application of their abilities. There were times when Curuthannor had wished for the skill, but seeing the aftermath of this one's distant touch, he couldn't want it any longer. To have the responsibility for a person's existence in one's hands, be able to take a life without knowing whether the individual deserved it . . . It was a cruelty that would stain the soul, no matter how it was used.

At least with a blade, one was forced to look the opponent in the eyes, and *choose* to kill or not. It wasn't a random act, there were no unintended consequences. So long as you felt justified in your actions, as long as your purpose was for the good, you could go to sleep knowing you had chosen your own best path forward.

The scroll, meanwhile, lay inert on the ground, untouched by any of the other guards. The buzz of magic was gone, the intended action taken. The seal no longer held any power, yet Curuthannor was careful not to brush his foot against the parchment. Why risk it?

"Move it," the guard at his back pushed Curuthannor with the butt of his pike.

"Where are you taking me?"

"A death on palace grounds warrants immediate justice. King Othin doesn't tolerate violence inside these walls."

Right, Curuthannor thought. *As if 'immediate justice' wasn't also violent.* "You're taking me to the king?"

"Don't hope for mercy," the guard snarled.

The truth was, King Othin was known for enormous shifts in temperament. He could go from amenable and charismatic to violently angry between one breath and the next. It had only gotten worse since the death of the queen a half century before. She had balanced him, smoothed out the emotional highs and lows. Her death had been devastating to many in the realm, but none more so than her companion of two thousand years.

Curuthannor mentally braced himself, hoping for an agreeable mood.

The guards led him across the courtyard, down a narrow alley, to the postern at the southeast corner of the palace. Tall towers with golden spires seemed to lean over him in judgment.

He had done nothing wrong. Nothing whatsoever. He only needed the chance to prove his integrity.

Drawing near the heavily guarded servants' entrance, Curuthannor's gaze was drawn to the inlaid image of the crown on the sun that was the king's sigil. Human servants bustled in and out, their gazes downcast, out of fear or respect, Curuthannor didn't know. They didn't pause in their work even to stare at the spectacle of the high elf prisoner being escorted through their workspace.

Passing through the kitchens, one lone human woman dared pause kneading dough for the nightly feast. Dark circles weighed heavy beneath her eyes, and a deep scar crossed her left cheek, but the clear blue of her gaze met Curuthannor's for one brief moment in time. Immediately, the high elf chef who ran the kitchen slapped the poor woman's hands with a wooden spoon.

The servant returned to work without complaint.

Curuthannor shook his head. His father used humans in the smithy, but they were treated as respected employees, not abused as slaves. Tasked with the feeding of the forge fires and equipment maintenance, their jobs might not be interesting, but they were honorable. How could the king condone such treatment of another sentient being?

The guard stabbed him in the back with the blunt end of his pike, interrupting Curuthannor's musings. He had problems of his own to worry about right now, he needn't be distracted by the plight of the changelings.

The guards pushed Curuthannor up a narrow flight of stairs and into a mirror-lined hallway. Every surface seemed to be polished to a reflective shine, even the white marble floor. The guards heavy-soled boots echoed with each footstep, making it sound as if an entire army was invading, rather than six men and a prisoner.

Finally, they reached the two-story gold-plated doors that led to the throne room proper. Inside, the king would be waiting. Inside, Curuthannor would learn his fate.

Two of the guards pushed open the heavy doors. The remaining four shoved Curuthannor through the deceptively beautiful passage. Like the hallway outside, mirrors glazed the walls, but this time they were carefully positioned to blind the new arrivals.

Curuthannor's eyes burned, but he would not close them against the glare. He was stronger than the king's fear.

But not stronger than the king's ability to manipulate the energy around him.

King Othin sat on his shining golden throne, listening to the hushed words of some advisor or penitent. To all the world, he appeared a most beneficent ruler. Even Curuthannor felt himself drawn to confess his sins and trust in the wisdom of his king. It was only too bad he had nothing to confess, except perhaps his failure to procure the iron needed for his blade.

Curuthannor and his guards stood on the entry pedestal, waiting to be acknowledged. Through the glare of the reflected light, Curuthannor couldn't tell if the king had deigned to notice him. However, after several long, painful moments, the steward approached.

"What are you doing here?" the angular man hissed. He was tall and thin, with a pointy chin and bony shoulders that seemed to cave in around his narrow chest. Long fingers steepled in front of the concave space, their nails shaped into even longer points.

The guard whispered a few words in the man's ears. His eyes grew wide. One of his hands traveled up to cover his mouth.

"Oh dear. Oh my," the man mumbled. He turned and wound his way through the small assembly toward the throne. He pushed his way up the final few steps to whisper in the king's ear, interrupting whatever conversation His Majesty had been having with the courtier.

Curuthannor cringed internally. One didn't interrupt the king. The steward might have the privilege, but Curuthannor—the subject of the interruption—would pay the price.

King Othin sat up, his gaze snapping toward Curuthannor and the guards still waiting at the entry.

"Come forward," King Othin ordered.

The guards didn't hesitate, shoving Curuthannor toward the throne with force. Curuthannor stumbled, but kept his feet, striding with fading confidence. Intentionally or not, Lhéwen had set him up for a fall.

"Report," the king commanded. His voice boomed through the stiff room. With the exception of the robes and gowns worn by the courtiers, there wasn't a single soft cloth to dampen the sound.

The guard leader took two steps forward, then kneeled with his right elbow on his right knee and his head bowed. The butt of his pike knocked against the floor. Curuthannor followed suit before the other guards could force him into position.

King Othin was his ruler. He had no qualms about that. The man might be emotionally high strung, but he had led the Upper Realm to become the most powerful of the new faerie realms.

"Your Majesty," the guard intoned. "We caught a traitor attempting to infiltrate the castle. He was thwarted, but it cost the life of one of my men."

"I am innocent," Curuthannor interrupted. "I was sent by Princess Faeliel's handmaiden with a message intended for your hand. I had no knowledge of the enchantment on the seal."

King Othin shifted in his seat, the creak of the ancient wood ringing through the silent room.

"Where is my daughter?" he demanded, his voice cold.

Curuthannor's gaze snapped up to meet the king's. How could he not know where she was? He had sent her to treat with the dark elves. Hadn't he?

Curuthannor's heart sank at the realization that he was neck-deep and sinking in the mire of court politics. The last thing he wanted or needed.

"She is in the Shadow Realm, Your Majesty. I saw her two days ago at the court of the shadow king and met with her handmaiden just yesterday. I was under the impression it was a sanctioned trip, that the princess had been named your new ambassador to the Shadow Realm."

"The scroll he carried instantly drained my brother and second in command of his life's energy," the guard interjected. "Even if he speaks the truth of the princess's whereabouts, he cannot be trusted. He is an assassin."

"Rindae has crossed the line," King Othin snarled.

"The shadow king has done nothing," Curuthannor argued.

The king flicked his fingers and pulled all the energy from Curuthannor's muscles. He slid to the floor in a boneless heap, barely able to lift his arm.

"The man doesn't deserve that title, and we will hear no further lies. Send the assassin to the Pit," the king ordered. "We will decide what should be done with him later. Sound the trumpets. Put the kingdom on alert. Rindae will pay for his treachery."

"Mercy!" Curuthannor pleaded, but his voice came out a bare whisper.

The Pit. He couldn't go to the Pit. There was no coming back from there. He would be forgotten and drained.

The soldiers pulled him to his feet, one on either side dragging him by the armpits away from the throne and out of the king's line of sight.

"Your Majesty, please! Mercy! I am the son of Hatholdammon!"

His pleas fell on deaf ears. The king didn't even twitch at the name of the smith currently crafting his greatest weapon.

A richly dressed noble watched the proceedings with sympathetic eyes. With a start, Curuthannor realized he recognized the man, one of his father's more frequent customers. He couldn't recall the man's name, but he remembered the onyx encrusted dagger at his belt. His eldest brother, Namba, had laid the stone. He had been inordinately proud of the work.

"Sir, my father is Hatholdammon, Master Smith of Rómesse Gulch. Tell him what has befallen here. I am innocent. I swear it on all the gods."

The man's eyes flicked to the side even as the back of one of the guard's hands slammed across Curuthannor's cheekbone making his head ring. Curuthannor could only hope for sympathy to override fear.

CHAPTER 21

Curuthannor's feet dragged behind him. The king's energy drain was beginning to wear away with the distance from the throne, but Curuthannor wouldn't go willingly to the Pit. He wouldn't make it easy on the men who had so maliciously twisted the truth to punish Curuthannor for faults not his own.

One of the men rushed forward to open the lid of the hole they intended to throw him in. The Pit buzzed with intense magic. Even from a distance, Curuthannor could feel the malice emanating from its depths.

"No," he croaked, trying to bring his feet underneath himself to back pedal away from the void. "You cannot put me in there. I have committed no crime."

"The king has spoken." The suspicious guard slammed the butt of his pike into Curuthannor's kidney, as if to make his point clear. Pain spiked through Curuthannor's body. "You killed Alimno. You deserve to die in the Pit, and more."

Curuthannor grunted and bent over, wheezing, but used the opportunity to examine his surroundings. There were always options. Maybe not many. Maybe only one. But there would be some way to fight this.

Except, right now, there were six angry armed guards, and Curuthannor was injured with his hands tied. They had professional training. He had a father who drilled him in the weapons they crafted, but little real-world experience.

Still, he wouldn't go easily into the dark. Even the glimmering light of the Upper Realm sun would barely reach the bottom of that hole. He didn't know how he knew it, but he did. It had been designed to suffocate the spirit of any man who entered.

He wouldn't be one of them.

Slowly but surely, his spirit replenished his body. He had to do something. Anything. The legs were the easiest targets, the soldier's pikes nearly useless in close quarters.

As Curuthannor took more of his own weight, the guards' holds on his arms loosened. Not much, but it was enough.

Curuthannor dropped to the ground and rolled, surprising the suspicious guard before he could bring his weapon to bear. The guard tripped, falling over top of Curuthannor's prone body. Curuthannor didn't stop.

Scissor kicking at the feet of one of the bowmen, Curuthannor nearly brought the next man down, but the bowman was faster. He jumped, clearing the hurdle of Curuthannor's legs just in time. Curuthannor used the momentum to swing his legs underneath him and rise to his knees.

Sensing a strike from behind, Curuthannor turned his shoulder. A blow to the meat of his bicep knocked Curuthannor off balance and made his right arm go numb, but that didn't much matter since he still didn't have a blade or even a free hand.

Curuthannor dropped and rolled once more. An arrow bounced off the smooth stone of the courtyard. Curuthannor popped into a crouch. It was a move he had perfected playing with his brothers in the fields around their home as a child. It was a lot more painful to his knees as a grown man on a hard surface.

Ignoring the bruised kneecaps, Curuthannor lunged forward and swung his back leg around in a wide kick aimed at the waist of the nearest guard. The man grunted from the force, but his heavy metal armor absorbed most of the impact and gave Curuthannor yet another bruise to add to his collection.

Maybe he could use their weight against them. The hole was still open, the lid pulled back. A guard with a bow stood near the edge, arrow nocked but not yet aimed. Curuthannor ran forward, landing a two-foot kick to the man's stomach before he could react. He stumbled back and fell into the oubliette with a startled scream.

Curuthannor landed on his back, the wind knocked out of his lungs. A bladed pike swung down at his head. He rolled out of the way just in time.

The guards pressed in around him, every weapon bared and pointed at his chest or neck. With the guards working together, the last of Curuthannor's options had expired. The scarred leather armor he wore wouldn't block a crossbow bolt to the chest. He was going to die.

Three men with pikes thrust forward, their steps and blades in sync. Two bowmen stood behind, arrows drawn and ready to loose. A razor sharp pike edge sparked against the stone where Curuthannor had just been laying. He slid his body backward, avoiding the cut, but nearing the edge of the Pit.

The third bowman had fallen in already, but Curuthannor couldn't hear his voice. What had happened to the soldier? What would happen if he fell in as well?

Pikes thrust forward again. Curuthannor shuffled back a little more. He could feel the edge of the Pit with the side of his leg. He dared not look over his shoulder.

"By the king's command, you have been sentenced to the Pit. Enjoy your stay." The guard swung his foot forward. Curuthannor could do nothing. The heavy leather boot connected with his stomach, the impact sending him over the edge.

Nothing but air streamed around him. He screamed, but the

sound was deadened by the magic of the Pit. He fell and fell some more. A seeming eternity passed.

The crunch of bone against stone and more screaming pain. Darkness claimed him.

C uruthannor woke with his head pounding. His brain felt like it would explode through the eggshell of his cranium. His body ached, as if he had been placed on his father's anvil and beaten with the heavy hammer. Above him, a mere pin-prick of light showed the entrance to the hole in which he fell.

Curuthannor shivered. Cold permeated his leathers and sank deep into his bones. His breath blew out a puff of condensed air, yet his skin was damp and clammy. Combined with the mineral scent of stone and gentle rot of frigid earth, there was no mistaking he was in some kind of cave beneath—or perhaps within—the castle mound.

"Hello?" he called. His voice echoed back at him from a distance. The cavern must be enormous. So what happened to the guard he kicked into the hole before he fell? Where had he gone?

When no reply came to his call, Curuthannor faced the truth. He was going to have to find a way out on his own. The only good news was the rope binding his hands had come loose in the fight. With a few more twists of his wrists, the foul twine dropped to the floor. He gently prodded the area and hissed as the salt from his fingers stung the exposed raw skin.

Though dim, the room was too well lit for the sole illumination to come from above. He faced away from whatever light source had been provided. If he was going to find a way out, he needed to get that light. But first, he needed the motivation to move.

Curuthannor closed his eyes and grit his teeth. This was going to hurt. He rolled over with a gasp and tears blurred his vision. His ribs throbbed and pain contorted his body. He still couldn't even contemplate standing.

A lump beneath his hip reminded him of the last of his mother's travel cakes, still wrapped in their beeswax shells. When the guards had removed his weapons, they hadn't bothered with the soft pouch on his belt. For that small favor, he would forever be grateful.

With all of his injuries, removing the cake was no easy task, but with careful fingers he pried the crumbled sweet bread from its casing. The first bite was like a whole-body balm. Energy trickled through his veins, his mother's secret recipe not only soothing his injuries, but also soothing his spirit. Love had always infused her food, but perhaps for the first time he realized that she put more than flour and butter in her cakes, she also mixed in her own energy to fuel her family. The knowledge stunned his aching, homesick heart.

Pouring the last few crumbs into his mouth, he finally felt able to contemplate his surroundings. He wasn't healed, but his mind had cleared and his body would respond. He didn't know how long he'd already been in the Pit, but it was time to do something about it.

His gaze found the light on the wall, a flickering torch that danced in an unfelt breeze. The wall behind the flame, wriggled and squirmed. He blinked, clearing the sticky gunk from dry eyes. The wriggling didn't stop. Another blink, and a third, and finally he could focus on what he was seeing: a writhing mass of serpentine bodies with thousands of legs swirled around the torch.

Curuthannor scrambled upright. Gorge rose from his stomach, threatening to send him back to the ground, but he swallowed it down. He couldn't tear his gaze away from the mass of creatures huddled around the light. Or was it the heat?

Several deep breaths later, he felt like he almost had his body back under his control. He took a few tentative steps toward the torch on the wall. More of the worm-like creatures had gathered around the limited flame. At least, it seemed like there were more of them. Approximately the length of his forearm and the width of his finger, each of the creatures had hundreds, possibly thousands of legs. Luckily, they didn't seem to notice his scrutiny, focused as they were on the torch.

Curuthannor was going to have to remove it from the wall if he wanted to be able to see where he was going. It was the only light in the room.

He didn't think the creatures would appreciate that. Gods, he hoped they didn't have teeth.

Clenching his jaw to steel his resolve, Curuthannor reached for the wooden grip of the torch. One of the creatures ran up the length of the wood. Curuthannor snatched his hand away. As soon as the wyrm removed itself back into the mess of its brethren, Curuthannor grabbed the stick.

It wouldn't budge. A wyrm ran across the back of his fist. Tiny pinpricks like needles penetrated his hand in a rapid tattoo of pain. His hand began to go numb.

Curuthannor snapped his hand back, shaking off the creature. Luckily, it was one of the smaller ones and hadn't yet wrapped itself around his wrist. He swallowed. A scuttling sound along the floor made him drop his gaze. The wyrm had returned. Wriggling and squirming across the stone floor, it raced toward Curuthannor's booted foot.

Curuthannor stepped back, but the thing launched itself forward. It latched onto the boot and raced up the laces. Curuthannor shook his leg, but the creature held on. It circled around his ankle, climbing higher. The leather protected him from the piercing appendages, but the wyrm seemed determined. When it reached the top of his knee, Curuthannor used the back of his hand, the hand that had already been stung, to fling it off of him. The thing squealed.

A river of shining segmented bodies streamed down the wall, away from the torch, all heading for Curuthannor. He had their attention now. And he carried no weapons to stop them. Heavy leather boots could still do a lot of damage. Stomping his feet, he crushed their insect-like bodies beneath his heels. Hissing screams met his ears. He backed away, the light growing dimmer the farther he traveled.

A shriek—like the protective cry of a mother eagle—reverberated around the room. The rapid thud of thousands upon thousands of footsteps pounded from somewhere within the cavern. Unable to pinpoint the noise, Curuthannor didn't know where to turn, where to run. He couldn't find an escape.

The running steps grew closer. Curuthannor continued to stomp on the small wyrms that swarmed toward him. Unable to stop them all, they began to climb his body. He swatted those he could reach, but they circled around to his back. Something found its way beneath his leathers. Pins and needles pricked his skin through the thin cloth of his tunic. Numbness began to spread across his shoulders and down.

Curuthannor spun, adrenaline surging in his panic. His brain shut down. He wanted these things off him.

More pinpricks on his bicep. And his neck. He was being overwhelmed. Soon he would have no sensation left in his entire body. Control slipped away. A scream erupted from his throat.

The horror appeared. The dim light of the torch glinted off smooth scales nearly as tall as Curuthannor himself. Its rounded head opened to reveal layer upon layer of jagged teeth. Another screech pierced Curuthannor's brain, sending his hands to his ears. It made little difference.

The smaller wyrms scattered in front of their mother. Paralyzed in fear and the venom that must be coursing through his veins, Curuthannor could do little but watch as the wyrm approached.

What was this thing? He had never heard of nor seen a creature of this size. Was it an insect? A mutated dragon?

The thing had more legs than Curuthannor could have imagined in his worst nightmares. Each leg vibrated with rigid bristles like the whiskers on a mountain cat. The legs moved in a wave down the creature's body, sliding its torso along the ground with a grating sound.

The wyrm slowed its approach, as if examining Curuthannor and taking his measure. The elf was no match for the wyrm, not without his weapons, not with the numbness spreading throughout his body. He swayed on his feet, struggling to remain upright. His will to fight drained away.

The wyrm drew closer, its jaws opening in a blooming flower of razor sharp blades. It lunged forward, its speed unimaginable. The jaws latched onto Curuthannor's chest and shoulder. He screamed, but the sound faded away with the last of his spirit.

CHAPTER 22

"She's gone, Your Highness," Tecindo reported. His face remained perfectly neutral, a skill that Daeturion admired in his assistant. No matter what happened, no matter how dangerous the mission or how damaging the information, he never reacted. He was calm in all things.

"The handmaiden?"

"Yes, Your Highness. Her name is Lhéwen. After leaving our company in the hall, she went to the Crossroads and spoke with the bartender. She was asking about the merchant involved in that bar fight."

"Curuthannor." Daeturion remembered the man. According to his brother's memories, Curuthannor had been impressive in that fight, knocking down many of the king's warriors without taking a single life.

"Yes."

"But you say she's gone, now? Where did she go?"

"She opened a portal to the Upper Realm. She's gone back to her king."

"Is she a spy, do you think?"

"I think it's unlikely. If she is, then she wanted us to know where she was going. She made no effort to conceal her actions or evade watchers. If I had to venture a guess, I would say she was fleeing scared."

Daeturion thought back to her memories of the princess's seduction. Lhéwen hadn't been scared so much as horrified. There had been an urgency to her thoughts: something time sensitive. If only he knew what it was.

"Watch the return portals. She will be coming back."

"Are you certain, Your Highness? She seemed distraught."

"The princess is her only friend, her only family that remains. Whatever she's doing, she will return. She has no other choice."

A fact which Daeturion could use to his advantage.

CHAPTER 23

Sweat burned Rothruinil's eyes. Her arms ached. Her legs felt like jelly. She ignored it all and spun into a whirling series of kicks and strikes aimed at the straw-filled dummy on its wooden stand.

Ever since Valyaro's funeral, she had thrown herself into training. She woke up before dawn to be the first on the training grounds, and went to bed exhausted each night, closing her eyes to a dreamless sleep so she wouldn't have to think about Valyaro's last moments, or those of his wife.

Both had died horrific deaths, and somehow Rothruinil knew it had been her fault. She had been honored with the leadership of the fire dance. She shouldn't have pushed it so close to King Othin and his guard. She should have eased away, not increased the intensity of the dance. The other Tirnor had been following her lead.

With a wordless scream, Rothruinil jumped and landed a spinning hook kick to the dummy's head, tearing the stitches in the sack cloth and knocking the straw man to the ground in a puff of dust.

"Powerful, but sloppy," a familiar voice commented from behind her back.

"Father," she gasped, trying to catch her breath without letting him see her fatigue. "I didn't hear your approach."

"I expect not. You were a bit far gone in the moment."

Rothruinil grunted an assent while she found a rough towel to wipe her face.

"Are you all done berating yourself, then? Ready to do something a bit more productive with your time?"

"What do you have in mind?"

"Walk with me."

Unable to deny her father and king, and curious if he would finally reveal what had been decided about King Othin and the Upper Realm, Rothruinil fell into step as he led them away from the training grounds and toward the palace.

"King Othin is demanding our support against the dark elves."

"Demanding? What right does he have to demand anything? He drained Valyaro for no better reason than his own impatience."

"You're not wrong. It'll be a long while before we can trust him, if ever. But he is the high elf king and he is powerful. His army is skilled and well trained."

"As is ours."

King Thanûr nodded. "Aye. We can light fires. They can drain energy. Which do you think would win?"

Rothruinil's eyes narrowed. "Fire can turn their cities to dust."

"Before they drop our entire army to its knees?" Thanûr lifted his eyebrows. "Perhaps we would win. Perhaps not. It's hard to say. It's not something I'd like to be testing now, though. I'd prefer to wait until we have an advantage. Strike when they're least expecting it, not when they're ready for us."

"You can't seriously be considering aligning the Summer Realm with the high court. That way lies madness. I'm certain of it."

"Even so, King Othin may be the aggrieved, not the aggressor."

"What are you saying?"

"King Othin is convinced—so he says—that King Rindae kidnapped his daughter. He believes she's been stolen away to the Shadow Realm."

"I don't believe it."

King Thanûr shrugged. "Maybe not, but the high elves can't lie. It's a habit born of honor and a population that includes truthsayers."

"That doesn't mean he can't, just that he won't, or at least that he shouldn't."

Thanûr dipped his chin in acknowledgment. "Still, a grieving man will do terrible things. I won't be forgiving him, but I can still empathize."

"You can't be serious."

"If what he says is true and our positions were reversed, I'd do most anything to bring you home. It's something you won't understand until you have a child of your own."

Rothruinil pursed her lips. To have a child, one had to first find a connection that was more than physical. Spirit and soul, as much as biology, had to be involved. Even then, it was a precious responsibility to bear children amongst the long-lived elves. Somehow, she doubted she would experience it.

"For now, I have only agreed to send someone to look for her. Someone who can observe without drawing attention, someone who can think and act both rationally and quickly. Someone who has the sense to walk away from a fight, but can defeat anyone who forces her hand."

Rothruinil lifted an eyebrow and smirked. "I suppose you had someone in mind."

King Thanûr smiled. "Find Princess Faeliel. Report back what you discover. I won't needlessly send our warriors into battle, but if the Shadow King has broken trust, it'll be war on his hands."

"What does mother think of all this?"

King Thanûr grimaced. "She and I are not in full agreement."

Rothruinil lifted an eyebrow. "She would join King Othin?"

"She would keep you here, to learn to rule from the safety of a throne rather than the dangerous reality of a battlefield. She has never been happy that you chose the way of the Tirnor."

"The clans will never accept my leadership if I don't prove myself capable."

"Agreed."

"I will go alone." It was a statement, not a question.

"Aye. You'll go alone, and you'll report directly to me, and only to me."

"Very well. I'll leave on the morrow. Do we have any people in the region I can contact?"

"There is a baker near the portal. He has lived in the Shadow Realm most of his life, but he remains loyal to the sun god. Do not share information with him, but he'll give you a place to stay. Otherwise, do what you can to remain anonymous."

"I will honor your faith in me."

"Always." King Thanûr wrapped an arm around his daughter and squeezed her shoulder. If there was one thing Rothruinil never doubted, it was that her parents loved her.

"**Y**ou know you don't have to do this." Queen Norgeledil sat on Rothruinil's bed while she packed a bag. "It was your father's idea, but he's not always right."

"We can't trust Othin."

"King Othin's proven his ability, and more, his willingness, to drain our people. If we defy him, he'll destroy us."

"You think so little of us? Have we been training for nothing?" Rothruinil shoved two tunics and a breast wrap in the satchel with a pair of leggings and length of bright colored cloth that could be used as a dress or a shawl or a hood, depending on the need. She would have to do her best to blend with the Shadow Realm populace, but she didn't quite know what that would mean.

"That's not what I said."

"No? But you want to surrender at the first sign of possible defeat, before we've even had a chance to test our mettle! The Tirnor are strong. We don't have to bow to the wishes of another king."

"I'll not risk our people in a war we cannot win."

"And who says we cannot win?" Rothruinil shook her head. Her mother was acting as if Othin was all-powerful, all-seeing, practically a god. "Othin is one man, one cruel, power-hungry man, but he'll not place his life on the front. Even for his trip here, he was surrounded by guards. He can only take one life at a time. We could reach him."

"And what if that life is yours? I'll not risk *you* against another king." Queen Norgeledil twisted her hands in her lap and turned her gaze down. It was a rare demonstration of vulnerability. "I haven't always understood your choices, but I've accepted them. But you shouldn't be going into dark elf territory just to prove a point."

"I'm not. If we must choose a side, I'll make sure we choose right."

"What if there's no right side?" Norgeledil reached forward and clasped Rothruinil's hands. "You were born after the colonization. You don't remember the Origin, or the wars that raged between resource-starved factions. Often there isn't a right side. Often the only right side is your own side."

"Then we'll know that, too. We can stand on our own. We don't need any of them!"

Norgeledil stroked the back of Rothruinil's hand. "You're still so young. We cannot cut ourselves off from our brethren, no matter how distant they may be."

"I feel like we're talking in circles." Rothruinil pulled her hand away. "Father has asked me to go, and I'll go. I'll do my part to lead our people on the right path."

Norgeledil's shoulders sagged. "Then you go without my blessing, but with my love. Be safe, my daughter."

On those words, Norgeledil stood and left the room, taking her doubts and her worries with her. Rothruinil watched her go, a momentary thread of remorse nearly forcing the words to call her mother back, but she remained strong. She believed in what she was doing, even if her mother didn't. The queen would see the value when Rothruinil returned with the facts of Othin's deception, for she was certain the high elf king was twisting the truth to suit his needs.

CHAPTER 24

The silvery portcullis of the western gate shone pink and gold in the setting sun. For a moment Lhéwen admired the sparkling rainbow of light it cast across the bridge . . . That is, until she realized its meaning.

Why was the castle barred? In all her years at the palace, she'd never seen the gates closed except when a visiting dignitary was in residence. For the safety and security of their guests, the king insisted the gates be barred, or at least that's what he claimed. But otherwise . . .

Lhéwen wracked her brain, trying to think of any other reason for the closure, but nothing came to mind. The king must be hosting someone important. It was a good sign that the king was maintaining his schedule, but she hoped that the guards would recognize her and let her pass.

Two tasks lay before her. First, she needed to tell the king of the princess's plan to remain longer in the Shadow Realm. She would need to choose her words carefully, or risk the king's wrath, but the reasoning was sound.

Second, she needed to uncover what had happened to

Curuthannor and the original message for the king. If he had died by the touch of the seal, she would find him. If someone had already found and reported the body, she might be able to claim it as a relative or something. She only hoped he could still be identified. The princess's magic was as much a curse as a blessing when used as a weapon.

She approached the gate and lowered her hood. Now that she'd passed through the press of the marketplace, she didn't need to worry about being accosted. In fact, it would be important for the guards to recognize her immediately.

"Halt," came a voice from the barbican. "Identify yourself."

Odd. While there was always a stately formality about the guardsmen, it wasn't usually harsh. Not like this.

"I am Lhéwen, handmaiden to princess Faeliel. I come with a message and must speak with the king."

"No one is to disturb the king."

Lhéwen took another step forward.

"Move away from the gate," the voice ordered, its tone growing fierce.

"What happened? Why are the gates barred?"

"That is no concern of yours."

Lhéwen ground her teeth, wanting to stamp her foot in impatience. She'd spent most of her life avoiding notice and carefully staying out of the limelight. Unlike the other handmaidens, she never wanted to be the center of attention, never tried to use her position in Faeliel's retinue to increase her own standing and visibility. But right this second she needed the guard to recognize her, to let her through the gate despite whatever had them all on alert.

"I am the personal companion of the princess. I must complete my mission."

"Then I suppose you have a scroll to hand the king as well?"

"What?" Could he be talking about Curuthannor's message?

"All missives will be processed through the messenger corps

and examined for malicious enchantments. You may proceed to the eastern gate and submit for inspection there."

"I don't have time for that," Lhéwen replied. "I must return to Her Highness as soon as possible. Surely, you recognize me?"

She'd been through these gates with the princess enough times, that even with her bland clothing and careful misdirections, the always alert guards would know her. They must. This gate had been complicit in so many of the princess's schemes, every guard had been bribed on more than one occasion. They wouldn't deny her now.

Unless . . .

"How long have you been stationed here?" Lhéwen asked, letting her ire bleed into her voice. "The princess will not be pleased by your obstruction."

"The princess has been kidnapped. If you claim to be her handmaiden, you should know this."

"What? The princess hasn't been kidnapped! I was just with her in the Shadow Realm. She was sent as an envoy to King Rindae."

The guard stepped forward toward the portcullis, the sun reflecting off golden armor with the king's sigil emblazoned on the chest.

"Traitor!" He shouted. "Guards to arms! Arrest this woman!"

Lhéwen gasped, her hand rising to cover her mouth.

"I am not a traitor!" Lhéwen replied, her eyes growing wide and panic pressing its talons into her heart. Traitors were sent to the Pit, a lightless spiritless void that drained its prisoners of their very will to live. If the prisoners were ever allowed out, they would be little more than walking, talking vegetables, their very essence drained from their bodies.

The portcullis rose from its moorings, the guard's expression fierce and determined. He wouldn't recognize her. He wouldn't listen. These guards were new, and they were serious. They were not her allies.

She turned and ran back the way she had come, toward the

westernmost hill, the hill of the sellswords and armorers. It was not her favorite marketplace—the weavers district took that honor, for obvious reasons—but it would do well to hide her. She didn't think the guards would chase her into the crowds of heavily armed men and women.

"Stop that woman!"

Then again . . .

Lhéwen ducked beneath a brawny arm and crawled under a table. She pushed her way out of the back side of one tent only to find herself in another. The merchant spun toward her, knife in hand and surprise in his eyes. He didn't move to stop her, but Lhéwen stayed as far as possible from him as she skirted around the table and out into a new street.

She ran down the road, away from the palace, taking random left and right turns, trying to put distance between herself and the pounding steps behind her. Finally, when she could no longer hear the guards, she found a darker than average corner behind a blacksmith's repair tent to hide in.

Lhéwen paused to listen for pursuit. She couldn't hear anything other than the pounding of hammer against steel. She slid into a sweaty, panicked heap and tried to catch her breath.

It didn't matter what the guard said or what anyone believed. She needed to get inside to find out what was going on and to set the record straight.

Thinking through her bag of trinkets and small enchantments she carried with her everywhere, she decided now might be the time to turn truly invisible. Lhéwen opened her belt pouch and fished through the contents. The charm she sought was a pendant crafted in the shape of a stylized gust of wind made out of twisted golden wire. A jeweler's apprentice had been practicing his craft one day when the princess had visited his master, and Lhéwen had fallen in love with the rough bauble. The apprentice had been so pleased by her praise, he'd given it to her as a gift.

Kindness always had value.

Unsure of what to do with the pendant—which was not refined enough for the princess to wear but warmed Lhéwen's heart—Lhéwen had used it for her own practice. Inspired by the swirling image and the princess's dismissal of its beauty, she'd created a charm that would turn the eye away, allowing the wearer to pass through a crowd like the wind through the trees. Or at least, that's how she'd romanticized it. She supposed it was really a simple 'do not see me' spell. Probably not even a sophisticated one by the standards of the great college masters. Lhéwen could tie spirit magic to an object to create enchantments, but had little manipulative skill of her own. Without the greater skill of another to twist the spirit, Lhéwen could only muddle with her own limited abilities.

Still, the charm worked. At least for a little while.

It only took a moment to activate with a puff of breath across the coils. The pendant vibrated with energy, and then went still. Even holding it, Lhéwen had a hard time looking at the metal that she logically knew lay in her hand. She pinned it to her cloak.

Now to test its effectiveness.

Passing near a small food vendor's cart, Lhéwen decided she was hungry. She wouldn't debase herself by stealing, but if she could take a flat bread, spread the butter and honey on one side, and place a coin in front of the baker without his noticing, she would consider the experiment a success.

The baker picked up the coin, looking around. He held it up with a question in his eyes, but not once did his gaze register the woman standing directly in front of him.

Lhéwen grinned, licking the last of the sticky sweet concoction from her fingers.

It was time to try her luck at the gate. The problem still remained, how to get them to open the portcullis. She didn't have a good answer for that, but she'd think of one on the way to the bridge.

She needn't have worried. Luck was on her side. She arrived at the bridge just as a wagon laden with shining weapons and armor was crossing to the castle. She hurried to catch up, giving the giant draft horse a pat on its rear. The animal snorted, but otherwise didn't fuss. She'd found that the charm had little effect on animals since their sense of hearing and smell was so much better than the greater fae who generally relied on sight and touch to understand their surroundings.

"Halt!" the guard at the gate commanded, just as he'd ordered Lhéwen. "Identify yourself."

Apparently, they followed a set script.

"I am Hatholdammon, Master Smith of Rómesse Gulch. I'm here with a delivery of arms for the king's guard."

Lhéwen frowned. Where had she heard that name before?

The guard turned back to speak with someone in the shadows. Within a heartbeat, a human runner was sprinting across the bailey toward the castle. Lhéwen admired his hustle, even if his speed was lacking compared to the elves.

The guard directed his gaze back toward Hatholdammon. "You are expected. You may proceed directly to the servant's gate. The arms master will meet you there."

"Certainly," Hatholdammon replied. He pulled on the horse's lead as the first portcullis groaned and was lifted out of the way.

The cart proceeded beneath the barbican, Lhéwen along with it, but the second portcullis wasn't immediately lifted.

The sour-faced guard approached. "Apologies, but I must examine the wares before you are allowed further into the castle. Security precaution in this time of war."

Time of war? When had the king declared war?

"That is understandable. I have nothing to hide," Hatholdammon replied. The man wore a scarred leather vest and trousers, but stood with the poise of a noble. His bare arms were corded with thick muscle, unusual for a high elf, but it made sense for a smith. He crossed his arms over his chest, and his biceps bulged even more. He wore a longsword on his left hip, and an axe on his right. An odd combination to Lhéwen's mind, but then, she was used to seeing the preening nobles with their decorative blades, not a man who was likely as skilled in the use of his weapons as he was in their creation.

The master smith from Rómesse Gulch. Didn't Curuthannor say that he was from Rómesse Gulch?

Lhéwen glanced at the man once more. He had the same blue eyes and strong chin as Curuthannor. They even had a similar build, if a bit thicker with muscle. Could this man be his father?

The blood drained from Lhéwen's face. She was truly glad he couldn't see her expression. His son was dead, and he didn't yet know it. When would he find out? *How* would he find out?

Meanwhile, the guard finished his inspection, finding nothing out of the ordinary in the cart. Every time his gaze ventured toward Lhéwen, his eyes flicked to the side. He wasn't looking for a second elf, so he didn't see one. Lhéwen didn't make a sound to betray her presence.

The second portcullis opened and the guard waved them through. "Direct to the servant's gate. No diversions."

"I heard you the first time," Hatholdammon replied, his expression hooded.

Lhéwen had no doubt that this was a dangerous man when he wanted to be. She kept close to his cart and the horse, hoping the sound of their movement would conceal the sound of her own footsteps on the hard stone courtyard. The tapping of her heels could give her presence away if she wasn't careful.

"You can come out now," Hatholdammon said, keeping his gaze locked straight forward as he continued to lead the horse toward the guards barracks.

Lhéwen wasn't sure she'd heard him correctly, or if he was referring to her. How could he know she was here?

"I can sense the enchantment. I won't give you away. Not yet, in any case. Tell me why I should continue to protect your invisibility."

"I am the princess's handmaiden, but they wouldn't let me

through the gate," Lhéwen whispered. No one appeared to be nearby, but she couldn't trust that the king's pet spies didn't fly overhead. "I don't know why. But I must see the king."

Hatholdammon's jaw clenched. He turned to face her directly, his furious gaze connecting and then sliding away as the enchantment pushed at his sight. "You . . ." he snarled, his face drawing down into hard lines. "Guards!" he shouted.

"No, wait, please let me explain." Lhéwen backed away. Her enchantment was still hiding her from view, but if the guards began searching for her in earnest, their gaze would not be deterred. Not completely.

"You framed my son for treason."

"No! That is a lie. I am sorry that he died, but he should not have opened the message."

A door slammed. The pounding of armor-clad running footsteps thundered across the courtyard as a squad of guards poured out of the barracks.

"He's not dead," Hatholdammon replied. "He's paying for *your* crimes in the Pit. I'll see that you take his place."

Relieved that Curuthannor was alive, that he hadn't been the one to break the seal, it took a beat or two to realize what he had said. Curuthannor was in the Pit. Which meant he'd been sentenced for treason. Which meant the guards at the gate hadn't been exaggerating when they threatened to send her there as well.

The blood drained from her face. The palace guards were nearly upon them. She had to turn away. She couldn't be caught. She wouldn't survive the Pit. Her will wasn't strong enough.

"I never intended for this," she said, stepping backward toward the west gate once more. "If the king had opened the missive, nothing would have happened. Only the hands of another would trigger the spell."

"What do you mean?"

The guards were only twenty lengths away. There was no time.

"I'm sorry," she whispered. "I never meant for anyone to get hurt. He shouldn't have opened it."

Lhéwen sprinted for the gate, but the inner portcullis had already dropped closed. She spun, looking for a way out, or at least a better place to hide.

She couldn't run to the palace. Someone would be sure to spot her, and it seemed she was unwelcome. Even if the other handmaidens were still residing inside the castle walls—which was unlikely given the princess's departure—they couldn't be trusted to keep her secret. If anything, they would use her as a pawn to increase their own stature at court.

The other gates would also be barred, and she knew none of the guards by name. The princess had always preferred the west gate, and it seemed the guard stations had been recently rotated. She couldn't count on a sympathetic release.

The guardsmen were speaking with Hatholdammon, who pointed in her general direction. Frantic now, Lhéwen knew there were just moments before the enchantment failed and she was spotted. Her only hope lay in the stables near the north gate. The horses wouldn't protest her presence, and she might find a shadowy corner in one of the stalls to hide in until nightfall. It was her best chance.

Keeping near the wall where she hoped the silvery gray of her travel cloak combined with the fading enchantment would help her blend with the stone, Lhéwen ran toward the stables and the protection of her equine friends.

CHAPTER 25

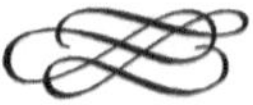

The guards ran off, chasing the girl across the courtyard. Hatholdammon had given them what help he could, but her words rang in his ears.

If the king had opened the missive, nothing would have happened.

Hatholdammon was a simple man, unused to court politics, but he knew the truth when he heard it. It might not be a magical sense, but he trusted his instincts. The woman hadn't intended for Curuthannor to fall.

Intent hardly mattered. Only the consequences.

He led trusty Tinnuroch toward the rear entrance of the palace grounds, where the arms master would find him. Normally, Hatholdammon would have sent one of the humans to deliver the first batch of weaponry to the king's guard, but Lord Rembon had arrived just in time. With the news of Curuthannor's sentence, Hatholdammon had no choice but to leave the running of the forge to Curuthannor's brothers and plead with the king.

The only question was whether the king would see him. The king might have commissioned the greatest sword known to elven-kind and placed an order large enough to keep the smith running for decades, but that didn't mean he would deign to hear him. Tunniel had warned that he was as likely to get thrown in the Pit with Curuthannor as he was to change the king's mind, but he had to try.

Hatholdammon hoped Arms Master Amath would be grateful for the early delivery of the soldier's arms and find it in his heart to assist a grieving father. Hatholdammon knew the man a little, though he hadn't visited in many years. He preferred the heat of his fires to the discomfort of travel. Still, the arms master should recognize him on sight, and hopefully had enough good will to bring him before the king.

Hatholdammon brought the wagon to a halt just outside the door, while Tinnuroch stamped his foot in impatience. The horse had liked the girl. Hatholdammon thought that was another strong point in her favor. Tinnuroch wasn't particularly jumpy, but he was known to fidget when strangers were near. Instead he'd settled right down when she'd tucked herself in next to his shoulder. He worried over the situation a bit while he waited for Amath, but ultimately decided the girl had caused Curuthannor's fall, and she would have to defend herself.

Amath shoved open the door with a boot, startling Hatholdammon from his reverie. The man must have been interrupted from a nap or something, because he was still lacing on a hardened leather gauntlet.

"Have you brought my gear?" the man asked without looking up.

"I have," Hatholdammon replied.

Amath's gaze snapped to Hatholdammon's face and he paused, surprise written across his expression. "Ah! Hatholdammon. I am surprised to see you. I thought you would send your man."

"Normally, I would." Hatholdammon debated how quickly to broach the subject of Curuthannor's imprisonment. "I felt today warranted a personal visit."

"Yes, it was quite a large order. The king will be pleased at the speed of this first delivery."

Hatholdammon grunted. Court etiquette was not his strong suit. He knew the rules—most of them, anyway—but he couldn't seem to bring himself to talk in circles around a subject. His sons were much better at that, thanks to the training of their mother. Tunniel was the second daughter of a low—but ambitious—noble. He had been livid when she'd chosen Hatholdammon as a lifemate. Not that it mattered much now. But she'd had a good influence on Hatholdammon as well. He could fumble along a little.

"I had several good blades in storage and only needed to sharpen them. But that's not truly why I'm here."

"Oh?"

"You have my son."

"Apologies, I'm not sure what you mean."

Hatholdammon gritted his teeth and blew a forced breath out his nose to calm the fury that threatened to boil over.

"Curuthannor is my son. You threw him in the Pit."

Amath lifted his hands and leaned back. "That was not me, though I heard about the tragedy. A gate guard was killed, you know. A young man drained to old age and death within a few heartbeats. But I did not know the killer was your son. And it was King Othin himself who gave sentence."

"Take me to the king. I must speak with him. This was not Curuthannor's doing."

"That is not how it works. You know that."

"Perhaps. But you can help me. Curuthannor is a good boy. Loyal. He was deceived."

Even if that girl had spoken the truth about her own intentions, she had still been a party to the spell that killed a man.

"You don't know that."

"I do. I would stake my life on it. I would request Sanyaro perform a truthseeking."

"It may already be too late. He has been in the Pit for more than a day. His spirit may already be broken."

"Not my son. He is not so weak as that." Hatholdammon let all of his love and grief pour into his words along with his conviction that Curuthannor was innocent. Curuthannor was strong. Stronger than his brothers in some ways. He would not be easily drained of his will.

Amath sighed. A frown furrowed his brow. He was going to do it.

"Come with me. We will take the weapons to the central armory, and if the king isn't locked away with his advisors, I will see if I can plead your case."

Hope bloomed in Hatholdammon's chest.

"I make no promises, however. If the king is in the war room, there is little I can say or do to help."

"Understood. It is appreciated."

Amath called out for a stable boy and four brawny human servants to help with the horse and carry the load, and together they proceeded through the servants' entrance of the castle and up a narrow flight of stairs to the armory on the first floor.

After cataloging the weapons and placing them in their temporary holdings, Amath dismissed the humans to their regular duties and led Hatholdammon toward the throne room.

"He will not be pleased to see you, nor like having his decisions questioned."

"I am aware, but I must try. Curuthannor deserves a chance. If Sanyaro says he did it, then he did. But he must be given an opportunity to defend himself."

"As luck would have it, Sanyaro is here. Sadly, he arrived just bells after Curuthannor was sentenced, otherwise he might have been called to advise the king on his decision."

"Perhaps." They both knew that was unlikely.

The two great men had been rivals for years. Even Sanyaro's self-exile did little to diminish their antagonism. Why he cared what happened here in the Upper Realm after taking a human woman as a lifemate, Hatholdammon hardly knew, but love did funny things to men.

The throne room doors stood open, with a view of the king in his golden throne, surrounded by cronies and advisors. It didn't look like a military gathering, however. Most of the men at the king's side were soft nobles, the kind of sycophants who would toady to any little thing the king said, which was why the king enjoyed having them at his side.

The court steward stood by the door, ready to announce new arrivals, a good sign that the king was open to petitioners.

"Arms Master Amath humbly presents Hatholdammon, Master Smith of Rómesse Gulch." The steward's voice rang through the assembled crowd, echoing off the polished marble and stone of the long hall.

The nobles of the hall turned to face the newcomers, their expression a mix of bored neutrality, casual interest, and mild hostility. Only two faces appeared reasonably friendly: Sanyaro, who stood at the base of the king's dais to his right side, and Lord Rembon, who gave an encouraging nod.

Amath strode down the three steps from the entry, Hatholdammon a half-step behind. The walk down the central aisle felt interminable. They finally stopped three lengths away from the dais. Amath bowed from the waist and Hatholdammon quickly followed suit.

The pair had been introduced, which meant it was the king's prerogative to address them, or make them wait. Tunniel had made this much very clear: do not seek to engage the king on the throne. Wait to be addressed. If it took three bells, it didn't matter, you waited in deference to the king.

Though he heeded the lesson, impatience ate away at his psyche while the muscles in his lower back began to throb. How much longer would the king make them debase themselves?

Finally, footsteps approached from the king's right, soft footsteps, shod in some kind of animal skin that Hatholdammon didn't recognize. It certainly wasn't the tough mammoth hide he was used to. And the man's robe was of fine quality, but plain, with no ornamentation on the hem.

"You come to plead for your son, yes?" Sanyaro asked. His voice was mellifluous and kind, but strong. Hatholdammon dared a glance up to see bright blue eyes staring at him with a knowing expression. Dark blond hair was braided back from the sides of his head, a single feather trapped in its weave.

Highly irregular.

"I have," Hatholdammon replied. If this truly was Sanyaro, the man already knew what was to happen.

"Good. Then we can finally begin." An enigmatic smile twisted Sanyaro's lips.

Hatholdammon quirked an eyebrow. If Sanyaro had known this was all going to happen, why couldn't he have arrived sooner to prevent Curuthannor's imprisonment in the first place?

Sanyaro chuckled quietly. "The future is a fickle beast," he said, as if responding to Hatholdammon's unasked question. "Sometimes the right outcome must wait for the wrong action."

Foreseers and their cryptic remarks. Hatholdammon had only ever been to one other oracle, but she had been similarly vague in her predictions. He'd sworn off any attempt at knowing the future after that. There was no point.

Sanyaro turned toward the king and cleared his throat. "Your Majesty, I believe there is a matter of utmost importance that must be addressed."

"Oh?" the king asked, glancing down at Hatholdammon and Amath for the first time. "And what might that be, most honored guest in our realm?"

"This man has a petition that may help us intercept your missing daughter."

CHAPTER 26

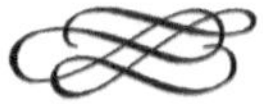

amn Sanyaro to the depths of the wastelands.

King Othin forced his breathing to remain steady and his expression implacable even as he seethed. The meddling augur should have wasted away centuries ago. He no longer belonged amongst the ranks of the powerful.

Unfortunately, Othin was the only one who seemed to realize it. Sanyaro was powerful enough to keep the other realm leaders from challenging him, but soon they would see his limitations.

Othin strode down the steps of the dais toward the smith, Hatholdammon. The man's eyes widened in fear, revealing the white around a pale blue iris before he quickly dropped his gaze to the floor. At least he knew how to show some respect, and more than a little fear. Now he would need to show a little sense.

"What do you know of our daughter? Where has the shadow king taken her?"

"I . . . I do not know, Your Majesty," Hatholdammon stammered. "His lordship is incorrect, I am not here with information regarding the princess."

That was a relief. Othin had been quick to drop Curuthannor in

166

the Pit before he could reveal any unwanted information of Faeliel's whereabouts. It would be much easier to control the narrative if Othin could spin the truth to meet his own goals.

"I am here to request a truthseeking for my son, Curuthannor, who you recently imprisoned in the Pit."

That wouldn't do.

Othin couldn't have the truth revealed. He needed his nobles to believe *his* truth. But they also needed to believe he was doing everything in his power to reclaim Faeliel.

"Lord Garamaen Sanyaro, what is the meaning of this? You say you will help intercept our daughter, but the smith denies any knowledge."

Sanyaro visibly suppressed a smirk. "Not long ago you asked why I had arrived unannounced to your court. I told you my purpose would be revealed in time. Hatholdammon, please restate your petition, and Your Majesty, please take the opportunity to listen."

Othin almost growled at the impudence, but held himself in check. Sanyaro was trouble, but he was still an elder, if only by a few centuries. He was also immune to Othin's emotional manipulation, but the smith wasn't.

"Well?" Othin demanded, lacing his words with a spike of fear to encourage the man's silence.

Hatholdammon hunched over further. Success. The man wouldn't say another word.

"Our time has been wasted," Othin said, pivoting on a silk-clad toe. "Get back to your forge and finish our sword."

"I have come to request a truthseeking for my son, Curuthannor, recently imprisoned in the Pit."

Othin's gaze flicked over to Sanyaro, who smiled and lifted his eyebrows in smug satisfaction. He'd interfered. He'd used his power to counteract Othin's. Othin was sure of it. The man was a canker in the midst of his glittering hall.

Othin couldn't confront Sanyaro, not without losing faith with his lords, but he could still physically intimidate the lesser blight in his house. He walked a measured circle around Hatholdammon's kneeling form, glaring at the back of the man's head. "Your time would be better spent on Thúlentur. Your son killed one of our guard. He has been convicted of treason. Perhaps we should look more carefully at those closest to him as well."

"That cannot be true. Your Majesty, I must formally request he be given an opportunity to prove himself innocent. If he is guilty, even I will not protest banishment to the Pit. I and my family are loyal citizens. We have always been loyal citizens. I do not believe my son had malicious intent when he arrived at Your Majesty's gate." Hatholdammon's words spilled from his mouth in an unstoppable torrent.

It was more than likely Sanyaro's influence, giving the man enough courage to speak against his king's edicts. If Sanyaro hadn't been present, Hatholdammon would have joined his son in the Pit.

"Then why is a highly skilled guard dead?"

"I do not know, Your Majesty. It is why I request a truthseeking. It is the only way to know for certain if Curuthannor's story is true."

"Your Majesty, if I may interject," Lord Garamaen Sanyaro interrupted.

"You have already done so. But please, do not feel beholden to protocol in our throne room." Othin couldn't help the sarcasm that dripped like syrup from his words.

Sanyaro didn't react, damn him.

"Curuthannor is the last person in this realm to have seen Princess Faeliel. As a part of the truthseeking, I would be required to determine if Curuthannor had been in the princess's presence, and if so, I would be able to see whatever he saw at that time. If Your Majesty allows it, there may be opportunity to learn of the Shadow Realm's intentions."

Othin let those words hang in the air for a few heavy moments as he returned to the throne. There it was. Cornered by Sanyaro's interference. He couldn't silence the smith or his son any longer. He would have to control the narrative in another way.

"At worst, you bring him here for the truthseeking, he is proven a traitor beyond a doubt, and he is returned to the Pit where the nildhoggr may deal with him," Sanyaro pushed.

Othin rested his hands on the golden arms of the gilded throne and straightened his spine. He stared at Lord Garamaen Sanyaro, knowing the hate in his blood was evident in his gaze, but unwilling to quench it.

He had no choice but to relent. "Sanyaro, it is most fortuitous that you have arrived. Send for Curuthannor, son of Hatholdammon. Let us see what information he might reveal."

CHAPTER 27

Lhéwen had always had an affinity with animals. It wasn't an earth magic ability to communicate or control their behavior, as some of the woodelves were reported to have, but they seemed to enjoy her company. Especially the horses. Her father had been a breeder before his fading, and Lhéwen had often worked at his side. If her magical enchantments hadn't been so strong and her service to the princess hadn't been required, she might have taken over the farm after his death.

Regardless, the skill had served her well over the years, never more so than in this moment. It helped that she was already familiar with the palace stables, since she was usually called upon to ready the mounts for the princess when she wanted to venture out on horseback. It hadn't happened nearly enough for Lhéwen's liking, but they knew her by sight—or more importantly right now —by smell.

The horses whuffled in greeting when she arrived, their fuzzy-soft muzzles reaching over stall doors to ask for a pat or a treat. Lhéwen couldn't provide either. Not with the guards closing in behind her.

"Shhh," she urged, racing to the fourth stall on the left and her favorite mare. The horses immediately quieted, though their ears pricked forward in curiosity.

The dapple gray horse was too dark for the princess's liking, and too rambunctious, but she had a mischievous streak that appealed to Lhéwen. She only hoped the mare was in fine spirits today and would understand her need.

With haste, Lhéwen opened the latch and slid the door just enough to let herself inside, then silently closed and locked it behind her. Giving Lómerocco a quick pat on her withers, Lhéwen pressed herself into the feed corner near the front of the stall but out of sight of anyone walking past. To further hide, she spread the golden hay over herself as best she could. Dust prickled at her nose, but at least she didn't have to crawl under the dirty straw in the back.

Lómerocco watched Lhéwen's actions with an equine expression of amused concern, then snorted. Her ears swiveled forward and back. She poked her head over the stall door to look down the aisle, then turned back to Lhéwen with a question in her eyes.

"I need to hide," Lhéwen whispered. "They can't find me."

Lómerocco bobbed her head as if understanding, then turned her body so her rear end faced the door. The horse shook her head, then craned her neck around to watch the entrance with one soft brown eye.

The external door slammed open and booted feet thundered down the central aisle.

"She must be in here. Find her," a gruff voice commanded.

The horses whinnied their displeasure as one by one, the stall doors were opened and searched. They were all too well trained to cause serious harm, but at least one booted toe was stepped on.

Lhéwen grinned upon hearing the cursing, but was careful to avoid moving and give herself away. The enchantment might hold even with their searching if she remained perfectly still. It was her best chance.

A guard approached. Fingers curled over the edge of the sliding door. Before he could do anything more, Lómerocco kicked the wood just inches below the man's fingers. The guard released his hold and stumbled back a step. Lómerocco kicked again.

"Sir, this one appears agitated," the guard said with an audible swallow.

Lhéwen grinned, mentally urging Lómerocco to keep it up even as she remained perfectly silent and still.

"Your job is to search the stall. I do not care what the animals are doing."

The horse whirled, careful not to get too close to Lhéwen's hiding spot and whinnied with gusto. She paced back and forth in front of the door while bobbing her head and snorting her displeasure. She whinnied once more.

If Lhéwen hadn't known better, she would have feared for her own safety. If she'd been in the guard's position, she wouldn't dare enter where she clearly wasn't wanted.

Apparently, the guard wasn't that smart, or he feared his commander more than the creature that outweighed him ten times over. The bolt on the stall door ground in its casing as the guard attempted to lift the handle and free the hook.

Lómerocco rushed the door, lunging forward to take a bite out of the guard's face . . . Or any body part that happened to get in the way.

Lhéwen heard a padded thump and assumed the man had fallen to the floor. Lómerocco was having too much fun to let that stop her. She reared up, pawing the air with her hooves, then slammed down to the ground. And again.

"I don't think she'll let us enter," the guard stated, dryly.

"Get a stablehand then. Someone must be able to control her."

Running footsteps sprinted away. Meanwhile, the other horses were learning from Lómerocco's example, their whinnies and thumps heard up and down the stables. Pretty soon the guards would have a full equine revolt on their hands.

"I've brought him," a new voice stated.

"Apologies, my lords, but what can I help you with?"

Lhéwen knew that voice. It was Erick, the human servant who cared for the horses and slept in the stables. She hadn't considered that he would be here, but of course he would be. And he would be able to calm the horses if anyone could.

Could he be trusted? He was only human, a changeling bound to obey the demands of the guards and unlikely to rebel.

She prepared herself to be discovered.

"We're looking for a woman who we believe entered the stables to hide. We must search all the stalls, but this horse is being difficult."

"Ah Lómerocco, my sweet. What're you doing?" Erick murmured.

The horse reared up once more, but some of the energy had faded from her protest. Another slide of the latch on the door. She snorted in response, her ears pinned back to her head, but she didn't bite or kick. She knew the hands that fed and groomed her.

"I'd best be the only one to enter," Erick said.

"As you wish," the guard commander replied, his voice sounding relieved. Lhéwen wasn't at all surprised. The high elves rarely risked their own when they had an alternative.

The door slid back just enough for Erick to enter.

"Search the stall. She may be under an enchantment that will make it difficult to see her, so walk through every corner."

"Aye," Erick replied, his hands lifted at waist height in a non-aggressive stance to calm the horse. He shuffled forward half a step. Lómerocco curled her head down and to one side, her gaze fixed on the new arrival. She bobbed her head and snorted, but made no further move to prevent Erick's entry.

"Shh," the stablehand murmured. "Shh. It's alright now. I'm here. What's got you so riled?"

His hand connected with her neck, gently petting down the fur to her shoulder.

"I'm going to just step around and check you out, now."

"I said check the stall, not the horse," the guard growled.

"I heard you, sir, but I'd rather not get kicked. I need to check to make sure she's calm and unhurt. I'll be checking the stall at the same time."

He ran his hands down her front leg. He crouched, looking beneath the mare.

His gaze connected with Lhéwen's.

The enchantment had run out.

For one brief moment, her heart stopped beating. This was it. She would be caught and thrown into the Pit to rot with the rest of the traitors.

And then he winked.

What was that supposed to mean?

Erick proceeded to check the rear foot. Lómerocco snorted and bobbed her head again, stamping that hoof into the ground before he could pick it up. He shushed her again, gently quieting her with a pat down the leg.

"I'm not going to hurt you," he said, his gaze all for Lhéwen. "Not to worry, now."

"Hurry it up, would you?" the guard urged. "If she's not there, we need to know it and move on before she gets away."

"I haven't seen her, yet," Erick said. "I'd like to think I would've but if you want me to check thoroughly it will be a few more minutes."

"Fine," the guard replied. "But make haste."

Erick grunted a noncommittal affirmative, but continued his examination of Lómerocco. He came around to the other side, closest to Lhéwen, staying close to the horse at all times.

"Check the corners, cretin," the guard growled. "She might be hidden."

"And get kicked? No thank you," Erick replied. "Just be patient, sir. I promise I'll be thorough if you give me a moment with Lómerocco."

The horse stamped her hoof again, pawing at the dirt and straw beneath her feet.

"She's still agitated, as you can see. Perhaps it would be better if you stepped back from the gate."

Was he truly trying to help Lhéwen? To keep her hidden from the guard's sight?

"Fine. The rest of you finish searching the stables, including the lofts and the stable hand's quarters," the commander ordered. "Leave nothing untouched. I'll stay here to make sure this changeling follows through on his word."

Erick hunched his shoulders at the insult, but continued to say nothing of her presence. Instead, he murmured sweet words to the horse as the guards continued in their own duties.

Lhéwen couldn't see the gate and daren't move for fear of being seen, but she thought the commander had stepped back based on how Lómerocco's ears relaxed. She wasn't surprised then, when Erick whispered a few words to her in the same gentle murmur he was using with the horse.

"What's going on, my lady?" he asked. "Are you in trouble?"

Lhéwen swallowed. "They've labeled me a traitor, but I must return to the princess."

"They say she was kidnapped, is that true?"

"Not at all!" Lhéwen hissed. "We were sent to the Shadow Realm to strike an alliance with the Shadow Realm. I don't know where everyone has gotten the idea she was kidnapped."

"That's not what the king is saying. He's calling us to prepare the war horses."

Lhéwen shook her head. How had it all gone so wrong?

"I was with the princess just this morning. She was not coerced to the Shadow Realm. She asked me to come, along with her guard. I helped her pack her things."

If the king is saying she was kidnapped, it was either a ploy to rile the nobles, or a facade to cover his own embarrassment.

"If what you say is true, you are in great danger."

Lhéwen couldn't help the soft snort that erupted from her nose. "I am aware of that. Erick, you must believe me. The princess has not betrayed her father, nor is she in danger."

Not yet.

The stable hand grinned. "You know my name." It was a statement, not a question.

"Of course!" Lhéwen replied, incensed. He might be human, and he might be a servant, but he was still integral to the functioning of the palace. "You are a worthy caretaker of the horses."

"You've always been kind to me, my lady. I will do my best to turn them away."

"Thank you, Erick."

With Lómerocco calm, Erick stood upright and patted the horse's shoulder. Then he turned and made a noisy show of examining the straw around Lhéwen, even going so far as to poke into the pile around her frozen form. He continued to the other three corners, giving each the same attention. When finally he was done, he exited the stall.

"She is not here, sir. I have checked every inch."

"Very well. Out the back, then. She will not have escaped the palace grounds."

It had been a long day of hiding. Squished as she was in the corner of the stall, her legs soon cramped and her backside lost all sensation. The only benefit to her position was the ability to prop her head between the feed basket and the side wall, which allowed her to intermittently doze between periodic searches by the guard. Lómerocco, sweet girl that she was, positioned herself to stand over Lhéwen, hiding her from view, at least a little. She might be a demon when she wanted to be, but she was also protective of those she trusted.

Lhéwen dared not move far or fast. The guards were making a

regular patrol of the stable, opening the stall doors and rechecking their search. She heard them mutter about footprints and dust patterns, looking for any sign of her presence. Luckily, all traces of her actual movements had been obliterated in their first frantic attempts to find her.

Now she could hear the footsteps of the guards echoing around the courtyard outside and shouts as wagons and packages were examined. That she hadn't yet been discovered had to be a combination of luck, positioning, Erick's earlier assistance, and Lómerocco's protective nature. The horse was a fine blockade.

Erick hadn't returned, whether because his duties called him away, or because he didn't want to draw attention to her location, Lhéwen couldn't be sure. However, since the guards hadn't marched in to take her to the Pit, she determined he'd been true to his word and hadn't reported her.

At long last, night fell and shadows lengthened through the stables. The sound of steel on flint roused Lhéwen from a drowsy stupor. An orange light began to glow from around the edge of the stall door as torches were lit between each horse's abode.

The stable hands were back to perform their nightly duties. The question was, were the guards standing with them?

Lhéwen pushed herself farther back into the corner, praying to all the gods that she could remain out of sight.

Just then, her stomach growled, the sound so loud even Lómerocco turned to look at her.

"I bet you're hungry." Erick's words were welcome, though Lhéwen couldn't be sure they were meant for her.

The stall door slid open, and Erick stepped in. He closed the door carefully behind him. No one else was with him.

"Easy now, girl," Erick murmured. His eyes widened then slid to the side and back, in a quick flick of motion. Someone else was here. Lhéwen heard no footsteps, but there were plenty of soldiers trained in stealth. There had to be, given the king's desire to know every last thing about his subjects. They might not officially be part of the king's guard, but they were certainly part of his arsenal.

Erick shifted forward, toward Lómerocco, but he set the bucket he carried on the ground near Lhéwen's feet.

"Your dinner's all ready for you," Erick murmured, his gaze all for the horse while he fed her one of her favorite pink apples. "Dig in now."

Lómerocco stepped forward, her ears pricked toward the bucket, but Erick held onto her head gently so that she wouldn't lunge for her feed.

"I said, go ahead and dig in."

Lhéwen's eyes widened. He wasn't talking to the horse, he was talking to her! He'd brought her food!

Careful not to move too fast or to make any sound, Lhéwen leaned toward the wooden bucket. Grain filled the vessel to the brim, way too much grain for Lómerocco's dinner.

Lhéwen grinned. So clever. The guards wouldn't know how much the horses were fed each night. She pushed her hand through the top layer of grain to find a warm loaf of bread and a packet of wrapped cheese and cold meats likely taken from the kitchen larder.

It wasn't much food, but it was enough to satisfy.

After she pulled everything out and leaned back, Erick released the mare's head to let the horse come forward for her grain. While she ate, Erick ran his hands over Lómerocco's legs and down her back, checking the horse once more, but they all knew the animal was sound. When he came back toward her head on the far side from the stall door, Erick paused, keeping his hands busy petting Lómerocco.

"I've arranged for an early morning exercise run for the horses," he whispered, keeping his mouth still even as he spoke clearly. "There will be a guard at the gate, but I trust her. She loves the horses nearly as much as you do. Be ready."

Lhéwen swallowed down a lump of emotion. Here was a

human, a man who had little enough freedom of his own, willing to risk it to help her escape. If that didn't define heroism, she didn't know what did. Before she could say a word, Erick crossed beneath Lómerocco's neck with the empty bucket and left.

Lómerocco snorted her satisfaction, her head bobbing.

Just a few more bells and Lhéwen would find a way to return to Faeliel and warn her of the news in the Upper Realm. She was sure, once the princess knew what was happening, she would return to the high court and confront her father. Together, they might be able to set everything straight, and achieve their original goal: a peaceful alliance between the two most powerful realms in the nine.

CHAPTER 28

The darkness that enveloped him pulled back ever so slightly. A gray light burned his eyes.

"Come now, Nilly," a scratching voice urged. "Time to let go. Ye've had enough fer now."

A squat nisse woman with spindly brown arms patted at the blackened carapace of the creature that yet loomed over Curuthannor's wasted body. The wyrm clacked its jaws at the woman, but didn't attempt to harm her. Instead, it begrudgingly backed away from Curuthannor.

"There we go now. That's a girl. Ye can save some for later." The woman shuffled backward and out of Curuthannor's line of vision, until only the tip of her pointed red hat could be seen behind the creature.

Curuthannor groaned. His head felt like it was filled with wool batting, his body barely had enough energy to twitch a finger. He had little left for the wyrm to save.

The woman continued to comfort and cajole the monstrous millipede away from Curuthannor and down a darkened tunnel, leading the way with a torch that glowed blue against the stone.

A kick to Curuthannor's side left him breathless and retching at the same time.

"The king has requested your presence. You will be offered a truthseeking."

Thank the gods.

"On your feet."

Curuthannor flopped to the side, his body still numb from the wyrms and his near-death. His tongue felt thick in his mouth and the left side of his face prickled with the sensation of thousands of needles pricking his skin.

A smaller wyrm flowed down his cheek and away, following its mother. Curuthannor shuddered. He couldn't tell if there were any others still winding their way across his body, but since the numbness was beginning to fade ever so slightly, he assumed they'd all been swept off him.

"How long have I been down here?" Curuthannor wheezed. His voice could barely be heard, even by his own ears. His lips and jaw weren't working properly to form the words.

"I said, get up." The guard kicked him again.

Curuthannor painstakingly lifted his left hand palm out to halt any further abuse. He rolled up to his knees, using his right forearm to push himself upright. He swallowed again. Licked his lips.

"How long have I been here?" His voice was louder this time, the words slightly more distinct.

"Two days," came the reply.

Was that all? It had felt like an eternity as his spirit was sucked from his body drop by drop. He closed his eyes, remembering the sickening pull on his aura. He might not be blessed with the ability to See the magical plane, but he certainly could feel it.

Knowing the guard wouldn't wait much longer before applying more forceful measures, Curuthannor made his way to standing.

"Follow me," the guard said.

"You're not going to bind me?" Curuthannor asked, unable to contain his surprise.

The guard smirked over his shoulder. "You're in no condition to run off anywhere. Your aura is so dim, even the nildhoggr would have a hard time finding you in the dark."

"Is that what that thing is called?"

The guard nodded. "Tormentors of the wicked, draining the spirit of any they find. Only the native nisse are able to control their hunger, and then only the priestesses of the dark are allowed beneath."

"Ah." That explained much. The Pit was feared by all, but only a few knew its true secrets.

Curuthannor followed the armor-clad guard as close as he could, afraid of being left behind in the dark cavern. The man held a single dim wisplight-lantern to light the way. It was the only source of light. His hand gripped the wood handle so tightly, the knuckles were white. Apparently even the guards were uncomfortable in this underground warren of torture. Curuthannor had to hurry to keep up, his feet dragging and stumbling on the smallest bits of gravel.

A spiral set of stairs appeared in the dim shaft of light. Curuthannor glanced up to see a glowing circle in the distant ceiling. At least a hundred stairs circled over and around themselves to reach the mound's surface.

"Get on with it," the guard said, pushing him toward the first step.

"I won't make it," Curuthannor replied, his voice bitter. The admission hurt his pride, but the thought of a single flight of stairs left him breathless and in pain, let alone the action of actually walking up them.

The guard grumbled in frustration, but waved a hand to send a small glimmer of energy in Curuthannor's direction. It felt like a mammoth had been removed from his chest, only to be replaced with a smallish griffin. He'd take it.

"Now get going," the guard prodded, pushing Curuthannor's shoulder toward the stairs.

For one brief moment, Curuthannor considered trying to fight his way free of the guard, but it would do him no good. He was too far outmatched, and fighting would only invite further recrimination.

Turning his face up toward the promise of light, Curuthannor began the long process of winding his way up the stairs to the surface of the world. Each step was a punishing struggle. Sweat poured down his brow and beneath his leathers. His breath came in panting gasps. Still, he persisted up toward the sun.

With a final push, he climbed out of the Pit and frowned.

Instead of rising out into the sunlight as he'd imagined, he emerged into a small room lit by the reflections of four great mirrors. They were positioned to capture and redirect sunlight toward the Pit entrance from a narrow window that ran the length of the room at the top of the wall.

But that wasn't what really had him frowning. Four guards stared down at him, their sharpened halberds pointed at his chest.

"Prisoner Curuthannor, you've been summoned for a truth-seeking."

This was more in line with the greeting Curuthannor had expected. The Pit must be enough of a threat they didn't feel they needed to send more than one guard down after him. Or maybe they wouldn't risk the lives of more than one guard against the nildhoggr.

"So I've been informed." He glanced back down the stairs toward the guard who pushed up after him with a cynical grin plastered across unapologetic lips.

"Step forward to be searched."

"What could I possibly have carried up from the Pit? You already confiscated my weapons before you threw me in there." They might have drained most of his energy, but he still had some fighting spirit left in him.

"Submit to the search or go back into the dark. It's your choice."

Curuthannor lifted his arms, reminding himself that he could put up with almost anything if it would prove he had no part in the assassination attempt. Another search was a waste of their time, not his.

Two guards stepped forward while the remainder maintained their ready stance. Their hands were quick, but thorough. Their purpose clear. They didn't rely on the work of others—which Curuthannor could admire—and they knew exactly what they were looking for. They didn't find anything.

The palace guard were excellent at searching for weapons. It suggested they did too much of it.

With that done, the guards stepped back and ushered Curuthannor before them. The room was bare but for a small table and three chairs against one wall. Only a single door gave entry and exit, and that was where Curuthannor was headed.

The room was located at the end of a long hall of cells, each with solid doors that gave no look at the occupants inside. Curuthannor didn't hear any sounds, however, so they were likely empty. There weren't often troublemakers doing enough damage to be confined to a cell. He was just lucky.

At the end of the hall, a long set of stairs led up to what Curuthannor imagined was the first floor of the palace, perhaps in a rear wing somewhere out of earshot of servants and nobles alike. The halls here were left entirely unadorned, the floors basic gray stone and the walls painted a clean, bright white. Not a single soul stirred in the corridor, save Curuthannor and his guard.

No one wanted to witness the prisoners, or put themselves in a dangerous position. Curuthannor could sympathize, not that he thought he was particularly dangerous.

Finally, they reached an intersection with a new hall, a much busier section of the palace. Human servants in the midst of cleaning and polishing the marble floor paused on seeing them, scuttling out of the way to press their backs to the wall while keeping their eyes downcast.

Curuthannor wondered what they saw when they looked at him. Was he still their superior? Or was he now lesser, more base, having been cast down into the Pit for his misdeeds. Alleged misdeeds.

Sanyaro would See the truth.

The golden doors of the throne room appeared once more before him. On seeing his entourage, the door guards immediately opened the doors and stepped out of the way. The crowd inside hushed, though a few of the noble ladies tittered behind their hands. Curuthannor was a spectacle, a source of entertainment for this particular crowd.

King Othin sat rigid on his throne, his posture matching the straight-backed chair with perfection. His hands rested on either armrest, his fingers grasping the front edge. Only his eyes moved, the rest of his body held as motionless as a condescending statue.

To his right, a man Curuthannor only knew by reputation stood with his hands clasped behind his back. Lord Garamaen Sanyaro, truthseeker of the nine faerie realms, the self-exiled former leader of the high elves of the new worlds. It was hard to miss him, with the feather hanging out of his hair. But Curuthannor supposed that was to be expected of a man who aligned himself with the humans in a region of limited civilization and less refinement. Curuthannor had heard rumors the man still lived a nomadic existence with the descendant tribes of his human children.

Sanyaro winked. Curuthannor's cheeks reddened at the realization that he'd been caught staring. He quickly glanced away, only to realize he'd been so distracted by the notorious elf lord, he hadn't noticed his own father standing just behind the source of his distraction.

"Father?" Curuthannor croaked, the word slipping from his lips before he could catch it.

Hatholdammon dipped his chin, his lips pressed into a thin line.

Curuthannor knew that look. It was a combination of worry, disappointment, and fury. Curuthannor hadn't seen that look since he was a boy caught playing too close to the forbidden mines.

The court steward lifted his staff and pounded it three times on the marble floor to gain the silence and attention of the crowd. Not that it was needed.

"Curuthannor, son of Hatholdammon, the Master Smith of Rómesse Gulch. Your honorable father has requested a truthseeking to determine the truth of your guilt," he intoned.

"I swear solemn oath, I had no knowledge of the purpose of the spell."

"Then you will submit to the truthseeking without complaint, and you will abide the findings and final judgment of His Majesty, our king?"

"I will." It wasn't as if he had much choice.

Sanyaro stepped forward, hand outstretched. "Relax and let go your mental barriers," he said. "If you do not fight me, this will not hurt."

He placed his hand on Curuthannor's forehead, thumb covering Curuthannor's third eye at the slight indentation above and between his eyebrows. Curuthannor's eyes closed of their own volition.

A moment later and Curuthannor blinked his eyes open.

"I, Garamaen Sanyaro, vouch under binding oath that Curuthannor, son of Hatholdammon, is innocent of all crimes currently attributed to his person. He is no traitor, nor is he an assassin. He was given the scroll by Lhéwen, handmaiden to Princess Faeliel, as he stated. He was taking the scroll to King Othin in good faith. All witnesses to this truthsaying are bound to hear and present this truth to any who ask. Let it be so."

The spell resolved with a gentle tightening around Curuthannor's throat and the smell of burnt silk. The sensation faded away like oil absorbed into wood.

"Wait—what? What has happened? Is that all?" Curuthannor

asked. To him, it seemed as if no time at all had passed. He simply blinked and everything was over.

"The truthseeking is over. Your interactions with the princess and her entourage have been revealed and no blame is placed on your shoulders," Sanyaro replied.

"So I'm free to go?"

"Not quite," King Othin replied, speaking for the first time since Curuthannor's arrival. "You will return to the Shadow Realm and bring our daughter home."

"Your Majesty," Curuthannor kneeled, head bowed, "I am no soldier, no spy. I am not the best man for this job."

"We are king here! You are but a smith's son! You will do as we command!" King Othin's voice echoed around the room with furious intent. Nobody stirred. Even the air seemed to hold its breath at the king's outburst.

Curuthannor pressed his forehead to the ground in subservience.

With an audible exhalation, the king brought himself under control, but his next words were tight, like a bowstring stretched to its limit. "You are the only high elf who has seen our daughter since she disappeared. You are the only man who has been in contact with her handmaiden. You are the best suited to find them, bring justice to any who conspired to take her from us. And you will do it immediately."

"Apologies, Your Majesty." Hatholdammon kneeled next to Curuthannor. "There is more you should know. I believe the handmaiden is here, in the palace somewhere."

King Othin snapped his attention to Curuthannor's father, who bowed his head as low as possible without falling over on the floor.

"Explain." The fury in the king's voice was a palpable thing.

"A woman snuck into the palace under a spell of obscurity. I called the guards, and they chased her off, but not before she told me she was sent by the princess, that the scroll that killed your guard was intended to be read by Your Majesty."

"So *a woman* was the assassin?"

"No!" Curuthannor shouted before he could stop himself. Abasing himself for his error in etiquette, he continued in a more respectful voice. "She is not an assassin. Nor a traitor."

"I cannot say for certain, but I agree with my son's assessment. She seemed fervent in her appeal. She said the scroll would have done nothing if opened by your hand."

"Guards! Double the watch. Find her." King Othin paused, his focus falling on Curuthannor and his father. "As for you two, return to your smithy and finish our sword. Should you fail, your entire line will be sent to the Pit. Is that understood?"

"Yes, Your Majesty," Curuthannor and Hatholdammon replied in unison.

Curuthannor swallowed the bile that rose in his throat. He had yet to acquire the iron. No longer just a threat of financial ruin, the lives of his entire family now rested in the balance.

CHAPTER 29

As soon as the throne room door closed behind him, Curuthannor's shoulder's slumped. Exhaustion and failure weighed heavy on his body and mind. His ribs sent shooting pain through his body with every breath, and his face felt swollen and stiff. The ordeals of the past few days had left him wrung out. He would need weeks of sleep to recover, and even then, who knew if the nildhoggr venom would ever fully leave his system. Any survivors of the Pit were typically left as lumbering simpletons for the rest of their lives. Curuthannor was only lucky his visit had only lasted two days. Any longer and he was sure he would have ended up as one of them.

A heavy hand thumped down on his shoulder.

Curuthannor winced at the painful contact, but turned to face the man who had given him life. "Father." He struggled to meet that man's gaze.

"You look awful, both physically and spiritually. Your aura is dim and drained. What happened?"

Curuthannor shook his head. His father's ability to See the bends and folds of energy always served to remind Curuthannor of his own shortcomings. Even if he became a master smith, he could never live up to his father's skill.

"The Pit is not kind to its guests," he finally replied. "There are things . . ." How did you even begin to explain the nildhoggr to someone who hadn't seen them, hadn't experienced them first hand? "I survived." That was more than most could say.

"I told them you would not succumb so quickly." Hatholdammon squeezed Curuthannor's shoulder once more, but with less force this time. The gesture was as much emotion as the ancient swordsmith was wont to show. "But how could you get yourself embroiled in this mess? You were only supposed to negotiate the deal with the mining master and then come home."

"About that . . ." Curuthannor paused. How could he tell his father that he failed? How could he explain that their entire lineage was now in danger?

"By all the gods, do not tell me you didn't get it. Without that iron, we are lost," Hatholdammon growled, reading Curuthannor's face.

"Prince Aradae bought every last bar before I could complete the deal." Curuthannor closed his eyes, defeat saturating his next words. "I failed."

"That is not an option." Hatholdammon's voice was hard. "We must have the black hills iron as we promised the king."

"Prince Aradae banned me from the realm. Or at least, he strongly suggested I leave. I cannot return."

"Of course you can. There's always a way."

"If I may intrude for a moment," Garamaen's voice interjected. "I understand you need a significant source of black hills iron to complete the king's order of arms."

The man had apparently followed them out of the throne room. Curuthannor hadn't even noticed, which was testament to his condition.

Hatholdammon quirked an eyebrow at the newcomer, but despite the pain radiating up and down his body, Curuthannor managed the more appropriate low bow for a man of his importance.

"Lord Garamaen, you honor us." Curuthannor's mother would have been proud. He'd even remembered to touch his fingers to his brow in the sign of highest respect for an elder. Even if he didn't look it, Garamaen was older than anyone else in the realm, including King Othin himself. Plus, he was Sanyaro, the truth-seeker. In a way, he outranked every other person in the nine, even the kings and queens who might be older.

Not that he looked the part in his plain white robe. Whether as a statement against the opulence of King Othin's court, or a simple lack of care, Garamaen could almost be mistaken for a palace servant, except even the servants were better clothed than the self-exiled noble.

"Not at all," Garamaen replied. "And please stand up. It is I who should honor you. You've done your realm a great service. Or you will have, once you're done."

Curuthannor straightened with a wince and a grunt. With his energy reserves so low and the bruises that he was fairly certain had colored his entire torso black and blue beneath his leathers, he could hardly manage to keep upright, let alone balance in a low bow for long. "I don't understand."

Lord Garamaen waved him away. "No matter. However, I think I can help."

"Help?" Hatholdammon asked, incredulous. "Why would you help us?"

Garamaen grinned. "Karma."

It sounded like a word he'd just invented himself. "Apologies, my lord, I'm afraid I do not know the meaning of 'karma'."

"Perhaps not, but you will. I'm afraid we all will, eventually. For now, just know that I have my reasons, not least of which is to attempt to minimize the damage this war will have on the nine realms."

"So it will be a war, then," Hatholdammon said. "I will need to bring on more humans to stoke the fires."

"Yes, you will. But first, let's get your son fixed up, shall we?" Garamaen turned his hand over, palm up, and reached toward Curuthannor.

Energy began to pour into Curuthannor's system. His spine straightened and his eyes closed in relief. He rolled his shoulders back and smiled.

"How's that, then?" Garamaen asked.

"Much better. I hadn't realized how much I hurt until it eased."

"Very good. Now then, you need black hills iron to complete the king's commission, of which, as it happens, I have a large supply."

"Why would a man like you need raw iron?"

Garamaen shrugged. "I don't. But I tend to know what will be needed before it is."

"Foreseers," Hatholdammon grunted.

"Yes, we can be difficult at times. It is often hard to understand the present when the futures are laid out before your eyes. Still, it's a blessing more than a curse." Garamaen threw an arm over Curuthannor's shoulders. "Shall we go then?"

"Go where?" Curuthannor was thoroughly confused. The man was mad, or so he seemed, yet he was also one of the most respected and honored men in all nine realms. There wasn't another foreseer with his skill, and no one with his unique set of abilities, including the diplomatic muscle necessary to forge alliances across divergent interests.

"To the Shadow Realm. Apologies, did I forget to mention that? We will need to visit my personal vault at the miner's hall to collect the iron. I will need you to assist me, while your father prepares Rómesse Gulch. You'll have at least a dozen new swordsmiths and armorers arriving within a fortnight."

"Are you mad?" Hatholdammon demanded.

Garamaen cocked his head to the side. "I do not believe so,

though I suppose it might be possible. Still, if you want the iron, you'd best follow along."

Without realizing it, Garamaen had walked Curuthannor and Hatholdammon down the hall, away from the throne room, until they now stood on the steps leading out into the grand entry garden, and the king's personal portal.

Garamaen strode to the arch with purpose, his fingers drawing the runes for Rómesse Gulch with speed and precision. The portal clouded and then cleared with a pop of displaced air, and Curuthannor could see the barest outline of the public courtyard in the village.

"Hatholdammon, you should go first. You can reassure your lady wife that your son is safe with me. We will return within a few days with the iron you seek."

The dip of Hatholdammon's chin was almost involuntary. He stepped into the portal without further argument. As soon as he was clear of the gate, Garamaen waved it closed.

"Now we're off to see a man about a key."

"A key?"

"Tharbatiron has been protecting my hoard. All we have to do is ask for it back."

"And if Prince Aradae confiscates it?"

"He won't." The words were said with the finality of a man who could See the future.

CHAPTER 30

A shuffling at the stall door alerted Lhéwen to Erick's return. He crept in on silent feet, carrying a light saddle and functional training bridle for Lómerocco. He wore a light riding cloak over his tunic and breeches, but his expression was strained. The finger he pressed to his lips was unnecessary. Lhéwen wouldn't make a peep.

Carefully, Erick slid the saddle over Lómerocco's back, tightening the girth with quick fingers. The horses had all been trained to stand perfectly still during saddling so that the riders could get their equipment on and off as efficiently as possible in the field, but the way Lómerocco's ears twitched back and forth had Lhéwen on edge.

When everything was checked and double checked, Erick motioned for Lhéwen to stand. The enchantment had worn off completely, and his gaze never left her face even as he removed his own travel cloak and threw it over her shoulders.

Leaning in, he pressed his lips close to her ear.

"Curuthannor has been released, but the guard has doubled its efforts to find you. They say you are personally behind Her Highness's abduction and the subsequent attempt on the king's life, and the murder of the gate guard."

"That's a lie!" Lhéwen hissed.

"I believe you. But I am just a changeling. My voice means nothing." Erick's expression turned sad and resigned. "My place is here, with the horses. It's easy enough to be ambushed in a dark barn before daybreak as I prepare them for their morning exercise."

"So I am to run, then? To take Lómerocco? That will surely prove their claims by virtue of my resistance."

"Perhaps, but what choice do you have? You've already hidden away in this stall for a day."

He was right, but the accusation—and the subsequent stain on her honor—still stung. What would she do? Where would she go? Back to the princess, she supposed, but to be deprived of the brilliant sun . . . forever? It was unthinkable. Unbelievable. Lhéwen's stomach turned over with anxious nausea.

"You must leave now. My friend cannot protect you, but she will turn a blind eye and will pretend that you are me for the time it takes you to get clear of the palace walls. Go out the Southern gate, as if you are taking Lómerocco for a morning run through the fields and vineyards. It's her usual routine and won't stand out. Once outside, you're on your own."

"I understand," Lhéwen said, taking the reins. She swallowed down her fear and forced a smile. "Thank you for your service." One didn't thank the fae, not without owing great favor, but Erick deserved it. He had risked much to help her. "I do not know what the future holds," which terrified her, "but if you ever need anything that I can help with, do not hesitate to reach out.

"My lady, you honor me."

"Quite the contrary. For now, take this." Lhéwen rummaged around in her belt purse for another pin, this one in the shape of a crescent moon. "It's a sleeping enchantment that will put you to sleep instantly, and wear off in four bells, or whenever you would otherwise wake. Just pin it to your shirt to activate it."

Erick bowed, sending a sheepish grin toward Lhéwen. "I was truly dreading the self-inflicted pain of a brick to my head. I appreciate the softer option."

Lhéwen chuckled. "Enchantments are my specialty. And that one is reusable, so don't lose it."

"I won't," Erick smiled, lifting the hood over her head and pulling it down around her face. His expression sobered. "Go now, quickly. My friend is on duty only until the next bell tolls."

With a nod and a click to the horse, Lhéwen strode forward and out into the dark.

She'd been on quite a few early morning rides, so Lhéwen knew the stable hand's routine reasonably well. Certainly well enough to fool the guards at the Southern gate. Or so she hoped. At least one of them would be purposefully ignoring her. Too bad she didn't know which one that would be.

All the same, she walked Lómerocco across the bailey toward the gate, keeping her head low and her hood down over her forehead. The cloak was long and heavy, made of a rough-spun cloth that showed little of the figure beneath. Lhéwen supposed that was a good thing, as she should be trying to look as much like Erick as possible. Luckily, as a human, even a tall human, he was reasonably close to her height. If he had been a high elf, her shorter stature would have marked her out immediately.

"Good morn, Erick," a female voice called from the gatehouse. Lhéwen wasn't sure what to say, if anything, so she simply bowed her head to the guard as she neared, which served the double purpose of further hiding her identity. The guard seemed to accept that, or perhaps this was Erick's friend. Either way, she didn't command Lhéwen to a halt.

"Portcullis up!" the guard ordered. The golden gate immediately began sliding upward. "Have a lovely ride. Lómerocco will take good care of you, I'm sure."

Lhéwen almost dared a glance at the guard's face, but stopped herself in time. This must be Erick's friend, but she couldn't risk being identified if it wasn't. Besides, Erick had said she would turn a blind eye, but could do nothing else. If Lhéwen revealed herself now, here, she might not be able to ignore the unauthorized passage.

Instead, Lhéwen kept her head down and her hand tight on the reins. She trusted that Erick would make use of the sleeping enchantment and would wake well-rested after the four bells wore off. His friend would surely find him safe in Lómerocco's stall.

After passing beneath the second portcullis, Lhéwen mounted Lómerocco and walked them across the bridge toward the produce markets that lined the road toward the southern valleys. Cresting the top of the hill, Lhéwen paused, staring out at the pastoral vista of fields and agricultural estates softly glowing in the beginnings of sunrise. In her mind's eye, she saw her father's land at the far edge of the valley, nestled between the king's own vineyards and the sandy beaches of the southern sea. Another fifty leagues down the coast, the village of Híthear had been steadily growing larger as the shipbuilders and fisherman expanded their trade to the southern continent.

She could go there, hide away from all the world, leave everything behind, not that she had much to leave behind. Her mother had died shortly after her father, fading like a sandcastle washed out to sea. She had no siblings. Faeliel was the closest thing she had to a family.

If she left now, she would abandon the princess to the Shadow Realm, without any knowledge of her father's political maneuverings. The princess would likely find a way to survive, even thrive, given her own skill sets, but Lhéwen would fare worse. The princess gave her the freedom and independence she needed to follow her passions, so long as they benefited—or at least didn't interfere—with Her Highness's activities. The princess gave her resources and access to a lifestyle that she could never achieve on her own.

If she ran, she would be forced to hide her true identity and live in secret in the wilderness. The creature comforts she'd grown used to in the palace would be gone. She would have to learn to hunt and forage, and she had no idea where to even start with that. She wasn't a wood elf, after all. And if the king's guard found her, they would be sure to send her to the Pit, no questions asked. They'd already done it to Curuthannor.

If she could convince the princess to return, all might not be lost. Perhaps this had all been a misunderstanding. Even if it hadn't, she'd chosen her side in this battle between father and daughter, and she couldn't switch now. Reconciliation was the best hope.

Lhéwen turned Lómerocco's head from the view and angled her down the grand causeway toward the central portals. The princess needed to know what was going on. She needed to be given a chance to return. And then all would be well.

The gods must have been smiling on her, because Lhéwen made it to the portal without further incident. There were few pedestrians out at this early hour, which was why Erick chose it for the horses' exercise. They could freely pass through the streets of the city and out into the greater plains for their run. Even the grand portal courtyard was mostly empty; two wood elf craftsmen entered the city from the Autumn Realm, but otherwise the portal remained closed. They glanced at Lhéwen and Lómerocco, but Lhéwen made sure to keep her hood down and neither man said anything.

Lhéwen rode around the entire courtyard, scanning the connecting streets for any sign of watchers. She didn't see anyone, but decided caution was the best protocol. She would find a place to release Lómerocco and go through the portal on foot, making several jumps to keep anyone from following her path. Paranoia wasn't her usual state of being, but there was always time to learn.

None of the townhomes in this area were wealthy enough to have stables of their own, so Lhéwen found a small secluded public garden a short walk from the plaza and dismounted under a broad tree. Stroking a hand across the mare's neck, she thanked her for her service.

"I wish I could take you with me," she murmured. "You'd be a good companion in the Shadow Realm, but I'm afraid you wouldn't like the dark. I know I don't. But I guess I'll have to get used to it. Princess Faeliel needs me, and I fear at this point I need her too."

Lómerocco snorted and gently stamped a hoof as if in response.

"Thank you, girl. You go on now, back to the palace. I can't have Erick getting into any more trouble than he already has. At least this way he won't have lost a horse."

Lómerocco would be able to find her own way back to the palace stables. She was a clever girl, so that wouldn't be a problem. And no one would dare steal a horse with the king's crest on her saddle.

With one final pat to Lómerocco's withers, Lhéwen wrapped Erick's cloak around her shoulders and pulled the hood down. She was lucky that part of her training as a handmaiden had been in portal lore and navigation. She had memorized codes for multiple cities within the Upper Realm, and even the largest public portals in the rest of the nine realms. She hadn't had much of an opportunity to try them out, but at least she wasn't stuck here.

Approaching the portal, Lhéwen glanced around once more. A pair of guards patrolled the far edge of the plaza, but their footsteps were unhurried. Lhéwen reassured herself that it was just the standard morning guard protecting the city.

She drew the runes along the stone. She would go to the remote village of Etsiramun first. It was one of the princess's favorite getaways and though rural, there was enough travel back and forth to the village that the location wouldn't draw attention.

As the connection between portals snapped into being, Lhéwen glanced once more over her shoulder. The guards were watching her now, but kept their distance.

She stepped through. The portal closed behind her. Lhéwen blew out a relieved breath. No one followed.

Etsiramun was bustling, however, as the villagers opened their daily market stalls. Although several large estates had grown up out of the scenic hillsides, the village itself was populated mostly by artists and fine craftsmen. There were clothiers and jewelers, painters and sculptors, and a few restaurants of renown. The streets were paved with flat cobblestones and tiles in decorative patterns, the artistic flair of the village reaching even the most practical of canvases.

The village fed Lhéwen's spirit. Unfortunately, she couldn't stay. Turning her back to the market, Lhéwen opened the portal to the next location.

The craftsmen of Etsiramun had strong connections to the Dwarven Realm due to the prevalence of high quality gems and master gemologists in the underground city. The jewelers were always traveling back and forth to pick up the best and brightest resources for their high-end pieces. No one would pay attention to Lhéwen's trip.

Quickly, before her nerves got the better of her, Lhéwen drew the runes for the Dwarven capital and stepped through the gate.

Torchlight and a short, bearded figure greeted her on entry into the Dwarven Realm. Though the dwarves didn't require light to navigate their subterranean home, they left the fires burning for the fae visitors who relied on sight more than sound and touch to understand their world.

"Greetings," the dwarf murmured, her voice echoing around the stone cavern.

Lhéwen could only assume the creature was a woman given the higher timbre of her voice and the style of her clothing, because both male and female dwarves had extensive facial and body hair.

"Greetings," Lhéwen replied, unsure of the proper protocol.

She'd met a few dwarves in her travels, but she'd never actually visited their home world. It wasn't a place Princess Faeliel had expressed any desire to see, given that it was underground and had no elven population.

"Where may I escort you?" the woman asked, her tone politely bored.

Lhéwen's eyes widened as she suddenly remembered that the dwarves required all visitors to have a guide through their city. It was a law created both for security of their high-value goods—the gems and precious metals they mined—as well as for the safety of the guest unfamiliar with the tunnels, shafts, and cliffs that comprised their homeworld.

Lhéwen stumbled across an explanation for her intrusion. "Apologies, but I am only passing through. I am meant to be going to the Shadow Realm. I must have incorrectly coded the portal."

"As you say," the woman replied.

Lhéwen cleared her throat but turned back to the natural stone archway that housed the Dwarven Realm's public portal. Their *only* portal as far as Lhéwen could recall.

She began drawing the runes for the Shadow Realm. It might have been a good idea to make a few more jumps to confuse any followers, but her nerves got the best of her. She couldn't explain why she was jumping from one gate to another anymore than she could explain why Faeliel had deceived her.

Painfully aware of the dwarf's gaze on her back, Lhéwen drew the runes for the Shadow Realm. The veil snapped into existence, connecting the dwarves with the dark elves. Lhéwen swallowed.

This was it. This was the final decision. There would be no going back after this. It was the final betrayal of her home realm and a declaration that she would bind herself to the fate of the high elf princess.

With a deep breath, Lhéwen entered the shadows.

CHAPTER 31

Curuthannor trailed behind Garamaen as they made their way down the gravel path into the Crossroads Amphitheater. The crowd was thick and boisterous, the mood celebratory.

Curuthannor didn't understand it. They must know that war was on the horizon. They must have heard the rumors of the Upper Realm's preparations. Surely, news had already crossed the portals.

And yet the dancing and drunken singing suggested no one cared a whit. Did they think themselves safe?

Garamaen pushed through the throng as if they weren't even there. He moved betwixt and between, flowing with the crowd without touching a single gyrating appendage. Curuthannor didn't have the same grace. He supposed it might be related to Garamaen's foresight—after all, if the man could truly predict every move, he wouldn't have to touch anyone he didn't want to—or perhaps his age, but the man had a knack for always being where the others weren't.

Curuthannor was hit more often than not by a flailing hand or stomped on by a wayward foot. Regardless, he was careful not to stray too far from Garamaen's back. The elder elf led Curuthannor around to the small outbuilding behind the bar, near the gardens where Curuthannor and Lhéwen had sat.

Where she'd arranged for his fall. He set that thought aside to dwell on later.

The single story building was modest in its design, just a simple stone structure with a wooden arbor crawling with vines near the front door. Two windows glowed with wisplight, indicating that Tharbatiron was within.

Garamaen knocked on the door, but entered without waiting for a response.

The dark elf inside looked up in surprise, but immediately smiled. "Garamaen, old friend," he said, standing from behind his desk. "What a wonderful surprise."

"Is it?" Garamaen asked, his voice sounding honestly confused. "I was sure you would have Seen us coming."

"So I did, but not the timing. My Sight is still not as precise as yours. Still, it is good to see you."

"And you."

With that, two of the oldest, most powerful elves in the realms hugged. Curuthannor had never seen the like. Elves were reserved. They weren't supposed to show emotion, or so he'd been taught. It was intended to remain a secret, internal, under the surface. Otherwise it could be used against you.

Tharbatiron was at least a millennia old, had perhaps been a child when this realm was first settled. Garamaen was even older, having known the Origin and helped to forge the first colonies in all nine realms. Still, both looked like they would live millennia more before passing on to the summerlands. Maybe once one achieved such great age and power, one didn't fear the force of emotion. Maybe they just didn't fear.

"And I see you've brought our young paramour back. I'm glad," Tharbatiron said, looking to Curuthannor as he ushered them all toward four leather chairs tucked away in the back of the room, near a corner armoire stacked with books and a single stubby white candle. Sadly, the titles weren't visible in the dim light. Curuthannor wished he knew what the dark elf was reading. He'd always thought a man could be known by the books he chose to read.

"Luckily, his stay in the Pit was brief. His father was quick to come to his aid," Garamaen said, bringing Curuthannor's attention back to the present moment.

"My father?" he asked, surprised.

"It was he who convinced King Othin to call for the truthseeking," Garamaen replied with a half-hearted shrug, as if the interaction should have been obvious.

"And he spoke with Lhéwen? I sent her in time?" Tharbatiron asked.

"Indeed. She spoke her piece. Unfortunately, but as expected, she was chased out of the palace grounds before she could inform the king, and Hatholdammon's words had little sway. King Othin has set his course."

"Most unfortunate."

"Agreed. But perhaps necessary."

Curuthannor was lost. The men spoke as if they were finishing each other's thoughts, perhaps had already discussed these issues, but were now just repeating them back to one another.

"But let me offer the latest confirmed news. The princess and king have become involved, as expected. They're practically inseparable. Hence, the celebration going on outside. Everyone thinks this is a sign that the crisis has been averted."

"Why haven't you told them the truth?" Curuthannor asked. It seemed the right thing to do, to make sure the people were prepared. King Othin wouldn't wait long to make the first strike.

"Who would believe a simple innkeeper?"

"Everyone knows you're more than that."

"Perhaps, but I'm not the king, nor do I want to be. I'm not a political creature, though I sometimes am forced to move in those circles. Everyone has their place." Tharbatiron shot Curuthannor a meaningful look.

Curuthannor grimaced. His place was back at the forge with his family.

"We do what we can," Garamaen replied. "We cannot control the actions of others, only encourage and persuade."

"On that we agree," Tharbatiron replied. "But I suppose you're here for your key?" Tharbatiron asked.

"Yes. The time has come. I knew I was buying up that iron for a reason."

"Then you're determined to go through with this?"

"We all have our parts to play."

"You risk a great deal."

"But stand to gain a great deal more."

"Fine, fine. I won't have this argument with you again." Tharbatiron opened a drawer in the corner cabinet, shuffling things around inside. "Sometimes I do wish for a little more light."

"Here, let me help," Garamaen replied. With a flick of his finger, the candle burst into flame.

"Appreciated," Tharbatiron said. "Ah, yes. Here it is." With a triumphant flourish, he pulled a thin brass key from the drawer and handed it to Garamaen. "I wish you well in your continuing journey."

"And I you," Garamaen replied as he stood from his chair.

The two men embraced once more, then Garamaen led the way back out into the night.

Perplexed by their cryptic conversation, Curuthannor could do nothing but follow in silence. Truly, he didn't know what to think of these men, nor what to say. They were peculiar, to say the least. But at least Garamaen had acquired the key. Hopefully now they could collect the iron for King Othin's sword and be on their way.

CHAPTER 32

The moon rose high and bright over the city of Nalakadr when Lhéwen stepped through the portal and into the Nalakadr daily market. The streets were crowded with fae of all races: goblins bought and sold metals, trolls pulled carts filled with strange-looking fruits and vegetables, dwarves manned stands of gems and jewelry, even a few high elves mixed in with the shoppers and merchants selling meat and grains from the Upper Realm.

Spotting a vendor with small cartons of Princess Faeliel's favorite breakfast berry, Lhéwen thought perhaps a small gift would help Her Highness overlook her handmaiden's short disappearance.

"How much for the red brickleberries?" Lhéwen asked, drawing her coin purse from beneath her borrowed cloak.

The vendor, a high elf man with long white-blonde hair and a shimmering blue robe that matched the color of his eyes, glanced her direction with surprise.

"Half gold," he replied.

Lhéwen's gaze snapped up to his apologetic face.

Seeing her shock, the man lifted his hands in a placating gesture. "I admit it's a steep price, but King Othin has imposed new fees on all imports and exports from the Shadow Realm. If I sell them for any less, I will lose money."

"These were to be a gift for Her Highness, Princess Faeliel, who is currently negotiating with King Rindae. Surely you can provide a better price?"

"It's true then? She's here? I had heard she might be in the city, but could hardly believe it."

"Yes . . ."

Before Lhéwen could say more, the man's eyes widened and a rough hand grabbed her upper arm.

"Let me go!" Lhéwen shouted. She struggled against the woman's grip, but the dark elf held on fast.

"By order of Crown Prince Daeturion, you are to come with me," the woman growled.

"I'm only buying some fruit!" Lhéwen shouted. "I've done nothing wrong!"

She scanned the busy marketplace for any sign of a friendly face or good samaritan, but even the stall-keeper backed away with his hands raised in front of him. Everyone else averted their gaze and continued on their own business.

With a sudden twist of her hips, the woman stepped behind Lhéwen, and simultaneously grabbed her other arm, forcing both behind her back in a rough prisoner's hold.

"I've been ordered to use minimal force, but that varies with the amount you struggle."

"Why?"

"I have my orders. I don't ask questions."

"Who are you?" Something about the long white braid that tangled around their feet seemed familiar.

"That doesn't matter. Are you ready to relent?"

Lhéwen forced herself to relax. It was clear she wouldn't be able to fight her way free. Perhaps instead of acting guilty by resisting, she could reason with the woman. Lhéwen straightened her shoulders and did her best to assume a confident air, despite the nerves fluttering in her belly.

"I am Princess Faeliel's handmaiden. You cannot arrest me without answering to her ladyship. I assure you there will be repercussions."

"Don't bother with the threats. I am not arresting you. As far as I know, the Crown Prince only wishes to speak with you. Will you come willingly, or do I have to increase the level of force?"

"No. Further force will not be necessary," Lhéwen replied. She would not cower or be dragged like a slave before royalty. She was Princess Faeliel's handmaiden, here to serve a purpose on a diplomatic mission. She would do her duty to her mistress with dignity and composure. She would play the part. "You may release me. I will come willingly."

Whether she sensed Lhéwen's change of heart or simply realized Lhéwen had nowhere to run, the dark elf let go. Turning, Lhéwen could see her face for the first time.

The dark elf had skin as black as a moonless night, and silvery eyes that seemed to sparkle and dance in the torchlight around them. However, her most notable feature was the long braid of white hair that she quickly picked up from the ground and wrapped around her shoulders like a scarf.

"You're the woman from the inn. The one who was listening to the musicians."

The woman jerked her chin down once in a rough nod.

"Here!" The produce vendor shoved a box of brickleberries toward Lhéwen. "Take these to Her Highness with my thanks. Anything she can do to repeal the taxes would be appreciated!"

"I will pass along your words," Lhéwen replied with as much dignity and hauteur as she could muster, then followed the dark elf with the long braid toward the black castle on the cliff.

CHAPTER 33

A quick knock and the door opened without Daeturion's leave. The only individual who could get away with the invasion of his personal space was his valet and personal assistant, Tecindo, and even he would only do so under the utmost urgency.

"Lhéwen has returned," the blood sidhe confirmed as soon as he entered the room. "However, she did not arrive from the Upper Realm. She came from the dwarves."

"What was she doing with the dwarves?" Daeturion mused.

He'd done his research on the woman as best he could in the hours since she'd left the city. She was not a noble, but had inherited her position from her mother. She had been with the princess for nearly a century, and with the death of her parents decades before, all of her personal connections had come through her role in the princess's employ.

She was a loyal citizen of the Upper Realm and dedicated to her job. There was no reason he could fathom she would have gone to the Dwarven Realm.

"Unknown. Ethires is bringing her here immediately, as ordered," Tecindo replied.

"Did she resist?"

"Mildly at first, as I understand it, but she relented quickly. No force was required, though Ethires will be able to give the full report."

"Send them in as soon as they arrive."

"Yes, sire."

As soon as the door shut, Daeturion leaned back in his chair to contemplate his strategy. If he chose the full interrogation mode, the young seamstress would likely shut down. She didn't seem the type to handle stressful situations well, if her reaction to the princess's seduction was any indication.

No, the better option would be to convince her of his good intentions, to win her confidence and trust. If he could manage that, he would have an inside eye into the princess's personal agenda. That alone was worth the effort.

Daeturion kept his hands busy straightening and putting away the documents on his desk. Though most everything sensitive was carefully encoded in case of loss or disclosure, he wouldn't tempt the woman to investigate.

Within a half bell, another knock on the door signaled their arrival. Daeturion quickly rearranged his personal presentation to appeal to the newcomer. He leaned back into the corner of his chair, placing his right elbow on the armrest and his left across his lap. It was a touch informal, but the dragon insignia carved into the wood above his head would remind her of his position. A slight smile with a modestly lifted brow would signal his good-humor. Approachable, friendly, yet still superior.

They entered the room, Tecindo stepping through the doorway first, followed by Lhéwen and then Ethires. Daeturion noted there were no restraints placed on the high elf's arms, nothing to suggest she had been forcibly coerced into position. The scowl on Ethires's face told a slightly different story, though if she were angry or annoyed, he couldn't quite tell.

The handmaiden dipped into a low curtsy, holding her position at the door. Ethires's scowl deepened.

"Welcome," Daeturion said, remaining seated in his chair. "Please sit. Ethires, you may go, but please wait outside the room to escort our guest to her quarters after our conversation."

Ethires pursed her lips, but did as she was told, leaving the room with a soft click of the door.

Lhéwen rose from her obeisance and gracefully flowed toward the nearest chair. After waiting to make sure the woman sat down, Tecindo took a position at the door, his back to the exit, on guard in case the high elf woman tried to flee. Not that she appeared so inclined.

Wide, blue eyes gazed around the room, pausing on a painting of the sun cresting above the Black Hills mountain range.

"Do you like it?" he asked after a few heartbeats. It was a good piece, one of his best. He was actually rather proud of it, not that many knew it was his own work.

The woman's gaze snapped to his face, then quickly down to the surface of his desk. "It is beautiful," she murmured. "Is it sunrise or sunset?"

"Sunrise over the black hills at the height of summer. I hiked several miles out of the city and up into the range to find the perfect spot."

"You painted it yourself?" Lhéwen's eyes turned back toward the image.

Daeturion grinned. She was an artist with needle and thread. It was no surprise that she would appreciate art of another kind.

"Yes. I don't have as much time as I once did, but I find the work helps the mind to think while the hand is busy."

"Truly?" the woman sounded incredulous, though she maintained a deferential pose. "I find the exact opposite. When I am working on my designs, my mind is blank. I am focused on the perfection of each cut and stitch."

"But isn't it in the clarity of art that thoughts and ideas are formed? When the noise of the everyday is muted, the important work is able to rise to the surface."

"Perhaps." Lhéwen said no more.

It seemed debate was not in her repertoire, though she didn't immediately agree. Not a toady then, but still a servant. She kept her back straight and her hands in her lap, poised in strict subservience.

Daeturion let a gentle smile soften his expression. She might not look up, but if she broke that careful facade, she would find a friendly companion, not an interrogator.

"In any case, I asked Ethires to fetch you after your journey to make sure all is well. I was concerned after seeing you so upset in the hall. You left the realm so suddenly, I was sure there must have been some kind of emergency."

"Your concern is appreciated," Lhéwen replied. "But as I said before, I am fully capable of completing my duties unassisted."

"I meant no disrespect. As I understand it, you have been a loyal servant for Princess Faeliel for many years. She speaks quite highly of your value."

Lhéwen's cheeks blushed and she twisted her fingers together in her lap. "I am honored."

Daeturion couldn't get a strong read on her. She still seemed troubled, distressed even, yet her tone and words gave nothing away. The compliment may have helped soften her stiff exterior, but it wasn't enough.

"It seems your mistress has made an impression on my king and I am hopeful this is the beginning of a new chapter in the relationship between our realms. As such, I want to assure you that I am at your service if she needs anything."

The woman's gaze jumped to his face and back down. "I don't know what you mean."

Her words were carefully neutral, her tone unassuming and non-confrontational. She was really quite the diplomat. She would make a great spy.

"It seems you may have left too soon then to know. Princess Faeliel and King Rindae have been ensconced in private negotiations since yesterday. I have chosen to take this new development as a good omen for our future dealings."

"I am but a humble seamstress, not included in the princess's plans. I'm afraid I don't have any information about her offer, if that is what you're asking."

"No, of course not," Daeturion was quick to deny, though he doubted its truth.

Lhéwen was a handmaiden, and would have been privy to the princess's personal dealings, if only because they were discussed in front of her. Royals often made the mistake of ignoring their servants, a mistake which could be capitalized upon.

Of course, there were ways he could have made her disclose everything, but he needed to earn her trust. If the princess was going to remain in this realm, he would need an ally within her circle.

"I was surprised King Othin sent his daughter to negotiate a treaty, however. I was under the impression he didn't give her such responsibilities."

Lhéwen shook her head so quickly Daeturion almost thought she was having a fit. "He doesn't." The woman's shoulders stiffened, though she didn't raise her head.

Daeturion lifted an eyebrow. She hadn't meant to say that.

"No?"

Lhéwen hesitated a few heartbeats, but Daeturion let the question linger.

"The princess is ready to demonstrate her capabilities," Lhéwen finally replied.

"I see. Then she is here without authorization."

Lhéwen's lip began to tremble. He'd pushed her too far.

"Please sire, let me return to my mistress. She will surely be missing my presence."

Plastering a concerned expression across his face, Daeturion moved around to sit in the chair next to the younger woman. He carefully covered her hands with his own and opened his mind to his magic. Within moments he knew everything Lhéwen had done and seen in the last two weeks.

He swallowed, forcing the visions of the past back into history where they belonged. He had all the information he needed now, but he still needed to foster the comfort and camaraderie Lhéwen needed to speak with him in the future. It was more important than ever to know what was going on behind the princess's doors.

"Something terrible has happened. I can feel it."

Lhéwen shook her head.

"I understand I am a stranger. You probably see me as an enemy, or at least not an ally. But please trust me when I say I will do anything I can to ease your time here in the Shadow Realm."

If he were lucky, that wouldn't be for very long. If what he'd Seen in her mind was any indication, there was no time to lose. They needed to push the princess back through the first portal and return her to King Othin with a sincere apology and reparations in her hands. The Shadow Realm couldn't afford to fight a true war. Not yet. They needed more time.

Unless . . .

If King Othin believed the princess had been kidnapped when she hadn't, and if she returned to the Upper Realm with success of some kind in hand, wouldn't that appease his power-hungry heart? A marriage contract could be the perfect compromise. Rindae would never bend the knee, nor should he, but Othin would gain influence in the Shadow Realm court.

The question was, would King Rindae—the man who'd sired two sons to two different women and yet refused to attach himself to any of his lovers—be willing to bind himself to the daughter of his enemy? They'd had days of 'negotiations' but that meant little to the king.

"But I can see that right now is not the time. You should go back to your mistress and assure her that you are well."

And when the princess left the king's side, Daeturion would be there to speak with him. One way or another, Faeliel had forced the king's hand.

CHAPTER 34

The goblin mound was in view before Curuthannor said a word. He waited until they passed beneath the high stone arch of the northern gate and were out of sight—and probably more importantly, hearing range—of any goblin pedestrians. Finally, when he felt his chance might be slipping by, Curuthannor opened the conversation.

"Master Ger refused to deal with me before. Why would he make a deal with us now? We haven't done anything to change his mind."

"Nor do we need to," Garamaen replied. "We're not going to see the mining master. We're going to see the hoard master, and verify my holdings."

"Your holdings?"

"Yes. Tharbatiron has been overseeing everything in my absence. I prefer to stay in the Human Realm as much as possible." Garamaen paused, his head shaking slightly from side to side. "Let me rephrase that. I prefer to stay out of fae politics as much as possible, and it seems any time I return to faerie—any of the other realms—I get pulled back into the conflicts I've tried so hard to ignore."

"Like performing a truthseeking for a simple smith's son."

Garamaen glanced at Curuthannor with an incredulous smirk. "Is that how you define yourself?"

"It's what I am." It was boring, and he wasn't particularly good at it, but it was still who he was.

"Interesting." Lord Garamaen looked away, pointing his gaze back up the trail toward the mining hall. "Well, a smith needs iron, and a good smith needs good iron. A great smith, like your father, requires the best iron money can buy. Which, luckily, I can provide. At a very agreeable price, I might add."

"What are your terms?" The elves never did anything without compensation.

"Oh, I'll give your father the iron for free. I have no reason to spend gold in the Human Realm." He cocked his head to the side. "At least, not yet. But I will require three unspecified boons from you, to be redeemed at the times and places of my choosing."

Curuthannor snorted at the outrageous request. "Is that all? You could ask for anything, and I would be required to comply. You could even ask me to sacrifice my life. For iron."

Garamaen shrugged. "This is true. What other options do you have at this point?"

"None."

"Precisely. Oh, and I'll also require your attendance at the king's feast tonight. Once he finds out I'm in his realm, Rindae will sadly insist that I am present. And this won't count as one of the boons."

"Then why do you need me?"

"I despise formal dinners. You'll be my excuse to avoid the dithering nobles."

They continued on the road to the miners' guild, the worn path twisting through the lower foothills of the mountain range. A small rodent-like creature darted out of the way, hiding beneath one of the thorny white rose bushes that occasionally dotted the landscape.

Garamaen looked up at the inky sky. The moon glowed through a hazy gray cloud, giving the orb a broad halo.

"Interesting that the shadow roses are already in bloom," he commented, his voice thoughtful and quiet. "It's not a good sign. The ash must be heavy tonight."

Curuthannor sniffed the air. There was no scent of fire or the sulfurous fumes of the volcano. "I don't smell anything unusual."

Lord Garamaen shook his head. "Not yet. But soon." He exhaled with a sad sigh. "Events are coming into alignment, then. Not much time. But I have to give it one more try."

"Give what one more try."

"Peace. Harmony. The existential need to find the best possible solution for the greatest good. But all that is a discussion for another day. Now we must focus on withdrawing my hoard."

Curuthannor shook his head. Lord Garamaen Sanyaro was an odd man, his thoughts too far in the future and too distant to seem rational or reasonable. However, the entrance to the goblin mound had appeared before them on the path, and it was time to take action.

Garamaen never hesitated. He strode forward and immediately looked up at the imp sitting in his nook beside the door.

"Orink, why is this door not open?" Garamaen asked, his voice mildly annoyed yet still cordial.

"Master Garamaen, your lordship, sir. Welcome back to the goblin hall." The imp shuffled from side to side, his hands twitching and twining together with nervous energy. "It's Master Ger's orders, sir. I will tell him you're here and ask if you might be let in."

"There's no need to involve Master Ger. He may continue to rest in his rooms. I'm here to see Wert."

"Wert? The clerk?"

The imp sounded shocked, but Garamaen simply held up his key.

"I have a withdrawal to make,"

"I'm sure Master Ger still wants to meet with you. I will do my duty and ask him."

"No, Orink. You will not ask him. You will open this door and let me in. It is my right."

Orink, as apparently the imp was named, bobbed up and down. "I have orders. Orders! The door stays shut."

Lord Garamaen closed his eyes and tilted his head to one side. "Yes, I see. You did have orders, but they were in two parts, right? First: do not disturb Master Ger when he's entertaining. Second: don't open the door. Am I correct?"

"Yes, yes. That's correct."

"Good. Then go get Wert."

"But—"

"Wert will let us in, and then you will not be violating any of your orders."

The imp's eyes brightened. "Be right back!"

Curuthannor snorted. "I had to grab the twerp's leg on a translocation to get inside last time I was here."

Lord Garamaen shrugged. "Find the leverage. Orink hates his job and despises Ger, but wants to do his duty. If you can find a way to appease the competing interests, you can find a solution that is amenable to everyone."

Curuthannor nodded. It made sense, but had never been stated quite so clearly before.

A few moments later, the heavy stone began to roll away from the entrance to the miners' hall. A scrawny underfed goblin with four eyes and a hunched back stood to one side.

"Sanyaro, a pleasure sir." The goblin dipped into an awkward bow, the weight of his hump listing his weight to the left.

"It is good to see you, Wert. Would you please escort us to my holdings?"

The goblin stepped back on an angle, gesturing for the men to move inside. "O' course, sir. O' course. But is something amiss?" Wert's eyes squinted even tighter together, and his mouth pinched as if he'd eaten something terribly sour. "I've personally weighed and measured every deposit and noted them in the logs. There've been no errors. Even Lord Tharbatiron's audits haven't found nothin'."

"I am certain that is true. Tharbatiron has done his job admirably well and so have you. However, I am not here for an audit."

Wert's shoulders relaxed and his expression smoothed. He handed Garamaen a dimly lit lantern. "If you don't mind carrying the light, I'd appreciate it. I spend my days in the hoard rooms." He said, as if that explained it.

As soon as Garamaen took hold, Wert turned and led them across the entry toward the right-most tunnel that curved sharply downward. "Then what can I help ye with? Not that I'm complainin' of the visit, but ye must understand this is most unusual."

"It's time to make a withdrawal."

The goblin glanced over his shoulder with wide eyes. "I'm sorry, sir, truly sorry, but we've been told no foreign sales. The whole mound was sworn to it."

"Then it's a good thing I've already paid."

Wert blinked a few times. "So ye have. I recorded payment myself."

"There can be no objection to withdrawing my holdings."

"I . . ." The goblin thought for a few heartbeats, the sound of his bare feet and long toenails clacking and scraping across the floor. ". . . I guess not."

"Good."

A small smile flickered at the corners of Curuthannor's mouth. This just might work. He might fulfill his duty after all.

They continued down the tunnel, ignoring the occasional dark openings and staying on the middle path. The space had clearly been dug from the stone by hand, ridges and uneven bumps in the walls and floor making the way treacherous, especially in the limited light of the single small lantern. There were no markings to guide them, at least none that Curuthannor could see. They could only trust that the clerk was leading them in the right direction.

At last the goblin stopped at a small side tunnel. A stone boulder larger than Tryg barred the way. "Here we are, sir. If ye'll give me yer key . . ."

"That's alright." Garamaen stepped closer to the rock, finding a small keyhole near the center of the rough door. "I can manage."

He slid the iron key into the lock and turned it one full clockwise revolution. A heartbeat passed, and then two. For a moment, Curuthannor questioned if something was wrong, but finally a clank and groan could be heard from within the room, and the door began to roll away as if pushed by an invisible giant.

Garamaen stepped inside. He lifted the lantern. Curuthannor's jaw dropped.

Surrounding him on all sides was a stash of iron larger than Curuthannor had ever seen in his entire life. Arranged in neat rows of stacked bars, the cavern extended back into the darkness beyond the reach of Garamaen's light, and—based on the echoes of their footsteps—had to be at least a dozen lengths before the end of the row. The entire store rooms at the Kremish mines he'd visited as a child couldn't compare to this stash.

Wert pulled a leather-bound notebook from a nook on the wall near the door. "How much'll you be needin' then?"

"All of it."

Wert's head snapped up. Four shocked eyes stared at Garamaen, then flicked their gazes around the room.

"All of it?" he squeaked.

"Yes. All of it."

Curuthannor was speechless. This much iron would take centuries to process. His father would have enough material to fulfill every noble order. And with the rest of the high court armorers unable to purchase the same, they would be the sole supplier.

Hatholdammon's smithy would become the unchallenged leader in arms and armor for the entire Upper Realm, perhaps all of the upperworlds.

"We will need help hauling everything to the surface. I will pay for porters, of course. Can you arrange for it?" Garamaen asked the immobilized clerk.

Wert blinked a few times and then shook his shoulders as if waking from a dream. "Yes, o' course." His gaze turned down to look at his notebook once more. "Are ye really sure ye want all of it?"

"I am certain. And you may cancel my standing order after this."

Wert shook his head, and drew a few markings on the page. "Give me some time and I'll have everything together for you. There'll be some papers for your signature."

"Understood. However, we are under a bit of a time constraint, so please be as quick as possible."

Wert nodded, backing out of the room. "As ye say. Be back in a quickie."

"Is it really going to be this easy?" Curuthannor wondered aloud after Wert left them alone. Curuthannor paced the length of the cavern down the aisle between pyramids of stacked iron bars. It was fifty strides before he found the far wall and turned around. He ran a hand along the rough metal, attempting to estimate the value of the hoard. If each bar was worth a quarter silver . . . it was still beyond his mathematical comprehension.

Garamaen tilted his head to one side and closed his eyes. "No, not entirely that easy. But really, there's nothing much they can do about it."

"Who? Master Ger?"

"The iron is mine. They cannot deny me my property."

"Where will you have it delivered? It's not as if the goblins will be able to take it all the way to the Upper Realm. They'd go blind from the light."

"Astute. The goblins will deliver it into the Human Realm. There's a desert I know of with good portal access and very little human activity. The local natives won't mind temporary storage. They wouldn't know what to do with the iron anyway. From there, you'll have to hire men to carry it through to your father's smithy. He'll be hiring a lot of new apprentices that I'm sure can take on the task."

"You have this all planned out, don't you?"

Garamaen tapped his forehead. "There's very little that I can't anticipate." He suddenly frowned. "It takes a deft opponent to thwart my Sight, though it can happen."

"I wouldn't bet against you."

"Good. Then we're in agreement."

Moments later the goblins arrived, pushing wheeled carts. In teams of two, each team choosing a different pyramid to tackle, they began loading the carts with the iron. Wert also returned with his notebook and charcoal.

"Delivery?" He asked, stylus poised above the parchment.

Rather than respond, Lord Garamaen leaned over and wrote the portal code directly on the report. "It's a wide cavern set into the cliff of a deep canyon. No one will be nearby, and the iron will be safe."

"It's yer material," Wert replied noncommittally. "I need ye to make yer mark here and here," he continued, pointing to the page. "We have no further obligation for the iron after it's delivered."

"Understood."

As Lord Garamaen bent once more to sign the indicated pages, rapid footsteps pounded down the outside tunnel.

Master Ger's rotund form skidded to a halt in the entrance to Lord Garamaen's hoard, blocking the way out for the first two filled carts.

"Lord Garamaen, Sanyaro, sir, apologies. I wish ye'd notified me ye were coming. We would've had a more fitting greeting for your esteemed presence."

Garamaen stood from his bent over position, rubbing his fingers together to smudge out the remaining charcoal on his fingers. "I didn't feel the need to bother you in your new position," he said. "But could you please step to the side and let the porters take my iron to its destination?"

Master Ger's eyes darted this way and that, taking in the scene. "Please, sir, ye must come sit with me for a moment. Wert, send the porters on a break. I'll have the ladies bring out some delectables."

"That is unnecessary, Master Ger. I'm afraid our time here is quite limited." Garamaen gestured to the waiting carts. "If you please?"

"I'm very sorry, sir, but we're under strict orders. I can't let ye take the iron from the mine. No foreign sales. I must insist we discuss this in my office."

"Wert, the good man that he is, informed me of the new restrictions. However, since I have already paid for the iron, it's not a foreign sale. I'm simply transferring my stock elsewhere."

"Yes, yes, I see that, sir, but truly, I must ask ye to come with me now."

Garamaen's lips pressed into a thin line before he finally turned to face Ger head on. "No. I will take my iron, as is my right, and that is the end of it."

Master Ger bowed his head and wrung his hands together. It almost looked like he was going to cry, but instead he turned and ran back the way he'd come, his girth bouncing and jiggling the entire way.

Curuthannor smiled. Sweet revenge. Sweet victory. Master Ger had blocked Curuthannor from making a purchase, but he'd still found a way to get the iron he needed.

Lord Garamaen didn't seem as pleased. "I suppose that was

necessary. He wasn't going to leave us alone, but now we might have worse problems on our hands."

"What do you mean?"

"Prince Aradae is coming. Let's get as much of this out of here as we can before he arrives."

Wert waved the two filled carts out the door while Garamaen walked to the nearest pyramid of bars and began helping the goblins load their cart. Curuthannor followed suit. As soon as the cart was full, Garamaen wrote the portal code on a slip of parchment he happened to have in his pocket and sent them on their way while Curuthannor began loading the next cart with the two-goblin team across the aisle.

They only managed to send off four more carts before Prince Aradae arrived with an entire squadron of the shadow guard, all bristling with weapons.

Curuthannor swallowed. It was one thing to break up a bar fight between soldiers, it was another to have the attention of ten highly trained men and women focused on you, with violence in their gazes.

"Halt." Aradae commanded. Immediately, the goblin porters dropped to the ground, their hands covering their heads. "By order of Rindae, King of the Shadow Realm and ruler of the dark elves, no iron is to be sold to foreigners from the goblin mound. Even to esteemed visitors such as yourself, Sanyaro."

"That's fine. I've already paid." Garamaen replied, still loading the iron cart. Curuthannor recollected himself and returned to his task, as well.

"Nor are you allowed to sell to any third parties."

"Who said anything about selling? I'm giving Curuthannor the iron."

Prince Aradae's brow furrowed. "Why, in all the realms, would anyone give away this much iron? I don't believe a word of it."

"You don't have to believe it, but it is the truth. And my reasons for doing so are my own."

Lord Garamaen Sanyaro kept his tone level, but there was still a note of challenge in his voice. If Prince Aradae pushed it much further, they all might get to see some of the ancient elf's fabled powers. It was rumored he was at least as strong an enervator as King Othin—able to drain multiple warriors of their energy all at once—and his fire magic was equally well trained. Secretly, Curuthannor couldn't wait to see what the great Sanyaro could do.

"I'm afraid that's not good enough in this time of political tension. My king cannot supply the enemy's army."

Garamaen straightened and faced Prince Aradae. "Then the Shadow Realm has declared war already?"

"Of course not!"

"Oh, good. You had me worried for a moment. But if there's no war, then there's no enemy. Yes?"

"War might not yet have been declared, but that doesn't change our current circumstances. That much iron, turned into weapons and armor, could be devastating. I state again, we will not supply our own enemy."

Lord Garamaen's single hand clenched, and his expression hardened.

This is it, thought Curuthannor, almost giddy with excitement. He gripped the hilt of his sword. The men and women of the shadow guard did the same. Curuthannor might die in this gods forsaken tunnel, but at least he'd go out in a blaze of glory and get to see one of the greatest of the fae at work.

Sanyaro's gaze raked across the black-clad and dark skinned group. The goblins had disappeared behind the iron pyramids, their movements ignored as the two sides clashed wills. Any moment the first blade would be drawn. Any moment, Sanyaro would unleash his full power.

Curuthannor would have a front row seat to it all.

Slowly, with obvious effort, Sanyaro unclenched his hand. His shoulders released. He gave Prince Aradae a grim smile.

"I see. Well, I suppose I shall have to take it up with your father directly at the feast tonight."

Prince Aradae's eyes widened. "The feast?"

"I see King Rindae hasn't yet told you the news. Yes, there will be a feast tonight, and it is critical that you attend, I think. I will see you there, and we'll finish our discussion."

Sanyaro stepped forward with a relaxed stride, the grim smile turning genuine as Aradae's expression shifted from shock to annoyance. Sanyaro patted him on the chest.

"Don't worry, dear boy. You won't be obligated to talk much. I, on the other hand, will need to find the calm before the storm. Curuthannor, follow me."

Curuthannor deflated, the adrenaline that had flooded his system in preparation for the fight draining away and leaving him oddly tired for not having actually done anything. But what was he to do? He couldn't start a fight. That wasn't his way, especially not for the simple thrill of seeing an elder in full battle mode. He finished fights, he didn't start them.

With a sigh, he stepped up behind Lord Garamaen Sanyaro.

The dark elves didn't move.

"Let us pass, Aradae. I will speak with your father. There's nothing more you can do."

Without a word, Prince Aradae stepped one foot backward and angled out of the way to let Lord Garamaen through. The rest of his shadow guard shifted as well, until a narrow aisle opened for their exit.

"Wert, do lock up, would you?" Garamaen called over his shoulder as he left. "I expect every bar to remain inside until I can get this sorted with His Majesty, King Rindae."

"O' course, sir. O' course. Have no worries," Wert replied from a shadowy corner at the back of the room. "Okay, you lot. Empty the carts and stack the iron back where it was. Nice and neat, now."

Curuthannor's shoulders brushed against the black leather of the guard as he proceeded through the gauntlet they'd thrown. He refused to flinch, instead meeting each individual gaze as he passed with his chin held high.

Even if they didn't get another bar of iron, the six carts that had already trundled out of the tunnels would be more than enough to complete High King Othin's commission, and outfit all of his generals from head to toe. Today was not a loss.

CHAPTER 35

Faeliel threw her head back on the pillow, a smile pulling the corners of her mouth. There was at least one good thing to be said for seducing the King of the Shadow Realm; he knew how to care for a lover. He'd hardly left her side since their first tryst in his office, as insatiable for gratification as she. They'd stopped for food and wine, uncaring of the time of day or the proper meal. At some point she had dozed, only to be wakened by soft kisses to her shoulder.

She hadn't minded in the least. She also had no idea what day it was, or how long they'd enjoyed each other's company.

They had ended up in the king's private chambers, a suite of rooms opulently furnished with deep cushioned couches and thick rugs. They'd only spent a short time in the front sitting area, but Faeliel had enjoyed the mix of textures on nearly every surface.

Two other doors had branched off the main sitting area, but they hadn't bothered with a tour. They'd gone straight from the sitting area into the king's bedchamber to find the broad bed with its natural woven branch headboard and silky sheets. She hadn't seen much of the rest of the space.

She opened her magical senses for a brief moment to make sure they were truly alone. Belegeth stood at the door with no other greater fae auras close by. Even the servants had been dismissed to give Faeliel and King Rindae their privacy. Sadly, the world didn't seem inclined to let them hide away any longer.

An aura of pulsing white light approached from the direction of the throne room: Daeturion, the king's son and heir to the throne, and one of the strongest users of soul magic she'd felt since she'd arrived in the Shadow Realm.

He paused at the door.

"I believe your son is here," she murmured, letting her lips whisper across King Rindae's earlobe.

"Let him wait," King Rindae mumbled into his pillow.

Daeturion knocked on the outer door, the sound urgent but not aggressive.

"I don't think he'll be denied." Faeliel nibbled the edge of his tall pointed ear. The skin of his neck prickled with goosebumps beneath her fingers and he let out a low groan. She'd discovered the erogenous zone at some point in their explorations, and delighted in his response. Hopefully it would keep his thoughts on the promise of her bed and not on the complications of political alliances.

"The sooner you answer it, the sooner you can return to the warmth of my sheets," she teased.

"Fine," the king grumbled. He pushed back the promised sheets and strode naked from the bed. Apparently, he was entirely uninhibited. Not that she minded.

While he was gone, Faeliel thought through the consequences of the sudden tryst. She'd anticipated a longer seduction, believing Rindae would hesitate to become involved with his enemy's daughter. She was glad to see she had been wrong. In fact, moving the timetable up a pace would prove a greater surprise to her father. She couldn't wait to truly be free of him.

She heard the outer door to the suite open and close, and quiet voices murmuring in the sitting room. Footsteps padded back to the bedroom.

King Rindae had put on a robe, but his bed-ruffled appearance still looked dashingly handsome.

"I apologize, but duty calls and can no longer be set aside."

Faeliel pushed out her bottom lip in a mock pout. She knew the requirements of his position, understood that he had an entire realm to rule, but she had hoped to solidify his attachment to her before he returned to his responsibilities.

"Isn't there anything I can do to convince you to stay?" She stood, letting the sheets slip away from her body, and strode toward her prey. Rindae didn't move, but his gaze heated as he looked down on her naked form. Pressing herself close, Faeliel gently drew a finger down the edge of his robe where it opened across his chest.

Rindae leaned into the caress, but his words were not the response she wanted to hear. "I'm afraid not this time, but I assure you, I will return as soon as the current problems have been dealt with."

Faeliel lifted up onto her toes, pressing her lips to the hollow beneath his ear. "Are you certain your son can't wait, just for a little while?"

Rindae's arms wrapped around her waist pulling her in tightly. She could feel his excitement from beneath his robe, but still he controlled himself.

"Return to your rooms and warm your sheets. I'll come to you as soon as I'm able."

"As you wish, my king." Faeliel dipped her chin and smiled up from under her lashes. Let him take the promise of those words to think on while she was gone.

CHAPTER 36

A glimpse of pale white flesh, and Daeturion turned away. He didn't need or want to see the woman in undress, and even if she tried to distract his father once more, she would be unsuccessful. King Rindae might be many things—lothario, narcissist, socialite . . . just to name a few—but he was dedicated to his realm and the dark elves he ruled.

Rather than wait and risk an unwanted encounter, he let himself into his father's private study and took a seat in the visitor's chair. Daeturion had spent many hours in this room, learning how to rule from his father. He'd read almost every book on the shelves that lined the walls from floor to ceiling, then been quizzed on their contents. To this day, he could still quote obscure historical facts and strategies from their pages.

The door opened.

"King Othin has declared war." Daeturion said without turning around. He didn't need to. His father's presence was unmistakable.

"And?" King Rindae wrapped the black robe tighter around his waist and sat down at his desk, reclining back as if Daeturion hadn't just told him that their entire realm and way of life was at risk of being destroyed.

"The princess has lied to us. She wasn't sent here on a diplomatic mission. She fled her father's control." Daeturion kept his tone level, but watched the king's reaction. He didn't seem shocked or surprised. Perhaps she had already confessed her intentions.

"How do you know this?"

"I intercepted her handmaiden, Lhéwen, on her return from the Upper Realm. Her memories are clear. She has been accused of aiding you in the capture of the heir to the golden throne and a price has been placed on her head."

"That doesn't mean Othin wasn't aware of his daughter's journey."

"Elves don't lie, father. He wouldn't swear to his entire court that she were kidnapped unless he truly believed it."

"Who's to say what words were used and in what context? He is clever and manipulative. Always has been. Even if he doesn't lie, I wouldn't trust a word out of his mouth."

So King Rindae was choosing to disbelieve the handmaiden in favor of the princess. Choosing to misinterpret Daeturion's information. Interesting.

"Still, we must make good with the Upper Realm. We cannot allow a misunderstanding to result in a cataclysmic war," Daeturion pushed. Time to test his father's commitment to the lady.

King Rindae lifted an eyebrow. "What are you suggesting then, my son? Should we swear allegiance to the foreign king to make amends?"

"Of course not, Father, but perhaps if she were to go home—"

"Do you truly believe that would end Othin's designs on our realm? Of all the realms, the dark elves have had the longest struggle to conquer and contain the native races. Now that we've done all the work to establish our dominance, Othin would take it for himself. He will not rest until he can claim dominion over our lands and our resources."

"Perhaps not, but it might delay his ambitions and give Aradae enough time to properly build a standing army."

Aradae was a strong warrior and had gathered a skilled group of soldiers over the centuries, but the Upper Realm's forces were more numerous than their own. If the fire sidhe joined the high elves, the Shadow Realm would be lost.

"He's had enough time for that already. Besides, returning Faeliel to her home realm in shame would be disastrous. She knows too much already," Rindae said.

Daeturion's eyes widened and he very nearly gasped. "You let her into your confidence?" His father had never before forgotten his priorities for a woman.

"No. But I understand her, and she understands me. She is a woman clawing for a bit of this life to call her own. She won't find it in the Upper Realm."

"Then you'll offer her asylum here? Oppose King Othin?"

Rindae had never been a man of personal commitment, and Daeturion had little hope that his father would be amenable to the suggestion of formally courting the princess—not after just a few days with her. After all, he'd spent decades with Daeturion's mother and never courted her. Marriage, even without a full life-mating, wasn't something to be entered into lightly, not when it meant potentially thousands of years with a single person. Still, if the king enjoyed her apparent attractions, it might be preferred over groveling and hoping for peaceful negotiation.

"That's not what I said." King Rindae's voice was calm but his eyes narrowed as his anger stirred.

The door slammed open. Daeturion spun to face the new threat, but it was only Aradae. His younger brother stormed into the king's office, fury etched into every pore while Tecindo carefully closed the door behind him.

"Lord Garamaen Sanyaro is here. He's taken his iron stores from the hoard and is *giving* them to the high elves." Aradae came to a stop at Daeturion's shoulder, one hand gripping the hilt of his current preferred weapon, a short double-edged sword of human make he had acquired during a stint with the desert-dwelling natives.

"And you let him?" Rindae demanded as he sat upright.

"Of course not! But how am I to keep one of the most powerful living origin elves from taking what he's already paid for? The man is insufferable, and far too powerful."

"How much does he have?"

"An entire cavern. Enough to outfit an army. It seems he's had a small standing order for years, and has stockpiled the iron over time."

Rindae leaned forward, his entire body tense. "That man meddles where he is not wanted. I suppose he took it all?"

"No, only a few cartloads. I managed to stop the rest from leaving, but only on his sufferance."

"A few cartloads is enough to outfit a legion. Father, we must act quickly. Return her to her homeland and beg forgiveness," Daeturion urged.

King Rindae's eyes narrowed and fury stirred in his voice. "I have refused to bend my will to Othin's for over a thousand years. I will not start now."

"You must! We are not prepared for war," Daeturion insisted.

"Does the commander of my forces agree with you?" King Rindae asked, turning to face Aradae.

"We've been actively recruiting, but thanks to the wretched time differential, we will always be at a disadvantage."

"But not unprepared."

Aradae dipped his chin, but Daeturion knew the truth. His little brother was doing his best to increase their security and add men to the ranks of his shadow guard, but the noble dark elf families had little interest in military service and the king had banned the lesser fae from serving in the guard.

"There may be another way," Daeturion ventured.

King Rindae lifted an imperious eyebrow.

"What if we don't send her home with reparations, but with an alliance?"

"What scheme have you concocted?" Rindae demanded.

"Court her. Make it official. Then we take the news of your future union to King Othin. It is an alliance we can all be glad of."

"I will not surrender—not even symbolically—to Othin."

"That's the beauty of it. This would be an alliance, not subservience. It will be the union of the millennium. High elf to dark elf, princess to king."

Daeturion watched his father's expression turn from affronted to speculative. He did love a good show, especially when he was the center of attention.

"Are you mad? King Othin will never let his daughter marry," Prince Aradae sputtered.

"Othin won't be able to do anything to stop it, and once the marriage is final, there will be no need for war. Blood is stronger than economics or power." Daeturion was confident the king wouldn't do anything to endanger or otherwise harm his only daughter. He had kept her as a political pawn, an enticing bait to attract the other realms, but Rindae was the only king left unpaired. The other elven rulers were either already lifemated, or uninterested in women.

"Which is why he's never let her court anyone in the past," Aradae argued.

"Perhaps it's been more a problem of an unsuitable match, than a refusal to let her court. But you cannot aim higher than a king for matrimony."

"This will anger him beyond reason. Without his wife by his side, there will be no one to control him."

Aradae could be like a canine with a fresh kill, unwilling to let an issue go. That could be a good thing when he was in the right, but right now he wasn't seeing the whole picture. Luckily, their father did.

"He may try, but we are not so weak. It's why he has feared us and is forever trying to bring us beneath his banner. Unlike Thanûr and Norgeledil, I know my own strength and have no fear of the Upper Realm. No, I think this idea has merit. Faeliel has a multitude of attractions I've only just begun to explore." King Rindae's lips lifted in a salacious smile.

"Father, their enervators will drain our armies to nothing," Aradae warned. "Dark elf bodies will lie thick on the ground before the high elves ever step foot on our lands."

"Then we will harness their souls to fight if necessary. Make your preparations."

Daeturion grinned at his father. "We must act fast, before Garamaen spreads word of King Othin's declaration. Our noble houses must be behind this union, must believe it is in their personal best interests as well as that of the realm at large."

King Rindae rubbed a finger across his top lip, pleased with the idea. "Yes. It will be perfect. We will hold a feast tonight and I will ask for Faeliel's hand in front of the entire court. Daeturion, you will arrange for everything. Call in the houses. Open the cellars. Spread the word. Let every man, woman, and child rejoice in the future of our realm."

"It will be done. But the news will spread quickly through the portals. As soon as she accepts we must send a messenger to Othin so there will be no misunderstanding. We must invite him to celebrate with us."

"How do you even know that she'll accept?" Aradae demanded.

"Oh, she'll accept. She all but promised herself to me already," Rindae replied with a smug smile.

"This is wrong. We should send her home, to her father and her people where she belongs. She will bring nothing but pain and trouble," Aradae insisted.

"No." King Rindae slammed his fist on the table. "*This* is the way we keep our sovereignty while saving our lands and our people from war."

"We will unite our realms through marriage and bind our interests with Othin's. There will be no need for competition or control if we share the same goals," Daeturion agreed.

CHAPTER 37

The hallway outside the princess's suite was deserted. Belegeth was not standing watch. No one roamed the halls. Lhéwen was entirely alone.

Daeturion had said Princess Faeliel had been spending time with the king. Perhaps she was with him now. But where to find them? She had no idea where they might be. The throne room? His public receiving room? Private quarters?

Given Faeliel's reaction before Lhéwen had left, the last seemed the most likely. Unfortunately, Lhéwen didn't know where his private rooms might be. Prior to her departure, they'd only ever been to the public spaces.

Shoulders drooping, Lhéwen unlocked the princess's suite. She had nowhere to go. There was nothing to do but wait. At least she didn't have to wait in the hall.

Lhéwen flopped onto the cushioned seat of the chaise beneath the window and covered her eyes with her arm.

She hadn't expected anyone to realize she had left the realm. They had, which meant they were watching her. She had been noticed. After decades remaining invisible in the high court, she'd failed to stay hidden in Nalakadr's shadows.

She blamed Curuthannor. If she hadn't met him, she wouldn't have been distracted by him. She would never have suggested a merchant carry a message from the princess, and Faeliel would not have enchanted the message to kill. Lhéwen would not have been forced by her own conscience to return to the Upper Realm without her mistress's permission, then find out that the woman she had felt as close to as a sister had lied to her . . .

No, this wasn't Curuthannor's fault. He hadn't done anything more than what she'd asked. She'd put all of the realms' responsibilities on him.

Nor was it her fault. Not really. She had been misled. Either the king had set this up as a means of justifying a war he'd wanted for centuries, or Faeliel had run away in yet another rebellion.

In the end, it didn't matter. Lhéwen was stuck here until the princess chose to return home. Without the princess's physical presence, there was no way to prove her own innocence. The king would have her beheaded on sight.

With that grim thought, Lhéwen drifted off into an uncomfortable sleep.

T he sound of the door opening jolted Lhéwen upright.

Faeliel entered the room wearing nothing but a thin silk chemise and loose tousled hair.

"Ah, there you are!" Princess Faeliel chimed as soon as she spotted Lhéwen.

Lhéwen quickly collected herself and dipped into a deep curtsy. "Your Highness," she replied. "You have returned."

"And where have you been?"

Lhéwen grimaced, but kept her face hidden. It wouldn't do for the princess to see her distress, but at the same time, she couldn't avoid the truth. Faeliel's reaction would tell her much about her true predicament.

"After your sudden energy surge, I knew the message had been opened by someone other than the king. There was no other explanation for your rapid change in demeanor. I had to find Curuthannor's body before anyone else did."

"Excellent thinking. I knew I brought you here for more than your skill with a needle. Did you find him? Was it gruesome? He must have died a very painful death, given the force with which I absorbed his energy."

"No. Rather, I don't know. I returned to the Crossroads to search for him, but he had left the Shadow Realm this morning, as instructed. He returned to the Upper Realm, but something happened."

The princess frowned. "Go on."

"Knowing that the king must be informed of the situation here, I decided to travel to the Upper Realm myself."

"You did what?" the princess's voice dropped and her expression turned hard.

Lhéwen hurried on before she could lose her nerve. "I went to the castle, to the west gate, as we always do, but the castle has been sealed shut. The guards have been rotated out. They didn't recognize me and I was barred from the palace."

The princess visibly relaxed. "So you didn't meet with my father? Then all is well."

"But the message never reached the king. The scroll was opened by one of the guards at the gate, who died almost instantly. I'm told Curuthannor was taken to the Pit as an assassin and traitor."

"The merchant's demise is most unfortunate," Faeliel dropped onto the couch where Lhéwen had been sleeping, flinging an arm over the back and crossing her legs in careless abandon, "but it's all for the best, really. So much has changed in the last . . . day? Two? I've lost track of time."

Faeliel giggled. By all the gods, she giggled like a young girl at her first public dance, gossiping about the handsomest man in the room.

"No, my lady, the news is much worse. Your father believes you have been abducted by the Shadow Realm and has judged me an accomplice. He has declared war! Were you not given this assignment by His Majesty directly?"

Faeliel sighed and cradled her forehead with a delicate hand. "Are you really so naive as to think the king would send me here? I have had to beg and scrape for every hairsbreadth of freedom I've earned since I was a child. He *still* believes me a child, or perhaps an imbecile, incapable of making intelligent decisions for myself."

"But he's launching a *war* over this! I could have been *executed* if I had been caught!"

"You should never have made that journey without my leave. Why do you think I wanted you to remain here and send the merchant? He was expendable."

Lhéwen had to physically bite her tongue to keep control of her emotions. No one should be expendable. Curuthannor was a good man, honorable and loyal. Princess Faeliel would have thrown that away on a whim.

"You told me this was an opportunity to prove yourself and your capacity to lead, to solve problems," Lhéwen said after swallowing down her ire. She kept her words carefully controlled and neutral. If Curuthannor had been expendable, it wouldn't be a stretch to think that she was as well.

"And so it is. I simply have to take it for myself. And I almost have. With a little more . . ." Faeliel's eyes twinkled and a suggestive grin spread across her lips. ". . . prodding, I believe we may be saved."

"Your purpose was to seduce King Rindae from the first. You never intended to return to the Upper Realm." Lhéwen's thoughts stuttered. For the first time, she realized the total lack of care the princess had shown. "You could have told me. Could have given me a choice! Now I'm bound to your fate, whether I will it or not."

Faeliel's voice grew cold and hard, like a jagged edge of stone. "I am your princess. Do not make the mistake of believing yourself my equal. You were bound to my fate the moment you joined my service."

Lhéwen recoiled as if slapped across the face. Never had Faeliel spoken to her in such a manner. Other ladies who displeased her had earned her wrath, and certainly some of the men who claimed too many advances, but never Lhéwen. She'd come to think of the princess as her friend, a surrogate sister.

Lhéwen could ill-afford to anger the princess. She couldn't return to the Upper Realm and she had nowhere else to go, no one else on whom she could rely. Princess Faeliel was her best chance of survival.

Swallowing her pride—not that she dared have much in the first place—Lhéwen gave the princess a proper curtsy and bowed her head.

"Apologies, my lady. I was shocked and did not mean to imply subversion. I would, however, appreciate understanding my own purpose here."

"You are my greatest lady in waiting: the best of my seamstresses, the most amenable to keeping our secrets, and useful with your little enchantments and design skills. That is all you need to know."

Lhéwen swallowed. In all her life, she had never felt more debased than at this moment. She finally understood that in the princess's eyes, she was nothing.

"Is there anything else?" Faeliel asked. "If not, you may return to your quarters until seventh bell. I will need you to dress me and attend me at dinner."

"Yes, Your Highness." Lhéwen kept her gaze lowered and her voice pleasantly neutral as she backed out of the room. She'd learned to disappear in the high court. It was like pulling on an old sweater: a little ill-fitting now, but familiar and warm, calming to the soul.

CHAPTER 38

As soon as they left the goblin tunnels and were free of eavesdropping ears, Garamaen's shoulders slumped and he began grumbling to himself.

"I should have done a better job of scaring that damn mining master. If he'd feared me a little more, he would have thought twice before running to Aradae. We might've gotten another couple of carts out of the tunnel. Still, I think there's enough to get started. And maybe I can manipulate this as a positive."

He rubbed a hand across his chin, ignoring Curuthannor's presence. His eyes gazed off into a distance Curuthannor couldn't see. Unfortunately, his feet kept moving over the rugged terrain Curuthannor *could* see and it was just short of a miracle the man didn't trip. Lord Garamaen Sanyaro was an eccentric sort, that was certain.

"Hmm . . . yes . . . that might work. Certainly not ideal, but better than the alternatives. Might save a few." Garamaen's words continued in a distracted, low rumble.

"What might work?" Curuthannor asked, hoping to draw Sanyaro's attention back to the present moment.

The elder elf blinked a few times, then glanced at Curuthannor as if recognizing his presence for the first time. "Apologies. Not to worry, I'm only cascading through a few possibilities. The good news is there's plenty of iron already through the portal to the Human Realm. Your father will be able to complete King Othin's sword."

His smile seemed tight around the edges, but he continued speaking. "The bad news is that Prince Aradae has informed His Majesty, King Rindae of our presence and we are expected at the feast tonight. There's no wiggling our way out this time."

"I thought that was the plan, anyway."

"Well, yes, but I always hope for an alternative. Formal social gatherings are not my preferred way to spend an evening."

Curuthannor looked down at the smudged and scratched brown traveling leathers. They were good in a fight, and good on the road, but not so good at a fancy noble party.

"I really don't think I should attend," he said.

"Nonsense," Garamaen replied. "I insist. If you're worried about your attire, I can speak with Tharbatiron about acquiring a new shirt and having the leather buffed and polished. The leipreacháni are good and fast. They'll get it done in time."

Curuthannor sighed, and Garamaen glanced his direction once more.

"As much as you dread this gathering, I dread it more. At least you don't have to attempt to negotiate the possible futures while having a civil conversation with self-centered royals."

Curuthannor didn't have a good response to that. Crossing beneath the northern arch once more, Garamaen followed the winding roads through the city back to the Crossroads Inn.

"Back so soon?" Tharbatiron asked when they arrived at the outdoor arena and pub.

"We will be invited to King Rindae's feast this evening. I'm afraid we may need rooms to ready ourselves."

"I thought that future had solidified. Your usual cottage is reserved, of course. I think I have another nearby for Curuthannor, as well. The feast should be entertaining."

Lord Garamaen grimaced. "I doubt it. He's still too wrapped up in the old ways."

"At least the news will be interesting. The inn will be practically pulsating with people."

"It's not already?" Curuthannor asked, mildly shocked. The crowd had grown even larger since their earlier departure, and the drinking heavier. They were nearing on destructive. In all his visits, he'd never seen the like.

Tharbatiron glanced at him and smiled. "No one parties like the goblins, and they've yet to arrive. Besides, so far all anyone has is rumor. Tonight, the king makes the announcement official. He and Princess Faeliel are courting."

Garamaen shook his head. "Foolish of them both. Enjoy the profits now. In a few months the tourist trade will be gone."

"There will always be those who choose to drown their sorrows in fine liquor and communal entertainment."

"I'm sure. Still, be careful, my friend."

Tharbatiron just smiled. "May I show you to your rooms? And is there anything else I can get for you?"

"Would you be able to arrange for someone to clean and polish my leathers?" Curuthannor asked.

"Most certainly. I could also arrange a new court robe, if you'd prefer?"

"That is unnecessary," Curuthannor replied. As self-conscious as he might be at a formal feast in his leathers, at least he would be comfortable. And prepared. The traditional robes that so many chose to wear were long and cumbersome, as likely to trip your feet as not. Besides, he hadn't the coin to pay for a more appropriate set of robes. "I prefer the practicality of the leather."

"As you wish. However, I insist on ordering a fresh set of linens to wear beneath. Your sleeves are practically falling off."

Curuthannor started to take offense, until he looked down at his arms. The innkeeper was right. The once-white fabric had turned gray and was streaked with dirt and grease from his travels. He hadn't even had an opportunity to bathe since his imprisonment and torture in the Pit. He suddenly realized he must smell as ripe as he looked.

"Apologies, I hadn't even thought—"

"Things have moved quickly. Not to worry," Garamaen interrupted. "Please, Tharbatiron, do what you can to make him presentable. Certainly a bath and shave, and the new linens. We haven't much time."

"I cannot afford to pay. Perhaps they can just wash the linens?"

Tharbatiron waved away the protest. "You are a guest of Lord Garamaen Sanyaro. Your coin is no good here. Not tonight. Follow me."

They proceeded down the pea gravel path away from the bar, past the outdoor stage, and toward the farthest corner away from the gates. Individual buildings dotted the landscape in this area, some seemingly built into the surrounding hillsides, others free-standing and made of heavy blocks of stone with doors at least three times Curuthannor's height. They continued past each one, heading deeper into the inn's property.

The freestanding buildings grew smaller as they passed, becoming more appropriate for elven guests. However, fewer and fewer lights lit the path, until only a single wisplight lamp lit the corner of each cottage. It made navigating the rocky path difficult for Curuthannor's high elf eyes, but he supposed the dark elves who typically rented these rooms would be able to see just fine.

"Here we are," Tharbatiron said, stopping before a white wooden cabin. He held out a key dangling from a silver keyring. "It's not the most lavish of our accommodations, but Lord Garamaen's cottage sits just over that small rise there, up against the outer wall."

"I appreciate it."

"The leipreacháni will be along shortly to assist you. If you need anything else, let them know and they'll send a message to me."

"My thanks," Curuthannor replied.

"Now you've done it," Garamaen teased. "Tharbatiron will hold onto that debt."

"True, but I won't hold it against you." Tharbatiron smiled warmly at them both.

"Get situated," Garamaen said to Curuthannor. "I expect we'll need to leave in two bells time."

"Not much time at all, then." Tharbatiron clapped his hands. "Go inside and bathe. Mick Artagan will be in to gather your clothes momentarily, but he won't disturb you. Just set your things by the door."

"I'll leave you to it," Garamaen said. "Get a bit of rest, if you can. We won't return here after we leave."

Curuthannor entered the small cottage with mild trepidation. He usually stayed in one of the less expensive communal bunk halls and paid to bathe in a separate heated tub. He didn't quite know what to expect in a private residence.

As soon as he opened the door, the room began to glow with soft light. The floors were paved in smooth stone and covered in plush rugs. Near the door, a small table and two cushioned chairs looked out the front window. A four-post bed pressed up against the back wall. Covered in luxe silk and fluffy pillows, it seemed far too luxurious for the average hardworking traveler.

On the far side of the room, another door stood slightly ajar. Looking inside, Curuthannor found the bathing facilities, including a copper tub that drew water from a pipe leading underground. He was relieved to discover the apparatus was the same as the tub he hired out. He knew how to start the water flow, and quickly began to undress, dropping his clothes to the floor after carefully setting his weapons in a neat arrangement on the table in the bedroom. He unwound the long braids in his hair and sank into the water with relief.

Days of stress and dirt washed away in the water. Muscles he hadn't noticed were stiff began to release. Even his hair was able to relax and flow freely in the steaming liquid. As went the muscles, so went the mind and he drifted in momentary peace.

After a time, footsteps clacked across the floor outside the bathing room. Curuthannor could just make out the quiet grumbling as the leipreachán crept through the cottage.

"He was supposed to the leave the clothes outside the door, nice and neat. Does he? No. So now Mickey has to go traipsing into a naked man's bath to ask. As if this job wasn't degrading enough. Hiring a leipreachán to clean clothes. I'm a master leatherworker, not a maid."

Curuthannor lifted his head from the hot metal behind him. A small grumbling man with a long red beard snuck into the room. A clay pipe hung out of the corner of the man's mouth and a cloud of smoke trailed behind him. *Just like a leipreachán*, Curuthannor thought. But what was he going to do? He needed to have his clothes cleaned, there was no other option.

"Apologies for the inconvenience," Curuthannor said, offering his best conciliatory smile. "I'm afraid I arrived unprepared and the bath was too inviting to wait."

"Harrmph," the man replied. He eyed Curuthannor from a distance. "I remember you. You're the sot who kept coughing at our smoke."

Curuthannor couldn't help the momentary shocked embarrassment. He hoped the warm bath explained the redness of his cheeks.

"We whittle our fingers to the bone working the leather. All we ask is a little relaxation at the end of our day. You get yours, don't we deserve ours?" The leipreachán nodded toward Curuthannor's bath.

"Of course—"

"I'll be back with your clothes in a bell. Don't you worry. They'll be clean and fresh, ready for all your fancy feasts."

"I never meant—" Curuthannor's words trailed off as the leipreachán disappeared through the door.

Curuthannor submerged his entire head beneath the water, feeling like a cad and a fool. It was too late now, though. The leipreachán was gone and so were his clothes. He could apologize better when the wee man returned.

When the water finally cooled to a tepid body temperature, Curuthannor got out and found a towel. There wasn't much to do in the room, and only a heavy cloth robe to wear, so after shaving and combing the tangles out of his hair, he lay down on the fluffy white bed. Within a heartbeat, he was deep asleep and insensible to the world.

A knock on the door woke him. For a moment he was completely disoriented.

What was he doing in fluffy blankets? Where were his clothes?

It all came back in a rush. His release from the Pit, the truthseeking, followed by the strange conversation with Tharbatiron and their trip to the mines. The confrontation with Prince Aradae and then back to the inn.

It was all a blur, but still hard to believe it had just happened in the last day. So much. It was no wonder he had slept so deeply.

The knock sounded again, this time louder.

"Curuthannor, it is time to depart."

Curuthannor jumped off the bed as if he had been poked with a sharp stick. He had overslept.

"One moment," Curuthannor replied. He never took long to gather himself, but this would test even *his* limits.

"Take your time," came the response. Luckily, Lord Garamaen's voice sounded bemused, not angry.

Glancing around the room, he found the stack of leathers and linens waiting for him on the chair by the window. He was glad to find the curtains closed as he dashed across the distance, taking the robe off as he went.

Throwing on his clothes as quickly as he could, he took a moment to brush and re-braid his hair, then tightened the laces on the leather vest and trousers before strapping his sword to the belt on his waist. The bracers for his forearms came next, except Curuthannor was forced to pause . . .

The linen shirt the leipreachán had provided had ruffles.

Ruffles.

Each arm, from the elbow down, was surrounded by puffy white cloth. In his rush to get dressed, he hadn't noticed the offensive design. He looked back at the table. Under the chair. There were no other options. Even his old bedraggled linen undershirt was gone—they had probably burned it. If this was some kind of leipreachán practical joke, he didn't appreciate it.

How was he supposed to put on the bracers? There was so much cloth poofing out around his forearms he wasn't sure he would be able to fasten the laces.

Still, he had to try. Lord Garamaen had said they weren't coming back to the inn, so he couldn't leave them behind. Besides, it wouldn't feel right to wear the rest of his armor without them. He would feel incomplete, and despite the relatively minor protection they offered, exposed.

Maybe the bracers would cover up the ignoble mess of a shirt. Curuthannor held the edge of the sleeve with the tips of his fingers, then carefully inserted the same arm into the hardened leather. The longest layers stayed in place, peeking out from the bottom edge nearest his wrist and lapping over the heel of his hand. It still looked entirely ridiculous. The shorter layers nearest his elbow stuck out at odd angles, simultaneously covering and bunching around the edges of the bracer. Meanwhile, the ruffles around his wrist were so compacted, they frilled around his hand like a lion's mane.

Using the fingers of his other hand, Curuthannor attempted to shove the ruffles in place, hiding as much as he could beneath the brown leather. At least the leipreacháni had done their job with his armor. The leather gleamed, and smelled as if it had just been purchased fresh from the leather smith.

"How's it coming in there?" Garamaen called, still outside.

Curuthannor swore he heard a hint of laughter in the prescient elder's voice. He let out a frustrated grunt, then opened the door. He couldn't keep the elder outside any longer.

"Apologies, Lord Garamaen. It appears the leipreacháni have chosen to play a practical joke at my expense."

Lord Garamaen took one look at Curuthannor and guffawed so loudly, Curuthannor was sure the palace would hear it.

"You must have done something quite offensive to earn that shirt. What did you do, steal his pipe?"

Curuthannor frowned. "No, but I did spurn their smoke at the pub when I was last here. And I forgot to put the clothes outside the door for pickup."

"That'll teach you. Well, I can help hide them some, but I'm afraid we must be going. King Rindae is relatively patient for a king, but we shouldn't test him overmuch."

With Garamaen's help, Curuthannor managed to get the layers of linen more or less under control. They still bunched at the elbow and frilled around his wrist, but at least he didn't appear like some kind of comical entertainer. As soon as Curuthannor was reasonably presentable, they began the trek through the city once more.

The crowd had gotten larger and more boisterous since Curuthannor's nap. Fae of all races danced in the streets, their shouts and cheers jubilant. The announcement may not be official, but the rumor mill had certainly spread the word of King Rindae's intended match. Everyone thought it signaled the end of the tension, a peaceful conclusion to centuries of fitful negotiations.

"At the feast, you are to remain at my side, as if you are acting as my valet," Garamaen warned, his gaze still scanning the crowd. "I won't require any real assistance, but do not wander. We cannot afford an incident. You may speak with Lhéwen when the opportunity arises—and you should—but do not attempt to converse with the dark elves. If they approach you, you may respond, but keep it vague. Understood?"

Curuthannor's brain hiccoughed.

Lhéwen would be at the feast. Of course she would be, she was the princess's handmaiden. And she would see him in this gods-awful shirt.

Curuthannor looked down at his arms once more. She was a seamstress, a premier designer. Not only had he played the fool as her messenger, now he would look the fool in her eyes as well.

In his distraction, a rotund goblin knocked into Curuthannor's shoulder, sending him careening into Garamaen. The elder elf caught him with an arm around his back and held him up before he could fall to the paving stones and be trampled.

"Are you well?" Garamaen asked.

"Yes, sir. Apologies. I understand."

"Good man." Garamaen paused, eyeing Curuthannor up and down. "Don't worry too much. If you play your words right, she might find you adorable."

"I'm not sure adorable is my preferred appearance."

"Better than dead."

"I suppose."

"In the future, I would avoid antagonizing the leipreacháni. You'll find that the lesser fae who serve the elves have just as much self-respect as the masters they serve, and their services should be similarly respected."

Curuthannor bit back a response. Unfortunately, the advice was too little, too late, and he would be forced to suffer the consequences.

CHAPTER 39

The princess strode through the doors of the grand hall, her hand placed on King Rindae's wrist in the elegant fashion of the high court, while Lhéwen followed three steps behind, wearing the mask of the meek handmaiden, though her lips wanted to curl in a snarl. Two bells spent preparing for this feast, and Faeliel hadn't said a word except to order one thing or another. She supposed it shouldn't matter. She shouldn't be surprised or upset. But Faeliel had been the closest thing to a sister she'd ever had, until this gods-cursed excursion.

Now the princess's true identity was being revealed. For once, Lhéwen could understand and agree with the other handmaidens who would complain about Her Highness's treatment or this or that insult. Lhéwen had always believed that their dissatisfaction stemmed from their noble upbringing. They expected preferential treatment and special privileges. As a common-born elf, her expectations had been set lower, and she thought she didn't mind being ordered around like a human.

Except, it turned out, she did. She had expected to be told the truth of their presence here, not tricked into assisting in yet another of the princess's rebellions. Lhéwen had become an accomplice in a complicated political agenda. She feared that of the two of them, she was the only one who would pay the price.

She should have followed her instincts and fled to one of the ocean villages. It was a mistake coming back here. The question remained, would she be able to correct it?

A bell sounded out across the hall, the lingering tone pure and ethereal, drawing her attention out of the unknown future and back to the present moment. The hum of the crowd quieted and every head turned toward the royal couple.

Lhéwen stopped when Her Highness did, clasping her hands in front of her skirt and keeping her gaze downcast.

Invisibility. The charm might have expired, but there was more than one way to remain overlooked.

King Rindae lifted his unencumbered hand, palm open to the ceiling. "Lords and ladies of the Shadow Realm, thank you for joining us on this most auspicious night. Not only have I reached an accord with Her Highness, Princess Faeliel of the Upper Realm, daughter and heir of His Majesty King Othin, we have also been graced with the presence of Lord Garamaen Sanyaro, Truthseeker of the Nine Realms."

Lhéwen's gaze snapped up, searching for the new arrival as hope bloomed in her chest. Though she had never met the man, had never before seen him, his reputation was legendary. He was the peacekeeper, the binder of Fenrir, the builder of worlds. His father had been part of the team who had created the portals, and he had been amongst the first to travel the dimensions. Whispers would have it he was supposed to have been crowned King of the Upper Realm, until he lost his hand and fell in love with a human woman. King Othin was quick to stifle that suggestion.

Perhaps, just maybe, he was here to help stop this madness. Perhaps he could help her extricate herself from the trap she'd found herself in.

There was only one man present who might be Sanyaro. He

stood at the back of the room near the wall, a bland, slightly amused expression plastered across his face. He was shorter than any other man present, save the human staff, with dull blond hair that had been braided back from his face. A single white feather hung from the end.

Next to him stood Curuthannor.

Lhéwen smiled and her carefully neutral mask cracked despite herself. He looked whole and hale, if a bit uncomfortable in the company he kept. His eyes kept darting this way and that while every other muscle in his body looked taut with tension. If he stood any straighter or more still, she might think him a colorful statue.

Curuthannor's eyes finally turned in her direction. Their gazes met. Curuthannor's jaw clenched and his eyes tightened around the corners.

Color rose to Lhéwen's cheeks. She had sent him on the mission that put him in the Pit. He must blame her. He must think she was responsible. Because she was. Maybe not entirely, but she had crafted the enchantment and tied it into Faeliel's magic.

He would never forgive her. She wouldn't forgive herself, either.

"As many of you know, I have been engaged in intense negotiations with Her Highness, Princess Faeliel, for the last few days. We have spent many bells together, contemplating the joint future of our realms. With Sanyaro's arrival, I believe the time has come to make it official," King Rindae continued.

Official? As far as Lhéwen knew, there had been no negotiations, at least not in words. Which meant . . .

King Rindae removed a shining silver ring from the breast pocket of his formal black robe and held it out on the palm of his hand. Princess Faeliel turned toward him with a beaming smile.

Lhéwen's heart lurched. She froze her face into the image of a smile.

"Though I have two sons by two women, I have yet to take a wife. Our time together has been brief, but I see a powerful future in the union of our two spirits and souls. So here, before the highest lords and ladies of my court, my friends and confidantes, I ask. Will you pledge yourself to me?"

Gasps echoed around the room and hands lifted to cover open mouths. Lhéwen remained motionless. She couldn't reveal anything, not one single emotion, not without endangering her already tenuous position.

"Yes, my king." Princess Faeliel's smile was brighter than the lamps that lit the room. Taking the ring from his palm with delicate fingers, she slid the metal band over the index finger of her left hand. She stepped closer to King Rindae, pressing her body against his, and the pair kissed, sealing their words before the court.

This couldn't be happening. Truly, this was madness. What was Faeliel thinking? Her father would never agree to a union with his enemy. She was not only courting the enemy king, she was courting disaster. King Othin would raze this land to the ground before he allowed his only daughter to court and marry the dark elf, even if . . . no, *especially* if there was a potential for a lifemate bond. That would mean the loss of one of his greatest assets.

When they finally stepped apart, King Rindae once more addressed the assembly. "Together, Faeliel and I will bring a new peace to our lands, a free but equal partnership between spirit and soul, light and shadow. With our union, the tension between our court and the golden throne will be released."

The king's sons began applauding, and soon the great hall erupted in excited noise, but King Rindae lifted his hands, once more quieting them before things got too loud to control.

"Come forward, Lord Garamaen Sanyaro. I would ask that you bless our courtship and usher our realm into new prosperity."

CHAPTER 40

She stood there, prim and proper with her hands clasped before her, giving nothing away of the treachery inside. Their gazes met and Curuthannor wanted to rush across the room and demand an answer. Of course, that would never do. Etiquette required he remain silent and still, just as she did.

They were delusional, all of them. These royals and their minions with their political schemes. If there was one thing he had come to realize in the past week, it was that he wanted nothing to do with any of them. They were power hungry and cruel, only interested in pursuing their own interests without regard for the greater cost.

Curuthannor's jaw clenched, every ounce of willpower focused on remaining in place. He almost didn't hear the announcement, but the applause snapped him out of his personal hell and into the insanity of the shadow court.

The princess beamed at the applauding crowd, her charisma turned up. It failed to work on Curuthannor. He felt it—how could he not?—but perhaps because he knew the truth of who she truly was, there was no attraction. She was a cold-hearted hag who was getting exactly what she wanted with no thought to the cost.

King Rindae lifted his unencumbered hand and quieted the gathering. "Come forward, Lord Garamaen Sanyaro. I would ask that you bless our courtship and usher our realm into new prosperity."

Garamaen stepped forward out of the back of the crowd, and Curuthannor was forced to follow. He had been ordered to remain close, to talk to no one but the woman who had betrayed him. He had no desire to do even that, if he could help it. Remaining in the great Sanyaro's shadow might buffer him from any interaction at all.

"King Rindae, you honor me, but I am afraid I cannot bless this union. I am not the lady's father, nor her king. I am simply the wandering truthseeker here to enjoy the evening meal." Garamaen replied after passing through the crowd to greet the king.

Curuthannor held back a snort. The man was perhaps the most powerful elf lord in all the realms, able to move with impunity through any of the courts.

Now mere steps away from the king, his consort, and her hand-maiden, Curuthannor's senses turned on high alert and his hand dropped to the pommel of his sword.

King Rindae's sons, the Princes Daeturion and Aradae, stepped forward out of the edge of the crowd. They didn't grasp their weapons, but they made their presence known.

Curuthannor immediately removed his hand from his weapon, but kept his arms at his sides where he could react quickly, if necessary. He didn't think there was risk of a physical attack, not here in front of the entire shadow court, but there were some very powerful wielders of spirit and soul magic amongst them. He was a common elf whose only magic was an ability to sense the energy patterns of artifacts and enchantments. He was outclassed on all fronts. His only weapons were the blades he carried and whatever focus and preparation he could muster.

"Nonsense, your support would be sure to sway any doubters in our favor," King Rindae replied.

"Perhaps we should take this to a more private venue?" Garamaen asked.

"I will not cower and hide behind closed doors." Rindae replied.

His son and heir, Daeturion, coughed lightly, and the king glanced his direction.

"However, since I can see that this will be a longer conversation, why don't we move to a more comfortable locale."

"That would be best," Garamaen replied. "Curuthannor is required to attend me, as well, but he may escort the handmaiden to your office."

Curuthannor grimaced, but King Rindae snapped his fingers and several human servants appeared to clear the way toward the doors at the back of the throne room. Garamaen followed King Rindae and Princess Faeliel, who remained hand in hand, and the king's two sons fell in line behind Garamaen. Curuthannor and Lhéwen had no choice but to walk together at the rear.

"Curuthannor . . ." she began after a few steps, but her words trailed off.

Curuthannor glanced at her from the corner of his eye and lifted a single eyebrow. "Do not say a word. It is done." Even if Sanyaro had encouraged him to speak with her, he didn't think there was anything to say.

Lhéwen bowed her head and watched her feet as they walked. Curuthannor couldn't help but worry she'd run into something or someone, with the way she failed to look where she was going, but they arrived at the door to the king's private chambers in one piece.

Lhéwen held him back before they entered.

"Let me at least fix this," she said, lifting her hands to hover near his arms.

The upper ruffles on his sleeves had come loose from their bindings and once again puffed around the leather bracers on his forearms. Lhéwen's bright blue eyes turned up to gaze at him, asking permission and forgiveness all at once. He could hardly say no.

"You may try," Curuthannor replied. "Lord Garamaen Sanyaro did his best to help, but there seems to be too much cloth to control."

"If you would remove the leather, I'm sure I can do more."

With quick fingers, Curuthannor unlaced the bracers and pulled them off, revealing the full horror of the shirt.

Lhéwen giggled, the sound tinkling like a trickle of water into crystal.

"This is leipreachán-make, yes?" Her fingers began to gently tug at the offensive garment. She didn't even look up to see his nod. "The leipreacháni are wonderful craftsmen, but their sense of style is lacking. Give them a design to put together, and they will outperform your greatest desires, but ask them to create something from scratch and you end up with—"

"Ruffles." Curuthannor finished for her.

"Precisely." Her eyes turned up to meet his gaze, their depths drawing Curuthannor in. She cast him a tentative smile, then returned to her work. She began carefully breaking the stitches holding the ruffles to the sleeve with a small hooked knife she'd pulled from a hidden pocket.

"Ruffles and lace and beaded trim are beautiful when used sparingly, but in excess they do nothing but obscure the underlying structure. Sometimes you must remove the outer layers to find the truth."

Her gaze lifted once more, but this time the look was intense and meaningful. "At times we may all be deceived by the apparent beauty in a design, only later to discover the ugly flaws beneath the surface."

She lifted away a cluster of ruffles to reveal a tear in the sleeve he hadn't even noticed.

"Perhaps a careful examination might be more prudent than simply trusting the designer."

Lhéwen visibly flinched. "I am sorry. So very sorry."

"Do not offer empty words. You arranged for my failure, left me to fade in the Pit," Curuthannor said, doing away with metaphor. He kept his tone level and cool, letting no emotion enter the discussion, but he couldn't let her quiet words and soft touches distract him like the ruffles on the shirt.

"I never intended for any of that," Lhéwen's voice was full of tears, but she kept her gaze locked on his arm as she finished removing the ruffles from the second sleeve. "I only followed the command of my princess. She wanted insurance that none would read the message except her father."

"That scroll killed a man. It could have killed me."

"But you did not open it," Lhéwen whispered. "I *knew* you wouldn't open it. You are an honorable man, it was obvious from the first. You are not one for treachery."

Curuthannor dipped his chin. "In that, you are correct. It is unfortunate that you cannot say the same for yourself."

"Curuthannor, please," Lhéwen begged. "Just listen to me. The princess only wants the freedom to live her own life."

"And she has no compunction at risking the lives of others to get it. No, Lhéwen, I will not let you evade responsibility so easily. You could have told me. You could have weakened the enchantment. You could have done many things, but you chose to send me off on your errand with a weapon in my hand and no concept of the danger I faced. Now King Othin is readying for war and your princess will do nothing to stop it."

"I came back to the Upper Realm to find out what had happened." She squeezed his arm, imploring him to understand, but he would not be dissuaded.

"So I was told. Yet you did nothing to free me from the Pit. Again, you could have turned yourself in, you could have placed yourself at King Othin's mercy and explained your purpose, but you didn't. You ran and hid and escaped the guard looking for you."

"I was scared. I didn't know," she whispered, the words almost inaudible. "I didn't think."

"I am not a political man. I do not pretend to understand the motivations of the royals. I only wish to serve my family and my realm to the best of my ability. The only reason I am here in this room is because Sanyaro commands it. If it were not for him, I would *still* be in the Pit. I have no desire to speak with you. Leave me be."

CHAPTER 41

Curuthannor and Lhéwen were the last to enter King Rindae's public office, the young warrior coming to stand at Garamaen's shoulder like a good valet. Garamaen glanced at the man's arms. They'd taken care of those gods-awful sleeves, so they'd had *the Conversation*. Curuthannor would come to regret his words, but Lhéwen had said her piece and they were on the right path regardless. That was good.

In the meantime, Garamaen, King Rindae, Princess Faeliel, and the two princes had found their own seats around the room. Garamaen had chosen a rather comfortable cushioned chair near the door. He wiggled in his seat for a moment, appreciating the firm yet cradling nature of the pillow. He would have to remember someday to ask Rindae who his upholsterer was . . .

He thought through the next few months and years. Sadly, he saw no opportunity for such a mundane conversation.

He turned his attention back to the king who now sat with his arm around Faeliel on a low-backed loveseat. If they put on any more of a show, they would need to find a stage.

Garamaen smiled, but he knew the expression didn't reach his eyes. Between the two of them, the palace wouldn't be large enough to contain their egos.

He still had to try to make them see sense.

Garamaen leaned back, but his gaze remained intensely focused on the dark elf king. He kept his voice level, but there would be no mistaking the danger lacing his words.

"This is a mistake, Your Majesty. I implore you to return Princess Faeliel to her father and request his blessing in the proper form. There is more at stake here than a simple marriage."

"I would bring the two most powerful realms together in a lasting peace. I don't believe there is anything *simple* about that," Rindae replied with a non-smile.

"Your actions and choices tonight will affect the future of the nine realms, but not in the manner you expect."

"If the future is decided, then why are you here?"

"I'm giving you one last chance to do the right thing, to save the nine realms from dissolving into hate and distrust."

"Nonsense," Princess Faeliel interrupted, her hand caressing her lover's knee. "With our agreement, I have made way for mutually beneficial terms. My father, King Othin, cannot deny the positive outcome."

"He can, and he will," Garamaen replied, calmly.

"*I* am not the one choosing hate. *I* am choosing love, building instead of conquering. If war is in the future, it is not of my making," King Rindae insisted.

Garamaen sensed more than saw Curuthannor stiffen behind him. He mentally willed the man to be still and silent.

Garamaen rubbed his forehead with his fingers. He could feel a deep headache building behind his eyes. "Your choices are your own. I cannot make them for you. But I tell you this: if you insist on pursuing this courtship, you will come to regret your fate."

"As you regretted lifemating with a human? Your choices have defined you, as mine will define me. Except my decisions will write me into the history books instead of out of them."

Garamaen's jaw flexed but he held his temper. He would allow no one to cast shame or derision on his lifemate. Of course, they also couldn't know that despite her short human lifespan, she yet remained at his side. They might not be able to physically touch any longer, but there was so much more to the lifemate bond than physical love. Their connection had, and would, continue to last through the ages, into death and beyond. It was a relationship the two self-centered royals across from him could never understand.

"Never once have I regretted the choices that brought me to Angeni. Never once have I looked back with longing on my life before her presence. I wish you luck in saying the same."

"I will usher in a new prosperity for my realm and unite both soul and spirit. Your fear will not lessen my determination to do what is right for my people and my realm."

Garamaen was blessed, or sometimes cursed, with the ability to See the future. All possible futures, in fact. Some were more likely than others to come to pass, but with every passing heartbeat and every new decision made by the peoples of the realms, the near future became clearer.

The far future was usually much harder to read. Unfortunately, thanks to Princess Faeliel's little rebellion, the next hundred years had become relatively solid in their probabilities. In fact, only a few branches remained for the fates of the nine realms. All but one resulted in intra-realm conflict the likes of which the fae hadn't seen since the portals first opened and the diaspora began. That one had such a slim likelihood of success, Garamaen didn't know why he bothered.

Still, he had to try.

"Grand words from a skilled politician. I hope you find the future I cannot See."

King Rindae gestured to Sanyaro's missing hand. "You do not See everything, my lord Sanyaro."

Garamaen shook his head and pursed his lips with disapproval. In truth, he *had* Seen the loss of his hand and had chosen the necessary sacrifice. It was a moral commitment he was proud of, and few others could boast.

"Princess Faeliel, do you understand the choice you're making? Have you thought of the consequences of your actions?"

Faeliel shrugged her perfectly shaped shoulders and tossed her glistening blonde hair over her shoulder. She'd chosen a gown with a wide neck that highlighted the curve of her throat. Her only jewelry was the silver cuff that curled around the edge of her ear. Garamaen was fairly certain that particular piece had been enchanted by the young handmaiden to increase the woman's attractions for her new king, but it didn't matter. He had long since inoculated himself against emotional manipulation.

"King Othin will be forced to see my happiness and the benefits of an equal partnership. There is no other option open to him."

"He *will* take action against you. This will not be a happy union."

Rindae scoffed. "She is a princess and heir to the golden throne. King Othin won't dare harm his own daughter. We will be safe together, here in the Shadow Realm."

Dark skin on light, a twining of two peoples with the twining of their leaders' hands. In another timeline, it could have worked. With a different ruler at the head of the most powerful army in the nine realms, it might have been enough.

Garamaen took a sip of the wine a servant had placed in front of him. A human servant. He grimaced. He hated seeing his beloved humans treated as beasts of burden, but now was not the time to win their freedom. Not yet. He peered into the distant future. In time, the humans would become strong enough to challenge the elves' supremacy. When that time came, another could take on that particular mantle.

He shook his head, clearing the errant thoughts. Sometimes his abilities could be distracting as he lost touch with the present in favor of the future or the past.

The wine was off. The cork had lost its seal and been infested with mold. Garamaen surreptitiously set the glass back down on the table at his elbow.

"King Othin is a vindictive man. He cares for his daughter, but he also cares about his reputation and that of his realm. He sees himself as the most powerful elf in the nine realms and anything that defies that image, including the disobedience of his daughter, must be squashed."

"The Shadow Realm is not an insect crawling about on the ground," Rindae growled.

"Perhaps not, but King Othin will attempt to stomp his golden slipper on your head all the same."

"Ridiculous," Faeliel replied with a sniff.

"I will say it again. If you do not return to the golden palace with a solemn apology on your lips, there will be war."

"Then let it come. I will not be so easily cowed."

Garamaen closed his eyes with a resigned breath. The last peaceful future had just faded from view, along with his appetite. War was inevitable.

"I hope you know what you are doing. I will leave you with a single piece of advice—don't be taken by surprise. Heed my warning and prepare."

There was nothing else to be said. Garamaen stood from the lovely chair and gestured for Curuthannor to follow. They couldn't force Faeliel to surrender herself—if they tried, Curuthannor would die.

The young man didn't know it yet, but he would become an integral part of the coming war. His would be a voice of reason in a time of chaos and confusion. Garamaen must do what he could to protect the man and unleash the warrior. Without him, the nine would be lost.

CHAPTER 42

"Stop," King Rindae commanded. "I have not released you yet."

Curuthannor felt himself pushed into the ground, as if each foot was as heavy as a mammoth. He moved his arm toward the hilt of his sword, but the movement was arrested in mid-air. Though his mind was his own, his body was no longer in his control.

No, not his body, his soul. His eyes turned toward Aradae, who stared at the pair of high elves at the door. His hands were held open at hip height, his fingers tense with immobility.

Lord Garamaen Sanyaro stirred next to Curuthannor, his shoulders rotating in their sockets as he stretched his spine upward to stand at his full height. He suddenly seemed bigger and more menacing than just moments before, finally appearing as strong as his reputation would have him. Curuthannor had never been scared of the man, but at this instant he would never dare oppose him.

"I cannot allow you to undermine our plans by returning to the high court," King Rindae continued. "You will stay here, as our guests, until such time as I deem the threat has passed."

"You dare try to command me?" Sanyaro growled. He snapped his fingers and the constraints around Curuthannor's soul evaporated.

Curuthannor drew his sword and moved in front of the elder elf. Sanyaro was far stronger magically, but he only had one hand. Curuthannor would be better in physical combat.

Aradae drew his sword as well and stepped forward to protect his father while his brother moved out of the way. He held the weapon in a tip-up ready stance on the back leg, matching Curuthannor's body position. Curuthannor was taller than the dark elf, which would give him the advantage in reach. But he'd seen the dark elf at the bar, and the man was fast and agile. Curuthannor couldn't let his guard down for even a fraction of a heartbeat or the man would be inside his guard and all would be lost.

Luckily, it seemed this would be a one-on-one physical fight. Daeturion clearly wasn't a fighter, if his pristine formal robes were any indication. He and Lhéwen had stepped to the back of the room, each on opposite sides of a floor-to-ceiling bookcase. The handmaiden's eyes were round with fear, but she didn't tremble or cower. She simply watched and stayed as far back as she could manage. Curuthannor approved, and hoped she remained there.

King Rindae may have been a fighter once, but now the king remained seated on the couch, his posture negligent and barely interested. He seemed more than willing to allow Aradae to take up the sword. Faeliel, however, sat up in rigid fury, her body poised to take action. She carried no weapons though, so Curuthannor felt fairly confident that her attempts to interfere would be magical, not mundane. Without his own protections, he could only trust that Sanyaro would be able to deflect any magic that came his way.

A buzzing began to build in Curuthannor's inner ear. Magical energy was being harnessed. He couldn't afford to look away from Prince Aradae, yet he could feel the change coming in the air.

"Lord Sanyaro," Curuthannor warned, but too late.

All at once a mist began to slide across the floor, writhing with loose forms of screaming faces. Something yanked on his energy, the magical connection pulling from Faeliel's hand. Curuthannor staggered, losing his footing even though he hadn't taken a step.

Almost as quickly as it began, the energy drain disconnected and the mist built up against an invisible line on the floor.

"You think to test my abilities?" Sanyaro's words snapped out with dangerous force. "Do not mistake my lack of political ambition for weakness. There is a reason I am granted access to any court I choose."

Aradae lunged forward, sword striking toward Curuthannor's shoulder. Curuthannor blocked, parried, aimed for the dark elf's throat. Aradae leaned back. The tip of Curuthannor's sword missed his adam's apple by less than a finger's length. The instant it passed, Aradae struck again, this time looking to slice open Curuthannor's guts from the side. Curuthannor spun to the outside. His sword lashed out. Aradae dodged. Riposte. Curuthannor countered.

The movement of the fight became a rhythm, each fighter trying to make his opponent miss the next beat. The clash of steel on steel, the metallic whine as the blades slid against one another, and the whoosh of air in and out of his lungs was the harmony to accompany the steady beat of his heart.

Aradae feinted to the right. Curuthannor followed, keeping the blades entwined but forgetting about the less lethal strikes. Mistake. Aradae's foot slammed into Curuthannor's gut, doubling him over. Aradae's blade came down in an overhead strike. Rather than fight to stand up and run into the other's man's blade, Curuthannor allowed his momentum to bring him to the ground and rolled out of the way. Aradae followed.

Curuthannor kicked at the dark elf's legs, but Aradae leaped up and over the strike with ease. He wasn't fast enough to avoid the return swing. Curuthannor's shin connected with the back of Aradae's knees, bringing them both to the ground.

"Enough!" Sanyaro shouted.

A thin line of fire suddenly leaped to life between the two combatants. Curuthannor rolled away from the blaze. The fire line widened and grew taller as Curuthannor and Aradae separated, until Curuthannor found himself lying next to Sanyaro's feet. The rug beneath the flame blackened and smoked, and the scent of burning wool seared Curuthannor's nose.

Aradae already stood on the other side of the fire line, his gaze fierce and sword still in hand.

The fight hadn't lasted long, but somehow Curuthannor knew it wouldn't be forgotten by anyone in the room.

"We are leaving. Do not try to stop us again." Sanyaro turned his back on the room, emphasizing his point. He had no fear of the men and women who would rule the Shadow Realm.

Curuthannor backed out with his sword still in hand. He wouldn't underestimate the dark elves.

CHAPTER 43

Lord Garamaen Sanyaro stomped his way down the passage toward the throne room and the feast of the Grand Hall. Curuthannor was forced into a stuttering jog to keep up. He still hadn't sheathed his sword, nor would he until they crossed the portal home.

"He thinks to control me. Me! Upstart little prick. Doesn't even know his history, let alone the future," Sanyaro mumbled.

Curuthannor continued to scan their surroundings. Guards were stationed every ten paces down the length of the twisting black hallway, but they made no move to stop the pair. It seemed the king had found his reason and chose to let them pass unhindered. Curuthannor wasn't sure anything could have stopped Sanyaro in his current mood.

He bumped into the elder's back. Intent on his surroundings he hadn't been paying close enough attention to the man in front of him. He assumed they would return the way they had entered. Luckily, Sanyaro didn't seem to notice. His attention was elsewhere—maybe elsewhen. For a moment, Curuthannor thought he might be lost in the crisis of his mind.

"No good. Can't go through the nobles. Too many questions, too many rumors. They must support Rindae's ill-advised plan or the realm will be lost. It won't do."

Sanyaro turned left instead of right, heading deeper into the palace carved out of pure obsidian.

Curuthannor hurried to catch up. "My lord, this is the wrong direction. We'll never get out of here this way."

"We'll take the underground way, the goblin-dug tunnels. They'll be empty. The goblins do love a good party. Tharbatiron will throw the best in the city. A lovely distraction."

"Sanyaro, sir, we will be lost for certain."

Lord Garamaen Sanyaro looked over his shoulder at Curuthannor for the first time. He lifted an eyebrow and tapped his forehead. "No need for maps when you can see every possible path forward. But take this." He removed a long thin piece of wood from a pocket within his plain linen robes, and handed it to Curuthannor. "Hold the thicker end."

Curuthannor did as asked, then flinched as the tip suddenly burst into a sparking, flickering flame. The light it gave off was brighter than it should have been, given its size, a welcome sight for eyes unused to the shadows.

For at least a half a bell they wound their way through the heart of the hardened mountain, their steps echoing off the black-glass walls. Sanyaro never hesitated at an intersection, never questioned his route, until they reached a cavern deep within the confines of the castle.

"We must wait here to let the announcement take root among the people. Tharbatiron has already stirred the crowd, but the king's words will confirm it."

"Here?" Curuthannor looked at his miniature torch, worried that it wouldn't last, but fire had barely damaged the wood. In fact, it hadn't descended more than a single knuckle-length toward Curuthannor's hand.

Truly, it was a neat trick. If his father had that kind of control over the flame in his forge, they would never overheat the steel and every blade would have the perfect constitution.

"Yes. It won't be long." He held his own light up to the etchings on the cavern wall, studying their design. The carvings seemed to depict some kind of half-horse half-dragon creature with a lizard's snout, long extensible whiskers, wings, and a horse's hooves and tail. Curuthannor had never seen the like.

"I'd forgotten about these," Sanyaro murmured. Curuthannor wasn't sure if he meant the carvings, or the creatures themselves. "Interesting. I wonder . . . it's possible." Sanyaro angled his head to the side, contemplating the drawings.

"My lord, we must press on. We must find a portal and return to the Upper Realm."

Sanyaro waved the stump of his hand in Curuthannor's direction. "There's nothing to be done for the high court at the moment. Anything I try or you try will only make it worse. We cannot be present or we are all lost."

Curuthannor shook his head, bewildered. Truly, the man spoke in riddles. He had to find a way to bring him back to the present moment. "I must return to my family. We must take the iron to them."

Sanyaro frowned, but continued to stare at the wall. "Yes. They will still need the iron. You must have a proper blade."

"My weapons are unimportant, but if we don't finish the king's blade on time, my family will be killed."

"Alright. We will go. I will ponder these complexities once we reach our destination. Perhaps there is a solution to be found. This way. We will take the king's own portal. He'll not be the wiser."

Sanyaro took the left path and picked up the pace. Curuthannor was glad that he would finally get home to see his brothers and mother again. He couldn't wait to see the looks on their faces when he pulled the iron through the portal. Six carts, and it was just a fraction of what they could claim if they could find a way to get it out of the Shadow Realm.

Which reminded him . . .

"Lord Sanyaro, sir, I am curious—not that I want to be demanding or overly anxious about it—but you never brought up the rest of the iron with King Rindae. Will we be leaving it behind?"

"For now. The goblins will protect it—they're honorable in that way—but it will be tricky to extract. Wert might be amenable to a deal of some kind, but it's the bribing of the porters that will be the problem. I will think on it some more."

All of a sudden, Sanyaro pressed up against the side wall and pressed a finger to his lips. Curuthannor followed suit and listened intently. The barest whisper of voices could be heard down the passage.

". . . the king is finally taking a queen," the first voice said. "The announcement's already been made."

"Political maneuverings. It'll never last."

"That's not what they're saying. The lady has her barbs in 'im good."

Lord Garamaen Sanyaro lifted his hand and closed his eyes. Energy buzzed from his fingers. His head twitched. Two thumps sounded from down the hall. Sanyaro paused an extra heartbeat before opening his eyes.

"We'd better hurry," he said, stepping forward into what turned out to be another large cavern with multiple tunnels branching off in every direction. "I only stole enough energy to put them to sleep. The portal is clear for the moment."

Crossing through the terminus, Curuthannor found that the far left tunnel wasn't a tunnel at all, but rather a portal built directly into the passageway. Sanyaro quickly drew the runes on the stone, setting Curuthannor's teeth on edge as always.

"No time to waste. Jump through."

Though he hated the portal's incessant buzzing, Curuthannor took the final steps and emerged into a canyon of striped red stone.

Curuthannor had never seen a portal so completely abandoned. Even the tunnel they'd just entered through had guards protecting it, but the canyon was eerily silent and devoid of any noticeable life.

"Welcome to the Human Realm," Sanyaro said as soon as the portal snapped shut behind him.

"Where is everyone?" Curuthannor shaded his eyes. The sun was hot and high overhead, a stark contrast to the dark, cold obsidian tunnels they'd just passed through.

"This is a remote portal I created about a thousand years ago, when a tribe of my descendants passed through the area. You're the first to visit since its creation. I have many such locations, some known to others, some not. This one is not. Everyone who helped in the creation is either dead, or entirely trustworthy."

Curuthannor couldn't decide if that made him feel proud or nervous. It wasn't always beneficial to one's health to be the first at anything. Still, the setting was beautiful, if stark and hot.

He turned in a circle, examining his surroundings. They stood just outside a small promontory in a cliff face. The arch they'd emerged through was one of several that jutted out from an over-hang that had clearly been carved by natural means, probably from flash flooding that ate away at the sandstone walls. Behind them, a broad cave large enough to encompass his family's entire home and smithy had been left empty except for the six carts of iron and primitive paintings of animals on the walls.

"I take that back," Sanyaro said, pointing to the iron that had been abandoned just inside the cave. "The goblins were here before you. Alas, I guess that means this secret is compromised. But we should be able to continue to use it for iron transport and storage."

Curuthannor walked toward the wagons. He ran a hand over the iron. These six wagons held enough iron to last his father years, maybe decades in the forge. They would be able to complete the king's current order, including the rest of the army requisitions, and still have some left over for custom jobs.

"Well, let's get on with it. Together we should be able to pull through the first cart and get your father's forge going."

"My thanks, Lord Sanyaro. This has saved us all."

Garamaen shook his head. "Do not thank me. You already owe three boons."

CHAPTER 44

Daeturion swallowed down the acid that burned his throat. He hated physical confrontation. He always had. Scheming and manipulation, the subtle art of gathering information and using it to his advantage—that he was good at. The rest he left to his younger, wilder brother.

"You must stop him, my king," Faeliel urged. "You cannot disregard his insolence. You are the king!"

"And how do you propose I do that?" King Rindae asked. "Magically, he is more powerful than all of us combined. He can counter our every ability. We might have bested him physically, if it weren't for that damned merchant warrior."

"I could have defeated him, given just a few more moments," Aradae growled. He'd sheathed his sword, and his breath had evened, but Daeturion could still see the battle-lust in the depths of his eyes.

It was true, he probably could have beaten Curuthannor, but Lord Garamaen Sanyaro had stopped the fight before blood was drawn. He didn't need to fight. To be honest, even without the blacksmith's son they never would have been able to block

Sanyaro's way. He commanded fire. He could have burned them to ash if he'd wanted to do them harm. No, Sanyaro was a man of peace and harmony, not war and discord.

"Who is he, really?" King Rindae asked.

For a moment Daeturion was confused by the question, then realized his attention had drifted. His father wanted information about the merchant warrior.

"As he said when we first encountered him, he is no one. Curuthannor, the untitled third son of Hatholdammon, a respected blacksmith with commissions from many of the lords of the high court—and according to the goblins, King Othin himself—but he has little of personal value to offer," Daeturion replied.

"How did he get so good with a blade?" Aradae asked.

"If you spent all day in a forge and didn't particularly care for it, wouldn't you take every opportunity to escape and practice with the blades you made?"

"That doesn't change the fact that the great Lord Sanyaro is leaving the realm without your permission. He must be stopped." Faeliel's voice had risen at least half an octave, her apparent panic getting the best of her.

They had to think rationally, not emotionally.

"No. Sanyaro is uninterested in fostering chaos. He won't return to the high court, not yet. The next move is our decision, and we must send an announcement to King Othin immediately," Daeturion replied. "This is still the best path forward."

"Garamaen is the best foreseer in all nine realms, and he cannot tell a lie. His Sight is true." Faeliel argued.

"Garamaen likes to think himself invincible, and his foresight infallible. He is incorrect," King Rindae replied. "There are ways to thwart his Sight. One day he will pay the price for his hubris."

Daeturion shook his head. "He believes what he says, but I do not think the future is as set as he Sees. There are always options." The fates wove as the souls chose, not the other way around. "But we must hurry to assuage any misgivings King Othin may have.

He must know that there is a way to cement a lasting accord between our realms without bloodshed."

"Is there?" Aradae asked. "I may not like the man, but Sanyaro has given us fair warning. If Othin wants his daughter, perhaps it is time she returned to her homeland."

"If I go back to the Upper Realm, I will never be able to leave again. My life will be over."

Daeturion had touched her hand. He had Seen her past, had Seen Othin through her memories. He was unmerciful, even cruel, obsessed with power and prestige. He would view her departure as a personal affront and she would be punished for it.

"What's more, he won't be satisfied until you have surrendered completely. Keeping me here is your best leverage against him." Faeliel's words rang with truth.

"Othin has been trying to gain a foothold in the Shadow Realm for centuries. Even if she returns, there is no guarantee he won't still open war in retaliation for her departure," Rindae added. "It might even be more likely. If she's not here, he won't pause to consider her safety."

"So you would allow yourself to be viewed as a hostage?" Aradae demanded.

"Of course not. Not to the people of the Shadow Realm, at least. I don't much care what my father's court believes, but I am here of my own free will. And our bond is strong. I can already feel the beginnings of a much deeper connection. You can't counterfeit a lifemating, so once our union is sealed, my father and all the rest will be forced to accept it. However, we should wait until it is done before telling him."

"If we don't tell him ourselves, he will find out through rumor and spies that you have declared a courtship, except instead of seeing the positive alliance, he will see subterfuge and betrayal. I state again, a messenger must be dispatched immediately. We cannot afford a delay." Daeturion was convinced this was their best and only realistic option. Whatever Sanyaro had said, whatever he believed, if they were to avoid war without losing their independence they needed to present their strengths rather than imply any weakness.

"Fine. I can see I will not win this argument, but let me warn you, a simple messenger isn't enough. My father must feel respected, even revered. We must send a proper envoy to request his blessing of our courtship."

Rindae lifted Faeliel's hand and kissed the inside of her palm. Daeturion barely withheld his grimace.

"Daeturion, you must go," the king said while holding Faeliel's gaze.

"Is this really necessary?" Aradae asked. Disgust practically dripped from the words.

Daeturion hid his grin behind a soft cough, but flicked his eyes from his brother to their father and back. Aradae got the message.

"Othin is as likely to take Daeturion prisoner in vengeance as he is to listen to your joyous news," he said, covering his true meaning.

Though Aradae had been careful to keep his words respectful, Daeturion knew he was equally disgusted by the rapid progression of this new courtship. Their mothers had once been on the receiving end of that suave grace, but they had each been set aside for other ladies after decades of loyal companionship and hope for the connection of a lifemating. Rindae had never offered a formal courtship, never made any promises to any of the ladies in his bed, never *married*, until now.

"Daeturion will be safe with my message in hand," Faeliel replied. She petted the king's arm and smiled up at him in reassurance.

"As Curuthannor was safe? Have you told our king what befell the last messenger you sent home?" Daeturion countered.

For an instant, Daeturion was sure he saw Faeliel's lip curl up in a sneer, but she quickly smoothed it over.

"Curuthannor was unknown and common. You are the heir to the shadow throne. None would dare."

"Except your father. In this, I must agree with Aradae. We should not enter the Upper Realm unnecessarily. However, I believe there may be an acceptable alternative, if you are willing to hear it."

"Go on," Rindae urged with a pat to Faeliel's hand, which had clenched on the sleeve of his robe.

"What if we invite the king to treat with us on neutral territory. Perhaps a location in the Human Realm would suit. Somewhere comfortable and easy to reach, but also easy to defend for both sides."

"What do you think, my love? Will your father be amenable to a meet?"

Faeliel lifted an eyebrow and blew a breath through her nose. "I suppose it may be the best solution."

"Then it is settled. Daeturion, you will arrange for it. Let us return to the feast now, before the rumors begin to grow from Sanyaro's departure. The lords and ladies of the court should be presented with the opportunities that will arise from the union. We must have their support." King Rindae stood and held out his hand to help Faeliel from her seat.

"Not just the lords and ladies of the court," the princess said as she took her new king's hand and rose from her cushion. "We should announce our union to the realm at large. Then *we* control the flow of information."

Daeturion lifted an eyebrow, impressed with her ladyship's astute suggestion. Information was power, and inclusion meant control. With both in hand, they could master any opposition.

CHAPTER 45

Footsteps stomped and swirled. Dark elves, blood sidhe, goblins, and trolls alike crowded the streets of Nalakadr, their cheers sporadically traveling like waves through the sea of fae. Even the bridges and balconies surrounding the upper levels of the twisting buildings were packed.

Rothruinil's eyes widened. This was not the reception she had expected. It seemed every soul in the Shadow Realm was out to celebrate.

"What's going on?" Rothruinil asked, grabbing the first blood sidhe that passed.

"Haven't you heard? Our king and the high elf princess are courting!"

Rothruinil nearly choked. She couldn't possibly have heard that right. "What?"

The man nodded in earnest. "This will be the party of a generation!" he shouted, leading Rothruinil in a twirl before disappearing into the crowd.

Forcing a smile, Rothruinil sidestepped out of the way of the portal entrance. More people were pushing through the veil, their faces lit with excitement. The outreaches of the entire realm must have heard the news and were coming in to join the celebration.

If only they knew . . .

But the high elf princess was here, at least that much was true. The question remained, was she here of her own free will, or had the dark elf king captured her, as King Othin claimed?

Progress was slow through the crowded streets, but step by step, Rothruinil approached the palace. Banners waved from the tops of the surrounding buildings, their brilliant colors seeming to glow brighter than the moonlight. The portcullis was lifted and the doors thrown open, but guards still stood on the bridge into the palace proper. A line had been clearly delineated where the casual bystanders could not pass. Everything up to that point was a mass of sweating bodies and swirling fabrics.

Grabbing a new dancing partner, Rothruinil twirled her way into a spot where she could watch the palace gates without being noticed.

Less than a bell later, she was rewarded. A gong chimed from the palace walls. King Rindae and Princess Faeliel stood on a wide balcony overlooking the entire palace grounds and out into the streets of the city.

Every breathless body in the area stilled to silence.

King Rindae lifted his hands, his left clasping the princess's in the air. She smiled up at him, her expression adoring and triumphant.

"Citizens!" the king spoke, his voice somehow enhanced to carry until it sounded like he stood right next to Rothruinil and the rest of the audience. "Your future queen!"

The crowd cheered, their voices carrying high into the black sky. Rothruinil forced herself to follow along, keeping up the pretense of a happy bystander.

Faeliel hadn't been kidnapped. She wasn't a prisoner. King Thanûr must be informed.

He had been deceived.

Rothruinil surreptitiously glanced around the courtyard surrounding Nalakadr's public portal. After a full night of revelry, the Shadow Realm citizens had finally retreated to their homes and burrows. At least, for the most part. A group of blood sidhe and their drunken meals staggered toward a blood bar on the corner, and a leipreachán slept on a black stone bench, but otherwise, no one was nearby.

Quickly, she coded the portal for home and stepped through the veil to Laernúra, the Summer Realm capital city. The path changed from smooth obsidian cobblestones to bumpy shell pavement, and the dim light of daybreak became brightest midday, but she didn't pause and her steps didn't falter. With each breath, the scent of sweetened ash faded, to be replaced with the bright florals of home. Though the tension eased from her shoulders, she couldn't pause to appreciate the sun god's glory. She had a job to do.

King Othin had lied. He was an oathbreaker. It could not be borne.

Twisting her hair into a loose tail, Rothruinil revealed the tattoos that crisscrossed her back and marked her as the daughter of the king and queen. She strode past the colorful tiled buildings and across the vine-draped bridges with a determined step. Everyone cleared out of the way with a lowered head, or risked her wrath. Not that she was concerned with the formality of her position— truly she could not care less whether the people gave their obeisance. No, she wrapped her heritage around herself as armor, to keep the people at a distance. The last thing she wanted or needed was an entourage. She didn't have the time.

Striding across the final bridge and onto the palace island, Rothruinil pushed her way through the dense tropical growth surrounding her family's fortress. A low growl met her intrusion.

Rothruinil grinned. She might not have time for the entourage of hangers-on, but she always had time for her babies.

She growled a response, though the rumble of her own throat was a thin reverberation in comparison to the echoing thunder of the barong.

A creature with the body of a great cat, the face of a red-skinned daemon, fangs as long as her forearm, and wings longer than Rothruinil was tall emerged from the shadows of the underbrush.

"You return. The hunt was successful?" Awgrria asked, her voice struggling to produce the words necessary for elvish speech.

"Of a sort," Rothruinil replied, running her hands down the warm fur of the cat's back. "I found my quarry, but she was not as we had been told."

Awgrria wrinkled her nose in distaste. "A lie?"

"Perhaps. Certainly an untruth."

"They are the same."

Rothruinil shrugged. Though sentient and capable of elvish speech, the barong could not understand the subtleties of the language. They thought of things in yes or no terms, their priorities on hunting, providing for their kits, and protecting their home. Anything else was deceit.

"I must speak with my father. Do you know where he is?"

Awgrria opened her mouth, drawing breath over her tongue and scenting the air. "His scent is on the wind from the north."

"Perhaps he is on the training grounds with the Tirnor."

"I will fly you there."

"I would appreciate it, but don't your kits need you?"

Awgrria had given birth to three healthy babes just months before. They were becoming little rascals, escaping their approved safe zone at every opportunity. Rothruinil knew they were driving their mother crazy, but the female rarely left her den.

"Their father has come to know his duty. I have time."

"In that case, please. You honor me."

Awgrria dipped her head and lowered to one knee, giving Rothruinil the ability to climb aboard her back. Despite the heat of the realm, the barong's fur wasn't hot or uncomfortable. On the contrary, the thin hair felt slick and cool against Rothruinil's skin. Awgrria ran a few steps and spread her wings, finding an opening in the leafy canopy to break through into the brilliant blue sky.

Rothruinil laughed out loud, the feeling of flight never ceasing to delight her senses. It was a rare treat from a creature that had never, and would never, be fully tamed.

Circling above the castle for a too-brief minute, Rothruinil marveled at the stone facade that had begun to crumble away as the vegetation ate at its surface. Given the heat, humidity, and relentless saltwater winds, it was a wonder the building had lasted so long. It was a remnant of the first settlers in this realm, the origin sidhe with fire abilities, who had come millennia ago to escape the dying world that was their home. Built in an ancient style with materials not native to the realm, it was a memory of a bygone era that was slowly but surely being forgotten.

As would they all pass beneath the sun.

In the past two hundred years, the king and queen had begun moving more of their royal proceedings outside of the ancient stone where they were better able to receive the sun god's blessing.

Spotting her father on the grassy hill where a group of eighteen Tirnor warriors sparred with their tavahatals, Rothruinil leaned in toward Awgrria's ear.

"Land there, next to the king," she said, pointing her finger at the cleared area where her father twirled his own weapon in a practice match.

Circling ever closer, Rothruinil watched and assessed her father's technique. She had trained with the Tirnor since she was a child, long before her naming day and rise to maturity. It had been a surprise to no one that she would choose the path of the warrior for her apprenticeship, least of all her father. But no matter how many centuries she put into the practice, her father still outperformed his child. Despite his thousands of years, his body retained the physique of a young warrior, thanks to the daily training that had become his habit.

His technique was flawless, the lunge and twirl of the short staff an extension of his body. His partner, Culuhatal, one of the most experienced tavahatal masters in the Summer Realm, matched him blow for blow. They didn't bother with the softer training weapons that wouldn't draw blood or break bones. No, they fought with the same hardwood clubs they would use in battle. They grunted and scowled as they danced around one another, their tavahatals moving at speeds that would destroy an early trainee. In fact, the only indication that this was training at all was the absence of fire.

As Awgrria neared the ground, the king lifted a hand, stopping the mock battle. Culuhatal retracted a final swing in an instant, the thick wooden bulb barely avoiding a strike to the king's arm. Both men gazed up at the winged lion and her rider with expectant expressions.

"Welcome home, daughter," King Thanûr said. "What news?"

Rothruinil sent Culuhatal a pointed glance. Taking the hint, the man cupped his hands around his mouth and called out to the other warriors, ending their matches.

"Return to the training hall," Culuhatal ordered. "Rest and eat. We discuss tactics in a bell."

The men cleared off the field and the king motioned for Rothruinil to follow him.

"So?" He asked, wiping his brow and bare chest with a cloth. "What did you learn."

Checking one more time to make sure no one else was nearby, Rothruinil shared the grim news.

"Princess Faeliel has not been kidnapped. High King Othin has lied to us."

"But she was there? In the keeping of Rindae?"

"Yes. With my own eyes, I saw the king announce that Faeliel will be the future shadow queen. According to the citizens, they are courting, hoping to form a lifemate bond."

King Thanûr wiped the cloth over his face, obscuring his expression. With a deep exhalation, he pulled the towel away.

"Is this another rebellion? Another one of the princess's antics?"

"If it is, it has gone too far, too fast. She has aligned herself with the shadow court."

"King Othin will not be pleased."

Rothruinil's eyebrows lifted in surprise. "Father, he has lied to us. His daughter wasn't kidnapped, she has chosen a lifemate. The Shadow Realm isn't declaring war, they're forming an alliance."

Thanûr shook his head. "That is not how Othin sees it."

"It is the truth."

"Perhaps. Regardless, she is there, and Othin wants her returned to him. Has the Shadow Realm begun its preparations for war?"

"No. I'm not sure what their plans are, but I saw no evidence of an increase in warriors or fortifications. The entire city was celebrating, dancing in the streets. There was nothing to indicate they even knew war was on the horizon."

"Then we wait. I'll not commit my warriors to a senseless war for Othin's personal vendetta." Thanûr strode toward the palace. "I refuse to be the instigator. Let Othin take the blame, and become the villain. I'll not be his weapon." Thanûr paused his steps, turning to face Rothruinil directly. "Go back to the Shadow Realm. Disguise yourself if needs be, but we need eyes and ears in their domain. We must know if and when they begin preparations, and understand their capabilities. I won't be the instigator, but we'll be prepared."

"Then we're joining King Othin? We're swearing his oath?" Rothruinil couldn't believe her father would disregard everything that Othin had done. He was volatile and vindictive, manipulative and unscrupulous.

Thanûr shot her an incredulous look. "Did I say that?"

"But you want to prepare for Othin's war."

"No. I prepare for war, but not necessarily Othin's war. I'll not let Valyaro's death be forgotten, but neither will I unnecessarily antagonize a powerful foe—and that's as true for the Shadow

Realm as it is for the Upper Realm. Their army must have grown enough that King Rindae feels he can oppose Othin's pressure."

"How do you know?"

"He would never have dared walk out of the summit otherwise."

"Then why don't we join with the dark elves? We can't support Othin."

"The golden army's not to be trifled with, and as Othin so poignantly demonstrated, neither is he. As a single combatant, he can do more damage to an army than any of our most elite warriors without ever joining the fray."

"What are you saying?"

"I'm saying that I'd rather we stayed out of it entirely, but if we must choose a side, I'll have it be an informed one. Now go. I've put Othin off for the time being, but his patience won't last long."

CHAPTER 46

King Othin paced around the enormous round table. Each of the major cities of all nine realms had been modeled and arranged along the edge, with their portal connections drawn in string. The table made alliances obvious, and the Shadow Realm had few. That meant they were isolated and insulated, their single portal the only known entry and egress from their capital city. It was a strong defensive position.

On the other hand, Othin's spies had reported just over a thousand soldiers in the shadow king's army on their last counting, and of those, only a fraction held enough personal magical power to withstand even the weakest of the high court's enervators.

Othin's assets were many and growing, his opponents few. He only needed to bring the fire sidhe beneath his command to assure his victory.

Thanûr and Norgeledil would swear fealty. They would have no other choice. He would make certain of it. When the time came, their soldiers would provide the first wave of attack, burning down King Rindae's precious city as they moved. With the energy drain on the unprotected foot soldiers, the fire sidhe would be practically unopposed. When they breached the dark palace, King Othin himself would see Rindae beheaded. He would claim the shadow throne for himself, placing one of his preferred puppets as protector of the realm.

King Othin snorted, and every head in the room turned to face him with a mixture of wariness and inscrutability. The council of high elves gathered at his command, there to offer what little knowledge and support they could muster. Despite their ambition, most were useless, though a few showed promise. Still, they all feared his powerful mood swings. They'd seen his treatment of those who displeased him. King Othin considered it a positive.

A knock on the door interrupted his planning. He nodded to the silent sentry to open it.

"We said we were not to be disturbed," Othin growled. He didn't even bother looking up, he knew exactly who stood on the other side. Rolimdornoron was the only person who would dare, but he'd better have a damn good reason for his disobedience.

"Apologies, Your Majesty. You are needed in the throne room. There has been a development."

Othin lifted an eyebrow and finally deigned to glance at his personal assistant and head messenger. Rolimdornoron stood framed in the doorway with his forehead nearly touching his knees in a low bow. He hadn't stepped forward into the room, and in his current position, he could see nothing of the table or the plans laid out on its surface.

The man knew how to give proper obeisance. Some of the other lords in this room could learn a thing or two from the lesser elf.

"Explain," Othin commanded.

"An emissary has arrived from the Shadow Realm."

"Throw him in the Pit. We will not treat with the Shadow Realm. Not after their treachery."

"He carries a scroll sealed with the princess's own signet."

"Your Majesty, it must be another trap," Tanco declared. He was the general of the golden army, and could be trusted to see the danger in any plan. "They are trying yet again to take your life. The scroll should be destroyed and the messenger dropped in the Pit immediately, before it can do even more harm than the last message from the Shadow Realm."

Othin was tempted to do just that, but he was also curious. What could the Shadow Realm hope to gain from a second attempt? Surely they would know he would suspect anything and anyone they sent to his court. And Sanyaro had judged the black-smith's son innocent of any wrongdoing. His scroll had indeed been sent from Faeliel. It was only too bad the parchment had been lost. Even Huginn and Munnin with their raven's curiosity couldn't find the remainder.

"Has the scroll been inspected?"

"The University has performed its tests and could find no evidence of magical manipulation, however no one dared break the wax," Rolimdornoron replied. "The messenger was also examined. He has sworn a binding oath that the message was given to him by the princess herself and that as far as he knows no harm is intended. He speaks the Truth."

"In that case, this is easily solved. We will watch him open the message. If he lies, or if there is another trap he is unaware of, then he will die."

"Your Majesty, I urge you to remain outside the room," Tanco said. "Your safety is of paramount importance. I will oversee the opening and deliver the message to you once we've proven its safety."

"I concur," Narchion, lord of the eastern province agreed. "It is sound advice, Your Majesty. The dark elves are devious and cannot be trusted."

King Othin pursed his lips in thought. He could not appear weak or scared in front of his lords. Even if they had pure inten-tions and his best interests in mind—which was unlikely given the ambition and ego in the room—he must always appear in control.

Perhaps it was time to once more demonstrate his power to his highest advisors.

Rather than saying anything, King Othin strode out of the room toward the great hall and his throne. The guards immediately fell into place, their halberds pointed forward in front of and on either side of their king. If anyone approached, they would eviscerate them. It was a lovely deterrent.

Othin listened for the footsteps of the rest of his entourage. Rolimdornoron scuttled along behind the guards, and the heavier tread of his advisors fell in line after only a moment's hesitation. Interesting.

The throne room guards pulled open the heavy gold doors as soon as they saw their king approaching. He didn't even break stride as he crossed the threshold and proceeded up the five steps to the golden throne. With a flourish, Othin sat and gazed out at the far entrance to the court. His advisors found their places in the hierarchy on the steps. No one but the king would sit.

"Send him in."

Rolimdornoron bowed from the base of the dais. "Yes, Your Majesty." He backed away down the long hall toward the penitent entrance, never bringing his gaze up from the floor and never turning his back on his king. King Othin allowed himself a fraction of a smile. Rolimdornoron was almost as well trained as the king's own guards, and he hadn't even needed to be drained of his individuality.

Moments later, the messenger was brought into the room. The dark elf looked like every other dark elf to King Othin's eye: black skin, shimmering white hair, pale eyes, and formal black robes with silver ribbon trim and Rindae's sigil—a dragon wrapping a sphere —emblazoned on the right breast in silver thread. The man squinted his eyes in the light, but approached the dais with a measured pace. He stopped two lengths from the foot of the steps and bowed with a flourish of his hands.

"Greetings from King Rindae, lord of the shadows and master of souls—" the messenger intoned.

Othin was quick to interrupt him. "We were told this message comes from our daughter, not our enemy. We have no interest in the deceits of Rindae."

The messenger swallowed and gently cleared his throat while maintaining his low bow. "Yes, Your Majesty."

He opened a small black tube worn like a sheath on his hip and removed a tightly rolled parchment. A black wax seal was pressed into the edge of the paper. He held the roll out on the palms of his hands.

Othin examined the sigil from a distance. It was truly his daughter's seal, the stylized knotted oak damaged on one edge. The black wax, however, was an ominous offering from the Shadow Realm. His daughter usually preferred the same golden wax he used on his own missives.

"Your daughter, Princess Faeliel, is well. She personally placed this message in my hands and bid me bring it to you and no other."

"Open it," King Othin commanded.

The dark elf glanced up, eyes wide. "Your Majesty, I am but the messenger. I am not worthy to see the message within."

"Then don't look at it, but you must be the one to open it. Do it now."

The messenger swallowed again. "As you wish, Your Majesty. May I borrow a slim dagger from one of your guards? I did not bring my own for fear of offense."

Othin nodded for the lowest of his advisors to hand the man his dagger. He could be magnanimous when needs be.

The lord in question frowned, but did as asked, handing the dark elf a jewel encrusted blade. "I want that back."

"Yes, my lord." The messenger didn't hesitate in his response nor alter his tone. Impressive. As well trained as Rolimdornoron was, even he would have taken offense at the implied theft. Instead, the dark elf messenger quickly inserted the tip of the knife beneath the wax and broke the seal with a quick twist of his wrist.

Nothing happened.

The messenger kept the scroll rolled, but loosened the edge to prove that the wax had in fact been broken. After returning the dagger to the lord, he once more held the parchment out on the palms of his hands.

King Othin curled his fingers in a quick 'bring it here' motion. The messenger—keeping his head bowed low—stepped up to the dais and leaned forward until the parchment was within reach.

Othin unrolled the scroll.

Dearest father, King Othin,

All is well, as am I. If it pleases you, I ask that you meet me and Shadow King Rindae in the Human Realm. We have much to discuss.

If you are amenable, please send word with the same messenger as brought you this scroll. He is trustworthy. A suitable location and portal codes will be negotiated upon his safe return.

Your loving daughter,
Faeliel

Othin rolled the scroll again and tapped it on his hand.

"Your Majesty?" Tanco asked. "What is the word?"

Othin considered how to present the news. He couldn't let his advisors believe Faeliel wanted to be in the Shadow Realm. After all, no high elf could stand the relentless dark for an extended length of time. The spirit craved the light even while the soul craved the dark recesses of the mind. It was why the high elves had chosen the brightest of the realms to work their magic, and the dark elves had chosen the shadows.

"Rindae wants to meet. The letter says Faeliel is well, but we do not believe the words on the page. There is force and manipulation behind the script."

"Then it is a trap. Guards, take hold of the messenger. We will not allow this treachery," Tanco replied.

"No." King Othin dropped the word with non-negotiable finality. "We will go to this meet. We will see for ourselves how the shadows have twisted our daughter. And we will bring her home."

This could be the opportunity he was looking for. It would take time for them to negotiate the details, and Othin could draw that time even longer. Especially since the Upper Realm moved faster than the Shadow Realm, his army would have more time to prepare than theirs. More importantly, his smiths would have time to finish his sword. And then, one way or another, the Shadow Realm would fall.

Yes, a meet would be to his benefit, especially after it failed.

"Tell Rindae we agree to this meet," Othin declared. They would see who was the stronger in the end.

CHAPTER 47

Faeliel stared down at her breakfast with bland disinterest. She'd had the same thing for the last three days: smooth milk pudding and toast. The brickleberries Lhéwen had acquired had long since been eaten. Even in the palace, the Shadow Realm meals were becoming flavorless and predictable, especially now that her father had increased the export taxes on agricultural goods once more. That would need to be one of the first things they discussed with the Upper Realm when they were married. She wasn't sure how much longer her taste buds would survive.

A messenger arrived, bowing before King Rindae and presenting him with a sealed letter on two outstretched hands. Faeliel lifted an eyebrow, waiting for the news.

"King Othin has accepted our invitation," King Rindae announced.

Lhéwen—on edge ever since the night of the announcement— flinched at the words, spilling red juice all over Faeliel's brand new gown. She'd commissioned it from the Shadow Realm's best seamstress—or so the other ladies of the court claimed—and it had arrived just yesterday.

Come to think of it, perhaps Lhéwen had been looking for a way to ruin the silk crafted by a competitor.

"Careful, or you will find yourself out of a job." Faeliel hissed.

"Apologies, Your Highness," Lhéwen murmured, quickly mopping up the spill with a spare towel. "I will ensure the gown is cleaned before the stain has a chance to set."

Faeliel ignored the comment, instead focusing on her new king while shooing away the clumsy hands of her maid. "My father will attend the meet? I am amazed."

In truth, she was more than amazed, she was shocked. She hadn't imagined her stilted formal letter would have encouraged High King Othin to lower himself to meet with his enemy. In fact, she'd hoped it wouldn't. She wanted more time to secure her relationship with Rindae, to confirm that the charm on her ear was working and her inkling of not just a marriage, but a possible life-mate bond of her own, were realized.

"Why so surprised?" King Rindae asked. "You agreed this was the best option and sent the invitation in your own words."

Faeliel shrugged. "The best option is to join our interests as quickly as possible. The more time you and I spend together—alone—the better." She smiled and lifted an eyebrow in suggestion.

"As enticing as that sounds, I must attend to court matters today. Daeturion is anxious to make arrangements for the meet and Aradae is intent on securing the realm in case of invasion."

"He shouldn't worry about that. Not yet. Father won't do anything until he has his new sword. It's probably why he's willing to meet at all."

"What new sword?"

"Oh, you know," Faeliel waved a hand with a graceful turn of her wrist that drew the eye up her arm and to the curve of her shoulder and décolleté. She'd practiced the gesture for bells in front of her tutor, a man her father had assigned to ensure she was as perfect a temptation as any lord could imagine. A man who had been tempted on several occasions himself. "The sword. It's why the merchant wanted the iron from the goblins."

"Master Ger did say something about a commissioned blade the merchant was bragging about, but we assumed it was a normal sword."

"Oh, dear me, no," Faeliel giggled. "My father doesn't commission plain blades. If I recall correctly, this particular weapon has been promised to enhance his ability to draw energy from his enemies and then store any excess in the metal itself. Apparently, the smith is quite talented."

"And you believe the merchant . . . what was his name?"

"Curuthannor," Faeliel replied. She felt Lhéwen stiffen behind her, freezing into immobility. Poor girl had a soft spot for the merchant, but had no idea how dangerous his position would be. He should have died taking the first message back to her father. It would have saved them all much pain and suffering.

"That's right," Rindae drew her attention back to the matter at hand. "You believe he was acquiring the iron for this blade?"

Faeliel shrugged once more as she lifted the spoon for another small bite of the pudding. She withdrew the spoon slowly, letting Rindae imagine what he would, then swallowed and licked her lips before responding.

"I have only heard my father speak of one new blade. He's been planning it for months, though he hadn't commissioned the work before my departure. Since Curuthannor was bragging about his commission from King Othin, I don't see how there could be anyone else." Faeliel paused for a moment, letting her new king process her words before she dismissed them. "But a sword like that takes months, even years to craft. And as I said, my father won't attack until he has his new toy in his hand. He will likely choose to delay and distract, but we can use that time to our benefit."

"How do you mean?"

"Well, for one thing, you need to ensure that your forces are immune to a spirit drain. It is my father's specialty, after all. Lucky for you, I am nearly as strong as my father and I have a secret asset."

"Oh?"

"My dear loyal Lhéwen is a master enchantress. We have discovered that by combining our abilities, we can enchant objects that can be carried and used by others without inherent spirit magic."

King Rindae lifted an eyebrow and grinned. "So you and your servant would make charms for my men? I hardly think that would be effective."

"We would make spiritual armor to prevent my father's manipulation of your energy. You cannot face him unprepared, even under flag of truce. He manipulates others to his side without realizing he's using his power. I have spent my entire life learning how to protect myself from his affect. If I am by your side, I can shield you as well. But I cannot protect an army."

Rindae glanced at Lhéwen, who was doing her best impression of a statue. Faeliel knew the woman didn't look like much, but that didn't mean she wasn't capable. "And you're sure this can be done?"

"I have capitalized on her skills for the last century or more. Why do you think I brought her along? She is far too useful to leave behind for another to find. But we will prove it. We will fashion the first of these charms for your approval, and they can be tested at the meet. Lhéwen will begin the process immediately."

Faeliel stood, putting a hand to the tied shoulder strap of her gown. "Luckily, my contribution won't begin until the charms are chosen and prepared. For now, this dress is ruined, and I'm afraid I'm all sticky. Perhaps you could help me get cleaned up, my king?"

CHAPTER 48

Lhéwen gathered up the princess's gown to have it washed before the stain set, not that it would matter much on the sheer black fabric. Most of the juice had passed right through the open-weave silk and she could hardly see the red smear. Lhéwen imagined the princess had actually been quite sticky, but she would enjoy getting stickier before she washed clean.

She shook her head. Faeliel was determined to free herself of her father's oppressive control. Lhéwen could understand that, but the princess was only tying herself to another master.

When Lhéwen chose to marry one day, and hopefully earn the bond of a lifemating, she would choose someone different. Strong, but not arrogant. Powerful, but still humble. Someone who would listen to her and honor her as an individual while treating her as a valuable partner. Someone who wouldn't resent her influence or use her solely for her skills.

King Rindae was none of those things. According to the gossip amongst the maids and servants, he was only interested in his own pursuits. He and Faeliel were made for each other.

Lhéwen's thoughts turned to the revelations at breakfast. If Faeliel was right, and her logic was sound, then Curuthannor and his family were caught in the middle of a dangerous game. The Shadow Realm would not arm its enemy, and King Othin would not give up his prize.

The protection charms were a good idea, if they worked. At least, they would be able to limit Othin's power enough to give the dark elves a chance to fight back. Soul magic, though strong in its own way, had no direct counter to the energy drain of the spirit masters. What could they do on their own, besides bring forth a heaving mist of souls from the daemon realm, like the one King Rindae had tried to threaten Sanyaro with? It hadn't worked then, and she doubted it would work on King Othin.

The question was, did Lhéwen really want to help the Shadow Realm defeat her true king? She was still a loyal high elf, even if her mistress wasn't. She could very easily sabotage the crafting of the charms so that they didn't work. Let King Othin take King Rindae out of the equation before the war ever began.

Perhaps that was the right answer. Perhaps it was time Lhéwen chose her own side in this war. Did she want to follow orders and stay here forever with a mistress who thought of her as little more than a tool? Or did she want to return to her home world a heroine for giving her king the means necessary to defeat his enemy?

For now, she had her instructions, and she couldn't outright disobey her mistress, not without severe and permanent consequences.

She took the dress to the palace laundry, then made her way out into the city. The king had suggested she start with the dark elf shops that lined the pedestrian walkways just on the other side of the palace moat. He assured her that the nobles of his court bought all of their finest jewelry from the artisans within.

The streets were crowded this time of day, or rather night. The midday sun had already passed overhead, giving its limited offering of light to this dark realm, and the residents had emerged from their homes to go about their activities. Now, three bells after sunset, the entire city was in motion.

Lhéwen dodged a troll with a wriggling sack tossed over one shoulder and jumped over an unidentifiable puddle. She'd gotten better at maneuvering about the city, and had finally convinced the princess she didn't need an escort. In fact, she drew less attention alone. With a hood over her head and a quick step, she was indistinguishable from the blood sidhe at a casual glance.

Lhéwen scanned the tables and trays at the first jewelry store she found. She and Faeliel would craft seven pieces, one each for King Rindae, Prince Daeturion, Prince Aradae, and the four additional dark elf guards who would attend the meet. They needed something small and shaped in pure silver, that wouldn't attract attention, yet with enough surface area to contain the enchantment. Unfortunately, this shop was dedicated to intricate gold designs embedded with semi-precious stones. None of it would work.

Lhéwen smiled at the shopkeeper and moved on.

Unlike the charisma enchantment on Faeliel's ear cuff—which Lhéwen was fairly certain King Rindae still hadn't detected, but which drew the spirit toward the wearer—or the invisibility spell Lhéwen had used on her ill-fated journey to the Upper Realm— which turned the gaze away—the counter-drain spell needed to block the wearer's aura like a shield. It would have been easier to put each person in a cage and enchant the cage than it would be to expand the effect of a small token brooch or pendant. It was a challenging problem, one that under other circumstances Lhéwen would have fully enjoyed solving.

She frowned, pushing through the doors of the second shop. No one was inside, but it didn't take long for Lhéwen to realize the goods were only plated in silver, not pure as she needed. Without saying a word, she left.

After passing several groups of dark elf ladies on leisurely strolls, who giggled behind their fans, Lhéwen began to realize this region of the city was more of a place to see and be seen than to shop for quality materials.

Entering the third shop, Lhéwen decided she'd had enough. She quickly passed a hand across the silver to test its efficacy, not bothering to even pretend to admire their design. Every bit of it was too hard to absorb the enchantment.

"Not pure enough and far too delicate," Lhéwen pronounced without preamble. "I need the purest silver in a size large enough to work with. None of this will do. Do you have anything else? Perhaps finer quality raw materials in back?"

"If you want a hunk of metal, why don't you go visit the dwarves?" The woman snapped, taking offense at Lhéwen's criticism.

Lhéwen refused to apologize. For the price the woman was charging, the metals should have been pristine. But the woman had offered a reasonable alternative, even if she meant it as an insult.

"Do you have a shop you would recommend?"

The woman curled a lip in disgust. "My supplier sets up shop twice a week near the portal. She should be there today. Go ask her yourself."

"I'll do that. Who should I ask for, and what name should I provide as referral?" Lhéwen asked. If the Shadow Realm markets were anything like the Upper Realm, she'd get a better deal and better service with a referral.

"She's Adwuna the dwarf. First tent in the line. I'm Olostiel, though I doubt it will do you much good."

Ten blocks and a half bell later, Lhéwen arrived at the portal courtyard, but paused at the commotion. A line of trolls emerged from the largest of the public portals, watched on either side by the black-clad shadow guard. Each troll carried a block of stone the size of three horses on its back. They walked twenty paces to set their block in place along what appeared to be the beginnings of a low wall, then returned to the portal and waited their turn to pass back through to the other side.

Lhéwen touched the shoulder of another onlooker. "What's going on?"

The bronze-skinned woman turned to her with hooded eyes. "They're building a wall."

"Well, yes, I see that, but why?"

A delicate tracery of lines had been tattooed down the woman's chin, drawing Lhéwen's gaze. She was fire sidhe, that was certain. No other race bore those marks. Trade between all of the realms was quite common, but the woman's lean musculature and loose wrapped leggings led Lhéwen to believe this was no simple merchant. Like Curuthannor, she held herself with athletic poise that belied her training.

"I imagine it's intended to protect the city."

Short on words, the woman made it clear she had no intention of striking up a conversation. Still, Lhéwen was glad to meet another upper-worlder. Even if she wasn't a high elf, she was a foreigner in this dark land.

"I suppose that makes sense," Lhéwen murmured as her gaze was drawn back to the house-sized stone being placed by the procession of trolls.

"What do you mean?" the woman surprised Lhéwen by asking. "What do you know?"

Lhéwen glanced back. The woman's expression was intent, her gaze fierce. It made Lhéwen want to shrink away.

"Only that it's always best to be prepared," Lhéwen demurred, while taking a small step back. "If you'll excuse me, I'd best get my shopping done and return to my mistress."

Lhéwen pushed her way through the gathering crowd and crossed the portal courtyard staying clear of the trolls and their heavy loads. She'd do well to stay far away from the shadow guard, too. Only when she reached the opposite side did she bother to look back at the woman, but she was gone. As momentous as the arrival of the trolls was, even she must have other business to attend.

With a shrug, Lhéwen turned toward the row of tents that lined the streets on the other side of the portal.

"No good for business, I tell ya," a squat goblin growled, her hands on her hips. "We'll all be displaced for certain."

"Nonsense," a dark elf merchant replied. "The king is courting the princess. This is all for show."

"No one undertakes this much work for show," the goblin replied.

Lhéwen ignored their banter, taking it as the unfounded gossip it was as she wended her way through the customers and vendors of foreign goods. It took another half bell before she found the dwarves and their tents of gems and precious metals.

Each corner of each white tent was guarded by a bearded individual in heavy plate armor who carried an axe big enough to take off her head. Their armor covered every inch of skin, and even their helms had been designed to shield most of their face. The only way Lhéwen could tell they were actually alive and not simple metal statues was from the bit of flesh on their lips and the long braided beards that emerged from their chins. She supposed it would be quite itchy to keep that much facial hair within their metal casing.

Despite being shorter than human height and practically blind, the dwarves were not pushovers. According to the legends of the first diaspora, their guards could be as vicious and deadly as any race, using keen ears and extra sensitive touch to navigate their surroundings. In fact, rumor had it they were better fighters on average than most of the other races *because* they didn't rely on sight alone. It was why the origin elves had been unable to conquer the Dwarven Realm, choosing instead an economic peace. That, and the fact that the surface of their realm was a barren, weather-beaten land with worldwide storms that lasted centuries. The dwarves were tough.

Lhéwen paused momentarily before approaching the first tent. The guard didn't stop her, but she could feel his attention on her.

"Excuse me, I'm looking for Adwuna. Is she in?"

"I'm Adwuna," a deep voice responded from a shadowed corner in the back.

Lhéwen approached the table with slow steps, admiring the metal plating on display from afar. Already, she could see a broad silver torque that might suit her needs.

"Olostiel referred me to you. I'm looking for seven pieces of purest silver that can be worn on the body as jewelry. Olostiel's designs were too delicate and the alloys too hard for my needs. Do you have any stock that might suit?"

The woman emerged from the shadows while polishing a square of metal that had been hammered flat. Wiry red hair had been braided into long plaits, then twisted and looped in broad circles around the crown of her head. The wispy version of the female beard had been similarly braided beneath her chin and adorned with tiny gold and silver beads in a rather striking display of wealth and honor. However, it was the large gold discs that hung from her ears that really caught Lhéwen's attention. If she could get those in pure silver, they might be enough.

"Olostiel must be playing a cruel joke on you, my dear. I have refused her patronage ever since she tried to cut my rates on a completed contract."

Lhéwen allowed her disgust to show on her face. "I'm afraid I'm not surprised. She was upset that I didn't choose any of her wares for the princess's commission, though she refused to deal fairly with me as well."

"Then we are in good company and she may have referred you true." Adwuna waved a hand across her table. Her gaze never rose to Lhéwen's face, rather her pale cloudy eyes seemed to stare off into the distance just beyond Lhéwen's right shoulder. "Pure silver, you say?"

"Yes. As pure as I can find."

"I do have some beautiful pieces that I might be able to part with, but what do you need them for?"

"I am working on a complex enchantment that needs a carrier. It must be soft enough to absorb the magic and strongly conductive to project the spell outward."

"Interesting." The woman twisted one of the beads on her beard in mindless thought. "This is needed by the princess, you say?"

"Actually, it's for the king and his guards, though the princess has instructed my purchases."

The dwarf clucked her tongue in a rapid rhythmic staccato. One of the guards at the tent corner responded, followed by the other. Adwuna clucked again.

"I believe I have something that might work for your needs." She ducked beneath the table, withdrawing a velvet sack. "Hold out your hand."

Lhéwen did as asked and Adwuna emptied the bag onto her palm. A silver ring tumbled out. Thick enough to cover the thumb or mid-finger from base to first knuckle, the metal had been artistically hammered into a shimmering round. Lhéwen closed her eyes and attempted to imbue the ring with a small test spell designed to make the wearer just a little more likable. The ring took the magic and expanded it, broadcasting the spell far enough that even Adwuna leaned forward.

"This is perfect. Do you have seven of them?" Lhéwen asked.

"No. But I can have them for you easy enough."

"How much?"

"We will give you the rings at no cost on one condition."

Lhéwen lifted an eyebrow. The deal was too sweet, but she knew the sour was coming.

"King Rindae must swear for himself and all his heirs to uphold and support the neutral territory of Nidallvar, the Dwarven Realm."

Lhéwen frowned. "I cannot make such a promise. I am but the

servant of the princess, nothing more. But I can attempt to arrange a private audience. Would that be acceptable?"

Adwuna dipped her head in agreement. "I was told an opportunity would present itself, and to be patient. It seems our revered mothers saw true. You may tell King Rindae that Adwuna, speaker for the clans of dwarves, would have an audience. The rings will be ready on the morrow. Arrange the meet and return when the king is ready to speak."

CHAPTER 49

"Meet with a dwarf? For what purpose?" King Rindae scoffed.

Despite her increasingly tenuous position with Princess Faeliel, Lhéwen had managed to convince Her Highness of the necessity of these particular rings. The princess had in turn used her influence to arrange the meeting with the king in his public office. Now, three days later, Adwuna waited outside the room while her personal guards stared down Belegeth and the king's guard and Lhéwen struggled to make the king see the importance of this meeting.

"I have visited every dark elf jeweler in the city, and none have the purity of metal I need in a size that is suitable for the energy shields you require. The dwarves are the only supplier. If you want protection from King Othin's energy drains, you must speak with her and agree to what she asks."

"There must be someone else who can provide what you need. Even one of the other dwarf merchants might be willing to sell. Keep looking," King Rindae replied.

"The dwarf merchants have all left the city and returned to their homelands. Only Adwuna remains."

Faeliel leaned over the king's shoulder, pressing her cheek against his and trailing her hand down his arm in a full-skin caress. "Adwuna is the speaker for the clans. The dwarves would make strong allies if we can win them to our side."

Lhéwen swallowed. Adwuna had been very clear, but she supposed the princess had a right to attempt to change her mind. And Adwuna could also speak for herself . . . and all the clans, apparently.

King Rindae visibly relaxed, the princess's charms working their effects on the king. Lhéwen wished she had never suggested nor made the ear cuff for Faeliel. She was sure her efforts to seduce Rindae would have been waved away like a fly near a horse's tail if it weren't for the attraction charm.

"Bring her in, then," King Rindae acquiesced. "We will hear what she has to say."

Lhéwen bowed and backed toward the door. She supposed she should be thankful the charm and Faeliel's skills were still working, otherwise she never would have gotten this audience. Of course, she also wouldn't have *needed* this audience if Faeliel had just agreed to go home.

Adwuna leaned against the wall opposite the door and just outside the office with a stern expression plastered across her face. Her guards bristled with weapons.

"Please, come in," Lhéwen murmured.

"The guards must remain outside," Belegeth and the king's guard both said at almost the exact same moment.

The dwarf guards, though shorter than their counterparts and seemingly overpowered, stepped forward without hesitation to shield Adwuna.

"Stand down," Adwuna said. "I will meet with the king."

Lhéwen bowed again and opened the door wider. With a swoop of her hand, she ushered the dwarf woman inside.

"Welcome, Adwuna, speaker for the dwarf clans," King Rindae intoned as if he hadn't been trying to avoid meeting with her just moments before.

"Greetings, King Rindae. I am glad we have found a moment to speak."

"I am not so busy that I cannot greet the speaker of the clans."

Adwuna grunted, the silver and gold beads hanging from her chin tinkling as they bounced against one another. "Perhaps you should be. But that is not my concern. I have come to declare neutrality for all of the dwarf clans in Nidallvar. Our revered mothers have prohibited any dwarf from raising arms for the benefit of any elf. We will take no side between shadow and light, nor give preference nor aid to any realm save our own. We will trade fairly with all who swear to uphold our neutrality for themselves and all heirs."

"Straight to the point. Just like a dwarf," Faeliel murmured. Adwuna's sightless gaze drifted toward the princess, but her expression did not change.

"From this moment on, until peace returns, no elf may enter our territory or their life will be forfeit. All communication and trade will be conducted through the lesser fae or humans."

"And why, under all the gods, do the 'revered mothers' make this pronouncement now?" King Rindae asked with a snort. "We are at peace, and shall continue to maintain that peace."

"Do you swear to uphold our neutrality? To deal fairly?"

"You dare impugn my honor and that of my realm?"

Adwuna shifted, the layered ruffles of her skirts swaying with the movement. She placed her hands on her hips and scowled. "Already our traders have gone from these lands and your merchants and artisans are suffering. Your lady has one source of pure silver, and that's me. If you do not swear to our demands, the dwarves will side with your enemy and all trade will be banned in its entirety for as long as our revered mothers require. Your realm will find itself alone and isolated from all but the dead."

"I hardly think that's true," Faeliel replied. "The Shadow Realm is a power the others are unable to ignore."

"The roots of the world tree are strong, but the branches are numerous," Adwuna replied, cryptically.

"Your Majesty," Lhéwen interrupted, daring to step outside her modest position to try to bring this circular argument to a close, "I will state again, to complete my task I must have the purest silver. Adwuna and the dwarves are the only source of this silver. If all they ask is neutrality between two peaceful realms, what is the harm in agreeing to the terms?"

"Give her what she wants and let's be done with it," Faeliel urged. "I want you safe from my father, and your men as well." Then she leaned in and whispered something else in the king's ear which Lhéwen couldn't hear. Whatever it was, it seemed to do the trick.

"I agree to uphold the neutrality of the Dwarven Realm."

"You must swear it for yourself and all your heirs," Adwuna said.

King Rindae grimaced, but complied. "Fine. I give binding oath that neither I nor any of my heirs will attempt to breach the neutrality of the Dwarven Realm so long as I am alive."

Adwuna turned toward Lhéwen and held out her hand. Seven silver rings rested on her palm. "Our terms are then agreed, our contract sealed with the merchandise. I look forward to our future dealings."

CHAPTER 50

Sweat dripped into Curuthannor's eye. He wiped it away with his shoulder, leaving a smear of ash and grease behind. His muscles burned as hot as the forge in front of him, while the never-ending pounding of the hammer on steel reverberated through his brain.

Dousing the metal with a hiss of steam, Curuthannor looked up to find his father's critical gaze watching him.

"You must have patience with the steel," Hatholdammon growled. "Be gentle with it."

"I am pounding it with a hammer. I hardly think that's a gentle activity," Curuthannor replied. He was tired. It was the only excuse for the thoughtless remark. "Apologies," Curuthannor immediately rescinded the comment. "I mean no disrespect."

"You have not been sleeping well."

"He has been moaning in his sleep. Just one name. *Lhéwen*," Curuthannor's second eldest brother, Minyondor, teased while grinding the edge of a commander's sword.

"How would you know?" Curuthannor replied. "You've been out all night every night courting Tautamiel."

316

"At least I have a woman who will one day accept me into her heart. What do you have besides a name and a dream?"

"My freedom?" Curuthannor couldn't help making it a question. In truth, he was a little jealous of Minyondor and his growing attachment to the carpenter's daughter. Not that he would ever admit it. Nor did he have any interest in the lady in question.

Curuthannor swallowed. At least Nambamahtar, the eldest, wasn't present. If he were, Curuthannor would never hear the end of it. He decided his best option was to ignore and deflect. He turned back to his father.

"The sword guard will be finished in time for the final forging," Curuthannor promised.

The curved guard piece would wrap around the oak hilt and protect the king's hand. It was a critical feature of the blade, and had to be both beautiful and functional. Usually Curuthannor enjoyed crafting the guards—it was certainly more interesting than heating, pounding, and slowly cooling a flat bar of iron over and over for hours on end. It required attention to detail, but without the pressure of keeping every angle and edge perfectly straight and true. If he struck his hammer a hairs-width incorrectly, it wouldn't destroy the entire blade. It wouldn't matter at all. He could just polish it out later.

"I trust that it will," Hatholdammon replied. "But this will not do." He picked the guard out of the water with a pair of tongs. "You've burned the steel. It is too fragile to perform its duty. It will break on the first strike."

To prove his point, Hatholdammon struck the guard against the anvil halfway across one quillon. A thumb-sized piece of steel spun away onto the floor.

"Start over."

Curuthannor's shoulders slumped. There was no time. The ritual final forging of the blade must begin at sunrise on the day of the summer solstice when the light and spirit were strongest.

Without each piece prepared and in place, the work could not begin. He had failed his family once again.

"Take a rest. Calm your mind." Hatholdammon interrupted Curuthannor's self-loathing. "When you return, you must focus on the task at hand and allow no further distractions. Minya will help you maintain the forge temperature."

"I could craft the hilt," Minyondor offered. "This edge is nearly finished."

Curuthannor didn't think he'd intended any insult, but it certainly felt like a stain on his honor.

"No. I will do it. It is my task, my only contribution. I will have it done."

"Good." Hatholdammon turned away, moving on to inspect one of the helms that had just been dipped in its final coating of gold.

Curuthannor watched his father as he spoke with Hadhion and placed an encouraging hand on the younger man's shoulder. Disgusted with his own inferior work, Curuthannor threw the inadequate guard into the waste bin with perhaps a bit too much force.

"You heard father. Get out of here," Minyondor said. "You'll make another critical mistake in your current state."

Curuthannor grimaced, but took the advice and headed outside into fresh cool air.

Situated in the village of Romésse Gulch, Hatholdammon's forge was farther from the capital city than most other craftsmen preferred. However, it was also in a narrow, rocky valley that butted up against the Crimson Mountains, so-called because when the sun dipped below the horizon, the sunset painted the mountain faces shades of pink and red. Though not as flexible and strong as the goblin iron, the Crimson Mountain mines were Hatholdammon's preferred source of local iron and being close to the source meant he had first choice of the supply. Or he did until the other armorers moved into the area. Now the entire valley rang with the clang of hundreds of hammers on steel.

The king's army requisition had been so large, Hatholdammon had been forced to subcontract most of the orders. But only Hatholdammon and his sons would work on the king's blade. Only Hatholdammon himself could forge the magic into the pure silver, steel, and diamond that would enhance the king's power and store the excess energy.

Curuthannor could barely be trusted with the steel guard that would protect the king's hand. Especially if he continued to force the metal into shape too quickly. He needed to get a hold of himself and rein in his thoughts. He was never this distracted.

In truth, it wasn't the work that left him sleepless at night or made him wish to pound the metal into oblivion, it was the thought of Lhéwen in the Shadow Realm, friendless but for the princess. It had been two months since he had gone with Lord Garamaen Sanyaro to collect the black hills iron. Two long months since he had seen her in the flesh. And yet he still couldn't shake the memory of her panicked expression as he'd backed out of the room that night. It was like an itch between his shoulder blades that he couldn't reach.

Was she safe? Was she happy? Was she even still alive?

The princess may have chosen the traitor's path, but that didn't mean Lhéwen had. She certainly hadn't looked pleased to remain behind. Then again, how would he know? She was a talented enchantress, but still a common elf, like him. Maybe she wanted the chance to break free of her own ignoble origins and earn a place amongst another people. Would they accept her? Could they?

Curuthannor shook his head and kicked his boot through the gravel of the main thoroughfare. Without conscious thought, his legs had carried him to the village portal. He gazed up into the sandstone arch with a mixture of hope and despair. So little separation between space and time, and yet it was insurmountable. A step that could change a life, or end one.

He crossed his arms over his chest and turned away.

CHAPTER 51

Lhéwen laid the seven silver rings in a row on a soft velvet cloth. She touched each one, feeling the open energy in the metal, the willingness to accept instruction. Princess Faeliel would construct the energy shield while Lhéwen wove the matching pattern into the ring itself.

Or so went the theory. So many things could go wrong. Intentional or not.

One would have to work. Only one. They would want to test the enchantment, to make sure that the princess couldn't drain the wearer, and therefore neither could her father.

The rest . . .

Lhéwen had decided to end this all and go home. If King Rindae died at the meet with King Othin, there would be no need for war. Daeturion would fall in line, she was sure of it. How could he not? If his father wasn't strong enough to stand against the High King, even with a protection charm in hand, then surely the son would see the folly in continuing to defy the Upper Realm. Faeliel would have no choice but to return to her life in the Upper Realm and Lhéwen would go with her. She would stand in the light again. She would leave the princess's service and find a small cottage where she could design and sew. Maybe she'd even be able to save enough gold for a horse of her own.

Only . . . Was failing to protect the same as murder? She might not be the weapon or the wielder, but she had the power to save a life and refused to use it. Could she live with herself if she caused the death of another?

No, the arrow was not to blame for the direction it flew. The kings would make their own choices. Lhéwen was choosing not to take a side.

Satisfied with her logic, Lhéwen lifted the tray with its precious, yet unassuming cargo and entered the sitting room of the princess's suite. She paused at the threshold.

The princess sat on the low-back chaise lounge, as expected. What wasn't expected was the presence of King Rindae and a hunched green creature with long ears, sharp teeth, and skinny, bowed legs who wore nothing but a rough fire-scarred leather apron around his waist.

Swallowing down her surprise and agitation, Lhéwen proceeded to set the tray on the low table near the chaise.

Princess Faeliel smiled, but it didn't reach her eyes. "Lhéwen, my dear, King Rindae has requested to witness our enchantment, and show this gremlin how we perform the working. I hope that is acceptable?"

Lhéwen swallowed. She generally liked to keep her enchantments small and private. She had never done a working in front of an audience before, but neither could she say no to the shadow king.

"Yes, my lady," Lhéwen bowed. "Though I'm not sure how much the gremlin will be able to learn. I'm afraid I work by instinct and have never had a student."

"My name is Whixle," the gremlin growled. "But don't worry

yourself. I'll see what needs to be seen, understand the working as it's happening."

"Much like yourself, Whixle is a promising enchanter, but he is also a smith," King Rindae replied. "And if we are to produce enough rings to protect every guard, you will need some assistance."

Lhéwen gasped. "Every guard?" She wasn't a machine. They couldn't possibly expect her to produce that many enchantments.

"Of course. Though I firmly believe we will remain at peace with the Upper Realm, there may come a day when the unthinkable occurs. If it does, we must ensure the safety of our fighters."

"Yes, Your Majesty," Lhéwen murmured. Her thoughts were spinning in circles. She wasn't a traitor, but if she crafted these rings for the shadow king and his army, she would be acting against her own realm. The shadow guard would suddenly have the advantage over the high elf warriors. But if she sabotaged the enchantments, the gremlin might know. Moreover, people would rely on her work. They would believe they were protected. When that protection was tested, they could die.

What to do?

Lhéwen repositioned the rings again, though they waited in a perfect line for their workings.

"Shall we get started, then?" Princess Faeliel asked.

"Yes, I am anxious to see how this may be done," Whixle added, his voice a grating whine.

Lhéwen placed her hands over the rings, making sure at least one finger touched each piece of silver. As soon as she felt the metal's resonance within her, she closed her physical eyes and opened her mind's eye to the magical spectrum. It was a task easier said than done.

After a few breaths, the colors of the magics in the room began to materialize around her. First, and brightest, was Faeliel's golden glow. She pulsed with metallic shimmer, but surprisingly there were a few darker threads beginning to splice through the bright light. Perhaps the influence of King Rindae? Evidence that the life-mating was taking hold as Faeliel believed? Lhéwen didn't know, but it hardly mattered.

King Rindae was next to appear, his marbled black and grey harder to see against the blackness of her closed eyelids. Still, his power and energy exuded from his physical form in a wide halo that touched much of the room around them.

Last, the gremlin—Whixle—emerged from the darkness. His aura was a sickly green color that seemed to want to reach out and touch the energies around it. Lhéwen felt herself mentally brushing away his questing energies, wishing he wasn't in the room, but it couldn't be helped.

"I am ready. Princess Faeliel, if you would please create a shield around yourself, I will use that for the pattern."

In an instant, the energy of Faeliel's aura changed. The edge of her golden halo hardened and grew darker, while the stronger energy within the princess's physical form pushed outward to support the edges. From one heartbeat to the next, nothing could touch her aura. Whixle's touch shrank away as if in fear, and even the gray tendrils that had begun to form from her bond with Rindae were ejected from her shell.

Quickly, Lhéwen began to weave the same energies into the metal beneath her fingers. She truly didn't know how she did it, only that if she had a pattern to follow—like the princess's current working—she could copy it and impress it onto other objects.

But this time, she made a mistake. She dropped a stitch in the pattern, leaving the smallest hole through which a powerful enervator could reach the aura of the protected person. She didn't know how much Whixle would See. Even if he could See the mistake, would he understand it for what it was?

Forcing her worries to the side, Lhéwen finished the working. The first ring was finished, just six more to go. Sweat beaded on her forehead. She had never done seven enchantments in a row, rarely seven in a week. There was not often that much need. The shields were far more complicated than anything else she had tried. Even the invisibility spell had been easier to manipulate. She swallowed, wishing for a glass of water but unwilling to pause her focus.

She began the second ring, dropping another stitch, but in a different location. She hoped if the gremlin saw the mistake, he would believe it was an accident, and not intentional. If he reported her, that one difference might be enough to save her from execution for disobeying her mistress.

The third and fourth each received their own unique mistake. No two rings would be alike, which was probably a good thing.

The more rings she completed, the more tired she became. Distractions became harder to ignore. She could hear the shifting and shuffling of the others in the room. King Rindae in particular seemed unable to sit still.

If he was bored, it was his own fault for insisting on being present.

Lhéwen brought her mind back around to her task, but too late. The fifth ring had not one, but two mistakes. Two locations where a connection from one aura could be made with the other. She grimaced, but pressed on. There was nothing to do about it now. The work was done.

Before she became any more exhausted, Lhéwen decided she had better make the test ring now, on the sixth version. It had to be perfect, and her own energy was wearing thin. She didn't have much time. Pressing the ring finger of her right hand deeply into the silver metal of the sixth ring, she forced her mind to attention. She could do this. She *would* do this.

The weave began with a simple twist and a hard pull. She followed the threads, thickening the energy as the princess had done. She found the shape of the pattern, building it layer by layer. She did not drop a stitch. The sixth ring was perfect.

Lhéwen gasped for air, her breath coming in heaving pants. Her mind's eye grew blank, a fog descending over her vision like a curtain. She could no longer See the auras in the room. She couldn't see anything.

"If it pleases the ladies, I would like to attempt the working for the final ring," Whixle proclaimed. "I think I understand what has been done, but I won't know for certain until the work is complete."

"Please," Lhéwen whispered. She could hardly make a sound, could hardly move. Her own aura was depleted.

"Take your hands off the metal," Whixle ordered. "I'll take your place."

Lhéwen nodded, unsure if her head moved, or whether anyone could see it. She opened her eyes, her physical sight nearly as dim and gray as her magical vision. She took a half step back from the table, tripped, and fell.

No one moved to help her as Whixle stepped forward. She slumped to the floor. Her eyes closed. Darkness claimed her.

L héwen woke to the slow clapping of appreciative hands.

"Well done, Whixle. I knew you had the ability within you," King Rindae said.

"You have granted me a fine opportunity, I will not waste it," Whixle replied. "Now that I have the pattern, I will be able to craft as many such items as you choose. I only need the silver."

"Now aren't you glad you made the deal with the dwarf?" Faeliel simpered. "Your entire army will be protected."

"They work?" Lhéwen rasped, her throat dry and sore.

Had Whixle made a perfect version, or dropped a stitch in the pattern as she had? Which ring had they tested? Lhéwen forced herself upright to examine the tray, unsure of what had occurred since she had dropped unconscious on the floor. The rings looked untouched, still in the order she had place them in. But her magic was completely drained, she couldn't See Whixle's work to understand the truth.

"Of course, my dear. We had no doubt."

"You tested the rings?" Lhéwen asked.

"Yes, all of them. Each provided a shield for my love."

Lhéwen inwardly groaned. If Faeliel hadn't noticed the dropped stitches, then Othin might miss his opportunity as well. And if the gremlin was able to craft enough for the entire army, then the high court would be powerless against them.

She had betrayed her realm.

"My king, you should order as many of the rings as Whixle can craft. Then your army will be unstoppable," Faeliel said, echoing Lhéwen's thoughts. "You can reclaim the iron that has been stolen before Othin's blade is complete."

"I thought it had already been taken to the Upper Realm." Lhéwen said, her head still woozy. How were they going to reclaim the iron if it was already gone?

"Lhéwen, dear, do not bother yourself with the conversations of your betters," Faeliel brushed a hand across the arm of the chaise she was leaning on and didn't make eye contact. "If you cannot perform your duties, please return to your rooms."

Lhéwen's face fell and her shoulders slumped. Any last fragment of goodwill or loyalty she owed the princess fell away. She might as well be human.

Of course, that could prove beneficial. It was a new level of invisibility to be so completely dismissed, even by her own mistress. Faeliel had asked her to leave, but her room was just on the other side of the door.

Dragging herself up to a hunched standing position, Lhéwen shambled toward her quarters, taking her time with each step. She may have betrayed her realm with the rings, but perhaps she could learn enough to help in some other manner.

"I would be happy to purchase the excess," Whixle said into the silence of the room. "It would certainly be useful in my own work."

"I have a better idea," Faeliel chimed. "If you can provide men at arms to recover the iron from the Upper Realm, then we wouldn't have to involve the shadow guard. Even better, if we are at the meet during the raid, my father would not be able to prove the shadow throne's involvement. He would be without his new weapon and without recourse to act against us."

"No," King Rindae replied, determined. "We cannot attend the meet if we are to do this."

"But the rings will protect us from my father's wrath," Faeliel objected.

"The rings will protect us from his magic, but there are many other ways he could take his vengeance. I will not put you in harm's way."

Lhéwen hid a smirk behind the closing door of her room. She had a sneaking suspicion that despite his big words and the limited demonstrations of his power in recent weeks, Rindae was not a man who would put *himself* in harm's way.

Lhéwen left the door open a crack and sat against the wall without turning on the light. She could still hear the faint conversation if she held her breath and didn't move. She wished she had enough magic left to enchant the metal knob to amplify the sound from the next room, but if she tried that now she was likely to fall unconscious once more.

"Then what do you suggest, my king?" Faeliel purred.

If Lhéwen wasn't mistaken, and she rarely was when it came to her mistress's moods, Faeliel was none too thrilled at having her idea dismissed. She would do well to remember and understand the feeling, though Lhéwen doubted it would have any effect on her behavior.

"Daeturion is the diplomat with the smooth words and manipulative nature. He will go to the meet and distract Othin. As soon as we confirm that Othin and his entourage have arrived, Aradae will take a team of guards to recover the iron. However, they will need help with the transport. Whixle, if you can provide suitable assistance, then you can have every bar of recovered iron so long as it is used in the production of arms and armor for my men alone."

"That is most generous, Your Majesty. I'm sure I will find a recovery team suitable to the task."

"And where will we be?" Faeliel asked.

"Conscripting soldiers from the dark elf lords of this realm. It is time they assisted in preserving their independence."

Lhéwen's eyes widened and she lifted a silent hand to cover her mouth. This was war. There was no pretending at diplomacy if they invaded the Upper Realm.

But what could Lhéwen, a mere handmaiden and seamstress, do to stop anything? She had no one to tell, no one to go to with this information. Daeturion had said if she needed anything, he would help, but he was firmly on the side of the Shadow Realm, and as far as she knew, already in the Human Realm preparing for the meet. He wouldn't want King Othin to have any more power than he already controlled.

To be honest, neither did she. These kings and their games were already menacing enough.

But neither could Curuthannor's family hand over the iron just because the dark elves demanded it. They had to fulfill their commission or be ruined. And King Othin was just as likely to kill them all as the shadow king if he thought they were considering treason. No, the smiths would fight and they would fight hard. Deservedly so. They'd been given the iron in free trade. And if Curuthannor was even a modest example of his profession, there would be as many fighters in the smithy as there were hammers to wield.

This was bad. This was very, very bad.

Lhéwen swallowed down her fear. She didn't know what to do. She wasn't a political creature. She'd spent her entire life learning how to disappear in plain sight.

She couldn't leave Curuthannor to his fate. Not again. She owed him a life debt, one she swore she would repay. She would make up for her mistake.

There had to be something. No, someone.

Tharbatiron could get a message to Curuthannor, she was sure of it. If not to the smith, then to Lord Garamaen Sanyaro, who would certainly want to help. They would find a way to stop this.

CHAPTER 52

Tall stone arches towered at least three lengths overhead. Draped with the colors of each realm, the northern pillars shone in gold while the southern pillars seemed to absorb the dying light. Torches had been lit around the space and their light flickered along the pocked and cratered surfaces of the ancient portals that encircled the clearing.

This was the oldest portal crossing in the entire Human Realm. The first elven settlers had created the stone monuments on their first crossing, giving access to all of the realms in a single space. Every realm was supposed to have one such space, but things had changed since the original diaspora. Not that any of that mattered for the moment. Only two realms would be gathering for this meet.

Daeturion walked the circle once more to make sure nothing had been overlooked. The kings and Princess Faeliel each had their own throne. They had decided the princess would sit at the right hand of King Rindae, but at a slight angle so that King Othin's throne would be aligned precisely between the two shadow thrones.

For that's what they would present on the morrow: a united pair.

Daeturion had been preparing the meet for weeks. Making arrangements, designing the space, negotiating the size and armament of the entourages, and ensuring the time differences were accounted for so that both sides would arrive in the same hour.

Tecindo, meanwhile, had been running himself ragged coordinating all of the incoming information from Daeturion's spies. Daeturion had men and women watching the movements of the princess and her handmaiden, keeping vigil in the Crossroads Inn, monitoring the activities in the city, and even following his little brother. If he had dared, he would have set a watch on his father as well, but in truth it was practically unnecessary. The king and princess were together more often than not, and Lhéwen was the perfect unwitting informant. Or, she would be once he was able to return to court.

Other than Lhéwen brokering a deal with the dwarves, there had been no suspicious behavior noted by the network. It was too bad the dwarves had declared neutrality, but neither was it the worst news. The dwarves were strong, that was certain, but continuous access to their metals and armor was more of a benefit than having their axes in with the guard. Besides, eventually Othin would pursue the bearded folk and when he did, they would be more inclined to assist the Shadow Realm to maintain their own independence. Better to agree to their terms now and reap the rewards of goodwill later.

Only a few more bells and this meet will be done. They would present the courtship to King Othin, who would be forced to recognize the intended marriage. They would open the way for a more prosperous nine realms with a union of equals.

The portal from the Shadow Realm buzzed behind him. Daeturion turned to watch Tecindo approach with soft steps. The blood sidhe's dark hair swept over one eye, obscuring his expression, but it didn't look bright.

"My lord, I'm afraid I come with news that will sour your plans."

"Our plans. What is it?"

"King Rindae and Princess Faeliel will be unable to attend the meet due to fears for their safety."

"What are you talking about? Fears for their safety?!" Daeturion's voice bounced off the surrounding stone, making his words louder than they should have been.

"They request that you take their place in the negotiations, and wear this ring as a means of shielding yourself from any magical manipulation by the high elves." Tecindo held out a beautifully hammered and polished silver ring.

"What are they afraid of?" Daeturion asked, eyeing the metal without touching it. It wasn't doing any visible harm to his assistant, but he would be a fool to trust an enchanted artifact without testing it first.

Tecindo's expression was inscrutable. "I was not present at the meeting, nor were any of our spies. All I know is that your father and the princess will be going on a grand tour of all the noble estates in the Shadow Realm. A messenger was sent to Prince Aradae with a similar ring to this, but I do not know the contents. I have set a closer watch on your brother to observe his next actions, but I wanted to bring this to you personally."

"You have done well. I will return to Nalakadr. I must speak with my father directly."

Tecindo stepped forward and his eyes tightened around the edges. He gripped Daeturion's arm with uncharacteristic intent.

"There is no time. If you walk through that portal, King Othin will arrive to an empty meet. The Shadow Realm moves too slowly."

Daeturion grimaced. Tecindo was right, which would be disastrous at best. His father had perfectly timed his defection.

"What of the guard? Will I have no protection?"

"I will stand by your side," Tecindo offered.

The portal snapped open again, and a warrior woman strode through the gate. Belegeth, personal bodyguard of the princess.

"Her highness, Princess Faeliel has sent me for your protection." She held up her hand to reveal the thick silver ring on her thumb. "The rings were enchanted by the princess and her handmaiden. They will shield you from both energy drain and emotional manipulation."

"Have you tested their efficacy?" Tecindo asked, a sour bitterness creeping into his tone.

"I do not have the magical prowess, but I trust Her Highness. She would not leave us here to face her father without assistance."

"As you say," Tecindo replied. He turned back to Daeturion and dropped his voice low. "There is no other option, my lord. I will not leave you."

Daeturion smiled at his assistant, gripping the man's hand briefly before letting go. They'd become close over the years, and Tecindo had proven his loyalty time and again. But he wasn't a fighter.

"You honor me, but you should return to the Shadow Realm and find out what's really going on. I will need a detailed report on my return."

"You think I can't take care of myself?" Tecindo hissed with a snake-like sibilance. In an instant, his form changed. His shoulders hunched and his fingers curled into long-taloned claws. Inch-long fangs snapped down from the top of his mouth and his jaw seemed to expand beyond its limits.

Daeturion leaned back in shock.

"You forget that I am full blood sidhe. My kind are trained from birth to hunt and drain our prey. I may not have much skill with a sword, but I am faster than any elf and more than capable of defending you from attack."

"Prove it." Belegeth's double-edged axe arced overhead.

Tecindo spun. Belegeth's axe swung down. Tecindo launched himself forward and shoved her arms to one side, using his body as a battering ram. They tumbled to the ground and Tecindo slammed his hand across her helm, pulling the metal away from her face. He landed on top, poised to strike like a viper.

"Halt," Daeturion commanded. He didn't think that Tecindo would have actually drawn blood, but he didn't know how Belegeth would react. "You've made your point."

Tecindo's fangs retracted back into his mouth and he released his hold on Belegeth's head. At that moment, Daeturion saw the dagger in the woman's hand. She clenched her hand on the grip.

"Do not draw blood, either of you," Daeturion ordered. "We do not have the time nor the energy to waste. We must prepare."

"And I *will* remain by your side," Tecindo reiterated.

"As you wish." Daeturion took a deep breath and blew it out through his nose. "This very well may end in tragedy, but if this is how it's to be, we'll have to rearrange things."

It wasn't the first time his father had left him to handle a delicate situation, just the first time the stakes had been this high. He couldn't be surprised, however. They could still deliver the message, even if it wouldn't have the same impact as seeing the king and princess together. But they would have to be creative.

"The thrones must go. Both of them. We will stand, and we will bow. Belegeth, you must speak for the princess. Share your words of Her Highness's current situation. You must convince King Othin that his daughter is safe and that she is happy."

"I am no orator," the woman replied as she collected her helm from the dusty ground a length away. Daeturion caught her briefly touching her neck and checking her fingers for blood. Tecindo hadn't broken the skin, but it had been close.

"You must try. Princess Faeliel should be here to speak for herself. Since she is not, you are the next closest to her. Surely the king will trust your words."

Belegeth shrugged. "It is possible. It is also possible that he will believe I was complicit in whatever scheme he's imagined. He has not been known for rationality since the queen faded."

"I understand, but there is no alternative. I will speak for my father."

Daeturion glanced around the meet space, considering the possible presentations. King Othin should be at a higher level now, not on equal ground. It would give him a sense of superiority and advantage.

"This is less than ideal. Worse. But I am not called the silver-tongued dragon for nothing."

"I had assumed that was some kind of innuendo," Belegeth murmured without a hint of humor in her tone.

Daeturion let the comment pass. He didn't have time for banter. "If we can convince King Othin to let me touch him or one of his entourage, I may be able to show them our memories of the two together to prove our claims. I will also offer another meet—though I doubt King Othin will be inclined to agree given this insult—but perhaps if we arrange it in his territory or in another of the upper worlds instead of purely neutral ground, he will appreciate our good intent."

It was their only hope.

CHAPTER 53

Lhéwen stumbled through the streets of Nalakadr, weaving between pedestrians and leaning on every stable surface available. She had to get to Tharbatiron before King Rindae enacted his plans. She had so little energy left. Everything had gone into the making of the six rings, but she would not let Curuthannor down. Not again. He needed to know what was coming.

Dragging her feet the last few steps to the great wood gate of the Crossroads Inn, Lhéwen paused to catch her breath. The doors stood open, but for the first time she really looked at the wall and the entrance to the popular lodging and drinking establishment. She realized the true scope of the massive structure. It wasn't just an inn or a pub. It was a fortress hidden in plain sight.

She didn't have the time to admire the stone architecture or wonder at the protections Tharbatiron had built into the walls over the millennia. She entered the deceptively pastoral enclosure, doing her best to keep her eyes open and walk upright. With her gaze trained on the amphitheater and the bar just beyond, she forced her feet to move her forward.

Tryg spotted her first, coming around the back of his bar with his usual rag and glass in hand.

"My lady Lhéwen, are ye alright?"

Lhéwen shook her head in response but had to throw a hand out to the side to keep her balance. "I must speak with Tharbatiron immediately," she said. "It is of critical importance."

"He's in his office. I'll take ye there myself." Tryg set down his chore and offered a thick arm for her to lean on.

Lhéwen dipped her chin and swallowed, grasping the proffered support with gratitude. It was like hanging from the branch of a thousand year old oak.

The torches on the path were all lit and glowing merrily, but they did little to lighten Lhéwen's apprehension. Would Tharbatiron be able to do anything? Would they get to the smithy in time?

Tryg pounded on Tharbatiron's door.

"Enter!" came the immediate reply.

Tryg pushed on the wood ushering Lhéwen inside. Lhéwen's slipper caught on the stoop and she would have fallen if it weren't for Tryg's quick reflexes. He caught her and lifted her in his arms, carrying her across the threshold like a groom with his bride, except not the groom Lhéwen would have chosen. The image of Curuthannor's strong jaw and blue eyes flashed through her mind, but didn't linger.

"Look who I found wandering in through our gate." Tryg's voice vibrated through Lhéwen's skull.

"What has happened?" Tharbatiron's voice asked.

Lhéwen suddenly realized her eyes were closed. She forced her eyelids open, only to find a hairy troll arm blocking her view of the room.

"Put me down, please," Lhéwen's voice came out a barest whisper.

"Here, let me help," a third voice interrupted. Lhéwen thought she recognized it, but she couldn't be sure. After all, Lord Garamaen Sanyaro had left this realm and hadn't returned as far as she knew.

As Tryg set her feet on the ground a wave of energy flooded her system. Lhéwen suddenly felt as if she'd just woken from the best night's sleep of her life. Her cheeks flushed and her eyes opened wide. Sure enough, Lord Garamaen Sanyaro, master of spirit and soul and fire, sat in a cushioned armchair drinking tea with Tharbatiron.

His gaze searched her face. "So, it has begun."

"Then you know?" Lhéwen asked.

"King Rindae will reclaim the iron," Garamaen said with a heavy sigh.

"We knew it was a possibility. Our brave shadow king will send his sons into danger while he dances and plays at home," Tharbatiron said.

"Daeturion will be forced to treat with King Othin on his own. It will not go well." Sanyaro replied. He stood and lifted a sword belt from the floor. Using the stump of his right arm to hold the belt in place, he quickly buckled his weapon to his side.

"We must warn Curuthannor and his family. We must prepare them," Lhéwen urged.

"I'm afraid it may already be too late. Rindae's lack of planning and last minute decisions have aided his cause. Much depends on our next few choices."

"What are you saying?" Lhéwen asked.

"You must go to him. Get him out of there."

"But how am I to leave? I cannot use the portal without the guards—and ultimately Faeliel—discovering me."

"Luckily, I have a solution for that," Tharbatiron replied.

The ancient dark elf stood from his chair and led the way out of the office building toward the stone-columned gazebo in the night-flowering garden where she and Curuthannor had once sat. Lhéwen and Sanyaro trailed along behind, the truthseeker smiling with a knowing expression.

Tharbatiron crossed the gazebo to the farthest pillar away from the amphitheater and office. A small indentation on the side of the column caught Lhéwen's attention.

"Is that . . ." her mouth gaped.

"A portal? Why yes, it is," Sanyaro replied.

"Like Garamaen, my father was one of the creators of the gateways. He taught me the method of their creation, as Garamaen's father taught him. Together with the help of a few others, we have created hidden exits outside of the public eye, places only we know about that can be used in times of need."

"This is such a time," Sanyaro assured.

Tharbatiron placed a finger on the entry stone and began to draw runes. "I will open the gate to your canyon lands in the Human Realm."

"We will connect from there to the mines of the Crimson Mountains. If we hurry, we might be able to beat Aradae and his men to the sword."

CHAPTER 54

The portal to the Upper Realm opened with a crackling hiss. Two guards from the golden army stepped through with their swords drawn. They scanned the area, but there was little for them to see. Daeturion stood poised with his hands across his chest, waiting for the king's presentation to bow, Belegeth knelt one pace behind and to his right with her axe planted in the dirt and her hands clasped on top, and Tecindo knelt three paces behind and to Daeturion's left with his head bowed.

The guards' expressions never changed. They stepped back through the portal and returned almost instantly with four more guards and King Othin on their heels. Each guard wore a full set of gilded plate armor, with the king's crest—the crown on top of a nine pointed star—embossed on the chest piece. Their hands gripped the hilts of their sheathed swords. They marched in perfect unison, the matched pairs mirroring each other's actions.

These weren't just golden army soldiers, these were the king's personal guard, rumored to be the most deadly soldiers in all of the nine realms with the exception of the elite fire-wielding Tirnor of the Summer Realm.

Daeturion swallowed. They'd allowed each of the kings a six-person entourage, but only two were supposed to be guards. The rest should have been advisors and witnesses.

Already Othin broke the terms of the meet. Then again, King Rindae hadn't even bothered to appear.

King Othin paced the short distance to stand in front of Daeturion, who bowed as low as could be deemed appropriate for the heir to the throne of another realm. He couldn't debase himself, that would be seen as surrender, but he could at least show deference.

"Welcome, Your Majesty, King Othin. Your presence today is an honor."

"Where is our daughter?" King Othin asked without preamble.

Daeturion held his bow. "I'm afraid she and King Rindae have been delayed. Please, sit. Would you like a refreshment? Perhaps some wine or fruit? This area of the Human Realm is terribly dry and dusty, I'm afraid."

Daeturion flicked his fingers toward Tecindo. The blood sidhe immediately rose and hurried to the serving table to fulfill whatever King Othin demanded.

King Othin scowled, but found his throne beneath the golden canopy Daeturion had provided for shade and comfort.

"We will neither eat nor drink anything from these lands. What is the delay?"

"In truth, I am not certain," Daeturion replied. He straightened from his bow as King Othin sat down. "But I have been instructed to act on my father's behalf."

"He arranged this meet, and yet he is not present to participate? Is there no honor left in the Shadow Realm? But we are not surprised when he would stoop so low as to kidnap and indoctrinate my daughter and heir."

Daeturion pushed his shoulders back, but kept his hands and face open and relaxed. He wouldn't let the taunts bring him to anger. He had heard far worse said about his father from within the shadow court.

"Let me assure you, Your Majesty, Princess Faeliel was not kidnapped nor manipulated in any way by any of the dark elves in the Shadow Realm. When she first arrived, we believed she had been sent on your orders to negotiate a new alliance."

"Nonsense. We never would have given our own daughter in such a perilous task. *She* is not expendable."

Daeturion took a deep breath, forcing down the anger at the implied insult. He would not react.

"Of course she is not expendable. In fact, that is precisely why we are here today." Daeturion smiled. "We have joyous news to share. The time spent in political discussions and negotiations has brought King Rindae and Princess Faeliel close. King Rindae has a deep and profound respect for Princess Faeliel's political acumen and keen mind. More, his heart and hers have become entwined."

"Impossible. We will not hear these lies." King Othin stood from his chair as if to leave. His portal remained open. It was only a few steps away.

"I swear a solemn oath to all the gods, King Rindae and Princess Faeliel are courting and intend to be lifemated." The chiming of a bell that was felt more than heard echoed off the stone pillars around them.

"A solemn oath is a sacred thing," Othin growled.

"Indeed. I speak the truth and I swear to it. They are destined for one another."

King Othin's nostrils flared and the blood rose to his cheeks. Daeturion had to do something, and fast.

"If you will allow me to touch your hand, I can show you what I have seen from my own memories."

King Othin's guards stepped in front of their master, blocking Daeturion's path.

Daeturion quickly lifted his hands in surrender even as Belegeth stepped to his side, axe in hand.

"If you will not see it in my memories, then hear it from Princess Faeliel's own guard." Daeturion stepped to the side to encourage Belegeth to speak.

The woman scowled, but complied. "I am not a diplomat nor a lady, so excuse my rough words," Belegeth began. "Your daughter, Princess Faeliel, heir to the golden throne, spends every possible waking moment with King Rindae, and most sleeping ones as well. They are besotted and they are courting. She seems content."

King Othin's lip curled. "Besotted? Content? What is this? Why is she not here to speak for herself?"

"She feared Your Majesty's wrath for choosing a dark elf for a husband," Belegeth replied.

Daeturion winced. The woman was honest, he'd give her that. But he wished she would choose her words more carefully.

"Your Majesty, I hope you will see this as a blessing from the gods themselves. For the first time since the diaspora, two souls from two realms will bring their worlds closer together. Their joy will be the bridge between our lands, forever ending the tension between our peoples. Their union will unify the upperworlds and the underworlds, bringing us all to greater prosperity."

King Othin laughed, the sound emanating from deep within his diaphragm. "If you believe that, then you are a fool."

CHAPTER 55

othruinil took a sip of the hot citrusy tea from the bright
ceramic mug in her hand, then set the cup down with a
soft rattle. The café wasn't far from the Nalakadr public
portals. In fact, it was one of the first storefronts a new arrival
would see upon entering the Shadow Realm capital. Sunny yellow
curtains hung from the archways around the patio, and dual flags
of the Summer Realm and the Shadow Realm held place of honor
above the door. It was a little taste of home in the dark of the seemingly endless night, but the true benefit was the view that it
provided.

Within days of Rothruinil's return to the Shadow Realm, dark
elf soldiers had commandeered the portal and taken control of all
movement into and out of the city. Trolls carried block-cut stones
from a quarry on the other side of the gate, and stacked them in a
wide circle around the broad arch that was Rothruinil's only way
home.

The wall had been installed quickly but carefully, the trolls
working without pause for weeks. At first, the local residents had
scoffed at the idea, believing it was all for show, the king and his

sons puffing up their chests and pretending at strength to impress the king's new consort.

Then word of the new iron export ban had gotten out and the merchants all believed that the dark elf lords were using the wall as a means of further taking control of trade in the city. Even the dwarves had closed up their shops and returned to their underground caves in the Dwarven Realm.

But it was the high elf servant's words that stuck with Rothruinil. She'd said, "it's always best to be prepared." There were only a few high elves in this city, and only one that warranted a servant. The woman had been the handmaiden to Faeliel, Rothruinil was sure of it. Which meant the dark elves were preparing for war.

The proprietor of the café, an average-looking fire sidhe with the traditional shaved head and tattoos of their people, approached her table with a kind smile.

"Can I get you some more tea? Or perhaps you'd like somethin' to eat?" The man's warm tenor still carried the lilt of their home world, an accent Rothruinil was trying hard to cover along with her tattoos.

"That would be much appreciated," Rothruinil replied. The food here was as authentic as the tea. It would be a lovely distraction as she watched her exit become impassable.

The man grinned. "I'll bring your favorite, then."

She'd been lucky this little café existed, and that her father had pointed her in this direction. The apartment above was comfortable, if small, and the food was excellent. It was the only comfort she could enjoy in this sun-forgotten realm.

Rothruinil frowned as the last stone was dropped into place. The new wall sealed the city from within, a tidy solution to the defensive problem of portal travel. Of course, a big enough force could probably break through under the right circumstances, but victory would come at great cost.

Worse, the Summer Realm had no knowledge of the new defenses. The guards had been letting individuals pass through the portal unhindered when there was a pause in the line of trolls, but they personally coded every location, which meant even if they didn't stop her—which was unlikely—they would know a fire sidhe had passed through. She couldn't risk that kind of exposure. There had to be another way home, but she had yet to find it. Until she did, she was stuck, and so was her intelligence.

For now, she was glad she had a place to stay and an ally to ward off the inevitable homesickness.

A sudden increase in activity near the new guard gate drew Rothruinil's attention outward. Soldiers had been on duty at the wall all day, but after the last of the trolls had left, the soldiers had settled into a bored attention. Now, the small cluster of men and women straightened their backs, lifted their chins, and placed clasped hands on the hilts of their swords.

The common street bustle increased as individuals jostled into each other. Rothruinil scanned the crowd, looking for the source of the pedestrian commotion. Whatever it was, it was coming closer.

The first of the black-clad warriors appeared at the end of the wide avenue. They walked in loose groups of three to five, their expressions grim but focused. They didn't have the tight control of her father's well-trained forces, but they were still an intimidating group in black armor that bristled with weapons. They monitored the surrounding crowd with intent as they moved, and Rothruinil could almost hear their thoughts evaluating every individual in their proximity. By Rothruinil's count, nearly fifty warriors made up the party. Civilians cleared a path.

Prince Aradae led the way, his expression grim and determined. Rothruinil had met him once, long ago, and he hadn't much changed in the interim. Gray eyes so pale they almost looked white stood out against his dark black skin, and the tight knot of white hair did nothing to relieve the severity of his expression. He'd chosen a heavy scaled armor that somehow managed to bend and flex with his every movement. He wore it as if it were as light as a silk robe, but Rothruinil imagined the extra weight would be a burden in battle. The Tirnor warriors of her homeland eschewed any armor for that very reason. They preferred speed and stealth over defensive might.

Still, the workmanship was immaculate and his flexibility seemed unhindered. If she could manage it, it would be interesting to find the name of the maker. Perhaps she could find a suitable set for herself.

Behind the dark elf soldiers, a long line of warriors wearing red caps pulled wagons, two to each cart. Bulging with muscle and strapped with weapons, the new warriors were neither dark elf nor blood sidhe, perhaps not even greater fae. If anything, they looked like oversized goblins that had been bred for battle.

What were they doing? Rothruinil couldn't figure it out. Were they short on supplies? Expecting a siege? Just as she couldn't get messages out, she also hadn't been able to receive any messages from the upperworlds in weeks. Had something happened that hadn't been made common knowledge amongst the common fae of this realm?

Before they reached the new portal wall, a group of archers split off from the rest of the group and jogged up the outer stairs to the bolt holes and crenellations at the top of the formidable structure. The rest proceeded through the gate and out of sight.

Rothruinil's lips pressed into a thin line. Wherever they were going, blood was about to be shed, and there was nothing she could do to stop it.

CHAPTER 56

As the sun crested the horizon, its light broke across the valley floor. The first ray touched the face of the eastern stone pillar. The buzzing of summer solstice magic hummed a quiet discord in Curuthannor's brain. The ceremony had begun.

Hatholdammon stepped forward toward a shrine that had been prepared for just this moment. Covered in golden silk, the flat surface would hold the pieces of the sword as it was slowly assembled over the course of the day. He extended his hands before him, the nearly finished blade lying flat across his palms.

The black hills iron had been liquified in a crucible with the leaves of the ash tree and charcoal burned from its wood, then hammered with careful precision into shape. Sixteen steel bars had been created to ensure at least one would be of high enough quality to deserve the king's enchantment. Curuthannor, Nambamahtar, Minyondor, and Hadhion had each taken turns at the anvil as the master smith watched with a critical gaze.

Only after all sixteen bars had achieved the necessary size had Hatholdammon taken up his own tools. He carefully polished a small section of each piece to reveal the hidden pattern in the metal. He examined their surface and tested their strength and elasticity. At last he made his selection and began the process of shaping the bar of steel into a sword worthy of a king.

Hatholdammon had ground and shaped the bevel, crafting the dual-edge that would soon be sharpened to a razor's edge. The runes that would hold and direct the enchantment had been carved into the fuller that ran a third of the length of the blade, and the sword had been painted with clay to control the temperature as it was fired. After weeks of work, it was ready for today's final heat treatment, the process that would give the weapon its hardness and flexibility, and magical power.

"All-father above, we welcome you to this circle of spirit and iron. We pray that you bless our efforts and find pleasure in the sword we craft in your name." With a bow, Hatholdammon laid metal on silk.

As his father stepped back, Curuthannor stepped forward. It had taken all of his focused will, and he hadn't slept, but Curuthannor was pleased with the final polished design. Shaped like the wings of a bird, the guard would curve down on either side of the blade, then connect to the hilt via rings of gold and silver.

"All-father above, we welcome you to this circle of spirit and iron. We pray that you protect the hand that wields this sword and shape its purpose toward righteous good." Using two hands in a reverent bow, Curuthannor laid the cross-guard on the shrine next to the blade.

Minyondor—who had carved the ash wood hilt by hand and helped Curuthannor to size and refine his guard design—approached the shrine next. "All-father above, we welcome you to this circle of spirit and iron. We pray that you guide the hand of the wielder."

Nambamahtar laid the final component of the king's sword on the shrine: a flawless diamond the size of an orange. Held in place by pure silver wire, it would act as the pommel and counterweight the sword, and would also store the high king's excess energy for later use. "All-father above, we welcome you to this circle of spirit and iron. We pray that you preserve and sustain the spirit of the wielder."

During their prayers, the sun had continued to move across the sacred circle, and as Nambamahtar stepped away from the shrine, the first ray of light touched the stone altar. The entire valley seemed to resonate with a bell-like tone that rippled outward from the shrine and echoed off the faces of the mountains.

Like his father and brothers, Curuthannor wore no shirt or armor, but the heat of the forge kept most of the chill at bay. At least for his chest. His back could have used a bit of extra warmth, but he didn't dare shift or turn to alleviate the discomfort. Every movement of this ritual had to be precise or the gods might not bless the sword with the promised enchantments.

Hatholdammon stepped forward once more, removing the blade from the shrine. He seated the coated steel between a set of long tongs, and placed the tip touching the dirt of the sacred circle.

"May the essence of the earth give strength and flexibility," Hatholdammon intoned.

He paused for three heart beats, then thrust the blade into the fire of the brick forge which Curuthannor and his brothers had painstakingly built to house the long blade. The heat of the flame was controlled with a pair of directional bellows that Curuthannor and Minyondor pumped in tandem to bring the fire to a constant temperature along the full length of the sword. The metal began to glow.

"May the heat of the forge purify the steel," the three men said together.

Meanwhile, Nambamahtar prepared the quenching bowl with the purified oil. He took a hot stone from within the forge and dropped it into the water, bringing the temperature just high enough to avoid warping the sword, but not so high as to soften its structure.

When the color of the iron turned to golden straw, Hatholdammon removed the blade from the fire and thrust it into the waiting oil.

"May the blessed oil clarify its purpose," Hatholdammon and Nambamahtar chanted.

The hiss of steam blasted from the quenching basin.

Curuthannor held his breath, anxious to see the final product. His father was a master smith, and the sword would be nothing less than brilliant, but somehow he was always a little surprised that what had once been a lump of raw iron could be turned into the elegant blade of a warrior.

Hatholdammon pulled the steel from the oil and held it up to the sky. "May the mountain air quicken every strike and cushion every parry."

The crackle of energy built around the sacred circle. The gods were listening, the magics were flowing, and the sword would own its purpose.

Hatholdammon brought the sword across his naked arm and stared up the length. He said not a word, but the expression in his eyes looked pleased with the work. Which was good, considering they wouldn't have another chance to craft this sword again for a year.

Now that the blade was hardened, it was time to sharpen and polish. Hatholdammon would focus on the blade, but Curuthannor and his brothers were needed to spin the grinding wheel. Several bells later, sweat coated their backs but the sword was sharp and nearly complete.

While Hatholdammon returned the blade to the shrine, Nambamahtar placed the crucible filled with pure silver into the fire of the forge. The metal would be needed to conduct the enchantments from the runes across the hilt, to the diamond. While the silver turned molten, Hatholdammon once more painted the edges of the runes and engravings with clay to build a barrier in which to receive the precious metal.

At last satisfied with the work, Hatholdammon stepped back and Curuthannor stepped forward. It was time for the final assembly and to set the enchantments in the blade. He took a deep cleansing breath before touching the guard.

"May the hand of the wielder remain steadfast and true," Curuthannor said. He lifted the guard from the golden silk and threaded it onto the sword tang. Metal scraped across metal and clanged into place. With the single strike of a small jeweler's hammer, Curuthannor pinned the guard in place.

He stepped back, relieved that his part of the ritual was over. He was required to remain until the ceremony was complete, but only to assist the others. His shoulders relaxed and a weight lifted from his mind. The remaining responsibility was minimal at best.

Minyondor stepped forward to attach the hilt. "May the World Tree bring harmony between sword and wielder." The ash wood slid home, requiring only a light tapping with a rubber mallet to seat it against the guard and knock the pins in place.

Nambamahtar was last. "May the spirit within and without obey the will of the wielder." He fastened the diamond to the pommel then wrapped the pure silver wire around the wood and metal of the guard, lining it up with a shallow groove in the fuller of the blade.

The trickiest part of the entire crafting was next; the pouring of the molten silver into the runes and channels that connected them. The design had to be carefully filled with the molten silver, else the steel corrupted and enchantments lost.

Hatholdammon lifted the sword to the sky once more, checking the final placement of every piece, then laid the blade on a wood block that would keep the flat of the sword precisely level.

After once again checking every angle of the sword, Hatholdammon took the tongs and the crucible and carefully tipped the narrow spout toward the first of the runes. Silver poured from the basin in a slow but steady drip. As it filled every gap, every crevice, Hatholdammon laid the enchantment.

"May Ansuz receive the spirit," he said. On the last word, when it seemed like the silver would overflow the bounds of the clay, Hatholdammon stopped the flow. The metal settled.

He moved on to the second rune. "May Algiz give protection."

And the third, "May Sowilo recharge the life force."

The final rune connected them all. "May Tiwaz bring success in battle."

With the silver poured and resting, they could close the ceremony and give the blade its final polish.

"May the silver—"

Screams broke through the early afternoon air. Distracted, Curuthannor didn't hear the rest of his father's words. He turned, his gaze raking across the valley toward the village. The blood drained from his face and his stomach turned.

Smoke billowed from one of the forges. Not the usual thin wisps from a controlled flame, this was a thick black cloud that mushroomed up into the pale blue sky.

Curuthannor's nostrils flared. Something had caught fire. His gaze connected with Minyondor, but his brother gave a small shake of his head. They couldn't interrupt the ceremony or all might be lost. Hatholdammon had to finish the prayer and polish the edge of the blade. The work had to be precise.

Still, Curuthannor couldn't ignore the increasing clamor from the village. Men shouted and women screamed. Whatever was happening, it was spreading, and fast. Metal clashed against metal.

Rómesse Gulch was under attack.

CHAPTER 57

Aradae stood at the front of the line before the portal, his team of sixteen men and women of the shadow guard lined up in pairs behind him. Behind them, eight heavy carts each pulled by two hired red cap mercenaries waited to extract as much iron as they could before the smithy was destroyed.

The plan was relatively simple. As soon as they received word that Othin had arrived at the meet, they would draw the runes to the Crimson Mountains portal. The guard would immobilize any of the high elves in the area, while the red caps collected the iron and hauled it back to Nalakadr. Hopefully they would meet little resistance, but given the merchant warrior's skill with a blade, they were prepared for a battle.

Unfortunately, that was also why the gremlins had insisted on hiring the red caps for the venture. They claimed they were not skilled enough fighters, though their sharp pointed teeth led Aradae to believe otherwise. Meanwhile, the red caps were battle-hardened warriors, and notoriously blood-thirsty. Closely related to the goblins and gremlins, the lesser fae creatures grew to human height, which made them proportionally the strongest of the races, except for trolls.

Rumor had it, they consumed their kills as a sign of their prowess in battle. Aradae had never fought with or against them, so he could neither confirm nor deny the rumors, but he would send a pair of guards with each team to maintain control. The fewer the deaths, the faster the mission, the better the outcome.

Once the iron had been collected, the shadow guard would destroy the forge that would supply Othin's armory. So their king had ordered, and so would it be.

Aradae felt badly for the smith and his family, but it was a strong tactical play: remove the enemy's military power base while their leader was distracted elsewhere. And the information about the village was reliable, coming from Othin's own daughter.

His gaze raked across the new portal enclosure, glad that he'd had enough foresight to order the construction. The fortified wall was coming together nicely. It stood more than four stories high and two lengths deep and circled the entire portal courtyard. Four gates into the city had been built into the walls, their heavy doors reinforced with iron and easily barred from the outside.

The trolls had finished the work less than a bell earlier, their numbers doubled to finish in time. The price was steep, but if the worst happened, and the golden army followed them home, at least there would be a way to compress and contain any return attack. A dozen of Aradae's best archers stood on the top of the wall, arrows nocked but not drawn, ready just in case. Having them so close wasn't ideal, however. They really needed a tower or two. Aradae would create a new set of plans when he returned. Still, with the relatively narrow portal, only a few men could cross at a single time and even a small number of archers would be able to pick them off as they entered.

A blood sidhe messenger sprinted toward them, his feet blurring with the speed of his approach. He held out a scroll sealed with King Rindae's sigil.

Aradae broke the wax and opened the parchment.

"Prepare yourselves!" he shouted. "Draw your weapons! Now is the time!" He nodded for the portal guard to draw the runes.

The portal began to glow. The energy field snapped into place within the confines of the broad stone arch. Aradae bounced lightly on his toes, pumping adrenaline through his body. Unlike his father, he would be the first through the gate, leading from the front, not asking his warriors to fight and die when he was unwilling to make his own sacrifices.

The final rune was drawn. The portal clouded, then cleared, revealing the bright light of the Upper Realm. Aradae squinted against the glare and blinked away the tears. Yet another disadvantage of dark against light, and another risk they hadn't considered, but would have to mitigate.

He took a final breath, then charged through the gate.

The portal spit him out on the street of what should have been a small mining village with a single smithy and a few ancillary artisans. Instead, row after row of tents and hastily built lean-tos crowded the area. Already, Aradae could see the thin smoke from at least a half-dozen forges. He'd memorized a map the princess had given him, but the information was clearly out of date.

A few pedestrians gaped as the dark elf soldiers emerged from the portal, then scattered. At least the ringing of hammers covered the sound of the shadow guard's arrival and the shouts of warning. Aradae had not been prepared for the size of this encampment. They had thought it would be easy to determine their targets. They had thought the iron would be obvious. But with this many smiths and forges, there was no single place to go.

"Quickly," Aradae shouted to the men and women behind him. The plan had changed with the complexity of the scene. "Two soldiers with each cart. Find the iron, destroy the forges. Shut down any resistance but do not instigate. If they willingly surrender, they may live. No mercy for any who take up arms."

"Yes, sir!" the men and women of the shadow guard confirmed in unison. They'd been drilling for this. They knew the stakes.

The red caps looked to their own commander, a man with a thick scar that ran from the top of his forehead, across his left eye, and then curled back across his cheek to the point of his chin.

"No unnecessary deaths. Kill only those who take up arms against you," Aradae repeated.

"As ye say," the commander replied, before turning to his company. "Get to it."

The red cap mercenaries grinned, revealing maws filled with sharpened teeth.

Aradae could only trust that the hired swords would follow his orders. If he could have refused their assistance, he would have, but they needed someone to pull the carts and the gremlins had been adamant. It had been a necessary but reasonable requirement when they thought the village was little more than a single estate.

Aradae jogged down the only paved street in sight, the road covered in flat stone, likely the castoff from the not-too-distant mines. On one side, a series of small buildings made up the village proper. The signs hanging above the doorways indicated the mundane shops of baker and butcher and mining supply. They were not of interest to him. It was the forges with their supplies of iron, weapons, and armor that were his focus.

He pointed the first cart team in the direction of one of the larger tents. Smoke curled from a pipe chimney. They entered to the sound of a woman's scream. The sound was silenced and a red cap cackled with glee. They must have found some iron.

Aradae moved on.

A man exited another tent at a jog, heavy hammer on one shoulder, the handle gripped in two thick hands. His expression was tight and determined. He lifted the hammer. Aradae sliced him across the midsection before the hammer could be brought to bear.

The second team ducked beneath the canvas overhang.

More men and women came out of their tents and shelters. Some gasped and ran to hide. Aradae let them go.

A woman in a heavy leather apron ran toward him with a red hot blade of unsharpened metal in a leather-covered hand. Aradae dodged the unwieldy strike—easy enough with the woman's unbalanced weapon—and sliced her arm across the bicep, cutting to the bone. She dropped the unfinished blade. Her eyes widened as Aradae's sword pierced through her apron and into her heart. Violence offered received violence in turn.

The repetitive sound of hammer against anvil shifted to the clashing of swords. Despite their greater numbers, the residents of the village were no match for Aradae's warriors, and the street soon filled with the bodies of the untrained smiths who dared a confrontation.

Aradae's target was a small two-story stone house that sat back off the main street. It looked perfect and pristine, a lovely little cottage in which to raise a family, if one was interested in the glittering facade of the high elves. The walkway to the front was bordered with pink and gold roses that grew up and over a trellis that covered the pedestrian path. The peaked roof was supported by filigreed wood arches, and the window casings contained colored cut glass that reflected a rainbow of light.

As the largest estate in the area, Aradae was sure this was the smith's home. Ignoring the brick paved path, Aradae cut through the yard, looking for the smithy and any other outbuildings that might contain the iron. Curuthannor's father was in charge of this entire operation, and therefore would have stashed the majority of his new-found wealth near his own forge, doling out the necessary bits to the other smiths only as necessary to complete their tasks. Anything else would have been too generous to comprehend.

Aradae was pleased to find he didn't have to go far. Behind and to the side of the house was a single-story three-sided structure. With four chimneys rising from the back, the smithy was just as Princess Faeliel had described. And sure enough, a third smaller outbuilding on a heavy raised wood foundation sat just a few lengths away. The wood was freshly cut and hastily built, not made of the same shining gray stone as the rest of the structures. Locked from the outside, it had to be the iron stores.

Aradae motioned the last team forward. "It must be in there. Get it, and let's go."

Aradae glanced around, looking for any sign of the merchant warrior or his brethren. A shadow skirted around the far side of the building. He nodded for one of the soldiers to investigate, but the fires were dim and the smithy was eerily silent. Every other tent or lean-to had been bustling with activity, yet the master of all was missing. Where could they have gone?

Aradae twirled the ring on his thumb, the promised enchantment making him nervous. Eventually they would come across an energy drain, but Aradae had only been given three of the purported protections. He wore one, the red cap commander had been granted another, and the third had been given to the commander of the shadow guard archers on the portal fortification wall. Everyone else would be susceptible to the spirit drains of the high elf masters.

A yelp of pain brought Aradae's attention back to the iron store. One of the red caps had touched the lock on the door, but now her arm hung loose at her side. She jerked her shoulder, but her entire arm flopped around like a soup noodle hanging from a spoon.

"I can't move my arm! All I did was touch it!" the woman cried.

"Did you really think we would leave the last of the black hills iron unprotected?" a woman asked.

Aradae spun around. Flashing green eyes were the first thing he saw. The high elf woman stood on the back stairs of the house, closing the door behind her. She was unarmed and looked like nothing more than a genteel wife. She wiped her hands, then flipped the towel over one shoulder in the practiced move of a woman used to working in the kitchen. Yet the scowl in her expression marred the pleasant exterior, and the twitch of her fingers warned Aradae that she might not be all that she appeared.

He stepped between the woman and his team, drawing her irate gaze. "We are here to reclaim what is ours by right of creation."

"Lord Garamaen Sanyaro, truthseeker and mediator of the nine faerie realms, bartered in good faith. That iron was his, and now it is ours, by right of trade," the woman replied. She might look the country wife, but there was clearly more beneath the surface.

"Prior to the trade, King Rindae, lord of the Shadow Realm and all dark elves, liege of goblin, gremlin, and troll, banned all exports of black hills iron. Sanyaro removed the iron in violation of the king's law." Aradae took a step toward the woman. An extended conversation wouldn't do anyone any good, but if he could contain her, they might be able to extract the iron without bloodshed.

"Perhaps, but Sanyaro had purchased the iron prior to the edict. It was his to give where he chose. Do not attempt to gain entry to the iron," the woman warned, her gaze never leaving Aradae's face though her words were meant for the soldiers behind him. "The next attempt to break the lock without the proper key will end in full paralysis."

"Then give us the key."

"I will not." Her fingers twitched toward her pocket, the gesture subtle enough that had Aradae not being watching her with intense focus, he might have missed it.

"I would prefer not to end your life over such a trivial matter. Give us the key, and return inside."

The woman shook her head, her lips lifting in a disdainful smirk. "I may not have a sword, but I am not defenseless."

She pressed her wrists together. Aradae felt a tug on his aura, but she couldn't gain hold. The woman's eyebrows furrowed, and her scowl deepened. Her gaze flicked to the shed behind him. He couldn't let her drain his warriors. He took two quick steps and lunged. She lifted her arms as if to block his thrust, but the steel was sharp and her flesh was weak and unprotected. The blade sliced through her hands as if they were nothing. The tip pierced her chest and pushed her back against the closed door of the house. Aradae tugged the metal free.

Eyes blinked slowly in shock. The woman slid down the painted blue door, her body leaving a smear of red behind her. Her mouth opened and closed, gasping for air.

"May the gods welcome you into the summerlands," Aradae whispered.

"You may take this iron," she wheezed, "but the sword will save us all. You will not prevail."

He reached a hand into her pocket and removed the key. He tossed it to the red caps behind him.

He would have to thank the enchantress for the ring.

"What did she mean, 'the sword will save us all'?" asked the red cap whose arm yet remained limp.

Aradae shook his head. "The only sword I can think of is King Othin's commission. That's why we're here for the iron. They can't be allowed to craft the enemy's greatest weapon."

"It sounds like the sword's already done," the other red cap growled.

Running footsteps approached from the street. "Prince Aradae, sir! Something is going on down the valley. Some kind of ritual forging is already in progress."

"May the wastelands rise up and take them," Aradae whispered. They had already lost too much time. "You two get this iron back to Nalakadr." Aradae ordered the team he'd come in with. He turned to the runner. "Find every unencumbered shadow guard warrior. We're going to get that sword."

CHAPTER 58

Hatholdammon staggered and dropped to one knee. "Tunniel," he whispered. His gaze lost focus. His hand clenched above his heart. He seemed to shrink in on himself, leaning to one side until he finally toppled over into the dirt of the sacred circle.

"Mother?" Curuthannor asked. He turned once more to face the village, which he could tell even from this distance was rapidly deteriorating into chaos. "They must be at the house! We must go to her!"

"We can't leave until the ceremony is complete," Nambamahtar replied. "Else all is for naught. If we're not slaughtered here today, we will be slaughtered by the king's own hand when we fail to deliver his promised sword. Hadhion is there. He will help her."

Curuthannor swore. He tore his gaze away from the distant village to once again face the shrine. Movement on the other side of the circle caught his attention. Two figures were sprinting toward the sacred circle from the mouth of the crimson mines. One appeared to be female. The other . . . did he have a feather in his hair?

"It's Sanyaro!" Curuthannor said, as recognition dawned. Hope rose in his chest. If the ancient elf were here, not all was lost. He would be able to turn the intruders away.

Curuthannor turned his focus to the woman. Golden hair shone in the afternoon sun. A breezy gown whipped into a frenzy behind her running feet.

Lhéwen. Curuthannor's thoughts tangled. What was she doing here? Why would Sanyaro have brought her here, of all places and times?

Nambamahtar kneeled by Hatholdammon's side, drawing Curuthannor's attention back to the present moment. "Father, you must complete the sword. Polish the silver and sharpen the steel. There is little time."

"Tunniel. She's . . . she's gone!" Hatholdammon moaned. He curled into a fetal position, hugging his arms across his chest.

"Father, get up!" Curuthannor shouted. "Sanyaro is coming. He will protect mother. You must get up and finish this!"

"It's too late. Nothing matters," Hatholdammon moaned.

"It can't be too late. Hadhion is there." Curuthannor replied even as his heart fell to the dirt of the sacred circle. Hadhion wasn't a warrior. He hunted game. Curuthannor was the best with a blade. He should have been there to protect her.

"Tautamiel," Minyondor stepped toward the burning tents as if in a daze.

"Minya, no!" Namba shouted. "The sword must be finished!"

Minyondor didn't seem to hear him. He took another step, and another, his attention focused on the village. He broke into a run.

"Stop him!" Nambamahtar commanded.

On instinct bred of being the youngest of three brothers, Curuthannor lunged, catching Minyondor around the ankles and dragging him to the ground. Minya twisted, his heel catching Curuthannor across the jaw and making his ears ring. Curuthannor grunted, but didn't let go. Minya growled and kicked at Curuthannor's shoulder.

"Minya, it's too late. The village is all but destroyed!" Curuthannor said. "If she's still alive, she's hiding. Her father will keep her safe."

Minyondor's boot slammed down again, but Curuthannor didn't give up even as he lost his hold. "The best thing you can do is keep yourself alive and help finish this sword. King Othin will not let this attack go unanswered."

"I must go to her! She could be dying!"

"You have no weapon!"

Minya rolled over, finally twisting out of Curuthannor's grasp. He scrambled to his feet and sprinted toward the village. "I will find one!"

"Can you do nothing right?" Namba demanded.

"He kicked me in the face!" Curuthannor rubbed his jaw as he picked himself up off the ground. "Father?"

Nambamahtar shook his head at the same time that Hatholdammon moaned his wife's name once more. They had been lifemated in truth, their bond deeply felt. Lifemates rarely outlived each other by more than a few days or weeks. Even those that did were never the same again. Othin's own erratic behavior was evidence of this truth.

"Can you finish it? Can you imbue the steel with the final enchantments in the grinding?" Curuthannor asked his eldest brother.

Nambamahtar shook his head. "I don't have the skill. I can do some, but it won't be nearly as strong as father's workings."

"There has to be something we can do."

"Your father is the only smith in this age capable of this level of enchantment," Sanyaro panted. He remained outside of the sacred circle, but pressed his only hand onto the sparkling stone, leaning on the pillar for support as he caught his breath.

Lhéwen arrived a moment or two later. She sucked in heaving gasps of air, clearly unused to the speed or effort of the exercise.

"I came to warn you," Lhéwen heaved, "but too late."

"Not too late yet," Sanyaro replied. "The sword has not been taken."

"My father cannot finish it," Curuthannor replied. "It is only half complete, and already the ceremony has been disrupted. Even if he could finish the working, the enchantment may not hold."

"Leave your father to me and Lhéwen. You are required for other things." Sanyaro thrust the hilt of his own sword toward Curuthannor and nodded his head toward the village.

Five black-clad warriors approached with determined steps. At their head, Aradae, Prince of Shadow and Commander of All Souls. He couldn't block the effects of Aradae's magic. The prince would string him along like a puppet, just as he had done in the shadow king's office.

"I will protect your soul and give your father the energy he needs to complete his task, but you must protect the circle," Sanyaro said, as if reading his mind.

Curuthannor spun the gently curved blade, testing its weight and balance. The single edge was decidedly sharp, the tip angled up for the thrusting strike. The handle had been wrapped in silk cord, soft and flexible, and unlikely to slip in the hand. It was a good weapon.

"Your father made it for me before you were born," Sanyaro said. "It has served me well over the years, crippled though I may be. It will serve you better."

Curuthannor turned the blade on its side, looking for his father's mark near the hilt. The curved cross was obvious. Curuthannor didn't know what to say.

"Prepare yourself," Sanyaro said before Curuthannor found his words. "They're nearly here."

CHAPTER 59

This *gods-damned sword.*

Garamaen stared down at the seemingly innocent looking weapon, the steel shining from the grind, the pure silver inlay now hardened and fused with the steel beneath. So close to done, and yet it would do nothing for anyone in its current state. Finishing the work would give Othin his greatest power. Not finishing it would destabilize the fragile network that struggled to hold the nine realms together. No matter what he did, there would be war, but the task now was to minimize the damage.

The sword must be finished.

Curuthannor stood at the edge of the circle between the two southernmost pillars, seemingly outmatched. He was a brave soul, that one. His aura shone in pure white, a gleaming halo of honor and loyalty. He was needed in the dark future that lay ahead.

With a twist of his hand, Garamaen lay a shield around the high elf's aura, protecting him from harm to spirit or soul. The dark elves wouldn't be able to touch him with their magic. In truth, that gave Curuthannor the advantage, even in a five to one battle.

Garamaen turned from the imminent fight and focused on the man who had lost his soul with the death of his lifemate.

"Hatholdammon, Master Smith of Rómesse Gulch and Enchanter of the First Order—"

Lhéwen snapped her attention to Garamaen, her eyes wide. Garamaen had forgotten that Hatholdammon had hidden much of his past from the next generation. Few but his wife—may her soul pass to the summerlands—knew that he had been numbered amongst the greatest enchanters born to the nine realms. He may well have rivaled the origin elves who helped create the first portals.

"—you are called to serve the nine realms. Stand and face your task," Sanyaro finished.

"Tunniel . . ." Hatholdammon groaned. He turned an anguished gaze up to Garamaen, imploring him for mercy. It was a mercy the man could not yet obtain.

"She is gone, but you cannot yet fade. Protect your sons. Protect the future. Finish what you have begun."

Hatholdammon closed his eyes. His face seemed to age in an instant. He wanted to fade, wanted to let go of the mortal body and join his lifemate in death. Garamaen understood Hatholdammon's pain all too well, though he had been granted a skill that gave him comfort that others could not share.

A brush of sweet air caressed Garamaen's face. His own lifemate had joined them, their bond as strong in death as it was in life, their continuing connection the only reason Garamaen hadn't followed her into the afterlife.

She is with me, Garamaen's human wife, Angeni, whispered through soul speech.

If you can hear me, tell him I am here, Tunniel said. *Tell him his greatest vengeance will be to finish the king's blade and take it to Othin. It is what the shadow warriors want, and what they cannot have.*

"Tunniel is with us now. Though you cannot see her or feel her, she will always be by your side. Small comfort, I know, but she has a message for you. She says 'your greatest vengeance will be to finish the sword.' If you cannot do it for anyone else, do this for her."

"Please, Father. I will help you, as much as I am able, but you must do this," Nambamahtar encouraged.

Hatholdammon pushed a hand into the ground and levered himself into a sitting position. His eyelids drooped and his shoulders sagged, but he was moving, and that was good. Garamaen fed him more energy. It would do nothing for his emotional state, but at least he would have the strength to polish the sword to its final state.

Garamaen turned to the young woman by his side. She might not have Hatholdammon's training or innate magical power, but she was more skilled than she realized. "Lhéwen, you must strengthen the enchantment as Hatholdammon sets it."

Lhéwen shook her head, her eyes wide with fear. "I cannot. I am just a handmaiden. A seamstress."

"You have served the princess for more than a hundred years. You have created thousands of enchantments in that time. Not only that, you mimicked the magic of others, and broke the pattern when necessary. You are far more than a 'seamstress'."

"But he's an Enchanter of the First Order," Lhéwen whispered. "I will only get in his way."

"He has just lost his lifemate. He needs your help."

Lhéwen took a deep breath and stepped forward as Nambamahtar lifted his father to standing.

Hatholdammon ran a finger down the new silver inlay. "May the will of the All-Father be done."

He lifted the sword from its holder with reverent hands and began the careful process of rubbing the edge across a whetstone. The sword would be finished.

"Go. Help your brother," Garamaen commanded, speaking to Nambamahtar. "The shadow guard cannot be allowed to claim this sword."

CHAPTER 60

Curuthannor waited, and watched. Aradae and four shadow guard warriors approached with rapid steps along the village path. There was no point in their trying to hide. There was no cover for at least ten lengths around the sacred circle, so there would be no surprises. Still, he was outnumbered five to one.

The silk cord beneath Curuthannor's hands shifted as he squeezed. He held the sword in a relaxed, but firm two-handed grip at his side, the tip of the blade extended toward his enemy. He shifted his weight, found his center of balance on his right foot. The left prepared for the first step.

Aradae might be one of the strongest wielders of soul magic Curuthannor had ever encountered, but he had to trust that Garamaen was stronger and would be able to protect him. So long as that held true, they were evenly matched. But Aradae had the advantage of both armor and numbers. The shadow warriors could overwhelm him and swarm the circle. Aradae could get one good strike across Curuthannor's bare skin and take him out of the fight forever. If either of those happened, Curuthannor's father and brother would die. Lhéwen would die.

He couldn't let that happen.

Curuthannor calmed his mind, centered and focused himself on the task at hand. He couldn't let them get too close, couldn't let them spread out around him. His only hope was to attack, starting with the weaker warriors. At times, the best defense was a powerful offense.

From standing to a sprint, Curuthannor rushed the oncoming soldiers.

First, the man on the left. He was big and slow, strong, but unable to match Curuthannor's speed. His heavy greatsword swung overhead but Curuthannor was already inside his guard. The curved blade of Sanyaro's weapon found a seam in the plate and pierced the leather beneath with hardly a whisper of resistance. Curuthannor spun. Pulled the blade free. Ready position.

Duck. A second swing from another warrior passed overhead. Curuthannor launched a kick to the man's stomach and knocked him to the ground. A quick lunge. Curuthannor's blade penetrated the man's throat between chest and helm. The soldier gurgled and coughed, choking on his own blood, but he wouldn't last long, unable to breathe.

Meanwhile, Aradae had flanked him on the left. Curuthannor parried and spun out of range. He wasn't ready to test his mettle against the dark elf prince.

The woman was next in the target list. Fast. Two daggers. She spun in a flurry of sharp edges and unconventional kicks. Forced backward, Curuthannor could barely keep up with the unrelenting blows. A blade found a hole in his defense and sliced across his forearm. Hot blood dripped down his hand.

Aradae and the second man were behind him now. Curuthannor felt the strike coming. Ducked. Rolled. The sword passed overhead, a little too close for comfort.

He couldn't afford to be surrounded. He somersaulted out of

the confines of the tight circle and found his feet, immediately turning to face the enemy once more.

A smith's heavy hammer smashed into the fifth warrior's temple. Blood and brain exploded from the dark elf's skull. The man fell. Behind him stood Nambamahtar, a disgusted sneer lifting the corner of his lip. He wasn't paying attention.

"Behind you!" Curuthannor yelled, but too late. The woman warrior was already on him, her blades slicing through Nambamahtar's unprotected skin and leaving criss-crossing trails of red across his chest.

Curuthannor ran toward the fight, but Aradae stepped between them. Curuthannor narrowly blocked a slashing strike that would have spilled his guts into the dirt. He crossed his sword over the top of Aradae's blade, sliding the steel up toward the dark elf's shoulder. Aradae lunged back out of the way.

Curuthannor spared a glance for his brother. He was still on his feet, but Curuthannor could see bone through a slash to one shoulder and enough cuts across his torso to fell a small tree. The woman continued to hassle him, even as he stumbled.

Steel flashed in Curuthannor's peripheral vision. He blocked a head strike and turned that into another slice across Aradae's shoulder, but the dark elf twisted out of the way.

Nambamahtar brought the hammer around just as the woman went for a final killing blow. Her dagger struck home, but so did his hammer. Her body flew to one side and fell in a heap. Her helm was crushed and misshapen. Her dagger remained buried in Nambamahtar's chest.

Nambamahtar fell to his knees. He dropped the hammer and both hands reached up to grasp the dagger.

"No!" Curuthannor shouted. He sprinted to his brother's side, momentarily forgetting Prince Aradae.

Confusion and shock and disbelief painted Nambamahtar's face. He turned his gaze to Curuthannor. "Little brother," he whispered. He fell to one side. His body lay still.

Violence and anger welled up from somewhere deep within Curuthannor's breast. He screamed out his rage, turning toward the man who had caused it all.

Prince Aradae stood just a length away, his expression closed and wary.

"You will not get away with this," Curuthannor promised. "You will pay."

"Give me the sword and no one else has to die."

"No one else will die but you."

Curuthannor sprang forward. His vision bled to red, his only focus the dark elf before him. His sword was a blur. He spun into a whirling attack, the sword in perpetual motion. Aradae backed away, but blocked every strike. Curuthannor couldn't find a hole in the other man's defense.

He screamed again. His fury generated new energy. His rage fueled the onslaught. Aradae would not get away. He would not succeed. High then low. Low then high. Kicks intermingled with sword strikes.

Curuthannor was inside the other man's guard. Aradae's blade skidded across Curuthannor's back, scoring a hit to his shoulder blade as Curuthannor brought the pommel of his sword into Aradae's exposed temple.

The dark elf's eyes rolled back into his head and he slumped to the ground.

Curuthannor took two steps toward the stone columns of the sacred circle as the berserker rage drained away. Fire coursed down his back. His vision swam, but there was no mistaking Hatholdammon standing at the shrine with the tip of the king's sword shining in the last rays of the setting sun. Lhéwen stood at his side, her arms lifted to the sky in a mirror of his father's position. The blade was complete.

Curuthannor's legs gave way. He fell, bleeding into the dirt.

CHAPTER 61

Lhéwen gasped, her feet taking flight before her brain had the chance to form coherent thought. "Curuthannor!" she screamed as the man slumped to the ground. He'd stood up to the dark elf soldiers and won, yet in the end he still might not survive. She reached his side and gathered his unconscious body into her lap, ignoring the blood that now smeared her dress and arms. His chest rose and fell, and that was all that mattered. That, and keeping it going.

Gashes covered Curuthannor's unprotected skin, some of them deep enough that she could see bone, others mere surface scratches that bled more than she thought they should have. She ripped white silk strips from her gown, shoving the fabric into the worst of the wounds to staunch the bleeding. She tied a tourniquet above a deep laceration on his bicep. She did everything she could think of, but it wasn't enough. The blood continued to flow.

"Sanyaro, please, you must do something," Lhéwen begged. She had no skill for magical healing. She'd never had the need. She couldn't weave a pattern she didn't know. But she couldn't let Curuthannor die here, not like this.

373

"Rest now, Hatholdammon," Garamaen said, his words carrying over the empty distance. "Tunniel is waiting for you."

In moments, Hatholdammon's body appeared to age, shriveling in upon itself as the man faded from the mortal world. Lhéwen lifted her eyes to the sky, sending a quick prayer to the All-Father, asking him to bless Hatholdammon's journey to the Daemon Realm and find him a place amongst the summerlands.

But Curuthannor was still amongst the living and needed their help. He would survive, if they could stop the bleeding.

"I don't know what else to do," Lhéwen said. Her voice sounded high pitched and panicky, even to her own ears. "He needs a healer, but I do not have the skill."

Lord Garamaen Sanyaro closed Hatholdammon's sightless eyes and left him curled as if in sleep.

"The wounds are deep, but not mortal," he replied as he approached. "You have prevented his death. His body only requires some extra energy to speed the process along."

Sanyaro knelt by her side. He held his left hand and the stump of his right arm over Curuthannor's body. He closed his eyes and cocked his head to the side. "There. He should awaken momentarily."

Lhéwen brushed a loose hair off of Curuthannor's battle weary face, but it stuck in the dried blood that smeared his cheek. She picked it away, then tried to wipe the red away with a bit of less dirty cloth from her dress. Without any water, it did little to clean him up. Luckily, the cuts beneath the fabric appeared to have been sealed, if not entirely healed.

Meanwhile, Sanyaro took the borrowed sword from Curuthannor's hand. His gaze searched the burning village in the distance, where shouts and the occasional crash could still be heard.

"The king's sword is finished," Sanyaro said as if talking to himself. "The shadow guard will be coming soon for Aradae and the bodies of their brethren. The sword cannot fall into their hands. Curuthannor is our only option, our only hope."

"What are you saying?" Lhéwen demanded. "Curuthannor is in no fit state to fight."

Sanyaro shook his head, turning back to face Lhéwen and her charge. "Not fight. Run. He must run with the sword to Othin and tell the king what has happened here today."

"Can't you take it?" Lhéwen asked. Curuthannor needed rest. He needed time to heal. Not pass through the portal into what was probably yet another dangerous situation.

"No. Othin won't trust the sword if he sees it in my hands. Besides, I can hold them off while you escape."

"Then I will take it. I will find somewhere for Curuthannor to hide and heal, and I will go to King Othin. Curuthannor should not go anywhere in his current state."

Sanyaro shook his head.

"You face the same problem as I. When he learns what has happened, he will blame you as much as anyone. You are the princess's handmaiden, after all. You cannot be trusted." Garamaen turned back to the village. "I will hold them off. Get Curuthannor up, take him to the portal in the mines. Few know of its existence. Code the gate to the meet and get Curuthannor through. Then go back to the Crossroads Inn. Tharbatiron will be waiting for you."

"I cannot go back there! Why would I? I am nothing but a servant to the princess. I have no value to her, except as a tool for her own schemes. I will not betray my realm. Not again. Not intentionally. Not ever."

Sanyaro pursed his lips in a sad smile. "You are already a traitor. Even I cannot protect you, and I would if I could. If you go to the meet, your life will be forfeit. You must return to the Shadow Realm, but do not worry, you will find a way to redeem yourself, and soon."

Sanyaro twirled the sword in his left hand. The stump of his right was held out to the side for balance. "Get him up and go. Now. They are coming. If they see you, all is lost."

At that exact moment, Curuthannor's eyes fluttered open. His gaze connected with hers, and Lhéwen let out a relieved sob. She pressed a hand to his face. "Thank the gods," she whispered. "You're alive."

"Go!" Sanyaro shouted.

"Quickly," Lhéwen urged, deciding to trust Sanyaro and his visions of the future. Not that her future mattered much. If the only thing she did for the rest of her life was save this one man, then she would be redeemed in her heart.

She levered Curuthannor up to standing and pulled his arm over her shoulder. Four dark smudges appeared at the edge of the village just as another tent erupted into flames.

Lhéwen urged Curuthannor toward the shrine and the finished king's blade. She grabbed the weapon and shoved it into Curuthannor's hand, then urged him into a staggering run.

"Where are we going?" Curuthannor demanded between gasping breaths. He leaned heavily on her shoulder, but they kept up the pace, even as one foot wanted to drag behind.

Despite the energy Sanyaro had given him, it was clear to Lhéwen that he didn't have enough.

"To the forgotten portal in the mines," Lhéwen replied. "Sanyaro wants you to take the sword to King Othin at the meet. I am to return to the Shadow Realm until I can prove my loyalty to the Upper Realm."

Lhéwen glanced over her shoulder. The black-clad soldiers were half the distance from the village to Sanyaro, but they moved slowly and with caution. Good.

"You cannot go back there," Curuthannor gasped. "You don't belong there."

"While I agree with you, Sanyaro has made it clear that I will die if I remain. I have to earn my return to the light, and I will. I'll find a way. Somehow."

"This is madness. This whole thing is utter madness."

Lhéwen didn't have a response. She could only agree, and that would do neither of them any good.

They reached the entrance to the mines a few moments later, and Lhéwen led the way through the abandoned tunnels to the forgotten portal. She began drawing the runes for the meet, glad that she had memorized its location from Daeturion's plans. The portal began to buzz with magic, the crackling blue energy flowing across the arc. The view changed from the darkened walls of stone to a dusty clearing and Daeturion's surprised expression.

His face brought her own recollection. "Daeturion and Belegeth are at the meet. King Rindae and Princess Faeliel have abandoned them, but they each wear a ring that will shield them from an energy drain. If it comes to that, you must remove the rings."

"Are they your creation?" Curuthannor asked. "Like the enchantment on the scroll?"

Lhéwen's face heated and her thoughts tangled. He knew. Of course he knew. "Sadly, yes. I tried to damage the spell, to leave an opening for King Othin or another to reach through, but I'm afraid I may have failed. If King Othin tries to drain them and fails, you must take the rings off their fingers."

Curuthannor frowned, but dipped his chin in acknowledgment.

"I never meant to betray you or our home. I only meant to serve the princess to the best of my ability. Please believe me."

"Gods help me, I do," Curuthannor replied.

Lhéwen blew out a relieved breath. "Thank you. Now go," Lhéwen urged. "And find me when this is all over."

"I will," Curuthannor promised. He grasped the king's blade to his chest as Lhéwen pushed him through the veil to the other side. As soon as she saw him arrive safely in the distant land, she closed the portal and began drawing her own runes.

She traveled through the canyon gate in the Human Realm, then coded the portal for the hidden gazebo. The veil opened and the view darkened. Tharbatiron relaxed on the other side, drinking a glass of wine at the table under the gazebo.

It wasn't home, but at least a friendly face was waiting for her.

CHAPTER 62

Curuthannor fell to the ground just inside the portal. He gasped, the pain of his wounds becoming more apparent with the fall. One eye was swollen near to shut and the other blurred with sweat, tears, and blood. The white cloth over his bicep had turned red and the sliced flesh beneath throbbed with every angry beat of his heart. He pushed at the dirt beneath his hands, struggling to rise. Without Lhéwen's support, he feared he didn't have the strength.

"What is the meaning of this?" King Othin demanded.

Curuthannor swallowed and willed himself upright with the last ripples of his spirit. If he was destined to fade, at least he would die in service to his king and his realm. The dark elves could not go unpunished.

"The dark elves have attacked the forges at Rómesse Gulch." Curuthannor's throat was hoarse and his voice cracked as the horror of the evening caught up with him.

Mother. She was gone. His father would fade with her, if he hadn't already. And Namba was dead with a dagger through his heart. Who knew what happened to Minya. He might yet live, or he might have died trying to find his betrothed.

His entire family gone in one dark afternoon. Everyone he loved, dead or missing. He had no one and nothing.

Curuthannor swallowed down his emotions. He didn't have time to mourn. There was too much at stake.

Finally able to gain enough leverage to get to his feet, Curuthannor faced his king, who sat in a throne flanked by guards under a canopy of gold cloth. To his left stood Daeturion, heir to the Shadow Throne and Prince Aradae's brother.

Curuthannor lunged toward the dark elf. Lifted the king's sword. Lashed out with uncontrolled fury and the last of his energy.

The princess's guard stepped between them and knocked Curuthannor back to the ground with the butt of her axe, preventing him from reaching his target.

Curuthannor doubled over, barely able to breathe, barely able to move. He groaned and rolled over. Coughed.

"Explain yourself," King Othin demanded.

Curuthannor struggled up once more. He bowed as low as he was able without falling again. It wasn't as deep as propriety demanded, but hopefully his bedraggled and beaten appearance would earn him some grace.

"Rómesse Gulch is gone. My home is lost. My mother and father are dead."

Curuthannor clenched his jaw, fighting against the rising tide of grief. He placed the sword across his palms and presented the king's blade to its master. "My father's last great act was to finish your sword. May it find honor in your hands."

"Seize him!" King Othin ordered.

For a moment, Curuthannor feared the order was for him, but the guards quickly surrounded Daeturion instead. The guardswoman growled and clenched the handle of her axe and the little man by Daeturion's side released his fangs and claws, but there was little that they would be able to do with eight of the king's personal guard surrounding them.

"Oathbreaker," King Othin declared. "This meet was manufactured in deceit, the neutral territory has been forfeited. I claim rights of the aggrieved."

King Othin stretched out a hand toward Daeturion and his entourage. Immediately, the blood sidhe servant dropped to his knees, his face growing gaunt and his breath raspy as his energy was drained. Daeturion and Belegeth, however, were seemingly unaffected.

"Their rings," Curuthannor gasped. "They wear rings enchanted to block your ability to drain their energy. You must remove them."

One of the king's guard stepped forward, but King Othin halted him with a snap of his fingers.

"These rings were crafted by our daughter, Princess Faeliel, and her handmaiden. Yes?"

Curuthannor nodded, realizing he had just implicated Lhéwen in the princess's treason. It would be even harder for her to prove her loyalty now. There was nothing he could say in this moment that would make it any better, however. Drawing more attention to her role in the process would only make it worse.

"Our daughter believes she is our equal, but she is wrong. No silver bauble can be made to thwart our power. Not now. Not ever." He rose from his throne and took four slow steps forward until he was within grasping distance of the sword's hilt.

"Your Majesty, can we not find common ground? Is it impossible to enter a future of joy and cooperation instead of war and strife?"

Daeturion spread his hands as if to reassure them all of his honesty and pure intentions. Curuthannor saw him for what he was: a power hungry and deceitful blackguard, just like his father, King Rindae.

Curuthannor lifted the sword once more toward his king. He

would see the Shadow Realm fall, the king and his sons destroyed with his own father's greatest creation. They would pay for their treachery at the point of the very weapon they had hoped to destroy.

"Cooperation must be built on a foundation of trust. How can we trust a realm that would offer peace from one face and attack from the other? A realm that sends its sons with charms and enchantments to thwart us?" King Othin asked. "You say our daughter is content, that she is bonded to your king, but we see no reason to believe you. Our judgment tells us that this, too, is a deceit, and there is only one possible punishment for an oath-breaker."

King Othin's lip curled in a vicious smile as he lifted the sword from Curuthannor's outstretched hands. "I see a flaw in your shield, Daeturion, son of Rindae, Shadow's Heir." He pointed the sword at the dark elf. "Now meet Thúlentur, the master sword of spirit." He twisted his wrist to bring his palm to the sky.

Prince Daeturion gasped. His right hand clutched at the shirt over his heart, while his left opened wide toward the king in entreaty.

The princess's guardswoman stepped forward, as if to protect the prince, but halted in mid-step, her expression torn.

Othin swung the sword in her direction. "You are loyal to our daughter, but you should first be loyal to your king."

The high elf's eyes widened, and her mouth worked, but no sound came out.

"It must feel quite distressing. It wouldn't have been so painful if you weren't wearing those dreadful rings."

Prince Daeturion's face was gradually losing its color, the surface layer of his skin turning ashen and gray. His cheeks began to hollow as if he were being suctioned inside out.

Curuthannor couldn't feel sympathy for the man. Wouldn't allow himself to pity someone who had been involved, even remotely, in the death of his family. Of his entire village. As far as he was concerned, the Shadow Realm could fall into the chaos that it had fostered.

"You see," King Othin continued, "Thúlentur amplifies our power, turning a stream of energy into a raging river, and your shields have a flaw. Rather than protect your auras, the rings narrow our focus, providing the tiniest exit through which that river may pass. In the end, they will only serve to increase and prolong your agony."

The guardswoman dropped her axe. Her hands twisted against the silver that encased her thumb, but it would not slide over her knuckle. "Mercy, my king," she begged, her voice a throaty murmur.

She didn't deserve it. She had chosen her side in this battle. She had chosen to follow a woman with no honor, with no compassion. A woman who would do anything for herself and nothing for anyone else.

Then again, so had Lhéwen, yet for some reason Curuthannor couldn't bring himself to hate the seamstress in the same way he hated everyone else involved in this mess. Somehow, he'd already forgiven her part in the conflict. But at least she had attempted to make amends. After all, she had said she had tried to unmake the rings' enchantment. It was her handiwork that had given Othin the flaw he needed to break through the rings' shields.

Lhéwen had been tricked. The guard had knowingly followed, else why would she have stepped forward to protect the prince?

"Would you swear loyalty? Leave your mistress behind and return to the Upper Realm?" King Othin asked.

She dropped to one knee, one hand resting on her upright thigh, the other pressing into the ground, holding her body steady. "Gladly, my king. Please."

"Your Majesty, during my short stay in the Shadow Realm, the guard was never far from the princess's side. She cannot be trusted."

"Of course she cannot be trusted. Not yet. But we can be

magnanimous." King Othin paused, turning a critical gaze on the woman who now lay prostrate on the ground. "We will let you keep your life, if you execute the dark elf heir."

The woman bowed her head. "As you command."

Prince Daeturion's face shrank and his eyes seemed to pop from his head. "No," he whispered. "Please."

King Othin turned his sword back to the dark elf, releasing the guard from its hold. She took a deep gasping breath, then another, before she stood and reclaimed her axe.

"May the gods have mercy on your soul," she said.

The axe swung overhead and down. The shriveled, shrunken thing that had been the heir to the shadow throne rolled away.

"Well done." The conniving smirk that crossed Othin's face said he wasn't done yet. "Guards, take her to the Pit. Belegeth, you are sentenced to one week at the mercy of the nildhoggr and her children."

Four guards immediately surrounded their comrade and pointed their swords at her chest. There would be no escape. Curuthannor shuddered, visions of thousands upon thousands of legs and squirming bodies shooting through his memories. Curuthannor might not trust the woman, but he didn't wish the Pit on anyone—except perhaps Prince Aradae. He wouldn't mind throwing the dark elf into that dark hole, but he also wouldn't bring him back out again.

"But, Your Majesty, you promised a pardon."

"We promised you your life. And you shall have it—after one week in the Pit. We shall see how much life remains after their gentle ministrations." He turned his attention to the blood sidhe who yet breathed on the ground. "Bring him and the body. We will prepare a gift for Rindae and his mistress."

"And the smith's son?" a monotone voice asked.

King Othin looked over his shoulder with a calculating glance. "He has proven his loyalty and delivered our sword. Let him return to his home and bury his dead."

With those words, King Othin strode toward the portal and returned to the gilded halls of his golden palace.

CHAPTER 63

Lord Garamaen Sanyaro, Truthseeker and origin sidhe, master of fire and soul and spirit, could do nothing to prevent this outcome.

The war had begun. The damage had been done. There was nothing left but to mitigate what damage he could.

The dark elves would need a ruler when all this was over. Aradae was a good man, even if he didn't know it yet. He needed some training, needed some diplomatic confidence, but that could be learned. There were players in this game who would help him.

Like Curuthannor, this was a man that would be needed for the future, at least the future Garamaen hoped to usher into existence.

Unfortunately, the three men who approached only saw the destruction on the field, and a crazy man with a feather in his hair standing over their fallen commander. They drew their swords, as Garamaen anticipated. They didn't know who he was, which was fine. He preferred his anonymity.

Garamaen glanced over his shoulder. Lhéwen and Curuthannor were out of sight, nearly to the tunnels already. They wouldn't see him or know what he did.

He lowered his sword and placed it on the ground. He lifted his arms in a show of surrender.

"Your prince yet lives," Garamaen called out. "Come and claim him."

The soldiers looked around, wary of a trap or ambush. They didn't realize that Garamaen could drain them of all their energy before they took another step, if he so chose. Or light every flammable inch of their under tunics and hair afire. But he would do neither of those things for it would get him nowhere. Instead, he stepped back, hand and stump still raised above his shoulders, allowing them free access to their dead and wounded.

Two of the three men stood guard while the third stepped forward, placing his fingers beneath his commander's chin.

"Who are you?" the man asked.

Garamaen sighed. Always they started with the mundane inconsequential questions. "Does it matter? Your prince lies bleeding from a blow to the head. He needs the treatment of a healer before his brain swells and he is no longer himself. I am not skilled enough to aid him further."

"What happened here?" one of the other guards asked.

"Prince Aradae fought, and lost. What more need you know?"

At that moment, Aradae groaned and rolled to his side, retching into the dirt. At least he wasn't in the sacred circle. The gods would not have looked favorably on such a desecration of holy ground. Nor would Hatholdammon and Tunniel appreciate their future grave so polluted, though he supposed it was unlikely they would be back to see. They had been taken to the gates of the Daemon Realm together, and there they would remain together, to rest in the summerlands until their next turn in the mortal coil.

"You're coming with us. If you won't answer our questions, you'll answer to our king."

Garamaen shook himself out of his reverie. "I'm afraid that won't be possible," he replied. "I have other matters to attend to at the moment, but you may tell your king what you will."

The closest guard lifted a lip in a snarl and brandished his sword. "It wasn't a request."

"I tire of this conversation." Garamaen flicked his hand toward the guards and drained their energy to the point of physical failure. The three men dropped to the ground, able to breathe and move their eyes, but that was about it.

Garamaen flexed his hand, the stolen energy now running through his veins. It was tempting to keep it, but like any drug, it would eventually wear off. He refused to become a leech.

"I'll be leaving now." He pointed a thumb over his shoulder, toward the mines and the forgotten portal inside. "When I am gone, I will return your energy. I suggest you forget about me, and leave the bodies of your fallen comrades. Return to your realm with the prince as quickly as you can manage. His brain doesn't have much longer before it will be damaged beyond repair. However, I will leave the final decision up to you."

With a shrug, Garamaen left the men to their misery and walked away. They would do as he said, too humiliated to tell anyone of their encounter with the crazy man with the feather in his hair. It would be a secret they kept to themselves until the day they died.

Sadly, that fate would come sooner than they anticipated.

CHAPTER 64

Rothruinil's eyes narrowed as the first of the carts returned through the portal. Each cart was stacked high with iron in various stages of production. The red caps retained the carnage of the battle in their pointed teeth, but few had any obvious wounds.

At least the dark elf warriors looked a little more battered. One of the women clutched her arm, which hung limply from her side like a wet noodle. Another man had bandaged a head wound, but the once-white cloth was already dripping red with blood.

Rothruinil had gone back up to her tiny apartment to watch the soldiers' return through her window. She was high enough that she could just see the portal over the wall from this vantage, a better view than the café at street level, though she missed the tea and flatbreads.

She had counted thirty-four warriors—including Aradae—and eight carts going through the fortress gate to enter the portal. They'd straggled back in twos and threes, but unless her count was wrong—and it wasn't—only nine of the shadow guard had returned. All of the carts and all of the red caps had come through the portal, but at least some of the shadow guard remained on the battlefield.

Aradae still hadn't come back. He was an active leader, the first on the field and the last to leave. She could admire that, except that she suspected this had been less of a battle and more of a slaughter.

They had gone for the iron. Some of the pieces on the carts were half-formed helmets and swords that hadn't yet been sharpened. How many innocents had died?

War was war, but everyone on a battlefield knew what they were there for. The craftsmen and villagers who had been working that iron didn't have any training. They were only doing their jobs, filling orders for their king and country. This had been a strategic attack, for certain, but one that would bring down the wrath of the high elves and all their bannermen. The dark elves had just struck the first blow.

The question was, which was worse, the dark elves who went to battle and slaughtered non-combatants for a bit of metal, or the murderous high elf king who would twist the truth to suit his needs? She'd rather not associate with any of them. There had to be a way to keep the Summer Realm out of this growing conflict.

Rothruinil's eyes drifted back toward the gate. The last of the red caps had returned at least a bell ago. Where were the other warriors? Where was Aradae?

Finally, the glow of portal's opening brightened the darkness of the city. The scene through the veil was definitely the Upper Realm. The golden light was unmistakable, as was the dark form being dragged through.

Rothruinil's heart clenched, though she couldn't say why. Aradae hung limp, draped between two of his men. Blood ran freely down his face, dripping onto the obsidian cobblestones and leaving a trail behind. She should be glad that the general of the Shadow Realm army had fallen. Though she didn't know what direct action he had taken in the struggle, it was clear they had fought and killed over nothing more than a bit of metal.

Her lip curled. Fire didn't need iron, but the metal would melt in a hot enough flame. The threat of the blaze was enough to end most struggles before they ever began, and the fire sidhe never needed to battle over resources.

The dark elves *and* the high elves could all go kill each other off as far as she was concerned. If only she could tell her father as much.

Still, Aradae wasn't dead, not yet, just critically injured. The dark elf forces weren't incapacitated, far from it. They had killed for the iron that would supply their arms and armor. They would be quick to put it to good use. But without proper leadership, their efforts would be scattered. Perhaps King Rindae or his heir could take up the slack, or perhaps there was a second in command who could do the job, but the transition would still take time. They wouldn't be ready to fight again immediately.

Meanwhile, the high elves had lost their supply. She didn't know how many forges had been destroyed, but given the piles of half-finished weapons, there had to have been quite a few. King Othin's army would be weakened for the lack, their preparations stalled.

Which meant the fire sidhe had time to maneuver, to position themselves outside of the conflict. They might have to enforce their sovereignty, but that wasn't necessarily a bad thing.

If only she could get a message to her father.

CHAPTER 65

The music was . . . not wonderful. The humans were talented enough, Lhéwen supposed, but the quality of their voices was rustic, their instruments brassy and sour. It was nothing compared to the ethereal choirs of the high elves who infused their songs with emotion and energy. Their magic allowed them to bring an audience to the greatest emotional heights and drive them to their knees in the depths of their sorrow. A lone high elf music master could enchant a crowd with a single note. The humans, without the amplification of the magic, could do little but imbue their own emotion into the melody.

Still, the love song honoring King Rindae and Princess Faeliel was tasteful, and Lhéwen supposed their efforts were noble. It was a piece that showcased their strengths, in as much as they had them. The woman's tone was pure, and the high notes rang through the rafters of the great hall. The man was a little less skilled vocally, the tenor too warbly for Lhéwen's taste, but his performance on the stringed instrument was decent. Had they attempted one of the elvish reels, his fingers would never have been able to keep up. Nor could they match the sorrow of an elvish lament. But the duet was passable entertainment for King Rindae's celebration feast.

Lhéwen stood behind Princess Faeliel's right shoulder, observing the performance and practicing her subservient mask even as her eyes burned with tears and fatigue. The bells she'd spent in the Upper Realm had been but moments in the slower moving Shadow Realm.

Tharbatiron had welcomed her home and given her a fresh gown, at which point her own emotions caught up with her. She'd sobbed in one of his cottages for at least three bells, stress and disappointment leaching from her soul. When finally she was presentable, she returned to the princess and made her apologies for her absence. Faeliel hadn't even noticed she was gone.

Maybe that was as it should be. Lhéwen was, after all, a simple handmaiden and seamstress. No longer a confidante, the princess only needed her for her skill with a braid and a needle and thread. After everything she'd been through, Lhéwen wasn't sure she wanted the princess's love after all.

It was time she made her own way and found her own purpose. If she were thinking strategically, she was perfectly poised to be a spy for the Upper Realm. She would watch and listen and remain invisible. Then, when she had something useful, she would find a way to tell King Othin or his generals. Or perhaps, Curuthannor. He would at least be willing to listen and not immediately assume she was a traitor. She just had to find a way to reach him.

Eventually, she would find an opportunity to prove her loyalty to her home world. She would not be exiled to the Shadow Realm forever.

Lhéwen sighed as the last chord drifted away on the humid air. Princess Faeliel stood, clapping her hands with enthusiasm. She, at least, enjoyed the show. King Rindae stood with her, grinning his pleasure, while the attending nobles clapped politely from their seats in the gallery behind.

"My king, you were absolutely correct about this evening's

performance. I thoroughly enjoyed it. What lovely voices. They were able to do so much, even without the use of magic."

"I'm glad you approve. We bribed them away from a human court some two hundred years ago. They're full changelings now, unable to return to their homeland, but I feel the reward was worth the sacrifice. They have been encouraged to study with some of our own apprentices."

"Truly? You allow the humans to apprentice?"

Lhéwen stifled a surprised intake of breath. King Othin would never allow such a thing in his court.

"No, not an apprenticeship. They serve at the behest of the early students and are able to sit in on some of the lessons. They are also allowed the use of the instruments during their rest periods. Few, however, have come as far as this duo."

The pair bowed their thanks for the compliment, though Lhéwen doubted the king or Faeliel saw. They were too engrossed in their own conversation.

Princess Faeliel extended an arm toward Lhéwen without taking her gaze from her suitor's face. She couldn't even take the heartbeat necessary to look where her hand was going, nearly knocking over the small table next to her chair, which held a now-empty crystal wine glass.

"I would love another song," Faeliel continued speaking to King Rindae. Her hand turned with an elegant twist at the wrist, expectantly waiting for a refill.

Carefully keeping her eyes downcast and her hands steady, Lhéwen poured out the last of the red liquid imported from the Upper Realm and placed the etched crystal in her ladyship's outstretched fingers.

"Anything my bride wants." King Rindae kissed the palm of Faeliel's other hand without taking his gaze off her face. He placed her hand on his knee, then clapped his hands for attention. "My lady would hear another."

"Something joyful," Faeliel added.

The duo bowed again, taking up their instruments. This time, the woman held a flat drum with a double-headed stick. They began to play, the rhythm faster and increasingly complicated.

Lhéwen returned to her station, straightening her spine and being careful not to lock out her knees. It wouldn't do to pass out during the princess's celebrations. But her thoughts drifted away from the spectacle before them.

Curuthannor had made it back to King Othin. She had seen it with her own eyes. But she hadn't heard anything since then. Even Tharbatiron had no information. She could only hope that he had delivered the sword and had been received with a hero's honor as he deserved. Sanyaro, at least, had said that Curuthannor was the only one Othin would trust. Anyone else carrying the sword would have been killed, but not Curuthannor. Still, she prayed that he was well and had found a way to grieve for his family.

So much had been lost in one afternoon.

The iron carts had paraded through the city to great fanfare. King Rindae had declared the battle a decisive victory and announced a celebration feast, despite the fact that Aradae had been badly wounded. According to the report of the palace healer, he would fully recover within a few days—good for Aradae and for King Rindae's mood, bad for the prospects of future Upper Realm battles. Prince Aradae now had a loyal following amongst the shadow guard, who had been flocking to the palace to hear the stories of the battle and of Prince Aradae's bravery.

Lhéwen thought it was all puffed up and exaggerated, but King Rindae encouraged it, using the tales to attract more of the dark elves into the guard. After all, as he said, what second or third son wouldn't want a bit of glory for himself?

They were all fools.

A commotion at the back of the room caused every head to turn. The music drifted to silence as three armed dark elf guards marched down the hall from the main entry doors. Their lips were pressed into hard lines, and Lhéwen could see the muscles of their jaws working beneath the skin. The assembled nobles moved hastily out of the way as they passed.

It wasn't until they were a mere three lengths away that Lhéwen noticed the fourth man, an aged blood sidhe carrying a golden bowl. He had been hidden behind the front guard. Silent tears streamed down the man's face, and his arms shook from the effort of holding the heavy lidded vessel, but his feet moved him forward at a steady pace.

"Your Majesty," the front guard said, his deep voice carrying a thread of emotion Lhéwen couldn't quite identify. He bent to one knee before King Rindae and lowered his head. The remaining guards followed suit. "We come with terrible news."

The blood sidhe gently set his bowl on the ground at the king's feet before abasing himself by laying entirely prone on the floor.

"What is it?" King Rindae asked.

"What is that?" Princess Faeliel asked at the same time.

The blood sidhe lifted the lid with a single shaking arm.

Inside lay Prince Daeturion's head.

Princess Faeliel screamed, pressing her feet into the ground and knocking her chair over in her haste to get away from the corpse. As the chair fell, her foot slipped, kicking the bowl and knocking it over. Prince Daeturion's head rolled out from the golden vessel in a lopsided wobble coming to rest at the feet of the female vocalist, who scrambled away, hysterical.

Shouts and sobs erupted around the room. Long white hair—still braided in the way Daeturion preferred—hung lank and wet around the bloody stump of a neck. Daeturion's mouth hung open, his white teeth shockingly vibrant. His eyes were blessedly closed, but the skin of his cheeks appeared hollow and ashen in the shadows of the wisplight.

Lhéwen rushed to Faeliel's side, helping her scoot away from the disturbing sight. Bile rose to burn the back of her throat, but still, she couldn't look away.

Daeturion had been sent to the Upper Realm to share the 'good' news with King Othin. He had taken King Rindae's place at the meet, was there when Curuthannor had delivered the blade and the news of the attack on Rómesse Gulch. Clearly, he had borne the brunt of King Othin's wrath.

King Rindae still sat in his chair, immobilized, even as Princess Faeliel pressed her face into Lhéwen's dress. The handmaiden did her best to comfort her mistress, but some small part of her heart was glad the dark elf heir had died. Perhaps now King Rindae and Faeliel would understand the power that they played with, and the lives that were at stake. She kept those thoughts to herself.

Finally, the king stood from his chair. His gaze never left the head of his eldest son, the heir to his throne.

"What happened?" he asked. Despite the chaos around him, there was no mistaking his words.

"There is a message in the bowl." The blood sidhe's voice cracked with age and sorrow. Had this broken man been Daeturion's assistant? Was it possible?

"Bring it to me," King Rindae replied.

The blood sidhe pushed up from the floor, crawling on hands and knees to the bowl. He pulled a soggy parchment from its depths, holding it delicately from one corner.

He kept his head bowed as he presented the paper on two hands to the king.

"Open it and read it," King Rindae commanded.

Lhéwen's eyes widened. *Here? Now?* It didn't seem the right time, not with so many courtiers and servants still present. There would be no containing the message within. Whatever King Othin had written, all would hear and share the news.

But maybe that was what King Rindae wanted. Shock and horror, used to bring his nobles to heel.

With shaking fingers, the blood sidhe unfolded the parchment and turned it over.

"A child for a child. Both are now dead."

Faeliel's sobs grew louder, her whole body heaving. Her hands tore at Lhéwen's dress and skin, clenching and unclenching without knowledge or reason.

King Rindae moved to wrap his arms around his bride-to-be, pulling her from Lhéwen's embrace. Faeliel pounded at his chest, her entire face clenched in grief. Whether an act or a true emotion, Lhéwen could hardly tell, but one thing was certain: King Othin would not take her home again.

Faeliel had made her choices, and now she would have to live with them. Lhéwen had made hers as well, and she, too, would have to face the consequences of her decisions. They'd been banished. Lhéwen had only known it sooner.

She swallowed, sobs aching to rise, to join in the princess's grief. She couldn't allow herself that moment of surcease or she might never recover. And unlike Princess Faeliel, she had no one else to lean on.

CHAPTER 66

Fearing what he would find, Curuthannor did as the king commanded and returned home. He crossed the portal into a nightmare. What once had been the main street of the village of Rómesse Gulch was now a wasteland of ash and blood. Only the two-story building that he had grown up in remained standing. It stuck out from the destruction like a tree in an empty field, except where the field would be green and growing, only death awaited.

Broken bodies lay strewn across the street, men and women, craftsmen not warriors, sliced to ribbons by the weapons they had once created. Those few who had been spared walked as he did, in near-catatonic states of delirium, looking for their loved ones amongst the wreckage. Tents that had once housed the temporary forges lay collapsed and burned to ash from the fires they had protected. Stone and metal were all that remained.

Curuthannor found Minyondor and his love first. A stab wound to Minya's chest had killed him. Tautamiel lay next to him, a small dagger in her hand and a slice across her throat. Though he had trained with the same weapons as Curuthannor, Minya had never been much of a fighter. He hadn't stood a chance against the shadow guard.

With gentle hands, Curuthannor arranged the bodies so that they rested in one another's arms and closed their eyes, as if in sleep.

"May all the gods watch over your souls and find you a place together in the summerlands," Curuthannor murmured. His throat closed and he fought to control his breathing. He couldn't break down. Not here. Not now.

Maybe not ever.

"I will return for you," Curuthannor promised. He would serve on the burial detail, ensuring that all of the men and women who had been cut from the weave of fate would find a final resting place.

For now, he forced himself to continue on through the city. He had to reach his home and his mother.

Curuthannor walked the path to the house, his feet heavy with trepidation. He didn't want to see, and yet he couldn't turn away. He swallowed down his fear and entered the house.

"Mother?" he called. There was no answer. He hadn't expected one, but as the last flame of hope died in his chest, he felt himself grow cold. He passed through the empty living space, where he and his brothers had played endless games of cards after dinner, past his father's office where Hatholdammon would stay up working on his designs, and into the kitchen, his mother's domain.

She wasn't there. For half a heartbeat, he let himself hope once more, but he knew it was useless. His father wouldn't have faded if she were alive. He turned the knob at the back exit and pushed to open the door. It moved only a fraction, then stuck. He shoved again, but the door wouldn't budge. Something was in the way.

Passing back through the house, Curuthannor walked around the side to the forge and iron stores at the rear. The doors to the iron cabinet had been broken open, the enchanted lock thrown to one side. Everything inside had been removed. The forge was cold as well, even the iron still in process had been taken.

Curuthannor turned, scanning the yard. His jaw clenched and he struggled to breathe through the angry grief.

She lay on the stoop, slumped to one side, her back pressed against the painted blue wood. A dark smear marred its surface. Her eyes, still open, stared at nothing.

With measured steps, Curuthannor approached the body of Tunniel, wife of Hatholdammon, his mother. Memories flashed through his mind. Her smile, calling them in from the forge for dinner, and every little graceful flourish of her hand.

Her hands. They were missing.

Curuthannor's breath stuck in his throat.

Her hands had been severed near the wrist, only the stumps of her arms resting in her lap. Blood stained her skirt and pooled beneath her body. Tears burned in Curuthannor's eyes. They had mutilated her. They had destroyed her. And for what? A bit of iron? A sword?

Swallowing down the raging grief enough that he could function, Curuthannor knelt by her side to give her the same honor he had given Minya and Tautamiel. Vengeance blossomed in his chest and he welcomed its fiery heat as a respite from the frigid sadness. He screamed his pain to the empty sky.

When at last his lungs were empty, he turned back to the smithy and the cold forges that should have been kept warm. Where was Hadhion? He should have been there to protect Tunniel. He should have done *something*. Yet his body was not present anywhere in the yard. He had run.

The question remained, had he run toward or away from the battle?

Curuthannor shook his head. It mattered little. Whatever had happened, Hadhion was gone along with the rest of Curuthannor's family. At some other time, he would have been glad for the disappearance of his rival, but right now he had greater demands on his emotions.

Curuthannor swallowed, not yet ready to face the scene at his father's sacred shrine, but knowing he couldn't avoid it forever. His father and brother deserved honor in death, and as the last living member of the family, Curuthannor was best suited to care for what remained.

Unable to bear leaving his mother alone, Curuthannor picked her up and carried her to her lifemate. Their souls had been united in life, it was only fitting they should be together in death. A sudden image of their bodies entombed together beneath the altar slab nearly overwhelmed him. It would be a fitting site for their grave. The only place that made any sense of their senseless deaths. He would see them honored in a way that would bring them together before all the gods of all the elements.

Curuthannor strode down the wide avenue, past the collapsed tents and smoldering ashes, to the edge of town and beyond. He set his sights on the tall stone columns that glowed in the gray predawn light. He'd lost time in the Human Realm and an entire night had passed while he had been away. In that time, the dark elves had taken what they had come for, and returned to their shadowed existence.

At least five of them had lost their lives. Curuthannor allowed himself a grim smile at that thought. He hoped their unprovoked attack sent their souls straight to the wastelands. They certainly deserved it.

His steps faltered as he approached the site of his father's and brother's deaths. The bodies remained untouched. Even the dark elves hadn't yet been moved or shifted by their brethren. They had been left behind, forgotten, which made sense from a race that would kill to reclaim the iron they had sold in fair trade. Double-dealing should be expected.

For the moment, Curuthannor chose to ignore the battlefield and instead focused on the real goal: his father's body.

Hatholdammon rested at the base of the enchanter's shrine. The forge had long since burned itself out, though warmth yet remained in the stone. The implements of the ritual hadn't been touched, but the magic had evaporated on the wind.

Curuthannor carefully set his mother's body on the ground next to her husband before letting his eyes see what they refused to acknowledge.

Tunniel had died in violence and yet with the exception of the bloody stain on her gown and the missing hands, she remained as she was, her appearance healthy and in the prime of her life. Hatholdammon, on the other hand, had willingly faded away upon her death. His body was withered and had aged nearly into decay. The skin of his face had tightened around his cheekbones, and wrinkles radiated from the corners of closed eyes and creased his thinned lips. Even the muscles of his arms had atrophied. His form had a hollowed look unfit for the Master Smith of Rómesse Gulch.

This wasn't Hatholdammon. This man was not Curuthannor's father. Only a shell remained of what once had been.

Curuthannor shuddered and the hair on the nape of his neck lifted. He suddenly realized this was the first time he had personally witnessed a fading. As painful as it was to see his father's body in such a state, Curuthannor couldn't imagine the pain Hatholdammon had experienced. Yet his expression showed none of the torment or the fear he must have experienced. Only surrender and relief.

Swallowing his revulsion, Curuthannor placed his blood-stained hands on the foreheads of his parents. He bowed his head.

"Gods above and those below, take these souls into your care. Honor them amongst the greatest of your creations." He paused and pressed his lips together to hold back his tears. "I will miss you both, terribly," he whispered.

His mother may have been his comfort and support, but his father had been the guiding force of his life. What would he do without their influence? With whom would he discuss his troubles or share in his victories? Who would push him to be a better man, to constantly improve his skills and pursue a better future?

Giving himself a few minutes of silence to grieve, Curuthannor finally gathered enough strength to find his brother amongst the dark elf dead. He had little care for the bodies of the enemy warriors—someone else could take them away to wherever they pleased—but Nambamahtar should be honored with the defenders of the village.

Namba lay on his side in the dirt, his legs bent underneath him at an impossible angle and one arm thrown over his head. His eyes remained open wide and staring, his last gasping breath gone from between gaping lips.

As horrifying as his father's faded body had been, this was somehow worse. Perhaps it was because the shock and pain were evident, or perhaps Curuthannor's guilt lay heavy on his soul, but he struggled to take the three final steps to his brother's side. Namba's death felt wasteful. Curuthannor might have prevented it if he had only been a little faster, or warned Namba of the threat a heartbeat sooner. Instead, the strongest of Hatholdammon's sons lay in the dirt and only the weakest, the youngest, the least worthy of the family legacy remained.

With shaking hands, Curuthannor lifted his brother's mangled body over one shoulder and pulled him into the sacred circle. He arranged the larger man into a prone position with his eyes closed and arms crossed over his chest. A shovel and a cart would be needed to do any more for his family, but surely the necessary tools could be found somewhere in the village.

Turning back to face the destruction of his hometown, Curuthannor counted the dark shapes on the ground just outside the stone columns of the circle. They hadn't breached the sacred space, for that Curuthannor was grateful, but there were only four. Someone had survived.

The woman lay in a crumpled heap, not far from where Namba had been, but the only reason Curuthannor knew she was female was from the shape of her armor. A bloody mess of brain pooled around the caved-in side of her helm. Her nose was gone and one eye had been blown from its socket. Namba's hammer had done its job, and done it well.

Nambamahtar's other victim lay in similar discomposure. The man didn't have a mark on his body, but his head was nearly gone. Only a lopsided cheekbone and his jaw remained.

Curuthannor's kills had been slightly less dramatic, but the men were equally dead. The first was a giant of a man whose hands gripped his stomach in death. Curuthannor's blade had sliced through the leather as if it wasn't even there. Curuthannor imagined that if he were to remove the vest, the man's guts would fall like broad noodles from his abdomen, though it wasn't something he wished to test. The second man lay with blood pooled around his neck and throat, his sightless eyes gazing up into the heavens.

Only one man remained unaccounted for: Prince Aradae. The leader of the attack had survived. The mastermind of the battle, the killer of innocents, the destroyer of Rómesse Gulch yet lived. Curuthannor hadn't finished his task.

Guilt and shame wracked his body, but in that moment, he knew what he needed to do. His family was dead. His home and the forge, gone. He'd never been a great smith, but he could wield a sword better than any man he'd yet met.

The Shadow Realm would pay for what they had done.

The recruitment line was longer than Curuthannor had anticipated. It seemed news of the destruction of Rómesse Gulch had spread across the realm, and every man or woman with weapons skills had leaped at the chance to defend their home territory from the threat of the dark elves. The ranks of the golden army were swelling.

New barracks were under construction inside the palace walls, and squadrons of men and women drilled in the courtyard. Meanwhile, patrol units paraded through the city, calling for more enrollment and watching for any sign of an attack. King Othin wouldn't be taken by surprise again.

"Name?" the clerk at the table asked as the man in front of Curuthannor passed beneath the portcullis and into the palace proper.

"Curuthannor."

"Home?"

"Rómesse Gulch."

The man's wide eyes looked up and connected with Curuthannor. "A survivor?"

Curuthannor nodded. "Yes, sir."

"Are you a smith? We need as many men skilled with iron as can be found."

"No, sir. I'm better at wielding swords than making them."

"Are you certain?"

"Yes, sir." On this, Curuthannor wouldn't budge. He wasn't destined for the forge. He was destined for the warrior's way. "I will only enlist if I can be guaranteed a place amongst the men at arms."

The man pursed his lips and frowned. "We have plenty of soldiers, but not nearly enough weaponry. Skills in the forge are in high demand."

Curuthannor leaned forward, letting the fury in his soul show on his face. "I will have my vengeance on the dark elves who destroyed my family. The hammer may be my past, but the sword is my future. No one will stop me."

The man lifted an eyebrow, but relented. "Fine. I'll enlist you into the footmen, but I'm noting training at the forge as well. You will have to prove your skill wielding a blade or you won't have an option but to take up the hammer."

"Understood." Curuthannor straightened up, once more hiding away his emotions beneath the rigid mask of control.

The man scribbled a note on a small piece of parchment and handed it over to Curuthannor. "Check in at the barracks. They'll get you started with a bed and basic supplies. The master of arms will issue a sword from the keep if you don't have your own. You can take the rest of the day to get settled. Drills begin tomorrow."

"Yes, sir." Curuthannor stepped toward the palace entrance, but the other man's voice called him back.

"Final warning, you'd better be the best or you'll be behind the forge by next week."

Curuthannor ignored the man's words. He would be the best. That wasn't a question. His only concern was how quickly they could get him through the portal into the Shadow Realm. He would find Prince Aradae on the battlefield and he *would* kill him.

EPILOGUE

"**O**ur daughter is missing."

King Othin didn't bother to look up from the war table. The summer queen could very well wait her turn.

The city models were now complete. The strings ran between known portal connections in a complicated rainbow of color. Unfortunately, they had failed to uncover any direct connections to portals in the Shadow Realm other than the city center, which was now enclosed in a fortress wall.

It was a strong defensive position. Reconnaissance had been limited, at best, and King Othin couldn't get any of his men or weapons into their dark city. The few merchant-spies who had tried had immediately been shot down. They were accepting no incoming traffic from the upper realms, and from what little he could tell, even travel between locations within the realm had been severely restricted. How could it not, with guards watching every entry?

It was something he was going to have to consider for his own portals. Already they had begun a similar construction around the portal hub in the capital, but unlike the Shadow

Realm, the Upper Realm had too many portals with extra-realm connections to contain them all. But he had men working on the problem, developing a way to monitor all traffic across all portals in the realm. They couldn't allow easy access for Shadow Realm spies.

"Did you hear what I said?" Queen Norgeledil demanded.

She stood before Othin with her arms crossed beneath her breasts, drawing the eye to the curling whorl of tattoo that traced a line from her bottom lip, down her throat and into her cleavage. The fire sidhe claimed the markings told the individual's life story, but Othin could make no sense of it. He thought it a rather ugly waste of an otherwise beautiful woman.

"How many of your portals have direct connections to the Shadow Realm?" Othin asked. He didn't much care about the fire sidhe princess. He cared about weapons and warriors and defensive strategies.

"My daughter is missing, and you ask me about portals?"

"And ours was stolen from us," Othin replied in terse majestic plural. With his daughter taken from him and his wife's soul gone to the summerlands, no one would ever again know his personal thoughts. "We have larger problems now."

"And this is one of them. The Shadow Realm has taken her."

Interesting, Othin thought. He turned his gaze back to the Summer Realm queen. They had something in common now, or at least she thought they did. No one had seen the note he'd included in the basket with the dark elf's head. No one in this realm knew that Faeliel had been exiled.

Meanwhile, Norgeledil was here without her lifemate, and without a guard. Had there been a disagreement in the court of the summer king? Perhaps he could use this to his advantage.

"We warned you that the Shadow Realm could not be trusted. We told you they were oathbreakers and reprobates. You did not listen. You chose to send your only child to the Shadow Realm to verify our word and now you have paid the ultimate price."

"How do you know that? How do you know we sent her to spy?"

"Our birds tell us many things."

Huginn squawked from his perch and ruffled his feathers as if in response.

"It was my husband's idea. I disagreed."

"Perhaps you should have disagreed more forcefully."

"Perhaps. But what's done is done. I must bring her home."

"And what would you give for our aid?"

Norgeledil's eyes narrowed, even as Othin smirked. They both knew how to play this game. She was far better at it than her soldier king.

"You'd use our misfortune for your own gain, when you also have a daughter missing? Haven't you any empathy for the suffering of others?"

"My lady, we are not allies. By rights, we should have our guards take you forcibly from our war room." The gold-armored warriors who stood on either side of the doorway stepped away from the wall as one and unsheathed their weapons.

"You need our fire for your war. Lay a hand on me and you will not have it."

"Stand down," King Othin commanded. In synchronized steps, the guards returned to a watchful at-ease. "You are here because we allow you to be here. We understand your pain and we will indulge your indiscretion. But our patience has its limits."

"Then let us be plain. We know you have engineered this war. Your daughter fled to the Shadow Realm under her own power, but you would use her rebellion as justification for your acquisition of the dark elf lands."

King Othin stared at the summer queen but said nothing. She was an astute creature. She could be a power to contend with, if she sought it. It was a shame really. A woman like that at the side of a more powerful king would have been formidable.

"I do not judge," she continued. "I only state the facts. Now our daughter is trapped behind the Shadow Realm's new walls, and we want her back in one piece. Our goals are aligned."

Othin met the woman's gaze. She was right. Now was the time to make things plain.

"Pledge your warriors to our service and swear that you will support our claim to the high seat, and we will bring your daughter home."

BOOK 2 COMING SOON...

Join my reader community!

You'll receive a free short story and be the first to know when The War of the Nine Faerie Realms, Book 2 is ready!

www.MeganHaskell.com

ACKNOWLEDGMENTS

No book can ever be born into the world without a team of people behind it. Even the first draft often requires a sounding board to bounce ideas and work through the rough spots in the plot. Which is why I'm so honored to have a robust group of people to help with *Forged in Shadow*. Endless thanks are owed, but here at least are a few of them.

First, I have to thank my husband. Without him, I'm not sure I would have started writing. He has encouraged me every step of the way, despite the fact that he doesn't read fantasy (he's a sci-fi, space opera, kinda guy.) He patiently listens to me prattle on about the book industry, and gives great advice on plot fixes, cover critiques, and every step in between.

My sister, Kim Peticolas, editor extraordinaire, has been a phenomenal resource during this entire process as well. She has helped with everything from copy editing, to world building, to graphic design, and more. If you need an editor or author consultant, she's a fantastic choice, and I'm not just saying that because she's my sister. (www.kimpeticolas.com) I'm incredibly proud to be working with her and thrilled that we've grown closer in our careers.

In addition to letting me grow up in a household that encouraged reading and introducing me to Tolkien at an impressionable age, my mom and dad have both been a supportive foundation for my writing efforts. My dad is an early beta reader and subject matter expert on all things military related, and my mom helps with the final proofing. I would get a lot more things wrong if it weren't for their help. They also buy books to give to hospital patients where they volunteer and spread the word to all their friends. That kind of constructive criticism and unconditional support is rare and precious. Thank you, from the bottom of my heart.

Forged in Shadow features the crafting of a Great Sword, a skill that I have never personally experienced first hand. Luckily, I found another subject matter expert to advise me. Thank you, Joy Fire (www.joyfireblacksmith.com), for all your advice and feedback on the early draft of *Forged in Shadow*, and please forgive any remaining mistakes. They are one hundred percent my own.

To my writer friends around the globe, thank you for always being there to discuss books and plots and stories and process and goals and achievements. The writing community never ceases to amaze me.

An extra special mention must go out to my partner in crime at The Author Wheel, Greta Boris. I can't wait to see what we do together.

To the T10: you know who you are, and you are my tribe.

To Allison Dillard, Beth Marcus, and the folks at the Monday morning O.C. Writers meetup: thank you for keeping me accountable while still understanding that life happens (and letting me vent when it does).

Many individuals have given input into *Forged in Shadow* as early beta readers and typo hunters, and I couldn't produce at the quality I strive for without them. Thank you Nathan, Joe, Sue,

Wayne, M'lissa, Erika, Shannon, Laureen, Renee, and Micala! There would have been a lot more plot holes without your help!

And also to my early Patreon supporters: AC, Bryce, Kristi, Dan, Jennifer, Renee, Mandy, Matt, Taya, Timandra, and Tonya... Thank you for believing in my work!

Last, to all my fans who have encouraged and supported my efforts over the years, I wouldn't be doing this if it weren't for you.

Thank you!

ABOUT THE AUTHOR

Escape into Myth, Magic, and Mayhem

I've been a fantasy reader for as long as I can remember. I've always loved joining extraordinary adventures in the written word, imagining myself alongside heroic men and women, fighters and warriors who strive to improve the world, or at least kill the bad guy. Ensconced in the safety of my bedroom, I explored strange lands with dangerous creatures. It was an addiction I was happy to accommodate, especially when my mom wanted me to do my chores.

Now it's my joy to bring new fantasy adventures to life, to give you, dear reader, a safe escape from your daily reality.

Join me, and let's fight some bad guys together.

www.MeganHaskell.com
www.TheAuthorWheel.com